Praise for the

"A mesmerising marriage betw̶̶̶̶̶̶̶̶̶̶ ̶̶̶̶̶̶̶̶cy romance
and urban fantasy that is both impeccably researched
and wonderfully paced. I devoured this series."
Sabaa Tahir, *New York Times* bestselling
author of *An Ember in the Ashes*

"An enormously satisfying conclusion to Alison
Goodman's brilliant trilogy. I read it in two huge gulps,
delighted by the breathless excitement, swoon-inducing
romance and clever plotting. A complete triumph."
Laura Wood, author of *A Sky Painted Gold*

"Georgette Heyer meets *Buffy the Vampire Slayer*
in this delicious blend of Regency romance and
dark fantasy. Tremendously good fun."
Katherine Woodfine, author of *The Clockwork Sparrow*

"The prose is as witty as Elizabeth Bennet herself
and the whole book is a joy from start to finish."
SFX Magazine

"Think Jane Austen meets contemporary supernatural
sass… This [book] has it all for fans of fantasy and
historical fiction – paranormal clashes, political
intrigue, smouldering romance, a handsomely
headstrong heroine, and bejewelled historical
detail. The writing fizzes with passion and panache
throughout, much like Lady Helen herself."

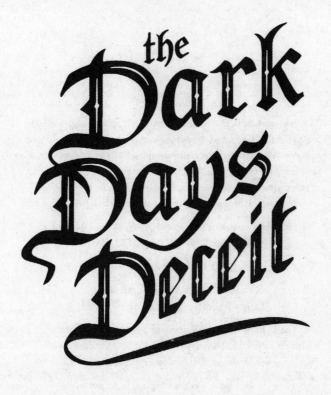

the Dark Days Deceit

ALISON GOODMAN

WALKER
BOOKS

First published in Great Britain 2018 by Walker Books Ltd
87 Vauxhall Walk, London SE11 5HJ

2 4 6 8 10 9 7 5 3 1

Text © 2018 Alison Goodman
Cover illustration © 2018 Larry Rostant

The right of Alison Goodman to be identified as author
of this work has been asserted by her in accordance with
the Copyright, Designs and Patents Act 1988

This book has been typeset in Sabon

Printed and bound by CPI Group (UK) Ltd, Croydon CR0 4YY

British Library Cataloguing in Publication Data:
a catalogue record for this book is available from the British Library

ISBN 978-1-4063-5898-8

www.walker.co.uk

MIX
Paper from
responsible sources
FSC® C020471

To Ron, for all the reasons,
and many other besides

My dear Helen,

Regarding your letter of 7th December, I understand that you would wish to continue your stay at Bath with Lady Ridgewell and Miss Cransdon. The company of such lively young friends would naturally eclipse that of your old aunt, not to mention the fact that your betrothed's country seat is so happily situated near that fair city. Nevertheless, I do remind you that I have not seen you since July, when the Duke obtained Her Majesty's permission for you to marry. Now that your nuptials are less than a month away, I insist that I join you to help prepare for your wedding and finalise your gowns for the ceremony and ball.

I had hoped you would return to London for such important purchases, but Lady Jersey has assured me that the warehouses and drapers at Bath are equal to the task.

I am aware that Lady Ridgewell has no spare room for me, but I have had an invitation from Lady Dunwick to stay with her and her daughter at their house in the Royal Crescent. Ever since they happened upon you and the Duke on the Brighton road before your official betrothal, Lady Dunwick has become somewhat adhesive. I will stay with her until other arrangements can be made.

I expect to travel in the next week and will write again soon with a firm date of arrival. I look forward to our reunion.

I remain always, your loving,
Aunt Leonore

Chapter One

Lady Helen Wrexhall refolded the letter and pressed its wax seal back together, as if she could lock away the news it contained. Aunt Leonore, soon to arrive at Bath. Lud.

Of course, she loved Aunt and wanted her to be part of the wedding, but it was a complication none of them needed. She tapped the edge of the letter against the hallway table. Her aunt and uncle, along with the rest of society, were under the impression that she had spent the last six months enjoying the delights of Brighton and Bath; not, in fact, training to be a warrior, masquerading as a man, fighting Deceivers, killing murderers, and becoming one half of the Grand Reclaimer with Lord Carlston. Helen shook her head. How was she to keep all that from Aunt? It was going to be impossible.

The sound of footsteps descending the stairs drew her from her thoughts. Lady Margaret appeared on the landing above, one red-gloved hand sliding along the banister, the other encased in a golden sable muff that matched the luxurious collar of her pelisse. Her brother followed behind, adjusting the capes of his greatcoat, his hat already upon his head.

"We are to the Pump Room for our daily dose of foul water

and gossip," Lady Margaret said, pausing at the bottom of the steps. "Will you join us after you have trained? We are all invited to breakfast with the Grays."

Helen shook her head. It was the fashion to breakfast with friends after taking the waters, but it was not one of her favourite diversions; she now had the appetite of a Reclaimer, and even when she restrained herself she ate double what a lady should eat in public. "Please pass on my regrets, and Delia's too. We will breakfast here and then the Duke is calling to take us to the porcelain showrooms. I am to choose a new coffee service."

"Another one?" Hammond asked, ushering his sister past Helen. "Is he restocking the whole of Chenwith Hall?"

"It is for the Queen, Michael," Lady Margaret chided. She addressed Helen. "Has his lordship arrived yet? He and Quinn finally returned late last night, did they not?"

"They are in the cellar," Helen replied.

She had not seen the men arrive, but had sensed Lord Carlston enter the house ten minutes earlier. The pulse they shared – a steady beat beneath her own heart's rhythm that confirmed their union as the Grand Reclaimer – had sharpened into a call. She felt the incessant draw of it, like a pin to a magnet. The two men had been gone a week; a dangerous foray into Napoleon's Paris to search for Carlston's traitorous wife, Lady Elise. Had they found her? Helen lifted her shoulders and let them drop, trying to shrug away the hollow unease that always came with the thought of that woman.

"We should go down and greet him," Lady Margaret said. "Perhaps he has orders for us."

"His lordship has made it clear the morning is for Reclaimers and Terrenes only," Hammond said, ushering her firmly towards the door. He cast a smile back at Helen. "Steer your betrothed away from French porcelain. We cannot have the Queen eating off the enemy's plate."

Garner, the butler, opened the door. A blast of freezing air swept into the hallway. Another bitter day, Helen thought, shivering despite the warm wrap of her woollen shawl. Outside, two wet footmen stepped forward to hold umbrellas over Lady Margaret and Mr Hammond as they made their way to the carriage. Garner closed the door against the elements and, with a bow to Helen, retreated to the butler's pantry.

"May I go down, my lady?" Darby asked. She wore the blue gown she kept for training and stood waiting on the top step of the staircase that led to the basement, clearly eager to reunite with Quinn.

Helen shook her head. They must wait a few moments more; she did not want to give in, quite yet, to the draw of the Grand Reclaimer bond. Darby, at least, knew her regard for Mr Quinn was built upon the man's worth. Helen's link to Carlston had been created by some heathen alchemical force that pulled them together regardless of the turmoil it caused.

She frowned at the empty hallway. "Where is Sprat? Did you tell her to come down?"

"I did," Darby said crisply. "She is most likely hiding from the idea of work, or she could be outside."

"Outside? Is she wearing her shoes? It is raining."

"I doubt it. She won't wear her shoes or her hose. I've told her over and over, my lady, but she won't listen to anyone but you."

Helen gave a nod of sympathy; Darby was trying so hard to help the girl. "I know, but we must keep in mind where she has come from. She needs time."

Darby's soft mouth tightened. "It has been a fair while, my lady, and she still cannot do your hair properly or sew a straight line."

"But she is an excellent pickpocket," Helen said, only half joking. Lord Carlston had used Sprat's more dubious skills on more than one occasion.

The quip did not draw a smile. "The other maids think she's been going through their belongings."

Helen's smile faded. "Has anything gone missing?"

"A few small things: pins and what-not." Darby paused. "She swears she's not touched them, my lady, but she bends the truth something awful."

"Well, we must not assume she is to blame. Nevertheless, I will speak to her about it." *Again,* Helen added silently. Rescuing Sprat from Kate Holt's bawdy house in Brighton had been an easy decision, but it seemed the girl was not interested in morality or training to be a lady's maid.

With no Sprat to ferry the letter upstairs, Helen tucked it inside her long cambric sleeve and finally led the way down the steps. The beat within her body quickened as they descended. While his lordship had been away, it had been vastly subdued; a blessed relief.

She pulled her woollen shawl more firmly around her shoulders. The basement was brisk at the best of times, but during the current stretch of dismal weather it was unbearably cold. There could be no doubt that their proximity to the River Avon added to the damp chill; the house stood in the middle of a handsome row along Great Pulteney Street near the bridge, one of the newer fashionable addresses. It lacked the space they had enjoyed in Brighton, but even so, the house was a godsend. Nearly all of Bath had been fully let for the winter Season and it had taken the Duke's influence to secure them lodgings at such short notice.

It could not be denied that her betrothal to the Duke of Selburn held many advantages, not least his constant regard for her comfort. The thought brought a smile. Not only was he refurbishing his country seat, Chenwith Hall, but he had also taken it upon himself to arrange a grand New Year's Day ball to celebrate their wedding. It was to be held in a new dance pavilion being built in the gardens at Chenwith, the crowning event of a huge Night Ice Fair that would mark their union. An enormous undertaking, but as the Duke said, their wedding celebration was to be attended by Royalty, so it must not be a meagre affair.

Mr Quinn was waiting at the doorway of the cellar, still clad in his thick coat. The windowless room currently served as their training area, and although not ideal – the only light came from oil lamps and the space was not large – it afforded the seclusion they needed as she and Lord Carlston tried to control their power. Only Quinn, Darby and Mr Pike, the bureaucratic heart of the Dark Days Club, knew that they were the Grand Reclaimer dyad – two halves of a whole meant to wield great power – just like their unknown nemesis, the Grand Deceiver. Yet, Helen thought, after five months they had very little to show for their efforts. It was true she could conjure the electrical fire, but they had no idea how to make the energy into a weapon, or, indeed, what role Lord Carlston was to play in the partnership.

"My lady." Mr Quinn bowed as Helen entered the cellar. "And Miss Darby, it is very good to see you again."

Behind her, Helen heard Darby whisper, "Are you well, Nathaniel?"

"I am now."

Helen heard the smile within Quinn's reply. Such sweetness between them.

Carlston stood beside the wine racks. The capes of his coat still glistened with rain and the yellow light from the lamps gave a golden hue to the planes of his face, reminding Helen of a gilded statue she had once seen of Michael the warrior-saint. The beat of their union thundered in her ears and she knew he felt it too. It was in the clench of his hand around the wine rack and the tension that coiled through his body as he fought the urge to step to her side.

He smiled, the carefully maintained space between them spanned by its warmth. "It is very good to see you."

"Indeed," she said. "We had thought to see you sooner." In her mind, however, she screamed: *Why did you take so long? Are you well? Did you find her?*

He raked his hand through his dark hair. "I was hoping to be back three days ago, but the news of Napoleon's impending return from Russia meant Paris was in turmoil, so we waited until things quietened down."

"Was your trip a success?"

His mouth tensed at the question. Clearly not. Then again, she was unsure what would actually constitute success. Lady Elise had been a spy for France and had betrayed Lord Carlston in the worst possible way, leaving him suspected of her murder. Her retrieval could only end in her execution and further scandal for his lordship. Yet he was determined to keep searching. Was it because he still loved her?

"Paris held no answers."

He looked away and wet his lips, the unconscious action bringing a shameful rush of heat through Helen's body. Even now, after so many months, she could still feel the touch of his lips on her own. The light, sweet touch of the Duke's mouth had not in any way subdued the sordid burn of that illicit memory.

"I am sorry to hear it," she managed.

He nodded and lifted one shoulder, as if throwing off the last seven days. "We have lost more training time than I expected.

Let us devote the rest of today to the problem of your power. I've had some ideas that may—"

"The rest of the day? But I cannot," Helen said. "I am engaged this afternoon to buy porcelain."

"Porcelain?" Carlston's hand tightened on the rail again. "With Selburn, I presume? Can you not put him off?"

"We must do it today or the order will not be filled in time."

His jaw shifted, his silence more eloquent than any comment.

"I am more than happy to forgo breakfast and work right through until the appointment," she added.

"Thank you," he said dryly. He took a few steps along the narrow space between the two wine racks, as much pacing as the room allowed. "Quinn, close the door. Make sure we are alone."

Quinn checked the corridor, then secured the door. He and Darby stood side by side, their unity and affection as clear as if they were holding hands. It all looked so natural, Helen thought. No confused questioning or divided loyalty.

"The trip to Paris did at least give me time to reflect upon our progress," Carlston said. He rubbed his eyes, his frustration palpable. "I feel like the third wheel on a racing gig. After all that we endured to bond, we do not even know how we are to share the power stored within you. Has there still been nothing from the Ligatus? I had hoped the new meditations would have had some effect by now."

His question brought a flare of guilt – she held the key to their power in her memory, but could not retrieve it. When the two of them had blood-bonded to become the Grand Reclaimer, she had simultaneously absorbed the Ligatus: a madman's journal written in the blood of slaughtered people and Deceivers. The author of that foul book, the rogue Reclaimer Samuel Benchley, had bound his victims' life knowledge and energy into its pages by alchemy. Now all their knowledge was locked in Helen's mind, frustratingly inaccessible, and their life energy an ever-present hum in her body.

"Nothing has come to me yet," she said, watching him pace across the brick floor again.

He stopped in front of her, eyes narrowed. "How hard are you trying?"

That was unfair. Helen crossed her arms. "I am meditating three times a day as you said I should. There is something at the edge of my mind. I just cannot catch hold of it yet."

She did, however, have a terrible sense of what it could be: the screams of a dying infant. There could only be one such pitiful voice in the Ligatus: little Timothy Marr, one of the poor Ratcliffe Highway souls brutally murdered for their blood by Benchley. Every time Helen meditated she heard the infant's distant cry, buried deep within her mind but slowly surfacing. More often than not it was accompanied by such an aching anguish that her own sobs wrenched her from the meditation. She had told no one of it yet. First she had to control her emotions so the little voice could emerge; and then she had to find a way to contend with all the others who howled their pain inside her.

Carlston paced back to the other side of the room. "I think it is time to try another way. I have asked Sir Jonathan to join us. He has studied mesmerism. You are aware of the practice?"

Helen wrinkled her nose. The field of mesmerism was even more disreputable than alchemy. "If I recall correctly, Mr Mesmer's theories have been wholly discredited in Paris."

"Mesmer has been discredited," Carlston conceded, "but Abbé Faria has developed a way to access thoughts hidden from the conscious mind, and he has had some success. Sir Jonathan assures me the practice is safe."

Sir Jonathan Beech was the Dark Days Club's senior Tracer,

responsible for tracking the progeny of Deceivers so they could be returned to full humanity by the Reclaimers. Not, Helen thought wryly, a theologian or physician qualified to delve into the hidden mysteries of the mind and soul. Nevertheless, she must try. She held within her not only the answer to their power, but possibly a way to destroy the Grand Deceiver and the Trinitas – a three-part alchemical weapon that, if brought together, could rip open a doorway between their world and the otherworld of the Deceivers and create a hell on earth.

"It would be prudent to continue with your own meditations," Carlston added. "The closer you can get to drawing on the information, the better for Sir Jonathan's methods."

Helen nodded, although foreboding prickled her skin. Little Timothy's anguish was just the tip of the pain buried within her mind. What would happen if Sir Jonathan brought out all the voices at once, as it had been when she had first absorbed the journal? She was not sure she was strong enough to withstand such an all-encompassing wave of despair again.

"When does Sir Jonathan arrive, my lord?" Darby asked, ever practical. "Will he be staying with us?"

"He arrives tomorrow and stays only two days. I have arranged a room at my lodgings."

At least Sir Jonathan would be gone by the time Aunt arrived at Bath, Helen thought. Which brought her to her own news.

"Lady Pennworth is coming here to help me prepare for the wedding."

Carlston, Darby and Quinn stared at her with similar expressions of dismay. It would have been comical if it were not so serious.

"You must stop her," Carlston said. "It is a complication we do not need."

"I know, but she will not be put off any longer. Besides, it would be deemed odd if she did not have a part in the preparations."

"Does she expect to stay with you?" Carlston demanded. "You will have to make some excuse. The risk of discovery is too great."

"She says she will stay with Lady Dunwick."

"Even so, she will demand your company every day. As it is, you are too distracted. With her here, we will make no progress at all!"

"I am not distracted," Helen protested. "I am doing as much as I can."

Carlston snorted. "You are forever at warehouses and shops with Selburn; and when you are here, your mind is on weddings, not training or the Grand Deceiver."

Helen felt the humming energy within her rise. "I am no more distracted by my wedding than you are by your search for your wife."

At the corner of her eye, she saw Quinn wince.

"Surely we do not need so much urgency," she added, trying to moderate her tone. "I know the Grand Deceiver holds the Colligat, but it is only one part of the Trinitas; and they cannot get their hands upon the second part since it is in here." She tapped her forehead. "Only we know I have absorbed the Ligatus, and it will take the Deceivers years to create another. Moreover, you have told me again and again that the third part of the Trinitas is safe – whatever it may be – so it follows that the immediate danger is past. We have time to gather ourselves, to train and find our power."

"Time to get married, you mean?" Carlston said acidly. From his fob pocket he withdrew a heavy disc of gold attached to a bloodstained ribbon. He held it up before Helen, its ornate etching of Bacchus glinting in the lamplight. It had belonged to the late Comte d'Antraigues, Deceiver and spy, and he had passed it to Helen after he was attacked by the assassin sent by the Grand Deceiver. "Louis gave us this for a reason. The Grand Deceiver is planning something and we must find out what it is."

"We already know what was being planned," Helen said. "To unite the Trinitas – but that is now secure. Besides, there has been no sign of Philip here or in London. Surely if the Grand Deceiver was planning something, they would send their harbinger of destruction. They have every other time."

"Do you really think the Grand Deceiver has retired defeated?" Carlston demanded.

It was clear any answer other than *no* would be wrong. "I see that *you* do not," she said.

He eyed her for a moment, as if she had disappointed him. "You and Pike have allowed yourselves to be lulled into a false sense of victory – exactly what I think the Grand Deceiver wants. We are meant to believe we have stymied their plan when in fact it is still in operation – a brilliant deception that is already halfway to defeating us. Louis did not mention the Trinitas when he gave you this fob. He told us to find the Bath Deceiver. Those were his dying words, and that is where the truth of our salvation lies. The Bath Deceiver holds the information we need."

"You speak as if we have not been searching," Helen protested. "To find one Deceiver amongst the hundred or so here in Bath is a monumental task, especially when all are doing their utmost to hide from us."

"In five months we have found only fifteen, none of them Louis's comrade. It is taking too long." He shook the fob on its ribbon. "I need you focused on the search and our training, not on your wedding. Can you do that? Or are you in too much of a rush to appease society and marry Selburn?"

Helen narrowed her eyes. "You think I am marrying the Duke only to save my reputation?"

He lowered the fob, his face set. She knew that expression –

he was deciding whether or not to step over a brink. A brink that they had, by mutual silence, avoided for months.

Do not do it, she thought fiercely. *Do not.*

"Knowing the man, what else could it be?" he said flatly. "You were compromised on the road to Barnes and you think the only way forward is to marry him. You are clinging to the delusion that you can be both a Reclaimer and the woman society expects you to be. The woman *he* expects you to be."

"Knowing the man?" she echoed. "You do not know the Duke. You see only your dislike of him. Selburn is offering me a chance to retain my reputation, that is true – but he is also offering far more than that. The chance of a family – my *own* family – and a life that holds more than reclaiming and killing. A life that is sanctified by God and society."

He blinked; the barb had hit home. He could not offer her those things. It was the truth, but still, she should not have said it. She had wanted to punish him for things he could not change: a wife still alive, and her own wretched confusion about their Grand Reclaimer bond.

"Your life is already sanctified by God and society," he said, his voice hard. "You have taken an oath as a Reclaimer. That is your life, and he is taking you away from it, away from your *duty*. What is worse, you are letting him."

Behind her, Darby made a soft sound of denial.

"That is not true!" Helen said.

Carlston leaned closer. "He is making you less than you are, Helen. He will not play second to a woman, and you are already stepping back."

"I am not!"

"Then show me I am wrong. Show me some damned focus!"

Helen drew herself up. She would show him focus. Concentrating all her outrage into her hands, she dragged the warm, ever-present thrum of otherworld energy up through her bone and marrow and flesh until it sparked into a blaze of blue fire that engulfed her fingertips. Heat throbbed through her body, a furnace of power. She cupped her fingers, the blue humming flame in each hand slowly curling around itself, until she held twin incandescent balls of hot energy hovering an inch above her palms. Dear God, she was holding them *and* maintaining them! Her breath quickened, the exhilaration bursting out in a small huffing laugh.

The jutting challenge in Carlston's face shifted into anticipation. "Can you throw them?" he whispered.

In the periphery of her vision, she saw Quinn edge Darby back against the door.

She raised her hands, the crackling, humming blue orbs shivering at the movement. She felt them slipping, the heat ebbing. *No!* She tried to draw more energy from her centre, but it was too late. Each ball pulsed with a flash of light, then broke apart into hundreds of harmless sparks. The tiny lights spun upward and hung in the air like a silent explosion of miniature fireworks, then showered down around them, flickering into oblivion.

Carlston released a long breath, his eyes dark with disappointment. "I thought for a moment..." He closed his fingers around the gleaming fob.

"I am sorry." She lowered her hands.

And yet, deep down, she felt a tiny treacherous sense of relief. It was all very well for him to seek their power with such fervour, but he was not the one who risked being consumed by the burning energy and howling despair of the Ligatus.

Chapter Two

Three hours later, Helen watched Sprat's reflection in the dressing table mirror as the girl considered where to place the next hairpin in Helen's coiffure. She was attempting to create a fashionable Roman style – arranged at the back, with two false braided pieces set atop one another – but it was fast collapsing into a lumpy side bun. Helen picked up a comb from the crowded table and ran her fingernail across its teeth, trying to find some measure of patience. The girl's ineptitude was coming hard upon the heels of the unsettling session with Lord Carlston, and Helen felt her nerves snapping with frustration.

She had not expected Carlston to challenge her commitment to the Dark Days Club, especially by way of her impending marriage to Selburn. Granted, she may be a little distracted by the wedding, but it was less than a month away now and such an important event required attention. She was not stepping back, as he had said. Nor failing in her duty.

She leaned forward and studied her face in the mirror. If his accusations were so unfair, why did they rankle so much?

The pale woman in the mirror stared back, her fingertips tracing the shape of her lips.

Yes, Helen thought, they rankled because of the one thing that neither he nor she could ever acknowledge again: *amore mio*. My love. Five months ago, he had said those words out loud, and now they crouched, silent and fierce, in every single moment they were together. A connection of overwhelming intensity and heat that was outside the bounds of morality and society.

More to the point, she told her reflection, it was probably not even real; an alchemical entailment on the Grand Reclaimer bond. Nothing more than a false sense of union created to hold them together. Not a glorious romance or the kind of foundation upon which one could build a life and a family. That took mutual respect and trust and strong friendship; the things she shared with Selburn.

Her reflection frowned. Not that her betrothal to the Duke lacked heat; no, it had heat as well, just not so … intense.

She sat back.

"My lady, if you keep movin', I'll never get this one in." Sprat held the pin poised above the top bun, her narrow brow furrowed in concentration.

Helen sighed. The girl really had no idea about dressing hair or maintaining a proper level of familiarity. "Try placing the pin on the other side," she said. "Otherwise the top piece will sit awry. Do you see?"

Training Sprat to take over Darby's role as her lady's maid had seemed like the perfect solution: a good situation for Sprat, and a release for Darby to pursue her Terrene duties. However, as Darby often said as she repaired Sprat's styling attempts, "not everyone has a flair for hair or fashion". And now, if the girl was stealing from within their house … well, something would have to be done about that.

"On the other side," Sprat repeated, committing the instruction to memory. She positioned the pin and pushed it into the braided bun. The sharp end ploughed a stinging trajectory across Helen's scalp that made her wince. "Sorry, my lady. Yer hair's gettin' long again and it's hard to see. S'pose you don't need it so short now." Sprat picked up another pin and eyed the false knot with misgiving. "Now that yer not goin' out much as Mr Amberley."

"I am still going out as Amberley," Helen protested, but in truth it had been weeks since she had last donned her male disguise to search for the Bath Deceiver. And her cropped hair had indeed grown out.

Sprat met her eyes in the mirror. "Not real often though, like before."

"It gets harder when you stay in a place as long as we have been here," Helen said. "I am more likely to be discovered."

Particularly when one was the Duke of Selburn's betrothed and recognised everywhere. Nevertheless, if what Carlston said was true – that she had fallen into a trap of complacency – then she must find her focus again.

"But don't you miss it, my lady? I'd much rather wear breeches than this." Sprat gestured to the green stuff gown she wore; neat but still a little baggy on her frame.

She had come to them half starved, and although good food had filled out the hollows beneath her shrewd blue eyes, she was still as lean as a winter fox and looked a good deal younger than her twelve years.

"I hear you don't like your boots or hose either," Helen said. "Darby says you are not wearing them."

Sprat bunched her dirty toes into the dressing room's thick blue carpet. "I do sometimes."

Helen turned on the stool to face the girl. "Sprat, you need to wear your boots and hose all the time. It is expected, especially if you are to be my lady's maid."

Sprat grinned. "Even in bed?"

Helen returned the smile. "You know what I mean. During the day."

"But you can't run in 'em, my lady. They slip, you see, on all the mud and you can't make the corners."

Helen knew she ought to point out that a proper lady's maid would neither be running nor cornering in mud, but some part of her – possibly the Mr Amberley part – was feeling more sympathetic than it should. "Yes, I know. Nevertheless, it is what I want."

"Yes, my lady. Shoes and hose all the time."

"There is something else, Sprat," Helen said.

The girl straightened, pale blue eyes wary beneath her knot of dull brown hair. She had a fine sense for trouble.

"I have heard that some of the other maids are missing pins and such. Did you take them?"

Sprat watched her gravely.

"Did you?" Helen pressed.

Sprat quirked her mouth to one side, clearly considering the dangers of telling the truth. "Yes, my lady." Her pale face brightened. "But I didn't sell 'em all."

"You have sold some of them?"

She gave a wary nod. "To a pawn in town."

"Sprat!"

"His lordship don't mind me thievin'," she offered quickly. "He asks me to fork every now and again for letters in gents' pockets an' such."

Helen bit down on what she thought of Lord Carlston's use of Sprat's talents, and said instead, "Where are the rest of the pins? You must give them back to the girls with an apology, and you must stop stealing."

"Even if I say I'm sorry, it ain't gunna get any better," Sprat muttered. "They're always ringin' a peal over me and callin' me nibbler."

Helen translated the cant phrases: the other maids were always scolding her and calling her a thief. "Well, what can you expect when you do actually steal from them?" She watched Sprat cross to the mahogany wash cabinet and squat beside it. "What are you doing?"

"I hid 'em in the wall," the girl said, digging her fingernails into a crack in the skirting.

"You hid them in *my* room?"

"No one was ever gunna look 'ere, were they, my lady?"

Impeccable thief logic. Shaking her head, Helen rose and walked over to Sprat's hiding place. A small section of the skirting board came free with a soft scrape, exposing a cavity in the wall's wooden structure. A folded letter lay inside, with a collection of hairpins set neatly in two rows beside it.

"Is that one of my letters?" She could see the missive was in Aunt's hand, from months ago. "Why on earth did you take that? Did you read it?"

"No, my lady. I ain't too good with readin'. I just like the squirly writin' on it, and the gold bits about the edge."

Such an odd thing to steal. Helen drew the packet out, her fingers brushing across silky cloth. What else was in there? She leaned closer: white silk, folded into four. Holy Heaven, a gentleman's silk handkerchief.

She dropped the letter and grabbed the girl's bony shoulder. "Stealing a handkerchief is a hanging offence, Sprat. At the very least, transportation to the colonies. Surely you know that!"

Sprat kneaded one hand within the other. "I'm sorry, my lady. Sometimes I can't stop meself."

"Whose is it?"

Sprat licked her lips. "The Duke's, my lady. I'm sorry. I'll give it back and 'pologise." She reached for it.

"No!"

Sprat snatched back her hand.

Helen softened her tone. "We must not give the Duke further reason…" She stopped.

Selburn had already suggested she send Sprat down to the kitchens and find a maid more befitting the needs of a Duchess. If he found out the girl had stolen from him as well, he would rightly expect Helen to dismiss her, and might even demand her arrest. Helen knew the Duke had no time for thieves: he had sent many a poacher to jail; and was barely polite to Mr Hammond and Lady Margaret who had once lived by theft in Paris.

"Sprat, you must leave the handkerchief in there and forget you ever touched it."

"Yes, my lady."

"And you must promise me you will stop stealing, especially from the Duke. When he and I are married, he will not have you in his house if he knows you are a thief."

Sprat nodded slowly. "I'll try, my lady. I'll try real hard, but somethin' comes over me and then I have to nab what I see."

Helen crouched down so their eyes were level. "When you feel like that, you must come to me. Immediately. We will wait together until the feeling has passed."

"Yes, my lady." It was said too easily, the girl's blue eyes far too guileless.

Helen clasped her shoulder again. "I mean it. If you thieve, you will not be able to stay with me. Do you understand?"

Sprat looked away. "I don't want to go back to the bawdy house."

"No, and you will not." Helen squeezed her shoulder reassuringly. "So stop thieving. And when that feeling does come upon you, come to me immediately. Can you do that?" She waited for the girl's nod. "Good. It is a promise between us."

She looked down at the Duke's handkerchief; as dangerous as a knife. "Now, take out the pins and close the wall up. We will never open it again."

Sprat collected the pins into her cupped hand and pushed the board back into place. "It's a good hidin' place though, ain't it, my lady? You gotta have a good hidin' place." She nodded sagely. "An' a good bolt-hole too."

Incorrigible.

Helen picked up the letter from the floor. "I don't want you to mention any of this ever again. Is that understood?"

"Yes, my lady."

His Grace, the Duke of Selburn, shifted his long-limbed body in the cane chair and peered out of the window of Molland's Pastry shop. A wall of rain sluiced Milsom Street creating a muddy river down its incline.

"It is even heavier now," he said to Helen, seated beside him. "We did well to go to the showrooms first. I have never seen so much water."

Helen looked past Delia, who sat opposite, and clicked her tongue. The poorer parts of Bath, set in the lower areas, would be flooded again. "That poor lady is half drowned," she said, watching a woman in lavender silk do a peculiar little hop to unwrap her sodden skirts from her ankles as she crossed the streaming road. The drenched gentleman beside her valiantly tried to keep her covered with an umbrella that sagged alarmingly under the violent downpour.

Delia turned in her chair to look as the woman hopped again. "How funny! She'll have both of them over in the mud if she keeps jumping like that."

"There, they have safely made the draper's shop. No one will drown on Milsom Street today," the Duke said, picking up his teacup.

Helen smiled, noticing that his usually straight fair hair had kinked rather charmingly at his nape in the damp heat of the shop. "The perils of shopping," she said.

The Duke laughed. "I think we survived our own ordeal very well. I am glad we settled upon the blue Chinoiserie pattern."

Helen nodded. She too was satisfied with the coffee set they had chosen. In fact, she was determined to be satisfied with the whole afternoon, despite Lord Carlston's earlier admonishments. There was something wholly agreeable about being warm and dry and eating cake while it stormed outside.

Their table was in the prime position before the front bow window and set apart from all others. The over-excited proprietor had ousted the table's previous tenants for the Duke – nobility did not often join the masses in a confectionery shop – and had also removed the nearest two tables for added privacy. Even with the extra space, Helen felt crowded by the press of fashionables and middlings, every table filled with bonneted ladies and damp gentlemen. A number more were gathered in the doorway, clearly waiting out the storm. Both large bow windows were fogged around the edges from so much warm breath and hot tea, and the air smelled of pastry, sugar and wet wool. Everything was movement and sound, except for one woman, seated nearby in a party of three, who watched their table with an odd intensity.

Helen shifted her position slightly for a better view of the lady and her two companions: an older woman and a man of about thirty. They were from the gentry, if their air of consequence and fashionable clothes were any indication. Something about the younger woman was familiar, although Helen did not recognise the face beneath the stylish cottage bonnet: large bright eyes a little too closely set together, a thin, rather pinched nose, and thick, mid-brown curls. Her blue-gloved hand was curled across her mouth, elbow supported by the other hand, as if she were musing deeply, or perhaps also trying to recollect if they were acquainted. Was she a Deceiver? She was not one of the creatures already known to them. Perhaps a newcomer then. The shop, with its chattering patrons, would be a prime target for a Hedon Deceiver seeking to nourish itself from human pleasure.

Helen found the handle of her lorgnette, hanging from its cord around her neck. The lenses of the spectacles were made of the same crystal prisms that were hidden within her touch watch, calibrated to expose a Deceiver if it was seen whilst feeding or if it had built whips. Although Helen had treasured the touch watch – a gift from Lord Carlston – it had soon become apparent that the use of its concealed three-part lens was too limited, especially for a lady. Consequently, she had quietly commissioned its maker, Mr Brewster, to refine his idea into something approximating a normal spectacle lens, with the aim of creating a lorgnette. She had received Brewster's third attempt only a week ago – a pair of round, tortoiseshell frames with an elegant horn handle and lenses only a little thicker than normal glass. A triumph of skill and perseverance.

Helen raised the lorgnette to her eyes. Ah, her instincts were correct. A swollen grey tentacle arched from the woman's back, its pulsing length sliding under the small table and across the lap of the oblivious gentleman. The undulating end caressed his chest as it suckled his energy, then reached across and latched on to the older woman's décolletage to draw upon her pale blue life force. Helen drew a steadying breath and lowered her lorgnette. For all the obscenity of the sight, the woman was skimming from more than one person and therefore within the dictates of the Compact between human and Deceiver. Even so, her air of recognition was troubling, as was her apparent indifference to Helen's scrutiny.

"Do you know the name of that lady, Delia?" Helen asked, tilting her head in the direction of the table.

"That is Mrs Knoll, newly arrived from York," Delia said. "She is here with her mother-in-law, the older lady next to her, who is taking the cure. The gentleman is Mr Josephs." Delia leaned closer. "He is a gazetted fortune hunter. I've heard that Mrs Knoll is recently widowed and has a decent fortune."

Delia's penchant for gossip and eavesdropping had decided benefits.

The Duke glanced at the woman, his haughty attention immediately turning her back to her party. "Just another impertinent gawper keen to see the next Duchess of Selburn," he said dismissively. He looked at Helen over the rim of his teacup. "Mind you, I can understand their fascination."

The expression in his eyes brought a flush to her cheeks. Yes, there was heat enough between them.

Helen glanced once more at the Deceiver. She and her companions were preparing to leave – gathering shawls, adjusting bonnets and paying their account. If Delia was correct and Mrs Knoll was newly arrived from York, she was plainly not the Bath Deceiver. Nevertheless, one to watch until Sir Jonathan traced her line.

As the trio departed the shop, Helen returned to the half-eaten tart on her plate: a particularly delicious combination of buttery pastry and tangy lemon curd. One of her favourites. She had already eaten a bacon pie, two sugar biscuits and a piece of the famous Molland's marzipan.

"You have almost finished," the Duke said. "Something else?"

She heard the amusement in his voice and sent him a side smile as she speared a generous mouthful. "I missed my breakfast."

"That is not like you. What occasioned such sacrifice?"

Helen hesitated. Why had she mentioned it? Now she would have to prevaricate; a sour note in the sweet day.

Before she could answer, however, Delia said brightly, "Lord Carlston returned last night."

At his lordship's name, the Duke's free hand bunched into a fist.

Helen narrowed her eyes at Delia. Her friend pressed her hand to her mouth, eyes stricken: *Sorry.*

The Duke placed his teacup back on its saucer, the porcelain meeting in a sharp clack. "How does his return occasion you missing your breakfast?"

Helen scanned the shop for over-keen ears. The din of chatter and the accompanying clink of crockery made it difficult to overhear any conversation. Nevertheless, she lowered her voice. "I forwent breakfast so that we could train all morning. To make up for the time he has been away." She may as well tell him the whole. "I have promised to train with him all of tomorrow too."

"He has only been away a week," the Duke said. "How long is this training regime to continue? You have worked hard for six months, and as far as I can see you have equalled Carlston in all areas."

It was true. She could now defeat three horsewhips at once – an approximation of a Deceiver with three energy whips – and disarm Lord Carlston in a knife fight.

"You are as capable as he is, perhaps even more so, and yet he continues to demand your time," the Duke added.

The force of his words, if not the sense, penetrated the nearby tables. A few faces turned towards them, but quickly turned away under Helen's scrutiny. One did not pry into a

Duke's business. Under the table, Helen motioned for him to lower his voice.

He drew an irritated breath, but obliged. "I know I cannot be privy to everything you do, but surely I deserve to know why you must spend so much time with another man. Time that seems to be increasing."

He had every right to be annoyed, but there was nothing she could do about it. He was not within the Inner Circle that had been sworn to secrecy. Only Mr Pike, Quinn and Darby knew that she and Lord Carlston were the Grand Reclaimer, and also that she had absorbed all the knowledge of the Ligatus. Of course, the Duke was no fool. He, along with Delia, Lady Margaret and Mr Hammond had all guessed that something momentous had happened in the attic in Barnes. It was only the Duke, however, who continued to press for an explanation. A reasonable request considering he was about to, unknowingly, marry one half of a supernatural dyad. Helen knew what Mr Pike would say to such a dilemma: this was exactly the reason why he had banned Reclaimers or Terrenes from marrying. A ban that had not withstood the Duke's rank or persistence.

Seeing that she was not going to answer, Selburn sat back. "Carlston cannot expect you to train over Christmas – it would be sacrilegious. And since that leads into our wedding week, I have had a rather good idea. A Christmas house party at Chenwith Hall."

"Oh," Delia said. "How wonderful."

Selburn did not understand Lord Carlston at all, Helen thought. It would not even enter his head that it was sacrilegious to train over Christmas, and he would, without a doubt, expect her to train right through her wedding week as well, to make up for any future deficit.

But since that observation would only add fuel to the fire,

she said, "It does sound wonderful, and Lady Margaret has not made any firm plans for us yet."

He shook his head. "You misapprehend me, my dear. The invitation does not include Lady Margaret, her brother or Lord Carlston." He made a small bow in his chair to Delia. "You, of course, are invited, Miss Cransdon."

"Thank you." Delia looked down at her plate, a picture of pleased modesty.

"We will have all manner of diversions," he added. "Dinner parties, dances, skating, sleigh rides. We could even tour Stonehenge or Avebury."

Helen stared at him. No Lady Margaret: had he lost his senses? "I cannot stay in your house before the wedding without a proper chaperone."

"But you will have a chaperone. Your aunt."

"My aunt?" Helen echoed.

"We have been in correspondence." He had the grace to look a little sheepish.

"She did not mention it in her letters to me," Helen said, trying to keep the sharpness from her tone. "Or, indeed, these plans for a Christmas house party."

"Of course not. It is my invitation to proffer."

So that was what Aunt had meant by *other arrangements*. "How long have you been corresponding?"

"A few weeks. Since she decided to come to Bath. It is of no consequence. The point is that you will be able to enjoy Christmas and the lead-up to the wedding without the added burden of Lord Carlston's demands. A short leave of absence, if you like."

"Lady Margaret, Mr Hammond and, yes, even Lord Carlston are my friends as well as my ... my colleagues." Helen realised her voice had climbed in volume and hastily lowered it. "I do not wish to abandon them. I want to celebrate the season with them."

"They can come to Christmas dinner, and I am sure we will meet them at other parties."

This was, Helen realised, the tip of a very large problem that had been brewing over the last few months.

She leaned closer, her voice barely a whisper. "Gerard." She paused at the intimacy of his Christian name upon her tongue. "You must understand that my association with Lord Carlston is not something I can leave willy-nilly, then pick up again at my own convenience."

"No, I do not understand that, since you will not tell me anything about your association."

She glanced across at Delia's rather too intense interest. Her friend straightened and politely turned in her chair, directing her attention to the vista of the wet street.

"You know there are things I cannot share," Helen said. "You swore your own oath."

Under the table, he took her hand. "Yes, to protect you."

She smiled and pressed the tight wrap of his fingers. "Even so, it is also an oath to a greater cause. When we are married, we must remain closely associated with Lord Carlston and the other members of the Dark Days Club."

"Why?" The Duke's long chin jutted. "As far as I am aware, a Reclaimer works with their Terrene and aides. Not with another Reclaimer."

"This time it is different." She withdrew her hand. "Please, would you consider inviting my friends?"

He sat back. "If you recall, five months ago Lord Carlston tried to choke the life out of me."

Helen recalled it far too vividly. She had burst into the Brighton drawing room to find Carlston, caught in the madness of their unfinished Grand Reclaimer bond, with one knee upon the Duke's chest and his hands crushing his throat. Then afterwards, the even worse moment in the salon when she had been forced to beat his lordship senseless to stop him from attacking her in his mania. His poor battered, bloodied face – it still haunted her at night.

She dropped her voice to a whisper. "You know Carlston was insane. His mind is restored now. I guarantee it."

"You say that, yet you offer no explanation how it happened. You expect me to take it on faith. Do you also believe he has magically lost his hostility towards me?"

Reluctantly, Helen shook her head.

"Just so," the Duke said. "He has certainly shown no remorse for his actions, and his dislike for me has only increased. Frankly, so has mine towards him. Would you have me take a man into my home whom I not only find objectionable in every way but who has also tried to kill me?"

"Of course not," Helen said. Lud, she had not meant to push the point into an ultimatum – especially not in a public place – but it seemed to be where they had arrived. "Nevertheless, I plan to spend the Christmas celebrations at Great Pulteney Street with my friends and family. You are, of course, welcome."

They stared at one another, both silent amidst all the clash and chatter.

"I believe the rain has stopped," Delia ventured.

Helen picked up her fork and speared a piece of the tart. She looked at the mouthful, then put the fork down again.

"If you are finished," the Duke said, his voice at its most formally polite, "I will call for the carriage."

That evening, after Darby had curtseyed and closed the bed-chamber door behind her, Helen threw back her covers, rose from her bed and picked up her night candle that still burned in its silver holder. She padded in bare feet and warm flannel nightgown across the carpet into her adjoining dressing room. Her candle threw its small light across her dressing table, the mirror catching a flash of her intent face lit eerily from beneath.

She contemplated the fireplace. Darby had raked over the embers; a few still glowed, but not high enough for her purpose. She would need to use the candle.

She crouched beside the washstand and felt along the skirting board, quickly locating the crack between the planks. One tug, and the small section came free. Inside the cavity, the white silk handkerchief seemed to glow in the soft light. Helen pulled it from its hiding place and bundled it in her lap. A small scrape of wood against wood drove the skirting board home, concealing all sign of the thief's cache behind it.

She stood, the handkerchief clutched in one hand, the candle holder in the other. An elegant embroidered monogram weighted one corner of the silk square. Helen studied the meticulous white stitching: an S, for Selburn, set beneath a ducal crown. Was it the Dowager Duchess's work? It was possible the handkerchief was a treasured memento of his late mother and here she was about to destroy it.

Maybe she should return it to him. Yet that would require a story to protect Sprat: something along the lines of the handkerchief accidentally dropped in the house, or on the street outside.

Helen shook her head. No, not a story, a *lie*. Admittedly a small one, but still the truth withheld from her betrothed. She was already walking a fine line in their relationship between truth, lies and omissions, and it was obvious from their awful stalemate in Molland's that he was, quite rightly, losing patience with so much secrecy. He had the right to expect honesty from his wife-to-be. A solid marriage had to be built on truth and trust.

The problem with the truth, however, was its consequences.

If she returned the handkerchief and admitted that Sprat had stolen it, the course of the girl's life would shift into Selburn's hands. He was the injured party and, although it was troubling to admit, she could not guarantee his mercy. He was already ill-disposed towards the girl. Sprat could lose her chance of forging a decent life – maybe lose her life altogether – for a square of silk that was probably just one of many in the Duke's possession.

Helen bunched her fingers around the embroidered corner. Sprat had led her to the Ligatus, and protected her after the foul blood alchemy in the journal had reclaimed Mad Lester and thrust her into a Reclaimer fugue; she owed the girl far too much to risk the truth.

One more lie of omission then.

She crouched before the hearth and laid the handkerchief across the grate. A careful dip of the night candle touched its burning wick to the corner of the cloth. The tiny flame grabbed at the embroidered initial, biting a black crescent into the exquisite stitching. Helen drew her head back as a stink like burning hair rose from the grate.

She watched until all of the white silk disappeared, transformed into black beaded ash, then picked up the iron poker and mixed it into the grey powdery remains in the hearth, ready to be swept away and dumped in the ash heap by the morning maid.

Chapter Three

FRIDAY, 11 DECEMBER 1812

Sir Jonathan Beech crossed to the drawing room window and peered down at the morning throng on Great Pulteney Street.

"It is raining again," he announced into the silence.

The weak winter light cast his round figure and extravagant grey sideburns into a silhouette that reminded Helen, somewhat irreverently, of the neighbour's fluffy Persian cat. She shifted in her armchair, trying to unseat her amusement. Sir Jonathan was here on serious business – to mesmerise her – although he had yet to broach the subject.

He turned from his study of the street. "I received your instructions about Mrs Knoll, the Deceiver you discovered. I have no information about her at present, so I've sent her particulars to Mr Ball. He is on his way north to reclaim a young man, and will go on to York to uncover as much about her as he can for our records."

"Thank you."

Sir Jonathan paced across to the table set near the window. "I see that you have been studying the Grand Deceiver folio."

Helen looked across at the brown leather archive case, still open. Lord Carlston had brought it back from the Home Office a month ago in the hope it would provide a new direction in the search for their nemesis. "It is the fifth time I have gone through it. I have not found anything of use. There is not much in it, is there?"

Sir Jonathan lifted a defensive shoulder. "It is as comprehensive as we can make it, Lady Helen, considering we only started to collect records seventy years ago when Mr Fielding created the Dark Days Club. Most of the information about the Grand Deceiver is from arcane writings from foreign cultures that no longer exist and we cannot translate. There is the Montblanc document though. That is useful, is it not?" He picked up the folio, flicking over the few pages within.

Helen bit her lip. She had quite forgotten that Sir Jonathan was also in charge of record keeping. "Yes, of course it is."

She had read the Montblanc translation at least ten times, trying to make sense of its poetic descriptions of the "daemons". One verse always stood out, more for its macabre beauty than its sense:

When the earth is fractured, and the poison pours forth,
bring the blood, bring the bone, bring the dead.

Accompanying notes about the verse, written by other Reclaimers and Tracers, had suggested many meanings, but it was Lord Carlston's neat question written in the margin that Helen found most pertinent: *Is the blood, bone and dead the Trinitas?*

"There." Sir Jonathan's finger had found a place upon a page. "All the Reclaimers agree that this verse says a Grand Deceiver will be charming and cunning above a normal Deceiver, and move from a lowly state to high rank. Is that not valuable?"

"Yes, you are quite right. Very valuable," Helen said. An act of contrition.

Sir Jonathan closed the folio and placed it back upon the

table. Another silence settled. It seemed a prompt was going to be required about the day's goal.

Helen waved an encouraging hand towards the sofa opposite. "Do take a seat, Sir Jonathan. Perhaps we can discuss how you plan to conduct the mesmerism session before Lord Carlston arrives."

There, she saw it again: the tension in the man's face whenever she mentioned Lord Carlston. She had first seen it six months ago when she had made Sir Jonathan's acquaintance at the reclaiming of little Jeremiah in London, and had already marked it twice this meeting. He had some history with Carlston that rankled.

"Are you sure you wish to discuss the process, Lady Helen?" He crossed to the sofa and sat down on the blue damask silk, neatly flicking back his coat-tails. "I do not wish to alarm you unnecessarily."

"I assure you, I find ignorance far more alarming. Is there much risk in mesmerism?"

"A journey into the mind and spirit will always hold risk, my lady." He shifted on the seat. "I cannot claim a great deal of experience in the practice of it."

"I see," Helen said, all amusement well and truly gone.

"Lord Carlston taught you the breathing exercise I sent down?"

Draw breath for four beats and release for seven. "Yes. It is quite straightforward."

Perhaps the only straightforward part of the whole exercise, Helen thought, considering the force of the Ligatus voices and blood-ink words that waited behind the dam of her consciousness. Carlston was convinced that Sir Jonathan and his mesmerism could finally break open that dam and allow her access to the Ligatus information. He seemed to have faith that, somehow, she would be able to discover the way to control the power within her, as well as uncover his role as the other half of the Grand Reclaimer.

Helen was not so sure – his lordship had not experienced the violent power of the Ligatus. It was hard enough to withstand the howling anguish and rage of the life forces caught in the book. How was she then to hold on to the sense in their voices or the squirming words that had come from a madman's pen?

"Good." Two nods punctuated Sir Jonathan's approval. "The rhythm is essential, you see. Although I will be instrumental in leading you to a place of trance, you must assist through breath regulation and focus." He gave a quick smile, meant to be reassuring. "But do not be concerned – you are always in control. You can break the trance at will."

By all rights, she should inform Sir Jonathan of the danger locked within her mind; but he was not a member of the Inner Circle and she could not break the vow of secrecy. It would have to be an oblique warning. Although if the process did work, he would know the truth soon enough.

Helen leaned forward. "Are you sure I will be able to break the trance? There are … *complications* … that may require me to do so."

Sir Jonathan's small mouth compressed even more tightly. "Ah, yes, the *complications*."

"You know about them?" Helen could not keep the surprise from her voice.

"Of course." Sir Jonathan observed her for a troubled moment. "Ah, you were not aware that his lordship and Mr Pike had informed me of the Grand Reclaimer dyad and the Ligatus."

Helen sat back. "No. I was not aware."

"I am honoured by the trust, my lady." Sir Jonathan bent his upper body into an awkward bow, the sofa creaking beneath him.

It had not been her trust, Helen thought, nor her decision to include him in the Circle. Was she the only one to abide by her promises?

"As I understand it," Sir Jonathan continued, "there are other life forces within you. Other energies. We have no way of knowing how those elements will" – he brought his hands together, interlacing his fingers – "interact with the mesmerism."

"I see." Helen looked squarely at him. "So I may not be able to break the trance. In fact, I may not be in control."

"There are always elements that cannot be figured into the Reclaimer equation." He unlaced his fingers. "Even his lordship has made—" He stopped.

"His lordship has made what?" she asked.

He shook his head, staring down at the floor.

"Sir Jonathan," Helen said crisply, bringing the man's attention back to her face, "I cannot help but notice the constraint between you and Lord Carlston. I do not wish to embark upon a dangerous process if the two people I am relying upon for my safety are experiencing some kind of enmity."

"I can assure you, Lady Helen, there is no enmity." He paused, searching for words. "There is regret and perhaps guilt, but it will not interfere with our work here today."

Regret and guilt? For what? Helen decided to step boldly. "You mean because of his wife, Lady Elise?"

"No!" Sir Jonathan's stubby hands rose into a flat wall of denial. "At least not on my part." He lowered his voice, a side glance checking the firmly closed door. "I must say, however, that from the very beginning I sensed something was awry with Countess Carlston. I traced her twice, you know, but her lineage was quite clean. Of course, it never occurred to me that she was just a common spy." He shook his head. "No, our shared regret concerns a boy in Exeter."

"What happened?"

"I'm afraid it has a rather sordid beginning. Not fit for a lady's ears."

"You must think of me as a Reclaimer, Sir Jonathan. Not as a lady."

He gave a reluctant nod. "As you wish. Near five years ago, I traced a Deceiver offspring to a landed family. The lady had been seduced by a Deceiver and the by-blow had been passed off as her husband's son. The boy had all the indicators of an offspring, including escalating insanity. Lord Carlston agreed with my findings and attempted to reclaim him. His lordship was well into the ritual when he realised that the boy was not an offspring but completely human. A poor child who had lost his reason." Sir Jonathan turned a heavy ring on his finger, his eyes focused upon the memory. "I had made a mistake, and Lord Carlston had acted upon it. I know you have witnessed a reclaiming, Lady Helen. You know how violent it can be upon the soul of the offspring. Lord Carlston did everything he could, but the boy was too ill, too weak to survive such an ordeal. He died in Lord Carlston's arms."

Helen bowed her head. It was as if she felt the boy in her own arms, watching the life leave his frail body. Sweet heaven, even in her imagination she felt crushed.

"How often are such mistakes made?" Her voice had retreated into a whisper. She cleared her throat and pushed past the vivid vision. "How often?"

"In twenty-two years of service, I have helped reclaim over two thousand souls back to full humanity. In that time, I have made seven mistakes. Four of them died; every one of them burned upon my soul." He touched his chest as if he felt that burn even now.

"But surely, after all this time, there are ways to avoid such terrible mistakes?" Helen asked.

"We do our best. I have made changes to the way we trace offspring, and Mr Pike reviews all reclaim orders. Nevertheless, innocents are killed in every war, Lady Helen." He leaned forward. "We must *all* contrive to live with that truth."

Helen rose from her chair and walked to the hearth, away from his implication that she too would one day kill an innocent. She had already killed Lowry and Lawrence – the first by accident and the second by intention – but neither man had been innocent by any measure. Even so, their deaths had dug claws into her soul. How would it be to cause the death of a child? She had a terrible inkling, drawn from the despair she felt when little Timothy Marr's voice rose through her mind.

She paused in front of the mantel mirror, the fire in the grate bringing warmth to her chilled body as she watched Sir Jonathan's reflection rub tiredly at his eyes. Why had he brought up such a thing? Because she had asked him, that's why. Still, it was not what she wanted to hear.

She turned to face him. "If you mean to reassure me, you are failing."

He gave a dry smile. "Forgive me. I meant to warn you."

Helen was distracted from answering by the sudden deepening of the Grand Reclaimer pulse in her chest: Lord Carlston had arrived.

A few moments later, she heard his voice greet Garner in the entrance hallway: *"We will show ourselves up."* She focused her hearing upon the other voices. Mr Quinn was also in attendance … and someone else. She concentrated, drawing a sharp breath as she recognised the man's cold voice.

"Mr Pike is here. You did not tell me he was coming."

Sir Jonathan stood, his plump hands tugging the hem of his waistcoat. "I did not … I was not expecting him."

Pike was the last person she wanted present; she would feel vulnerable enough without him in the room. Had Lord Carlston invited him? She paced across the hearth, the action bringing no relief whatsoever. Although she and Pike had come to a wary acknowledgment of the other's importance to the Dark Days Club, she had not forgiven his brutal coercion of her and Mr Hammond to obtain the Ligatus.

Sir Jonathan watched her cross the hearth again. "Mr Pike puts us on our mettle, hey?" The false joviality in his voice brought her to a halt.

"You do not trust him either."

He rocked back on his heels. "I respect his devotion to the Dark Days Club."

A knock sounded on the door.

Helen crossed to the centre of the room, smoothed the bodice of her gown and drew her shoulders back. "Come," she called.

The door opened to admit Lord Carlston and Mr Pike. If it was at all possible, Ignatious Pike, Second Secretary to the Home Office and bureaucratic head of the Dark Days Club, looked even more gaunt than when she had last seen him a month back in London at a covert meeting. Admittedly, he wore a new olive kerseymere jacket that fitted his stooped shoulders a little better than his previous efforts, but his collar and cravat were loose around his corded neck, and the lines that ran from his nose to his downturned mouth seemed more deeply carved.

It was perhaps also to his detriment that he stood beside Lord Carlston, whose fierce vitality was only enhanced by the severe elegance of his navy-blue jacket, perfectly tailored to his shoulders and, no doubt, a pig to get into, even with Quinn's help. For a moment, Helen missed wearing her own male garb, but she shrugged away the regret. For the next month, she was a bride.

She rose from her curtsey. "Mr Pike, I had not expected to see you today," she said, aiming the words at Carlston. She noted the quiet arrival of Quinn and Darby behind them. So this was to be a meeting of the newly expanded Inner Circle.

"Mr Pike is as eager as I am to find the power of the Grand Reclaimer," Carlston said pointedly.

"As are we all," Helen said, blocking the barb. She turned to Mr Pike. "Why was I not consulted about informing Sir Jonathan of the dyad?"

The Second Secretary gave his thin-lipped smile. "He could hardly attempt to draw out the Ligatus information without knowing about it, Lady Helen. Lord Carlston tells me that this method of memory retrieval has been very successful on the Continent."

Sir Jonathan stepped forward. "Indeed, Mr Pike. However, we must remember that in this case it is not Lady Helen's own memories she is recalling, but access to something... Well, something entirely without precedent."

Helen ground her palms together. "Quite so. However, my question to you, Mr Pike, was why was I not consulted about bringing Sir Jonathan into the Circle?"

"It is a necessity. Do you have an objection to his inclusion?"

"I can hardly have an objection now, can I?"

"Did you have one?"

"No, but—"

"Then let us stop quibbling." He turned away, the dismissal clear. "Shall we get started on the process, Sir Jonathan?"

The Tracer bowed. "Of course. I must say, however, that while the process has had some success, I cannot guarantee anything."

"I am not holding you accountable, Sir Jonathan, if that is your concern," Pike said.

His bluntness pushed the older man back a step. "I assure you … that is not what I… No, not at all…"

Carlston glanced at Pike, a wealth of irritation in the fleeting contact. "Your best effort is all that we ask, Sir Jonathan," he said.

"Yes, yes, my best effort," the Tracer murmured. He retreated to the rain-streaked windows and unsnibbed one of the folded shutters. "We must close these to block out the light. Lady Helen's chair too must face away from the window. Miss Darby, if you would light a few candles?"

As Quinn and Darby moved to arrange the room, Helen crossed to where Pike and Carlston stood, intent upon taking up cudgels again. Pike's dismissiveness was infuriating.

She caught a warning in Carlston's level gaze: *Leave it.*

She narrowed her eyes: *I will not leave it.*

"How is your wife, Mr Pike?" Carlston asked, abruptly halting her attack.

It was not an idle inquiry. The retrieval of Benchley's journal had not only brought the Ligatus power; it had also brought the intelligence that Pike's wife, Isabella, was a Deceiver offspring – an Unreclaimable – with a vestige rooted so deep within her soul that it pushed her into bouts of violent insanity. Four years ago, the poor woman had, unknowingly, killed the Reclaimer who had tried to restore her soul. The terrible act had forced her husband to abuse his position in an effort to hide the crime and her taint.

Pike studied Carlston from under a resentful brow. It was plain he had not wanted the subject raised. "Not well." He addressed Helen. "She has deteriorated greatly since you saw her in Brighton." He rubbed his mouth, as if he wished to wipe away his next words. "The periods of insanity are getting longer. Sometimes she does not know who I am."

Oh no, poor lady. And poor Pike. Although Helen did not trust him, or even like him, no one deserved the pain of seeing the one they loved descend into madness. For an instant, she saw an image of Carlston attacking Selburn in Brighton, insane from the vestige darkness.

"I am sorry to hear it, Mr Pike."

So this was what lay behind the man's brusque manner, and the reason why Carlston had brought him here: a reminder of the urgent need to discover the secrets of their united power and truly become the Grand Reclaimer. She had already restored the soul of one Unreclaimable through the Ligatus, and had promised to save Isabella Pike too; a promise that was plainly coming into its own urgency.

She glared at Carlston: *How dare you use Mrs Pike's sanity.*

He crossed his arms: *I will use whatever works.*

She drew a breath through her outrage and addressed the issue at hand. "Is it now time to reclaim Isabella, Mr Pike? You know that Lord Carlston and I will attempt it whenever you wish."

Pike ducked his head. "Thank you, but I cannot go ahead until we are sure you both have the Grand Reclaimer power under control. The risk to Isabella's life would be too great, and I could not bear…"

"Of course," Helen said.

Carlston's eyes were upon her, but she refused to look at his insufferable self-righteousness. She knew, just as well as he did, that their power must be the priority. It was not as if she were deliberately failing to find a way to control it. Had she not agreed to try this unholy mesmerism? Besides, it was not she who had gone to Paris for a week to search for a traitor wife.

"Lady Helen, if you would please seat yourself here," Sir Jonathan said, patting the back of the wing armchair that

Quinn had placed in the centre of the room with its back to the windows. A plain mahogany chair had been set before it. "As you see, I will be sitting opposite you and quite close. I hope that is permissible."

With a nod, Helen took her seat in the armchair and settled back into its velvet cushions, trying to appear at ease. A hard task, considering the anger still locked in her muscles and the sudden hammering of her heart. It was all very well to agree to be mesmerised, but now that it was imminent, the uncertainties of such a dubious process came rushing forth. Just how dangerous was it? What would happen if all the voices emerged at once? What if they did not come at all? Could she even be mesmerised?

"Lord Carlston, I believe you will be noting what Lady Helen says in her trance. If you could please take your position at the writing desk." Sir Jonathan waited until Carlston had seated himself at the secretaire. "And, Mr Pike, if you could be seated over there." He waved the Second Secretary to the sofa that had been set behind Helen's chair. "I believe we are almost ready."

He flicked out his coat-tails and took his seat opposite Helen, then frowned as Darby crossed to stand by the armchair. "No, Miss Darby, you must take yourself out of the way. Stand beside Mr Quinn, by the wall."

"I'm afraid that is not possible, Sir Jonathan," Darby said. She raised her chin, her stance somehow becoming broader and more threatening just by the straightening of her shoulders and spine. A trick she had learned from Quinn. "I am Lady Helen's Terrene and I stand by her side."

Helen glanced up at her and nodded her agreement, receiving Darby's sweet, swift smile in return.

Sir Jonathan turned to Carlston, clearly seeking his support.

"Do not look to me," his lordship said. "As Darby has stated, she is Lady Helen's Terrene."

"She stays, Sir Jonathan," Helen said, hiding a moment of wry amusement. It must be difficult for Sir Jonathan to reconcile the maid in her neat blue gown and white cap with the warrior aide she claimed to be.

"Well, you must not interrupt at any point," the Tracer warned.

"I'm sure she has no intention of doing so," Helen said. "Shall we start now?" Brave words, but her mouth was as dry as a wad of cotton.

"Before we do so, there are some rules that you must all adhere to," Sir Jonathan said, gathering everyone around the room in his sober glance. "Mesmerism requires immense concentration. Observers must be quiet at all times. Usually there are no words spoken between the mesmerist and the subject during a session, but Lord Carlston has requested that I speak to the life forces within Lady Helen and ask for information." Sir Jonathan nodded to Helen, his grave expression failing to hide the doubt behind it. "I am not sure if this is possible, my lady, but we will try. I also ask that no movement be made around the room that could distract Lady Helen or myself. Are we all agreed upon these stipulations?" He glanced around, receiving everyone's nod of accord. "Excellent."

I am with you. Carlston's voice, barely more than a breath, pitched for her Reclaimer ears. Helen shifted in her chair, a side glance catching an image of him in the candlelight: quill in hand, steady gaze upon her, his lips curved into his half-smile. Even through the remnants of her anger, she felt the anchor of his presence.

The wind outside slammed against the windows, the rain and grit within the gusts rat-a-tat-tatting against the glass in sweeping waves.

Sir Jonathan sat forward in his chair. "Lady Helen, I will be making what are called passes down your body with my hand, but I will not touch you. These passes manipulate the energy in your body. You must focus upon my eyes and not shift your gaze from them. Can you do that?"

"I believe so," Helen said, obeying the request. His blue eyes held solemn concentration.

"Then please start the breathing rhythm you have practised."

Helen drew her breath for four beats and, as she released it, counted out seven. Sir Jonathan lifted his hand an inch or so from her forehead. With forefinger extended, he drew a line down through the air, past her nose, her chin, her throat, her chest, stopping at her abdomen. He lifted his hand back to her forehead and repeated the downward pass, his eyes fixed upon hers, the flowing movement matching the release of her breath.

His fingertip passed her line of sight again, and again. It was not going to work. She could not be mesmerised. She swallowed; her mouth was still dry and a muscle near her eye twitched. How irritating.

His round face blurred a little – all this staring made her eyes tired. She was keeping the rhythm quite well, her chest rising and falling, and his fingertip passing, over and over. She could barely focus; easier to close her eyes. Yes, much easier.

In the soft darkness, she heard a buzzing in her ears; something stirring, whispering, rising in a slow arc, like a hive disturbed.

A soft, plaintive cry pierced the shifting hum.

"Is there someone who will speak?" Sir Jonathan's voice, low and steady.

The crying became louder, shuddering through her mind into her throat, building into a sob, spreading into a howl. An infant's cry.

"That is a child," Pike's voice said.

"Mr Pike, silence, please. Breathe, Lady Helen. Let the child go."

She released air, the anguish passing through her body, catching at the sobs in her chest. Behind it came a woman's gibbering screech. No sense within it, only terror. The wailing filled her ears. Shook her body.

"Breathe, Lady Helen!"

Other voices, rising through the darkness: a man cursing, another jabbering, and another and another, swarming into her mind. Too many of them, screaming, shouting, howling, squealing, their cries collapsing into scrawled words that glowed in her mind, pulsing, then exploding back into a buzzing, hissing, shrieking cacophony.

"VC!" she gasped. "Cannot trust VC!"

The letters erupted into flames, their warning consumed, the heat building and building inside her mind.

"What is VC?" Sir Jonathan's voice, far away.

But VC was gone. Other meanings exploded in front of her closed eyes: bright, hot, whirling Catherine wheels of understanding that burst into bright blue lights, falling into the darkness again, all their sense gone. And still the searing heat building through her body.

"The dyad power," Sir Jonathan said, his urgency jabbing through the clamouring voices. "How is the dyad power controlled?"

A voice rose above the others – a Deceiver – screaming a word that burst from Helen's lips. "Water!" She grabbed for the knowledge that followed the word, the sense of it making her gasp. This was the answer to the dyad power. "Water!"

"Does she need water?" Darby's voice, anxious.

"Be quiet!" Sir Jonathan's voice snapped. "Lady Helen, tell me about the dyad power."

She rocked, the boiling heat of the voices, the sound, the words surging through every vein, muscle, sinew, building into crackling, burning energy.

"Sir Jonathan, it is time to stop!" Carlston's voice.

Water. Yes. She held on to the meaning. Nothing else could be held. It was all burning.

"Lady Helen, sit still." Sir Jonathan, urgent now. "Listen to me! You must return to the room. Come back now. Breathe with me: one-two-three-four!"

She rose from the chair, feet braced wide on the carpet, the burning within her seeking a path. Yes, she understood the path. She thrust out her hands, eyes opening as the blue power pulsed through her arms.

"I know," she said, her voice crackling with energy, a taste on her tongue like air struck with lightning.

She whirled – glorious Reclaimer speed – her fingers dragging the air around with her: collecting it, moulding it, spinning the water contained within it into a silvery thread of droplets.

Around her, everyone had slowed, their momentum caught in normal time. Sir Jonathan rising from his chair, Darby reaching towards her, Quinn bending into a run. But the heat within her was too much to hold. Too much!

Screaming, she thrust out her hands, the silvery blue thread of water spooling out towards the back wall: a pathway, hanging in the air, waiting for the searing power. It burst from her, blue energy pulsing hot through her arms and fingers, propelled along the shimmering line. The thick surge of boiling heat consumed the water as it raced towards the far wall, leaving a wispy white trail of steam.

A body at Reclaimer speed launched itself across the room. Carlston. "Get down!" he yelled as he tackled Sir Jonathan, slamming them both to the floor.

The boiling power hit the wall and the boom of impact shuddered through the whole drawing room. Chunks of plaster and wood pelted down in a bruising rain. Darby dropped to the floor in a crouch as the force slammed through Lady Margaret's dressing room beyond, smashing a clothes-press into splinters and flattening a table. The ceiling between the rooms disintegrated, floorboards and beams crashing from the bedchamber above; a mangled chair dropped through and ruptured into pieces on the drawing room floor. The window shutters bowed and cracked, swinging from their hinges, the glass behind them fracturing, popping, smashing. The mirror above the hearth collapsed in a tinkling rush of destruction; the fire in the grate doused by black soot shaken loose from the chimney. Grey dust billowed, chalky and dank, filling the air with lung-clogging particles and grit as freezing rain gusted in through the broken windows.

The pulsing roar of energy built in Helen again, the whispering voices rising into soft howls and shrieks, the heat flashing through her body. She whirled, an uncontrollable impulse to surge into Reclaimer speed, to spin the air and water into pure power, thundering through her blood.

Carlston hauled himself to his feet. "Helen, stop!"

Another figure, on hands and knees, lunged through the billowing dust and soot. A strong grip locked around Helen's ankle: Darby. Blue power arced between them, a jolt of searing pain flashing from Helen's heart to her feet. Darby screamed, propelled backward across the room. She landed heavily on the wet carpet, her body rolling over and over until it slammed against a fallen shutter.

Silence, deep and shocked.

Helen rocked on her feet. The power was gone. The heat and pain, gone. The voices once again a hum in the background of her mind.

Dear God, had she killed Darby?

A shrill scream sounded from the floor below. And then another. Shouts from outside. Someone amidst the debris coughed and retched: Pike.

Helen staggered a step towards her Terrene. "Darby!" The cry was lost, caught in the parched dust of her throat.

All around, masonry and rubble slid and crunched as people stirred: Pike hauling himself upright from the toppled sofa; Sir Jonathan leaning against the wall, nursing one arm against his chest; Carlston on his back on the floor, wiping grit from his eyes; and Quinn crawling to Darby on his hands and knees, his eyes wide with fear.

"Jen!" It was half plea, half command. He pushed aside a splintered chair and reached for her pale cheek. "Jen?"

Darby shuddered and took a deep, gasping breath. Alive! Helen sagged, a hoarse sob shaking her on her feet.

"Nathaniel!" Darby grasped Quinn's arm, the reassurance curling the big man over her prone body. "I'm not hurt. It's all right. I'm not hurt."

"What the hell *was* that?" Pike demanded, picking his way across the broken furniture.

Sir Jonathan took a tentative step after him, then leaned back against the wall. "My wrist! I think it's broken."

Below came the sound of Mr Hammond's voice and then Lady Margaret's and Delia's, the sense of their shouts lost in the cries from the street and the gusts of wind and rain that slapped the surviving shutters against the walls.

Carlston stood up slowly, using an upended armchair for leverage. "Sir Jonathan, stay where you are. Helen, are you hurt? Is anyone else hurt?"

She tried to say *no*, but her voice was lost. Her legs buckled, the edges of her vision hazing into grey – she was going to faint.

She began to slide downward, then felt arms catch her as her knees hit the floor, her body lifted upright again and braced against navy-blue wool and firm muscle. The room tipped and lurched into a nauseating spin. She blinked and focused on Carlston's grit-reddened eyes, watching her in alarm.

He shifted his hold, cradling her head. "Where are you hurt?" Blood seeped from a cut across his cheek, leaving a wet track through the grey dust on his face.

"I found the power," she rasped.

"Are you injured?"

"Not hurt, just ... drained." The word was fitting: some of the buzzing power in her had gone, leaving a terrible weariness. At least the room had stopped spinning. "I know how to make it into a weapon." She wet her lips, tasting chalk and sweet, coppery blood. "Water."

He nodded. "I'll get you some."

"No!" She caught the lapel of his jacket, her grip oddly weak around the cloth. "I mean the Deceivers *use water*."

His face became intent. "In what way?"

"In the air, to make a path for their energy whips. I think that is how we can do it too."

She surveyed the destruction around them. Darby and Quinn were still huddled on the floor; Sir Jonathan had sunk into a squat against the wall; and Pike had worked his way to the doorway, no doubt preparing for the frantic arrival of Lady Margaret, Delia and Mr Hammond.

"Water," Carlston echoed, as if locking the new sense of the word into the puzzle of their power. He looked at the rain blowing in soaking gusts through the broken windows. "Well, at least we have plenty of it."

She gave a small, raw laugh, the sound stinging her throat.

He smoothed a wet hank of hair from her cheek, the gentle

path of his fingers calling up the Reclaimer beat in her body, turning her face into the curve of his palm, pressing her lips against his skin... Lud, what was she doing? She jerked her head back from the unthinking intimacy. "No."

"I beg your pardon," he said stiffly, shifting his grip to her shoulders.

"I can stand on my own, thank you." She pulled her arms free. Retreated one, two, three steps. Turned away.

Yet not even that space between them, nor her bone-aching fatigue, nor the freezing gusts of rain that drenched her, could obscure the pounding pulse that reached out towards him.

Chapter Four

An hour later, Mr Hammond picked up the decanter from the tray that Garner had delivered to the morning room and poured a generous measure of brandy into Helen's tumbler, ignoring her murmur of protest. He half rose from his chair and pushed the glass across the mahogany table; it left a dark wet trail through the fine layer of plaster dust.

"Another will not hurt," he said.

Perhaps he was right. Although she had changed her sodden gown, her hands still trembled from cold and fatigue. She raised the tumbler to her lips and took a mouthful. The fruity liquor stung her raw throat, but also stoked the comforting warmth in her chest and belly that the first measure had supplied.

Beside her, Darby sat wrapped in a woollen rug, her face still pale as she sipped at her own glass under the watchful eye of Quinn. He stood behind her as if on guard, flecks of plaster still salting his dark hair.

Helen glanced around the room. It was mostly intact, with only a few chunks of the ceiling shaken loose and a wide crack that had opened up along the inside wall. According to Mr Hammond's report, the real damage was upstairs. She had, more or less, destroyed the first floor and a good part of the second, both now uninhabitable. If it had not been for Darby, she might have brought the whole house down.

She stretched out her other hand; her skin showed no signs of the burning power that had rushed from her fingertips. The only indications were a strange pressure behind her eyes and the awful exhaustion that dragged at her every move, dampening even her ever-present connection to Lord Carlston.

"What about the street, Mr Hammond? Is it now secure?" Pike asked.

He and Carlston stood side by side in front of the hearth in an effort to dry their soaked clothes. Carlston had refused another brandy, but Pike swirled a second measure in his glass, a frown of concentration on his thin face.

Hammond took a mouthful from his own refilled tumbler. "Quinn secured it."

All attention turned to the Terrene.

"A cart-horse bolted, sending a cargo of coal onto the road," he reported. "Most of the load has been picked over by scavengers, and the hauler is crying foul, so he'll be around with his hand out before long. A few people on the street were cut by flying glass. Mrs Kent tended to them with the help of Miss Cransdon." He gave a respectful nod to Delia, who was seated opposite Helen.

"None had serious cuts," Delia said, a delicate flush colouring her pale skin; the excitement, no doubt, of finally being entrusted with a Dark Days Club task. "We sent them on their way with your story and a half-crown each, as you instructed, Mr Pike."

"Good." The Second Secretary sucked his front teeth. "It was the best I could do under the circumstances, although I will not be thanked by those trying to introduce gas lights to the populace. I have apprised the mayor and the constables of the 'accident' and they will inform the Bath Council."

"Mr Hammond will be dealing with the newspapers," Carlston added. "But if any of you are questioned, keep to the story that we were trialling the new gas technology and a lamp unfortunately exploded."

"That is all very well," Lady Margaret said from an armchair angled before the hearth, "but it seems somewhat unfair that my brother, Miss Cransdon and I are the only ones here who do not know the truth of what happened. Even Darby and Quinn know."

Hammond gave a slight shake of his head. "Not now, Margaret."

She sat forward. Her dark hair had come loose from its coiffure and large smudges of dust and plaster soiled her navy-blue gown. "Why not now? If we are to be in danger, surely we have a right to know what kind and where it is coming from?"

"You will be informed at the appropriate time, Lady Margaret," Carlston said. He ignored her mutinous glare and gestured to Hammond. "Anything else?"

"Lisbeth, the maid who was hit on the head by debris, has regained her senses. And, of course, Sir Jonathan has a broken wrist." Hammond nodded to the Tracer, who sat next to him nursing a splinted hand and a very large measure of brandy. "Most of the damage was to the building and not to us or any bystanders, thank God."

"Amen," Helen said, joining the soft declaration around the room. Thank the Lord she had not killed anyone. It was bad enough to have injured Sir Jonathan, Lisbeth and the poor people on the street.

Lady Margaret rose from her chair and restlessly paced a few steps, drawing her silk shawl around her shoulders. "As my brother said, the damage to the building is substantial. This is, for all intents and purposes, the only habitable room in the main part of the house. The drawing room and my rooms – including most of my clothing, I may add – are destroyed, as are the bedchambers above." She turned abruptly. "Will it happen again?"

Helen glanced at Carlston: *It may be just the beginning.* He tilted his head in agreement.

Lady Margaret caught the silent communication. "You think there is more to come! And where do you propose we live while there is an ever-present threat of explosion? The owner of this house will, quite rightly, expect us to—"

A loud voice in the front hallway stopped her mid-sentence. "What a mess! Where is Lady Helen?"

"Your Grace, she is currently in the morning room, but—"

"Out of my way. I will see her now."

"Ah." Carlston crossed his arms and leaned back against the mantel. "I believe your betrothed has arrived, Lady Helen."

"Word gets around fast here," Hammond murmured to Sir Jonathan. The Tracer frowned at him, clearly in no mood for flippancy.

Helen squeezed her eyes shut then opened them wide, trying to bring some sharpness back to her mind. Selburn would want to know what had happened, and the prospect of lying to him – again – exhausted her even more.

The door opened and the Duke strode into the room still wearing his wet greatcoat and gloves. He located Helen and took a deep breath. "You are not hurt."

"No," she said as he crossed the room to her side. "We are all quite well, except for poor Sir Jonathan here, who has broken his wrist."

The Duke nodded his commiserations to Sir Jonathan, but his attention was upon Helen. He took her hand, encompassing it within both of his own. The chill of the day had penetrated his gloves and the kid leather was cold against Helen's skin.

"There is a large crowd outside the house. What happened?"

"An experimental gas lamp exploded," Carlston said, straightening from his lounge against the mantel.

Squaring up for battle, Helen thought. Exactly what she did not need.

"This house has never had a gas lamp, Carlston." Selburn lifted Helen's hand to his lips, then released his hold. "What really happened, my dear?"

Carlston stepped forward and repeated, "An experimental gas lamp exploded."

Selburn whirled around. "I did not ask you."

Pike hurriedly inserted himself into the narrowing space between the two men. "Your Grace, this is Reclaimer business."

Selburn drew himself up to his superior height. "My betrothed is sitting in a house that is more or less destroyed. From what I can see, it is only by the grace of God that she and the rest of you are not dead. I demand to know what happened."

"Demand all you want," Carlston said.

Helen cleared her throat. "I destroyed it."

Selburn swung back, bemused. "*You* destroyed it?"

"Lady Helen," Pike warned.

She stood up. "No, Mr Pike, the Duke deserves to know the truth. As do the others." She nodded to Lady Margaret. "They are part of the Dark Days Club. Keeping this information from them is now more dangerous than revealing it."

"We have not discussed this!"

"We are discussing it now." She refrained from pointing out that he had not *discussed* Sir Jonathan's inclusion. "Lord Carlston, do you object?"

He observed her for a long moment, his eyes hooded. "I

would not have chosen this particular moment, but it was always going to be necessary to inform our aides. I believe this is the time, Pike."

The Second Secretary considered them for a moment, then gave a reluctant nod. "I suppose you are right." He addressed the room. "Nothing that is said here must ever go beyond this circle, by the seal of your oaths." He bowed to Helen. "My lady Reclaimer, you have the floor."

She pressed her palms together. How best to explain? Whichever way she framed it, the Duke would be hurt by the immensity of what she had kept from him.

"Selburn, please understand that I have been obliged to stay silent."

"Of course," he said, but his eyes were wary.

"You will remember that Darby and I confronted Lord Carlston in the attic of the Comte d'Antraigues's house in Barnes Terrace. I had obtained a cure from the Comte to save his lordship from his madness."

She glanced at Carlston, but he had averted his face. Was he thinking of poor Stokes? He still could not remember killing their fellow Reclaimer, and she knew the madness-induced lapse in memory added to the burden of his guilt.

"The cure required us to make a bond – an alchemical union," she continued. "Before he died, the Comte told me that the Grand Deceiver is a dyad of power – two creatures working together. The only way to combat the Grand Deceiver is to unite two Reclaimers into an opposing power. Lord Carlston and I are now that dyad: the Grand Reclaimer."

"What?" Selburn stared at her, aghast.

"That is not all," Helen said. "The Grand Reclaimer bond required a blood conduit. I used the Ligatus, Samuel Benchley's journal. It was written in blood, you see, and primed with power.

In the course of the Grand Reclaimer union, I absorbed all of the information and the life forces in the book." She paused; if Selburn had been appalled by the dyad announcement, her next words were going to horrify him. "I am now the Ligatus." She heard Delia gasp, but doggedly continued. "When Sir Jonathan mesmerised me to access its information, I accessed its power and that was what caused the explosion."

"Dear God," Hammond said. "You are carrying all that book's death and pain within you? How can you bear it?"

"It is not easy," Helen said.

She looked back at the Duke's haggard face; it was as if the shock had drawn his skin tight against his bones. He turned away, one of his hands flexing in and out of a fist. Not a good sign.

"It is always in the background of my mind, like a hum," she added. "But it is not only death and pain, Mr Hammond. It is also information and power."

Delia clutched the edge of the table. "You blew up the house? By yourself?"

Helen gave a wan smile. "It was a lot of power. Perhaps, with the Ligatus, even more power than a Grand Reclaimer usually holds."

"So you *can* control it? Like a weapon?" Delia asked, eyes round.

Helen met her friend's eyes, wishing she had a different answer. "No, I did not have control."

The admission silenced the room.

"No control over that much power?" Lady Margaret echoed. "Heaven help us."

Sir Jonathan cleared his throat. "Surely it is a matter of practice. And I can consult with my mesmerism instructor to find a less *explosive* method of drawing out the Ligatus information and power." He drew his injured hand closer to his chest. "Once I have healed."

The Duke turned to face Helen again. His awful haggard shock had given way to an alarmingly high colour. "Are you telling me that you are in some kind of blood bond with Lord Carlston?"

"I rather thought we had moved on from that point," Carlston said. "But yes, that is exactly what Lady Helen is saying."

"Lord Carlston, please!" Helen said. She did not need him stepping in to make more trouble.

Selburn pressed his knuckle against his forehead. "So this is why the two of you are always training? Always locking yourselves away?"

"You see now why I had to keep it secret, don't you?" Helen asked, but he angled his face from her, mouth set in a hard line. "We have been trying to discover the way to channel the power into something we can use against the Grand Deceiver."

"And now you have found it?"

"Lady Helen *may* have found the way," Carlston said. "That remains to be seen." He cast her a glance: *No more. This is Reclaimer business.*

"It is water," Helen said, a shake of her head refusing his silent command. She would have no more omissions, no more lies, between her and Selburn. "The Deceivers use it as a conduit for their power."

"Ah, like electricity," Mr Hammond said, sitting straighter in his chair. "I have read Mr Gray's theories, and he has posited that water is a *non-electric*. It does not hold the electrical fire, but rather allows it to flow readily."

"Exactly." Helen smiled, glad of another, more neutral voice.

"But how do the Deceivers use it as a conduit?" Delia asked.

"There is always some water in the air," Helen said. "As I

understand it, a Deceiver fashions the tiny water drops into a channel, and then sends its power through that channel to create a whip. I don't know yet how they manage to control and maintain the electrical fire within their whips for so long, or how they can manipulate them with such astounding agility. That is something Lord Carlston and I must discover and try to replicate."

She looked across at him. He nodded his agreement, his half-smile in place – he was clearly enjoying the look of resentment on Selburn's face. Yet that was how it must be, Helen thought. Only she and Carlston could find the answer.

"And where do you propose to replicate Deceiver whips?" Lady Margaret asked. She gestured around the room. "We cannot live in this house any longer, and there will be no others available so late in the Season, especially in the decent areas. Think how difficult it was to secure this place."

"We can hardly stay in Bath, Margaret," Mr Hammond said. "A town this size is not the place to learn how to make weapons from water in the air."

"So where do you suggest we decamp?" his sister demanded. "Or is that the extent of your contribution?"

"You are right, Lady Margaret. It is the next question we must address," Carlston said, the effort at conciliation softening her rigid stance.

Delia cleared her throat. "I have a possible answer." She addressed the Duke. "I hope you do not think this is forward of me, Your Grace, but just two days ago you kindly invited Lady Helen and myself to a Christmas house party at Chenwith Hall. Perhaps that invitation could include Lady Margaret and Mr Hammond and…" She trailed off, darting an anxious look at Helen. "It was what you suggested."

Helen glared at her. Had Delia forgotten the outcome of that suggestion? Selburn plainly had not, for he was refusing to look in Delia's or her direction.

With her chin lifted, Lady Margaret gathered her shawl closer around her body. "Miss Cransdon, you and Lady Helen have dined at Chenwith Hall twice, and neither invitation included my brother or me. The Duke has made it quite clear that we are not welcome in his home, and that our criminal presence would sully Chenwith Hall."

Pike held up his hand to block Lady Margaret's bitterness. "Miss Cransdon has made an excellent suggestion. Your Grace, would you be willing to extend your invitation?"

"The invitation was to my betrothed and Miss Cransdon, and that stands." Still he refused to meet Helen's eyes.

Lady Margaret gave a low, savage laugh.

"Your Grace," Pike said, "you swore an oath – just as we have all sworn – to serve the interests of the Dark Days Club. I am saying now, without equivocation, that inviting your comrades-in-arms to stay at Chenwith Hall will be directly serving those interests."

Selburn's jaw shifted. "I see."

"Are you a part of the Dark Days Club or not, Your Grace?" Pike pressed.

The Duke observed him for a long, chilly moment. "I am." He turned to Lady Margaret and bowed. "It would be my pleasure to host you and your household at Chenwith Hall."

Lady Margaret's eyes flashed – a clear desire to refuse him – but she gave a stiff nod. "Thank you. We accept your *generous* offer."

"Good, that is one problem solved," Pike said. He turned to Carlston. "When you are all settled, we must—"

"Wait!" Selburn said sharply. "Carlston is not invited. He has his own rooms; he does not need to stay at Chenwith."

"I do not recall asking for your hospitality," Carlston said.

Ignoring him, Selburn said to Pike, "I will not have him in my house."

"But, Your Grace," Delia said, "Lord Carlston and Lady Helen are the Grand Reclaimer. They must be together to learn how to defeat the Grand Deceiver." She realised all eyes had turned upon her again and ducked her head. "I mean to say, that is what we are trying to do, is it not?"

"Quite," Lord Carlston said kindly. "However, Miss Cransdon, you must understand that the Duke's sense of duty only extends as far as it is convenient for him. His membership of the Dark Days Club is purely recreational."

Selburn stepped towards Carlston, his hands clenched.

Mr Pike inserted himself between the two men again and said, "Your Grace, would you be so kind as to speak privately with me in the dining room?"

For a moment, it looked as if Selburn would push past the Second Secretary.

"I'm so sorry," Delia said breathlessly. "It seemed like such a good solution."

Her timid apology penetrated the Duke's fury. He gave her a curt nod of acknowledgment, then turned and walked out of the room. Pike sent Carlston a quelling glance and followed, closing the door behind them.

It was a strange request on Pike's part, Helen thought, considering he knew that both she and Carlston could listen to the conversation if they chose to do so. Perhaps he thought good manners would prevent them from eavesdropping, or maybe he was trying to preserve the Duke's dignity. Whatever the case, she should leave their discussion to play out in privacy. Yet...

She heard Pike close the dining room door across the hall, and looked at Carlston. Was he listening too? She could not tell; his face was at its most impenetrable.

"Your Grace," she heard Pike say, "I understand your hesitation—"

"I don't think you do. Carlston has tried to kill me twice, and now I find out that he is in some kind of infernal blood bond with my betrothed."

"You know he was in the grip of the vestige madness both of those times, Your Grace. I guarantee his sanity now. You must see that he and Lady Helen need space and time to develop their dyad power without fear of harming others or being observed. Chenwith Hall is ideal, especially at such short notice. And surely you would rather observe these training sessions than not?"

Helen's face heated. How dare Pike imply she needed supervision.

"Carlston does not need to stay at Chenwith for that," Selburn said.

"It will look odd for him to ride out of Bath every day to your estate. It will be noticed. Not to mention that it is twelve miles. It will take him a good part of the daylight hours to go back and forth. And when it snows, he will not be able to make the journey at all. I ask you, on behalf of the Prince Regent and the Dark Days Club, to allow Lord Carlston to reside at Chenwith Hall. At least until some progress is made in the control of the dyad power."

Helen held her breath and looked up to see Carlston watching her, his face still dispassionate.

Pike's plea was met with silence. "Your Grace," he added, "do I need to remind you again that you gave your oath?"

"I gave it for her, Pike."

Helen released her breath. She had always known the Duke had taken the Dark Days Club oath for her sake, but such gallantry struck her heart anew with tenderness. And fear for his safety.

"This is what she needs, Your Grace."

"You mean it is what the Dark Days Club needs." Selburn's voice was dry. "It is against my better judgment, Pike, but I will include Carlston. Only until Christmas, mind you. After that, I insist Lady Helen and I have time to enjoy our wedding week."

"Understood, Your Grace. Thank you."

Helen pressed her hand against her still-flushed cheek. It was, as Pike said, best for the dyad. She quickly turned away at the sound of the two men crossing the hall.

The morning room door opened, drawing everyone's focus.

"Lord Carlston, a room awaits you at Chenwith if you so wish," the Duke said brusquely.

Carlston bowed, his voice as expressionless as his face. "Thank you."

The Duke met Helen's eyes for a moment – still a little angry.

"Selburn," she began.

"I am glad you are unhurt, Lady Helen." His lips curved for a moment into a tight smile. He needed more time.

She nodded; it was the least she could do.

He bowed to her, then addressed the assembled company. "It will be my pleasure to welcome you to Chenwith this afternoon. We dine at eight." He walked out of the room.

Pike closed the door, the click of the latch overloud in the silence.

Hammond raised his brandy in a toast. "I cannot tell you how much I am looking forward to this house party," he said and drained the glass.

Chapter Five

"Helen dear, we are coming to Chenwith." Helen's shoulder shook beneath a firm grip. "Time to wake up."

The familiar voice and insistent hand finally dragged her from the soft cocoon of a deep, exhausted oblivion. She opened her eyes to see Delia's face three inches from her own. Her friend's lips were pursed in evaluation, a knit of concern creasing the smooth skin of her brow. One navy-gloved hand clutched the edge of the window frame, bracing under the sway of the carriage; the other still gripped Helen's shoulder.

"Ah, finally. We have been trying to wake you for the last five minutes." She peered more intently into Helen's eyes. "Are you feeling any better?"

"I'm well enough, thank you." In truth, she felt much the same – as if someone had sewn lead weights upon her limbs and poured treacle into her brain.

Delia raised the hem of her red pelisse away from the peril of her boot heels and retreated back to the seat beside Darby. "Forgive me for saying so, but you do not look it."

Ignoring the uncharitable observation, Helen asked, "How are you feeling, Darby?"

In all the hustle and bustle to pack their belongings and set out for Chenwith Hall, Helen had not had the time nor privacy to fully discuss the violent flash of power that had sparked between them. Or its after-effects.

"I'm well, my lady, now that I'm over the fright. Just an odd feeling here." She touched her forehead.

Indeed, Darby did look restored; her skin had returned to its pink health, and her eyes no longer held the bleary shock that had clouded them after the explosion.

Helen looked down at her own tan-gloved hands; she could feel a tremble in them. And she too had an odd sensation in her head. Not an ache as such, but more of a dull pressure.

Darby leaned forward. "My lady, I think I saw—"

"Miss Cransdon is right," Lady Margaret said over Darby's soft words. "You do not look at all recovered, Lady Helen. Do sit back, Darby, you are crowding us."

Darby drew her drab woollen cloak around her shoulders and pressed herself into the corner of her seat.

"I need rest, that is all," Helen said, unable to keep the irritation from her voice. Did the whole world need to comment upon her appearance? "We all need rest."

"You have just slept like the dead for the entire journey without any benefit," Lady Margaret added. "When we arrive, you should tell Lord Carlston that the fatigue has not lifted."

"There is nothing he can do about it," Helen snapped.

Lady Margaret laid her hand on Helen's arm. "Do not make the mistake of holding back information. Surely we have learned that lesson by now?"

Helen was in no mood to concede the point. She shifted her arm away from Lady Margaret's touch and peered out of the rain-splattered window. The journey to Chenwith Hall took an hour and a half by coach on a dry road, so taking the weather into account, it would probably be around three in the afternoon. Yet the winter light had already drawn in, and the relentless drizzle blurred the view beyond the winter-bare oaks that lined the estate's driveway. The oaks were famous in the region, planted by the first Duke of Selburn, and now the grand old sentinels of the Hall. They would have seen commoner, noble and Royalty all pass by; Queen Elizabeth had visited the Hall, as had their own Prince Regent.

Helen smiled. She may be arriving as a guest herself, but after New Year's Day this would be her home forever.

Ahead, she could just make out the figures of Carlston and Hammond on horseback, riding side by side, hats and greatcoats dark with rain, their mounts' hooves sending up sprays of water as they trotted through the puddles on the gravel drive. She scrunched her cold toes in her half-boots, trying to pinpoint a niggling sense of something awry that jangled beneath her weariness. She could not put her finger upon it. A need of some kind that crawled across her skin and shifted her on the leather seat.

She focused instead on the steady beat of her bond with Carlston – still there, of course. At least that was unchanged.

"I do hope I can have a bath before dinner," Delia said. "I feel as if I am still covered in plaster and dust."

"I am sure the Duke will arrange everything for our comfort," Helen said.

"Do you think he will want me to send away my staff?" Lady Margaret asked. "I do not want to lose Garner or Mrs Kent, or indeed Cook. It took me so long to find her, and if she is not suitably employed she will go elsewhere."

"The Duke said he welcomed your household," Helen said. "And he knows the value of a good cook."

She scrunched her toes again, finding some relief in the

movement. Was that what she needed? The release of motion? Perhaps she should stop the coach and walk to the house – the rain was not overly heavy. The thought, however, was too late. The coach rounded the last curve of the driveway, the vista opening up to reveal the magnificence of Chenwith Hall.

Like most of Bath and its environs, the Hall had been built from the local gold-hued limestone that even now, through the grey mizzle, held a honeyed glow. The residence was in the grand Baroque style, with a double-storey central block and two matching symmetrical wings that projected forward to create an immense rectangular courtyard at the front. All three inward-facing frontages were decorated with a Baroque exuberance of Doric columns, urns, cherubs and coronets; and not one of the fifty or so arched windows had been bricked in. The Duke of Selburn had not allowed the window tax to dim his life. Above it all soared the centrepiece of Chenwith Hall: a huge octagonal dome that crowned the central block, its gold spire reaching towards the heavens.

"What do you think of your new home, Darby?" Helen asked into the awed silence.

"Oh my," Darby breathed. "It is … oh, my lady." She shook her head.

Helen smiled. She too had been wordless when she had first seen the house – a totally inadequate word to describe the Duke's ancestral seat. Since then she had visited the Hall four times and her amazement at its grandeur had eased into mere wonderment.

The Chenwith estate was easily double the size of Landsdale, her uncle's country seat where she and her brother had lived after the death of their parents. Selburn had told her that Chenwith Hall had one hundred and forty-five rooms, could accommodate twenty guests and their servants, and boasted one of the largest libraries in England. The house sat at the centre of near fourteen thousand acres of parkland and employed over four hundred people, thirty of them just to maintain the gardens that had been landscaped by Capability Brown himself. The estate also supported twenty-two tenant farmers and their families, grew most of its own produce from three large kitchen gardens, and kept a sizable herd of dairy cattle.

And she was to be mistress of it all.

It was not an overly daunting prospect; from childhood she had been trained to run such a household, from reckoning the monthly candle orders at age eight, to organising her own ill-fated presentation ball with Aunt six months ago. No, the truly daunting prospect was how to combine the duties of a Duchess with those of a Reclaimer once she was married.

It could be argued that her mother, Lady Catherine, Countess of Hayden, had managed to do so, at least for ten years. The harsh truth, however, was that Lady Catherine's life as a Reclaimer had killed her and her husband, orphaning their children. Helen would not wish the pain of that loss on anyone, let alone the children she may one day bear. If she were to be blessed with a family – her *own* family – she would not allow the Dark Days Club to tear it apart. Her children must never suffer the grief that she had suffered, or be wrenched from all that was known and loved.

And now she had only three weeks before the problem became her life. Perhaps now that she had fully conjured the power stored within her, they could defeat the Grand Deceiver before her wedding and she could retire from the Dark Days Club. A grand plan, except they still did not know how to use the power as the Grand Reclaimer, and they had no idea where to find the Grand Deceiver.

The carriage ground across the gravel courtyard and drew

up before the front portico. A sweep of twenty honey-coloured stone steps led up to an arched doorway with the Selburn crest carved above it. At the foot of the steps, the senior servants waited in line to greet the arrival of their mistress-to-be. Fairwood, the butler, stood at their head, and beside him the small, spare figure of Mrs Clarke, the housekeeper.

Poor wretches, Helen thought. They were drenched, and the formality was unnecessary since this was not her bride-arrival. Perhaps it was the Duke's pointed reminder to Carlston that she was to be his Duchess soon enough. Not a propitious start to the enforced house party.

Two liveried footmen hurried forward, one to open the carriage door and let down the step, the other waiting with an umbrella.

Helen rose; the sooner they got indoors, the sooner the staff would be out of the rain. She took the footman's hand and found the step with her foot.

The uncomfortable sensation beneath her skin intensified, so much so that she inadvertently clutched the footman's hand with far more strength than any lady should have at her disposal. He winced, but doggedly absorbed the pain, only a flicker of his eyelids betraying his astonishment. She stepped down to the gravel, quickly releasing her grip. Lud, what was wrong with her? This was more than just fatigue. Every sight, sound and touch grated upon her nerves.

Beyond the carriage, Carlston and Hammond had dismounted and a groom was leading their horses towards the stables. Hammond lifted his hand in greeting, both men making their way across the gravel towards the steps.

Mr Quinn climbed down from beside the coachman and removed his hat, shaking the rain from it and looking for Darby's descent from the carriage.

The luggage coach drew up, the grind of its wheels sending

another twitch of irritation along Helen's shoulders. Geoffrey swung down from the footman's seat, then helped Sprat to the ground.

The girl was as wet as a seal, but grinning with delight. "Would you look at this place," she said loudly, heading towards the steps. "Lordy, it's as big as—"

"Sprat," Geoffrey hissed. He caught her arm and pulled her back, but all of the Duke's senior servants had already turned to stare at the girl.

She stared back, pasty skin flushed, her pointed chin lifted.

The footman with the umbrella stepped behind Helen and held it over her head. The rain pattered against the oiled canvas canopy in an uneven drum; so loud. She waved the man away, then gathered up the hems of her gown and pelisse and climbed the wet stone steps, counting them out of habit. Every rise, however, deepened an odd sense of weight along her spine. She tried to ignore it and focus on her count, but the sensation stopped her on step twelve. It was as if her feet were tethered to the stone.

"Lady Helen, is something wrong?" Lady Margaret inquired, arriving at her side. She had not eschewed the umbrella, and thrust it forward to protect them both.

Lord Carlston paused on the step behind them. "Lady Margaret tells me you are still fatigued. Do you need some assistance?" he asked.

Of course Lady Margaret had told him. Helen sent an irritated glance at her chaperone. Lady Margaret returned her glare, clearly as irritated by her silence. And never the twain shall meet, Helen thought sourly.

She looked over her shoulder and smiled reassuringly at the Earl. "Once I am inside, all will be well."

He did not look convinced. Nor did the very damp Delia and Mr Hammond behind him.

She looked up at the front door. Selburn had clearly abandoned the usual protocol of receiving new arrivals in the drawing room, for he stood framed within the stone arch of the doorway, his gold hair and the earthy colours of his jacket and buckskins in harmony with the honeyed colours of his home. It was as if he had grown from the stone itself, Helen fancied.

She returned his smile – albeit a little forced through the aggravations of her body – and pushed her limbs to climb the remainder of the steps.

"Welcome, my dear," Selburn said. His gaze was intent, with a flattering proprietorial warmth. He took her hand and folded it into the crook of his elbow. "I am so pleased you are here. Now Chenwith is complete."

He gave a small nod to Lord Carlston and the others. "Please come this way."

As he escorted Helen over the thick stone threshold into the foyer, she could not help craning her neck to look at the central dome. It was designed to draw the eye, and there could be no resisting its beauty. The huge base was edged in gilt to create a bright golden circle through which one viewed the soaring scene of Eros waking Psyche from her death sleep. The young god cradled his golden-haired beloved, one of his white-feathered wings curved around her shoulders as he lifted her pale face towards his kiss.

The dome rose from the support of four pillars, each one bearing a nymph – soft pastel Summer, bold Winter, warm Autumn and vibrant Spring – all lounging against tumbling cornucopias full of the fruit and flowers of their season. It was, Helen thought, peculiarly female. Most of the front-hall ceilings in grand houses depicted gods of battle and scenes of victory. Here was the triumph of love and lush bounteous beauty.

"You must all be cold and ready for the warmth of a fire,"

Selburn said. "I have arranged for you to be taken directly to your rooms." The Duke, it seemed, was immune to the dome's magnetic pull. How long would it be before she would walk through the hall without an upward glance.

Lady Margaret was still caught in its soaring beauty, her head back and one hand pressed to her breast as if it had struck her heart. Carlston and Hammond were divesting themselves of their drenched hats and greatcoats into the hands of two footmen. Delia, it seemed, had overcome the beauty of the dome and stood at the foot of the staircase, ready to go to her room.

Helen lengthened her spine, trying to throw off the awful heaviness that still pulled at her body and jangled her nerves. The grand staircase rose before them, splitting at a wide landing then sweeping around on itself in two separate staircases to the next floor. She swallowed, her mouth dusty and dry. The thought of ascending the blue-carpeted steps brought a tremor of revulsion.

"You are shivering," Selburn said. He chafed her hand and addressed his housekeeper. "Mrs Clarke, arrange a hot bath for Lady Helen and take her upstairs."

"No!" The word exploded from Helen. "I must..." She shook her head. She had to do something, but she could not name it.

"You must what?" Selburn asked, tightening his hold upon her hand.

The violent compulsion coalesced into a clear, ringing thought. *Ground.*

She pulled herself free. "I must go to the garden. Now!" She strode past the grand staircase, the soles of her boots rapping out her speed on the marble floor.

"Bring an umbrella," she heard Selburn order, and then the

sound of his footsteps behind her, but she could not slow her pace. In fact, she had to run.

She passed the Great Hall, its doors a blur of white wood and gilt flowers, across the central corridor of the house, past the open drawing room doors and the caress of the room's residual warmth, then through the smaller corridor lined with storage rooms that led to the terrace. Beyond it stretched the estate's formal garden.

Ground.

"Helen, wait!"

But her hand was already turning the brass door handle. She lunged out onto the stone terrace, the rain harder now and beating a soft tattoo on the stiff brim of her bonnet. She stood for a second, feeling the chilled air on her skin, the cold floor beneath her feet curling her toes. No, still too much stone.

She took the steps, counting as she ran down – twenty again, for symmetry – then onto the stretch of wet lawn that led to the huge central fountain: Atlas crouched beneath the burden of Earth upon his shoulders. A good distance beyond it was the hulking shape of the half-built dance pavilion, shrouded in rain and mist.

She stopped, her boots sinking into the sodden grass. The drag upon her body shifted, eased a little, the constriction on her chest opening so that she gulped and filled her lungs. She lifted her face to the sky and closed her eyes. The rain dripped off the brim of her bonnet, tracked down her nose and cheeks, wetting her lips with a taste of iron and green fir tree. So, the earth beneath her feet had some effect upon the power within her body. Of course, all Reclaimers needed to make contact with the earth to drain dangerous Deceiver energy from within them. Yet this was not a dispersal. It was a renewal.

Helen held out her hand. It no longer trembled. The niggling pressure in her head, however, had not changed.

She turned at the sound of approach. Selburn was descending the steps, a footman behind him struggling to open a large umbrella. Carlston was on his way too. She could feel it in the strong pulse of their Reclaimer bond.

The Duke slowed as he walked across the wet grass, waving the footman forward to hold the umbrella over her. "What is wrong, Helen?"

She shook her head; how could she explain something she did not understand?

Over the Duke's shoulder, she saw Carlston and Hammond burst through the terrace door. They both stopped, orienting themselves. Carlston started forward again, but Hammond grabbed his arm. Helen concentrated, catching the words he murmured close to Carlston's ear: "... cannot barge over there. It is his house. We are his guests. She is his betrothed."

Hammond was right. A man was sovereign in his own home; a guest did not impose himself upon his host's business. Carlston stared at her and Selburn, then he turned and followed Hammond back into the house.

"Is this something to do with the events at Bath?" the Duke asked.

Helen forced her attention back to her betrothed. "I don't know. Perhaps." She peeled a waterlogged curl from her cheek and wiped the wet residue from her skin. "I am feeling a little better now. I think I just needed ... some air."

"You seem improved, but you must tell me if you experience anything strange. I will not have you at risk."

"Risk is part of being a Reclaimer, especially a Grand Reclaimer."

"Nevertheless, you will be the mother of my children and I cannot have you in danger." He cupped her elbow. "Let us go back inside, out of this rain. You will catch a chill."

"No!" It came out too abruptly, the jerk away from his hold a little too violent. She drew a steadying breath. "I mean to say … I feel I must walk."

He looked up at the sky. "It will be dark soon."

"There is still a little light."

He studied her for a moment as if to gauge her determination. He should know by now that she said what she meant. "As you wish. I shall accompany you."

He took the umbrella from the footman, careful to maintain its shield above her head, and dismissed him with a wave of his hand. The footman bowed and retreated.

"I do not want you to get wet," Helen protested.

He smiled. "I was hoping you would invite me under too."

She flushed. "Of course."

He stepped beside her so the canopy covered them both, and offered his arm. Helen placed her hand in the crook of his elbow and allowed herself to be steered to the gravel path that ran alongside the lawn. With every step across the wet grass, the jangle of her nerves eased.

A low hedge bordered the fountain, the carefully manicured green circle interrupted at north and south to allow for the straight gravel path. They entered at the north, walking arm in arm alongside the stone god in the centre of the fountain, labouring beneath his burden. Water spouted from the curved trumpets of the four mermen around him.

The thud of the rain upon the umbrella and the clash of the cascading water forced the Duke to raise his voice. "If you do not mind, I will not take you past the new building."

"Why ever not?"

He smiled wryly. "It was to be a surprise. My wedding present to you for our wedding ball. A dance pavilion modelled upon the great hall in the Catherine Palace in Russia; windows instead of walls so it will feel as if we are dancing in the garden itself." He glanced sideways at her, a droll slant to his voice. "You were not meant to be here until Christmas week, when it is due to be finished."

"And now your surprise is ruined," Helen said. "I am sorry."

"Well, you have not seen it yet, so there will be some surprise."

"I promise I will not go to that part of the grounds until our wedding." She paused. "Thank you for allowing Lord Carlston and the others to come as well. I know it was not what you wanted."

He tucked his chin to his chest. "No, it was not. For all of Pike's arguments about the Dark Days Club, I did it as a favour to you."

"I know, and I am grateful."

"Good, because I am hoping that you will, in turn, do me a favour."

Helen glanced at him. A favour did not usually require an immediate return.

"Your friends will not be my only guests over Christmas. My younger brother and his wife arrived yesterday; and I believe Sir Jonathan will join us once a London surgeon has seen his wrist."

Helen looked back at the house. Lord Henry and Lady Georgina already in residence. Lud! Sir Jonathan was, of course, a trusted member of the Dark Days Club, but Selburn's brother and his wife were most definitely not. Helen had met them only once since the announcement of her betrothal and, although she had tried to find some likeable qualities in them, she had never come across two more irritating people. How were she and Carlston to train with them in the house? It would be near impossible.

"Does Mr Pike know that Lord Henry and Lady Georgina are here too?" she asked, carefully keeping the edge from her voice.

"I do not need permission to receive my family in my own home," Selburn said crisply. He stopped and turned to face her, clearly coming to the heart of the favour. "With Henry and Georgina here for Christmas, as well as your friends, Chenwith Hall is in need of a hostess. Will you stand as hostess, Helen?"

Good Lord, she had not expected that to be the favour. What was he thinking? She was not yet a married woman, and had just turned nineteen; how could she lend any respectability to the gathering? Besides, the hostess was the axis upon which a house party revolved. She set the menus, organised the entertainment, and ensured the comfort and engagement of all guests. A busy task at best, and with the added burden of Christmas and their New Year's Day ball, there would be little time left for anything else, least of all training to become a Grand Reclaimer. Surely he should know that.

"I must admit I have an ulterior motive," he added. "Before long, you will be mistress of Chenwith and all my other estates. Here is an excellent chance to acquaint yourself with the running of the house and its staff. I give you full leave to arrange everything as you wish."

So, far more than an invitation to act as hostess; it was a step into her life as the Duchess of Selburn. And the abrupt arrival of her dilemma.

She started walking again, hoping it would mask the delay in her answer. They rounded the far side of the fountain, leaving behind the cacophony of falling water. Somehow she must refuse him without causing offence or raising the spectre of the time she would soon be spending with Carlston. She led the way into the maze of formal hedged gardens affectionately known as the Little Labyrinth; a nod to the more famous labyrinth in Bath's famous Sydney Gardens.

He laid his hand upon her own, stopping her again. "I know it is not entirely orthodox for you to take on such a role. However, your aunt arrives tomorrow – she has written to confirm – so she can assist you. With Lady Georgina in residence as well, you will have enough chaperones to satisfy even the most poisonous of tongues."

"My aunt is coming *here*?"

"Yes, of course. And your brother and uncle too, in due course, for the wedding."

This collusion between Selburn and Aunt was gaining far too much momentum. Rather like an avalanche. She had to make her position clear.

"You do me great honour, but you must understand that I am here to train with Lord Carlston. Hosting my family and yours will make that near impossible."

His gaze was fixed upon the path, head down so that his full expression was hidden from view, but she saw the long muscle in his jaw tighten. "Helen, it is Christmastide. Of course I am hosting our families. It is the season for family. Even more so, since we are to be married in three weeks. I want us to be able to enjoy the Yule and the preparations for our wedding, *together*." He looked up and now she saw, far too clearly, the deep reproach in his eyes. "Only three weeks of your attention. Surely I deserve that? Do you have no room for me at all?" His voice held a new, unsettling note: exasperation taking on the hard armour of resentment.

Helen knew she had little experience in the ways of courtship and marriage. She did, however, have a great deal of experience in recognising danger, and the tone in his voice sent a shiver across her skin as if cold fingers had brushed her nape. Her imminent marriage was in jeopardy, and somehow his invitation to act as hostess had become a test. Perhaps not intentionally so, but a test nonetheless.

He had a right to some resentment, Helen conceded. She had spent so much time with Carlston over the past months, and she was not certain she could claim a pure heart – one of the cornerstones of a virtuous and true wife. The Grand Reclaimer union, that infernal alchemical bond, muddied everything. One thing was clear, however: she could not refuse Selburn's request. He was to be her husband; the man she would soon promise to honour and obey, and with whom she would make her home and family. If her marriage was to start with any hope of harmony, he must, for now, take precedence. It was, as he said, only three weeks. Surely she could find a way to both train with Lord Carlston and appease her betrothed.

Ignoring the relentless background beat of her Reclaimer bond, she took his hand. "I would be honoured to be Chenwith's hostess, Gerard."

He bowed, the formality at odds with the broad smile on his face. "Thank you."

She held up one finger: a caveat. "I must, however, be the one to inform Lord Carlston. And the others too."

The broad smile faltered. "You are too careful of his opinion."

"Nevertheless, I must be the one to tell him."

"As you wish." He tucked her hand into the crook of his elbow. "We should return now."

Although Helen would have preferred to walk further into the gardens, she allowed herself to be turned back along the path towards the huge figure of Atlas crouched beneath his burden of the wet stone world.

* * *

Carlston stood alone in the foyer, hands clasped behind his back, looking up at the dome. He turned at the sound of their footsteps. His boots and buckskins still held the tidemarks of their soaking, and his cropped dark hair had curled at the ends from the damp ride. He must be freezing, Helen thought, and yet he had waited.

"Does he think the world turns only with his supervision?" Selburn said under his breath.

"Lord Carlston," Helen said over the comment, "you should have gone up with the others."

"I wanted to ensure you are quite well."

"She is," Selburn said.

Carlston ignored him. "It seems your fatigue has lifted."

"It has," Helen said quickly before Selburn could interject again. He was only doing it to irritate Carlston. "As soon as I walked upon the ground, I began to feel…" She tilted her head, taking a moment to fully attend to her physical self. "Almost energised."

"Energised?" Carlston's brows lifted. "That is interesting."

"I was under the impression that the earth drained power from Reclaimers," Selburn said. "Why is this happening? Is Lady Helen safe?"

"I don't know," Carlston said.

Selburn sniffed. "I thought you were the expert."

"This is new territory," Carlston replied. "I do not presume to know everything. That kind of hubris is the domain of others."

The inference was clear. Helen looked between the two of them. Lud, they could not be together five seconds before the cudgels came out.

The Duke smiled, malicious mischief brightening his eyes. "I believe Lady Helen has something to tell you."

Helen sent an indignant glance at him. That was not in the spirit of the agreement they had just made. He was mistaken if he thought she would be drafted into his trump game.

"It can wait until we are all dry," she said and withdrew her hand from the crook of his arm. "Gentlemen, if you will excuse me, I shall retire."

"Of course. Mrs Clarke will show you the way," Selburn said. No contrition there, Helen thought. He walked across the foyer and called, "Mrs Clarke?"

"Was it only in the garden that you felt energised?" Carlston asked in a low voice. "Not out the front of the house as well?"

He was studying her so intently.

"No, not out front," she said, dropping her pitch to match his own. "In truth, I felt quite drained upon the steps."

"Upon the steps," he repeated slowly. His attention had clearly turned inward, his finger and thumb flicking together as he concentrated on some thought.

The housekeeper bustled into the foyer. "Yes, Your Grace?"

"Show Lady Helen to her suite."

The little woman bobbed a curtsy. "This way, my lady. We have the kettles on if you would like to bathe before dinner."

"Thank you, I would."

Carlston and Selburn bowed as Helen followed the housekeeper to the grand staircase. She did not look back as she climbed the carpeted steps; however, her Reclaimer sense – or perhaps it was her feminine sense – knew that both men silently watched her until she disappeared from their view.

Chapter Six

Helen followed Mrs Clarke along the well-lit first-floor corridor, the candles in the brass wall sconces flickering in the breeze of their swift progress. Paintings lined the passage: portraits of the Duke's grim-faced forebears, noble dogs in profile, Baroque landscapes and gleaming horses. Helen would have liked to linger – one of the portraits was definitely a Reynolds – but Mrs Clarke moved with a crisp tread that spoke of important matters still to be managed. She reminded Helen of a squirrel. Not in her features – although there was a hint of reddish-grey hair curling from under her neat white cap – but in the sense of bright busyness interspersed with sudden moments of inquiring stillness. According to Selburn, she'd had the running of the place since the Dowager Duchess had died three years ago. Perhaps she would not welcome a new mistress in her domain.

"I am not sure if you are yet aware, Mrs Clarke," Helen said, quickening her pace to walk beside the woman, "but the Duke has asked me to act as Chenwith's hostess over Christmas."

The housekeeper gave a quick nod. "Oh yes, my lady. He informed me this afternoon that I am to report to you and assist you in any way I can."

Did he now, Helen thought. So sure of her answer that he had already informed his senior servants. She pushed aside her pique. A husband and wife *should* be sure of one another.

"If I may, there is one issue that needs prompt solution, my lady," Mrs Clarke added.

"Yes?" So, she was to step into her role immediately.

"I believe Lady Margaret's house staff arrived with you. Am I to find employment for them here, or will they be moving on? I am sure, with Christmas and the wedding almost upon us, there will be work enough for them if Lady Margaret does not wish to dismiss them."

Here was her chance to show Selburn she was ready to take on the management of his households, and also repay Lady Margaret's generosity over the past six months.

"I know for a fact that Lady Margaret wishes to keep them, especially her cook, so let us find employment for them."

"Yes, my lady. Except..." Mrs Clarke cast Helen a sideways, darting glance. "I cannot answer for the kitchen staff. His Grace has placed Mrs Carroll, our cook, in charge of her kitchen. She is quite particular about whom she hires."

"I understand," Helen said. The message was clear: she was to handle the problem of Mrs Carroll.

"I believe His Grace has shown you around on an earlier visit," Mrs Clarke said.

"Yes, twice." Helen hesitated; could she admit that despite those tours she was already well on her way to being lost? Better to be frank from the start. "Even so, I do not entirely remember the layout of the house."

Mrs Clarke smiled sympathetically. "When I first arrived twenty years ago, it took me a good three weeks before I knew all its ups and downs. This is the Grand Corridor. It runs across the house, from the Great Chamber in the east," she pointed behind them, "to the Gentlemen's Wing in the west." She gestured ahead to a distant archway, a slight lift of her brow hinting at a wry sense of humour. "The Gentlemen's Wing is also called Bucks' Corner."

Helen smiled. Selburn had told her about the collection of rooms on the ground and first floors that he had set aside for his hunting cronies. A male world, as far from the main apartments as possible, and comprising a billiard room, smoking room, bedchambers, an absurd number of mounted deer heads, and a staircase straight to the cellars.

They passed oak double doors on their left. "That is the Courtyard Suite, my lady, where Lord Henry and Lady Georgina are residing," Mrs Clarke whispered. "Lady Georgina is currently resting, I believe."

Mrs Clarke stopped before another set of doors almost directly opposite the Courtyard Room, painted white with elegant mouldings picked out in gilt. "This is the Bamboo Room, my lady, with a lovely view of the gardens. His Grace had it refurbished for you." She opened the doors with a small flourish and stepped aside, a look of anticipation upon her face.

Mrs Clarke's excitement carried Helen across the threshold. A large white marble hearth framed the bright coals of a well-established fire, the reach of its gentle heat easing the chill upon her skin. Night candles had been lit and placed around the room, their flickering light reflected in the mirror above the mantel, and shimmering across the oriental bamboo-print wallpaper and gold damask canopy that hung above the bed.

Good Lord, Helen thought, looking up at the huge crowning centrepiece atop the bed's canopy: a gold dome edged by a Grecian frieze and topped by an urn of ostrich feathers. Selburn had given her the state bed – the most lavish furnishing in any noble house, built for Royal visits, even if that visit was only an ambition.

Across the room, matching gold damask curtains framed glass doors that led to a terrace, beyond which she saw the misty twilight shapes of the formal garden. The gold and green carpet, she realised, had been woven to match the wallpaper. She turned around, taking in more of the rich furnishings. Everything glinted with an edge or curve of gilt: two elegant mahogany bedside tables; a chaise longue upholstered in green velvet; an Egyptian-style table, its top a marvellous marble mosaic; and a night bureau fashioned to look like a set of drawers, inlaid with glowing mother of pearl. The opulence was a little dizzying.

"May I enter, my lady?" Mrs Clarke asked.

"Of course."

The housekeeper stepped in and sent a swift glance around the room, ending in a tiny nod. All was perfect. She gestured to two doorways set opposite one another at the terrace end. "To the right is your dressing room, my lady, and to the left your private withdrawing room. Water is being brought up for your bath now." She paused, then allowed a tentative smile and curtseyed. "Welcome, my lady."

"Thank you, Mrs Clarke." Helen gestured around the room. "It is beautiful."

The housekeeper straightened at the unexpected acknowledgment – a surprised squirrel moment, Helen thought irrepressibly – then gave a pleased nod and retreated, leaving Helen alone.

A private withdrawing room? How wonderful. She crossed to the door and opened it. A fire and the night candles had been lit here too, their glow showing a large writing desk and matching chair, two armchairs upholstered in rich blue arranged before the hearth, and between them a low table set with a gilt tea caddy and a blue and gold Sèvres tea set. A quieter room; more to her taste.

She heard the click of a door behind her, felt a familiar shift in the energy of the room. She turned, already knowing it was Darby who had arrived.

Her Terrene stood in the doorway of the dressing room. From behind her came the sounds of water being poured, two young male voices and a third female voice – Sprat – who seemed to be instructing her companions on how to fill a bath. By the curt responses, her advice was not being received well. The girl certainly had a way of irritating her fellow servants.

Helen smiled a welcome. Although it was returned, there was a rigidity to Darby's face and a flare to her nostrils that spoke of fear.

"My lady, your bath is prepared."

"What is wrong?" Helen asked.

Darby's eyes cut to the dressing room, a slight shake of her head reminding Helen they were not alone.

She stood aside for Helen to enter. A large copper bath had been set before the hearth, its calico lining draped over the edges, and a curl of steam rising from the water's surface. A kettle hung over the fire from an iron hook – supplementary hot water – and a large white drying cloth hung on a rack, being warmed for use.

Sprat and two young footmen, both clad in the handsome Chenwith livery, held water pitchers. Sprat bobbed a curtsey as the two footmen bowed and darted quick glances at their mistress-to-be, their curiosity not quite stifled by their training.

"Thank you," Helen said. "You may leave us."

The two young men withdrew. Helen heard their whispers along the hallway: *"Ain't she tall; she smiled at us – did you see?"*

"You too, Sprat," Darby said.

Sprat looked at Helen. "But I just found you again, my lady."

"Do as Darby says."

"Yer gunna talk about them Deceivers, ain't yer? I've took me oath, just like you and Miss Darby. Can't I stay?"

Helen shook her head. Sprat may have taken her oath to the Dark Days Club, but her idea of standing by her word seemed to be entirely contingent upon her own gain. "I know you have, but this is Reclaimer and Terrene business."

Sprat sighed and curtseyed. Darby closed the door behind her, and turned to Helen.

"Wait," Helen said, raising her hand. Sprat was still outside the door. "I can hear you breathing, Sprat," she called. "Go!" She listened as the girl's footsteps receded.

"She is shameless," Darby said.

"What do you expect? Kate Holt trained her to listen at doors."

"I know." Darby stepped up to Helen and began to untie her bonnet ribbons, her fingers trembling.

"Do not worry about that." Helen closed her hand around Darby's fumbling attempt to undo the wet bow. "Tell me what is wrong."

Darby drew away, bunching her hands against her chest. "I don't know if you'll believe me, my lady."

"I will always believe you, Darby. Surely you know that."

Darby nodded and gave a tremulous smile. "When you and I made our bond through the Ligatus, we were joined in both mind and spirit, my lady. But I didn't really understand what that meant until today." She took a deep, shaking breath. "I *saw* the Ligatus in you, my lady. When you channelled its power and I touched you, it went through me and I saw ... I felt ... I..." Her face contorted.

Helen grabbed Darby's arms, anchoring her Terrene through the memory. "You felt what?"

95

"Death. I felt Death. That power was within me for no more than a second or two, and I swear if I'd held it any longer, it would have killed me."

"That stands to reason," Helen said soothingly. "The Ligatus was built out of death."

"That's not what I mean, my lady. The Ligatus isn't meant to be in you, is it? It's not meant to be in a person."

"No. It is meant to be a book."

"Yet for the past five months you have been holding it blocked behind your mind, like a seawall holding back the waves."

"I have not held it back," Helen protested. "I've been trying to draw it out."

"No, my lady. I don't think you've known it, but you've been holding it back. For good reason. When I touched you, I saw the Ligatus entwined into your life energy." She jammed her fingers together and held up her laced hands. "Tight, like this. Sir Jonathan's mesmerism opened a rift in your mind, and now all that ghastly energy has a pathway into the world – through you. And from what I saw, I don't think it distinguishes between your life energy and its own."

Helen stepped back. "What do you mean?"

"I think it's seeking a way out, like water carving its course, wearing through your control until it can break through. And when it does, it will drag your life force from you, my lady. It will kill you, and it will kill me and Lord Carlston too. We are all bound to it."

Helen stared at her Terrene. "You cannot be sure of that."

"No, my lady, I can't." Yet Darby's drawn face held her certainty. "But ever since the explosion I've had an odd feeling in my head. It is not an ache, but…" She touched her forehead.

"Like a pressure behind the eyes?" Helen asked quickly.

"Yes." Darby released a ragged breath. "You have it too."

Helen nodded.

"I think it is the power forcing its way out of you. And—"

"And because we are bound, you feel it too," Helen finished. "If it is the same for Lord Carlston... Well, that would tell us something, wouldn't it?" She paced across the room. "Even so, Darby, the Ligatus is now part of the dyad power. It could give us the advantage. We need it to destroy the Grand Deceiver. We need all the power we can get to destroy the Grand Deceiver."

"I know, my lady."

"And yet you say it is going to kill us." Helen dug a knuckle into the niggling pressure in her forehead. "If it is woven into my life force as tightly as you say, we may not be able to remove it."

"Surely we must try?"

"How long until it breaks through?" Helen realised the question was futile. "Of course, you cannot know."

"Maybe if we found a way for me to see the Ligatus again?" Darby ventured.

"And have you thrown across the room once more? How do we know you would survive it?"

"I survived it last time," her Terrene said staunchly.

"No, it is too much of a risk. We need more information about how it works."

"The information is locked inside your head, my lady. If you try and get it, I wager that rift is only going to get wider."

"Then we must find another source of information," Helen said, pressing her palms together as if she could will that way to appear. "Carlston believes the Bath Deceiver has answers. Perhaps the creature will have answers about this, too."

A leap, but there was nowhere else to go.

"Perhaps," Darby agreed. "If you can find him. Or her."

Their eyes met in silent prayer: *God Almighty, help us.*

Helen stood alone in front of the swing mirror clad in her long bath shift. Darby had gone to the servants' meal. She had wanted to refuse the summons, to stay in solidarity after bringing such awful news, but Helen told her to go. The servants ate at five thirty, come what may.

Helen pressed her fingers to her forehead and leaned towards the glass. Her reflected eyes, amber in the soft light, watched herself move closer, their expression grave. Did the Ligatus reside only in her head? Or was it throughout her whole body, even now pushing its way through her skin?

She looked at the door, still firmly closed, and gathered the hem of the shift, lifting it over her head. It dropped to the blue carpet, a pile of fine linen beside her long feet. She had only ever seen her full naked body a few times before, and it took some seconds to overcome the self-consciousness of such an illicit view. The luxury of a long mirror was to contemplate one's dressed self, not to boldly stare at one's bare form.

She finally fixed her gaze upon her full length in the mirror. Pale skin and long limbs tinged old-gold by the firelight. Deep blue shadows accentuating the curve of breasts and waist. A training bruise, already faded into a brown smudge, across her ribs. And lower, the mound of Venus – *mons veneris*, to give its rightful, safer name: a dark, inverted triangle upon white skin. But no outward sign of the Ligatus. It sat within her like a canker, unseen and yet so destructive.

She placed her hands on her belly and drew them down her flanks, feeling the firm hold of muscle beneath her cold skin. Bone, sinew, blood, flesh. So much terrible power in such a frail, impermanent vessel. Why had she been chosen to carry it? Why did she have to wield it? A wave of fury closed her eyes and clenched her fists. *Dear God, is Darby right? Will it kill us?*

"Will it?" she said aloud. Not a prayer but a savage demand, the force of it opening her eyes.

The room was silent except for the tick of the mantel clock. No answer in its soft beat.

Before her, in the mirror, she saw only her own pale face. Her own hollow fear.

She turned from the glass and picked up her shift, pulling it back over her head, the garment enveloping her in soft shapeless linen. Slowly, she walked to the bath and climbed in, the shift billowing around her legs. Gathering the dripping hem above her knees, she lowered herself into the hot water. Its embrace warmed her flesh through the wet cloth, but could not touch the chill in her soul.

Helen paused at the bottom of the stairs and eyed the closed doors to the drawing room. The two footmen manning them stared resolutely into the distance, awaiting her approach. She adjusted her shawl over her elbows – a rich Norwich silk in blue paisley that matched the navy silk of her gown – and smoothed the cream kid glove upon one hand as she listened to the voices inside. Selburn, Carlston, Hammond and a light tenor that must be Lord Henry discussing the merits of a horse. Delia and Lady Margaret agreeing upon their dislike of the new fashion for velvet hunting caps trimmed with fur; and a sigh from somewhere near the hearth, no doubt the irritated exhalation of Lady Georgina.

Helen was the last one down. She had hoped to catch Carlston alone, or at least with only Dark Days Club members in the room.

She crossed the short space to the doors and nodded to the footmen.

"Helen, there you are," Delia said as she entered the room.

The gentlemen, clustered near the windows, suspended their conversation to bow.

Helen shot a glance at Carlston – the silent message clearly received by the slight draw of his dark brows – then curtseyed, rising to find Lord Henry rapidly crossing the floor to her with a wide, insincere smile. She politely returned the smile as he clasped one of her hands between his own, the grip a little too tight.

Lord Henry Annisford was a shorter, paler version of his older brother. He had the long Annisford family jaw, but unlike the Duke who had also inherited the matching patrician nose and firm mouth, Lord Henry's nose was just a little too short for his face and his mouth a little … wet. He wore evening dress, of course, and while the cut of his black jacket and cream silk pantaloons was excellent, Helen could not admire his up-to-the-minute yellow and pink striped waistcoat, nor the style of his cravat. The former emphasised his sallow complexion, and the latter was a rather ill-tied Mathematical, pinned with an ugly citrine circled by diamonds.

"My dear, how pleasant to see you again," he said, patting the hand he had captured. He turned to gather his wife into the conversation. "Georgina, my dear, what do you say?"

Lady Georgina, it seemed, was inclined to say very little. She smiled tightly from an armchair by the hearth, her long fingers plucking at the fringe on her green lace shawl.

The Lady Henry Annisford, formerly Miss Georgina Bale, was a sour expression away from breathtaking beauty. According to Lady Margaret, Miss Bale had been one of the Incomparables of her Season – those beauties who swept all before them – and had placed quite a lot of nuptial expectation upon the charms of her blonde curls, large green eyes and a perfectly proportioned profile that had prompted an ode from

Lord Byron. That expectation, however, had only taken her as high as the younger brother of a Duke; the famed profile, apparently, not quite overcoming the drawbacks of a meagre dowry and a foul temper.

"You are looking well, Lady Helen," Lord Henry said through his wife's silence. "Is she not looking well, Georgina?"

Another tight smile.

"It is a pleasure to see you both again," Helen lied.

Lady Georgina turned to the Duke, affording Helen ample opportunity to view the famed profile. It was indeed charming, and right at that moment offered a small, sensual pout. "Selburn, do we dine soon? I had thought we were keeping country hours."

The Duke broke away from the other men and crossed the room. "City hours, Lady Georgina. You know that very well."

She smiled at his approach, but the Duke was not heading towards his sister-in-law. He stopped before Helen.

"My brother is correct, Lady Helen. You are looking well indeed."

She saw the more pointed evaluation in his eyes and gave a small nod: yes, she had recovered. It was more or less true, if one didn't take into account the deadly power that was forcing its way out of her mind and body.

She managed to retrieve her hand from Lord Henry as the doors opened to admit Fairwood. The butler bowed and said, "Your Grace," in a tone of announcement.

Selburn turned to his sister-in-law. "There, Georgina, we are ready to dine." He bowed, and offered her his arm.

Although Lady Georgina's rank was equal to Helen's, her married state gave her the higher station and thus the Duke's arm into dinner. A most fortuitous order of precedence, Helen thought, as she took Carlston's arm: she would get her chance for a quiet word with her Reclaimer partner after all.

He clearly had the same idea, for he held back as the Duke and Lady Georgina departed for the dining room, then with a subtle lift of his hand sent a wordless command to Lady Margaret who was rising from the sofa to take Lord Henry's arm.

"Oh dear, my slipper has come untied," Lady Margaret immediately declared, peering down at her feet. "Do go on, Lord Carlston. We will not be far behind."

Mr Hammond and Delia, readying themselves to bring up the rear, drew back to await the resolution of the false emergency.

Carlston and Helen slowly made their way into the corridor. The Duke and Lady Georgina were already halfway to the dining room doors.

"We must find a way to extract you from this house and rent another," Carlston said, his tone for Reclaimer ears only. "We will not be able to get anything done with Lord Henry and Lady Georgina here."

Let alone Aunt Leonore as well, Helen thought. Even so, she could not just abandon Chenwith. She had promised Selburn she would stay, and she did not go back on her word. Besides, he was already looking over his shoulder at their slow progress.

"He knows we need isolation," Carlston added. She could almost hear the grind of his teeth. "Why did he not put them off?"

"They were already here." Helen waved away the difficulty of Lord Henry and his wife. "We have a more pressing problem."

He nodded. "We certainly do."

They looked at one another in consternation. Was it the same problem, or did they face two?

"We need to talk. Alone," Helen murmured.

Selburn and Lady Georgina had paused at the dining room doors, both of them looking back with expressions of impatience.

"Quite," Carlston agreed dryly.

"What has happened to Lord Henry?" Lady Georgina demanded.

At that moment, her husband and Lady Margaret emerged from the drawing room followed by Mr Hammond and Delia, and the procession into the dining room was completed in silence.

The table, a mahogany Chippendale custom-built for the room, had been reduced to *en famille* size and set with crisp white napery, crystal glassware and cutlery with the ducal crest engraved upon the handles.

Selburn escorted Lady Georgina to the chair beside him at the foot of the table, then turned and addressed Helen as she headed towards the seat on his left. "My dear, you are to sit at the head of the table."

Helen winced inwardly. By placing her at the premium position, Selburn had just informed the room that she was Chenwith's hostess. Well, it was done now. But, Lud, she had wanted to explain it to Carlston. She smiled tightly at her betrothed and backtracked to her appointed seat.

The meaning of the Duke's instruction dawned upon those around the table. Hammond looked across at his sister, brows lifted in surprise; and there was no mistaking the quick understanding in Carlston's stern expression.

Lady Georgina drew herself up. "Brother, you must not place Lady Helen in such a compromising position. She is not married, and does not have the age, the *gravitas*, to act as hostess, especially since the Queen will be staying."

"The Queen will be staying here on the night of the wedding,

Lady Georgina, so Lady Helen will, in fact, be married by then," Delia pointed out.

Lady Georgina glared at her, then addressed the Duke again. "A hostess is meant to bring respectability to a gathering, Selburn. By placing your betrothed in the position you are doing the very opposite. I am the only person here with the rank and reputation—"

"Georgina," Lord Henry whispered fiercely. "That is enough."

"No, Henry, your wife is quite right," Selburn said. "That is why Lady Helen will be assisted by her aunt, Viscountess Pennworth, who arrives tomorrow."

Helen risked a glance at Carlston. If his expression had been stern before, it was now positively rigid.

She busied herself with placing her napkin upon her lap as everyone took their seats. For now, she could take refuge in the etiquette of the table and devote her conversation to Lord Henry on her right while the soup and fish course was served. Hopefully by the first remove, when she was required to turn the table and speak to Carlston, he would have his reproach under control.

She barely tasted the bisque placed before her by the footman, nor did she listen to most of Lord Henry's conversation. Luckily he only required a minimal amount of nodding to keep his monologue in progress. Her mind fixed upon the problem of finding time to speak to Carlston *alone* without any possibility of being overheard. She had to explain, properly, about this whole hostess mingle-mangle, but more importantly, she had to tell him about the Ligatus. The drawing room after dinner would be too public, and she could not dally behind when it was time to retire. Nor, obviously, could he come to her room, especially with Lord Henry and Lady Georgina in the Courtyard Room opposite. At breakfast then? Perhaps, but privacy could not be guaranteed.

For Helen, the remove of the soup and fish came too quickly; it was quite clear by the frown upon his face that Carlston was still annoyed. Nevertheless, everyone waited upon her to turn the table conversation and broach the first course.

She surveyed the dishes: a rich beef and mushroom ragu, vol-au-vents, a roasted rabbit, a port-wine jelly, a ham, cutlets and three winter vegetables. The menu was not quite balanced, she realised. She remembered Georgina's scowl; had she ordered the menu, and perhaps thought to take on the prestigious role of hostess during a Royal visit? Well, now it was Helen's duty, and she would certainly not have a first table with so much dry meat upon it and not a sauce in sight.

She turned to Carlston, who looked pointedly at Lord Henry, now regaling Lady Margaret with an anecdote. "He and his wife for the whole of Christmas? Not ideal for our requirements," he commented acidly. "Not to mention the imminent arrival of your aunt."

"There is something else too," Helen admitted. "Do you have an odd pressure in your head, behind your eyes?"

He observed her for moment, his mouth set into a grim line. "Yes."

She bit her lip. All three of them with the same sensation.

"Do you know what it means?" he asked.

"Not here," she said softly, a glance around the table collecting all the obstacles to conversation now helping themselves to the plates set before them. Even Selburn, Hammond, Lady Margaret and Delia, she realised. When had she decided to keep the new danger from their aides? Only a few hours earlier she had been insisting upon honesty. She examined the decision. Part of it was uncertainty – Darby could be wrong; but mostly she wanted to inform Carlston about this before anyone else. He was the third point in this possible triangle of peril, and perhaps they would be able to find a solution together before alarming the others.

Carlston gave a slight nod, accepting the need for discretion, and picked up the silver serving spoon from the beef and mushroom ragu, angling it in query.

"Yes, please," Helen said.

He served the stew, leaning closer to place it on her plate. The rich earthy smell of sautéed mushrooms and meat rose up through the steam.

"I plan to ride at dawn tomorrow morning with a friend," he said. "I have something to show *him* nearby."

Their eyes met; he meant Mr Amberley, her male guise. So his problem required discretion too. No, not discretion – subterfuge. But was it feasible for her to ride out as Mr Amberley? It was certainly more feasible than riding out with him as the future wife of the Duke of Selburn. If Lord Carlston and Lady Helen were seen alone together, the scandal would rock the county. Yet even slipping out of the house was going to be difficult. She would need Darby's help and a good serve of luck.

"A local sight?" she asked, keeping her voice light.

"Yes, a particularly magnificent view," he replied. "I believe the picturesque can change one's life. The effect of the *sublime* especially."

His grave emphasis upon the word *sublime* brought a chill across her skin. One of their recent dinner discussions had explored the ideal of the picturesque, in particular its concept of horror and terror within the greatness of the sublime. Horror and terror – that was what he meant. Holy heaven, what was he going to show her?

"A morning ride is always beneficial," she said and picked up her fork, although the food on her plate suddenly held no appeal. "Especially at dawn."

He gave a small nod – their rendezvous was set. But although he smiled, Helen could see a worrying apprehension in his eyes. Whatever awaited them frightened even Lord Carlston.

Chapter Seven

SATURDAY, 12 DECEMBER 1812

Helen opened her eyes and gasped, sucking in air until her lungs pressed against her chest. Shrill wailing, somewhere near. She lurched upright in the state bed, fingers dug into the sheets and mattress, disorientated by the awful howls and unfamiliar shapes in the dark room.

"Who is there?"

She scrabbled forward, throwing off the bedcovers, not knowing where she was heading but compelled to move under the urgent anguish of the shrieks.

The screaming stopped, the sudden silence like a shock surging across her skin. She swayed on her knees at the end of the bed, panting, the ghostly shapes around her coalescing into the night stand and mosaic table. The cold air grabbed at her fingers, toes, chilling her throat with every hard breath.

She pressed her hand to her chest, the beat of her heart hammering against her palm.

No one in the room. No more screams.

It had been a dream.

She stretched her Reclaimer hearing through the house, and heard the slow even breaths of a multitude of sleeping people interspersed with the ratchet of male snoring, scrabbling rodents and a woman softly praying close by. No one else, it seemed, had heard the screams.

Of course not; it was a dream. No, a nightmare, from the Ligatus. The shrieking voice had belonged to the infant, Timothy Marr. Was this the rift, leaking the journal's energy into her mind?

She crawled back to the top of the bed and thrust her legs under the covers, gathering them around herself and wriggling into the abandoned warmth. Even so, she felt frozen, inside and out, the slight pressure behind her eyes magnified by the dark silence.

She listened through the house again, searching the different respirations until she found Carlston's familiar rhythm in a room on the floor below – slow, smooth, steady, the tempo in time with the deeper beat of their union. Curling into the solace of the sound, she closed her eyes, praying that the screams would not come again.

A half-hour before the household rose to start the day, Helen followed Darby out of the scullery entrance and across the cobbled kitchen yard. Darby shielded her lamp in case anyone was about, but as far as Helen could tell, their departure was unobserved.

The Temple of Venus, their objective in the north-west corner of the gardens, was a distant shape through the pre-dawn gloom. She was to wait for Lord Carlston in the temple; he would bring a horse for her, and together they would ride to his mysterious destination.

It was good to be outside. She still felt the remnants of the nightmare on her mind like a sticky cobweb. Hopefully a walk in the bracing air would brush it all away. She flexed her hands in her tan riding gloves, every breath curling into steam before her mouth, and was thankful for her woollen greatcoat, buckskin breeches and hessian boots. Poor Darby wore only her serge gown and short cloak.

"It will be a chilly exchange of clothes when you return," her Terrene said, as if she had caught Helen's thought. She patted the basket hanging from the crook of her arm as they crunched and splashed through the thawing snow that whitened the grass. "I have brought your thickest petticoat and the blue pelisse."

"I am more concerned about you, Darby. It will be a long, cold wait for us. And what if someone comes by and sees you? What will you say?"

"I doubt anyone from the house will venture so far," Darby said, then gave a mischievous smile. "Anyway, I will have Mr Quinn's company and that will be explanation enough."

"Darby!" Helen said, stifling her own smile.

Darby's lightness dropped away. "Are you sure I cannot accompany you, my lady?"

"His lordship wishes to show me something and has made it clear he wants to ride alone with Mr Amberley."

Darby nodded, her eyes troubled. "You will both be careful though, won't you?"

Twenty minutes later they reached the small stone temple set on a rise that overlooked the estate's patch of cultivated wilderness. The building was, Helen decided, a rather odd mismatch of styles, with three walls decorated with classical colonnades and a Moorish-styled open frontage to take in the view of the gardens.

Inside, it was much plainer, with a marble floor set in black and white diamonds, and faded frescoes upon the three walls. Darby set down the lamp and inspected the floor, brushing aside a few curled brown leaves before placing the basket of clothes in a corner.

She chafed her hands together, her fingertips pink from the cold. "His lordship and Mr Quinn shouldn't be long, my lady," she said, stamping her feet. "Mr Quinn said they would be here before dawn."

"Have you told Quinn about the rift in the Ligatus and the pressure in our heads?"

Darby stopped chafing her hands. "No, my lady. I didn't want to worry him, and I wasn't sure if it was to be kept secret."

"I think perhaps we should keep it between the three of us, for now."

It was an odd order – after all, Quinn was Carlston's Terrene – but some caution was tolling within Helen, and she felt obliged to listen to it. Besides, they had no evidence that the rift was real, so until evidence presented itself, it would be irresponsible to alarm any of the others.

She walked around the room, viewing the three dimly lit frescoes of Venus and her maidens painted by a competent, if not inspired, hand. How old were they, she wondered. The temple could be ten years old or two hundred.

Near the front, she paused before a faded rendering of Venus emerging from the sea upon a shell. A copy of the famous Botticelli painting, although the face and hair of Venus were not how Helen remembered them from the illustrations she had seen of the original. Was it a portrait of someone? She peered more closely. A face dominated by wide cheekbones and a pointed chin, blue eyes hooded in a sultry expression, and luxurious black wavy hair. If the rendition was of a real woman, she must have been fascinating.

She turned at the sound of thudding hooves. Lord Carlston, mounted on his heavy-boned chestnut stallion, Ares, and behind him Quinn on Faro, the big bay that the Terrene habitually rode from his lordship's stable, and presumably Helen's mount for the morning. Both men were muffled in greatcoats, their breath leaving a trail of vapour in the air.

Carlston reined in Ares on the flagged surrounds of the temple, the horse snorting at the constraint. Helen had seen his lordship ride many times, but even so his athleticism was always to be admired. He had such ease and command. Riding and dancing were the two activities in which a man could not hide any deficiency of elegance – and his lordship excelled at both.

"Good morning," Helen said. She almost curtseyed, then remembered she had no skirts, so made a rather odd bow.

Carlston surveyed the lamp. "You should not have lit—" He stopped, something behind her catching his gaze. Frowning, he leaned forward in the saddle, studying the wall at her back.

Helen looked over her shoulder at the Venus rising from the sea, then back at Carlston's frown. Intuition caught her breath. "Is that a portrait of Lady Elise?"

Carlston drew back, his horse sidling across the flags under its tightened rein. "Yes," he said curtly. "You should not have lit a lamp."

The painting, it seemed, was not for discussion.

"No one has risen yet, not even the housemaids," Helen said, walking away from the wall; a move, she realised, solely to shift Carlston's eyes from his wife. Good Lord, was she jealous of a daub of paint? And what was the portrait doing in her betrothed's temple?

"Then let us be on our way before they do," Carlston said. He motioned to Darby. "Extinguish the lamp."

Darby hurried to comply as Quinn dismounted and handed Faro's reins to Helen.

"He's a bit fresh, my lady, but he won't give you any trouble," he said, stroking the horse's dark muzzle.

Faro eyed Helen with calm interest and a soft whiffle of

grassy breath. He stood at around eighteen hands – big enough to carry a man of Quinn's stature, but slightly overlarge, perhaps, for Mr Amberley.

Quinn bent and offered his laced hands as a makeshift mounting step. Grabbing the pommel, Helen inserted her foot and launched herself upward, feeling the added velocity of Quinn's strength behind her own thrust. She flung her leg over the saddle and settled her seat, the big horse solid and unmoving beneath the grip of her knees. Quinn hooked her boot into one stirrup as she manoeuvred her foot into the other. Murmuring her thanks, she threaded out the rein and urged Faro to walk around.

"Keep safe, my lady," Darby called. She stood with her arms tightly folded over her chest and hands tucked under her armpits for warmth, her broad face pinched tight with concern.

"We should be back by breakfast," his lordship said to Quinn. "If we are not, you know what to do."

Quinn squinted up at him. "Aye. God forbid that it comes to that."

That sounded ominous. Where exactly were they going? And more importantly, for what reason?

Before Helen could ask, Carlston had turned Ares and was trotting down the rise, heading, she surmised, to the little-used north-east gate. She saw him bend forward in the saddle, opening the horse into a gallop. Any conversation, it seemed, would wait until they were well away from Chenwith.

With a nod to Darby and Quinn, she pressed her black beaver hat more firmly on her head and shifted her seat, urging Faro after his companion. The horse leaped forward and Helen gave a low laugh of exhilaration, the joy of riding astride and leaning into the horse's speed overshadowing any unease.

They were on the road to Bristol before Carlston dropped Ares back into a walk. Helen drew up beside him, easing Faro into the slower pace. Ares turned his head and mouthed Faro's bridle, the two jostling for a moment before settling into the journey.

"Last night, what did you mean when you asked if I had an odd sensation in my head?" Carlston said abruptly.

Helen straightened in the saddle, unsettled by the apprehension in his eyes beneath the brim of his hat.

"During the explosion, Darby thought she saw the Ligatus power trying to force its way out of me. We can't be sure, of course, but now we both have this feeling of pressure here." She touched her forehead. "I wanted to know if you had it too. And you said you did, so—"

"Thank God." He closed his eyes and lifted his face to the brightening sky. "Thank God!"

"It is not something to thank God about," Helen began.

He opened his eyes, the apprehension gone. "No, you don't understand. I thought the vestige darkness had come back. I thought I was going mad again."

She closed her hands around the pommel, forcing back the impulse to reach across and touch his arm, to reassure him that his mind was whole. Little wonder he had been so worried.

Even so, the truth was not much better.

"No, it is not the vestige. Darby thinks the Ligatus is going to rip the three of us apart."

He stared at her, making the awful connection in an instant. "Because we are all linked through the bond," he said grimly. "God's blood, we go from the frying pan into the fire. What exactly did she see?"

Helen reported Darby's description, then added, "We cannot be sure her interpretation is correct, but since you are feeling the same kind of pressure, there must be a link." She paused. "I had a nightmare last night. I thought I heard an infant screaming: Timothy Marr."

"A dream from the Ligatus?" He frowned at the muddy road ahead. "Perhaps it is another way we can extract information from it. We must find out what is really happening rather than just guessing at it."

"Darby offered to try to see the Ligatus again."

"What, under the same circumstances?" He shook his head. "Apart from the obvious danger to Darby, I'm sure the Duke would not appreciate us blowing up his estate."

"Might the Bath Deceiver know?"

Carlston rubbed at his mouth. "A good question. I thought the Comte d'Antraigues implied the Bath Deceiver knew only about the Grand Deceiver dyad, not our dyad."

Helen, who had been in receipt of the Comte's dying words about the Grand Deceiver, nodded. "Yes, that is the impression I received. Still, could it not be possible the Bath Deceiver might know something about us too?"

"I'd say the odds of it are not high, but it is probably our only way forward." He reined in Ares, who came to an obedient standstill under his firm hands. "Considering this new development, I am not sure it is a good idea to take you to the Wedding today."

Helen pulled Faro up too. "The Wedding?"

"The Stanton Drew stone circle. I wanted to test a theory about your reinvigoration yesterday. It is possible you can draw energy from the earth; and the Wedding, like all the stone circles, is a rich source of earth power. However, it may now be too dangerous to investigate."

"But what if I *can* draw energy from the earth? What does that mean?"

"I don't know. We are in uncharted territory, Helen."

"Will it give us an advantage over the Grand Deceiver?" she asked, ignoring the inappropriate use of her name.

"Maybe." He paused. "Probably. There is no greater power source than the earth."

So, Helen thought, this drawing of power could be their one advantage; a way to destroy the Grand Deceiver's threat to humanity.

"Our problem is that we do not know what kind of force we are facing," she said. "It could be just the Grand Deceiver, or a Deceiver army, or something even worse. It seems to me we are far too ignorant of their power, and our own power as well, and it makes us weak. I think we must take this chance to discover the extent of our power, even if we do not yet know what it will be used against."

Carlston gave a reluctant nod. "It is true, we are always on the back foot. Every Deceiver is generations old and remembers everything; whereas we have one life span and *must* learn it all – every Reclaimer, every time – from records that are, frankly, questionable. I agree that we need information, about them and about our own power. Having said that, we must consider the risk. If the mesmerism has, as Darby surmises, opened a rift for the Ligatus to force its way out of you, then drawing the earth power could make that rift larger through an influx of energy."

A larger rift? It was a horrible thought. Helen stroked Faro's neck, the horse's warm solidity steadying her. They were caught between the need to become a force that could destroy the Grand Deceiver and the possibility that the Ligatus would kill them before they could complete that duty.

"But you do not know that will happen," she said.

He tilted his head, conceding the point.

"As far as I can remember," she continued, "the pressure behind my eyes did not change when I was in the garden. That could mean the energy that I drew from the earth did not affect the rift."

"You cannot be sure of that."

"We cannot be sure of anything unless we test it."

"We could just wait."

"For what?" she demanded. "More information? Apart from the Bath Deceiver – whom we have not yet found – we have only the information we discover ourselves. Besides, what if we wait and the Ligatus kills us anyway? All of this will have been for nothing, and there will be no Grand Reclaimer to stand against the Grand Deceiver."

He lifted a shoulder. "These are good arguments, but…"

"But what?"

"I do not want to place you in danger."

Amore mio – it was in his eyes, in the soft tone of his voice. *My love.*

God help her, it rose in her too. The longing. An answer to his call.

"We are all in danger, Carlston. At least this is something we can do about it." She pressed her heels into Faro's flanks, urging the horse forward, away from the illicit yearning that dug at her conscience like a burr.

She took the lead for a mile or so, finding her composure in her mount's smooth pace and the brightening of the misty dawn into a cold, blue-skied morning. Fields stretched out on either side of the narrow rutted road, enclosed by low dry-stone walls, the grass a patchwork of melting snow and wet green earth. Black-faced sheep huddled in groups, the damp ground beneath their hooves milled into mud, the pungent smell of their dung mixing with the faint scent of chimney smoke. She glimpsed a farmhand trudging through a winter-bare apple orchard, and caught a snatch of his whistled tune. Otherwise, only the thud of their horses' hooves and the morning calls of the winter starlings disturbed the quiet.

She rubbed at the tight sensation across her forehead. Perhaps Carlston was right: testing his theory could be too dangerous. On the other hand, would it not be a dereliction of their duty to ignore the one advantage that could defeat the Grand Deceiver? More power meant more strength, and if the Comte d'Antraigues's warnings were to be heeded, they were going to need everything they had, and more, to defeat their enemy.

And if they did defeat the Grand Deceiver – a chilling *if* – did that mean the Grand Reclaimer would no longer be required? According to Sir Jonathan, destroying a Grand Deceiver did not destroy all other Deceivers; the creatures would remain hidden across England, and the Reclaimers would still be needed to control them. Would she and Carlston be expected to part ways and return to enforcing the Pact as independent Reclaimers?

Probably better for them both if they were no longer entwined through their power, she thought. And the dissolution of the dyad would certainly please Selburn. No doubt he would want her to step down from *all* her Reclaimer duties to take on her role as his wife. A reasonable expectation, but until they were blessed with children it would surely be a waste not to use her abilities.

Helen heard the jingle of tack as Carlston closed the distance between them. She kept her eyes fixed upon the road as he drew his horse alongside, the pulse of their union a soft throb throughout her whole body, from fingertips to toes.

"Have you told Selburn about the rift in the Ligatus?" he asked.

Her betrothed, it seemed, was on both their minds.

"No."

"I do not think we should tell him yet. Or anyone else for that matter. Not until we determine the truth." He cleared his throat. "Do you agree?"

A request, not a command – his way of stepping back.

He added, "If Selburn is told, he will want you to be rid of the Ligatus immediately. I would if I were him."

Helen glanced sidelong at the declaration. "I shall not tell him. For now," she conceded. "Why do you think your wife's portrait is in his temple?"

Carlston's brows rose; he had not expected the question. To be fair, she had not expected to ask it.

"It was painted by one of Elise's friends during a house party."

"You were at Chenwith for a house party?"

He gave his half-smile. "Yes, I came with George Brummell. Invited as a courtesy to him, I think, more than for my company. I certainly was not one of Selburn's cronies. It was where I first met Elise."

Helen nodded, an encouragement to continue. He had never spoken about his courtship of Lady Elise before. In her mind's eye, Helen glimpsed a bright summer's day, a lady painting her friend's vivid, beautiful face upon the stone wall, their laughter luring the gentlemen of the party from their conversations to cluster around both artist and model in admiration.

Carlston drew the reins through his fingers. "It was also where Elise and I fell in love, and I more or less usurped Selburn's hopes. I am surprised he has kept the portrait."

"You seem more aggrieved than surprised," Helen said, hearing a little too much edge within her voice. "It sounds as if you still have some regard for her."

His shoulder hitched. "I did love her once; then I mourned her. Now..."

"Now?" Helen pressed. "She betrayed you. She betrayed England. When you find her, what do you propose to do?"

"*If* I find her. We cannot be sure she is still alive. Or indeed if the information you received from the Ligatus was the truth or just Benchley's mad writings."

"Assuming she is alive," Helen persisted, "what happens when you find her?"

The muscle in his jaw tightened. "Are you asking if I intend to kill her? Do you actually think I would go against all human honour, against what we stand for as Reclaimers? We do not raise our hands against a normal human."

"I was not asking that at all," Helen said, although perhaps she was – she did not know why she kept upon the subject. "Even so, you cannot claim you have not raised your hand. You raised it against Selburn." He opened his mouth to protest, but she shook her head. "I do not mean when you were in the throes of the vestige madness. Before that."

"Ah." He gave a reluctant nod. "Just after Elise disappeared. Yes, that is true. He came to our townhouse with two of his cronies. Everyone thought I had murdered Elise, and Selburn had come to exact punishment. He did not stand a chance. I took the whip off him almost immediately and laid open his shoulder with one cut. Who was he to impugn my honour? To whip me?" He looked ahead, eyes focused upon the memory. "I stood over him with his blood dripping from the whip and realised I could kill him with the next cut. More to the point, I wanted to do so with every fibre of my being. So I broke the whip in half and threw it away. The next day I left England." He glanced at her, his face dark. "Did he tell you some other story?"

"He has not mentioned it."

"No, he would not. It reflects as badly upon him as it does me. And now he must feel as foolish as I do for believing Elise's lies and falling for her spy tricks." He drew a deep breath. "If she is still alive, and I discover she was indeed spying for

Napoleon, I will bring her back to face the courts for treason."

"As a Countess, if she is found guilty they will behead her."

"Yes," he said flatly.

And he would be a widower. The thought came, dark and unbidden. She curled the back of her hand against her cheek, holding back a flush of shame.

He glanced at her, the expression in his eyes too full. "It would not be revenge," he said. "It would be justice. I no longer feel anything for her except … regret."

"Regret?" The prompt felt too dangerous. She added quickly, "Of course, as you say, regret for falling for her spy tricks."

He stared ahead again. "Exactly."

They rode in silence, side by side, for another half-mile or so until Carlston pointed to a field ahead. A boulder, at least seven feet tall and hewn into a rough rectangle, stood upright in the earth. On either side of it were boulders of the same size and shape but recumbent upon the grass, their positions too orderly to be natural.

"That is part of the largest circle," he said. "Twenty-seven pillars altogether, although a good number are now on their sides."

Helen straightened in the saddle to see the extent of the monument. So far she could count only four stones; it must be immense. "Why is it called The Wedding?"

"The legend has it that a local couple married on a Saturday and the devil, disguised as a fiddler, enticed them and their guests to dance through into the Sabbath. For their sin, they were all turned to stone."

"Well, what can one expect when one dances upon a Sunday," Helen said lightly, but the sight of the ancient monoliths made the skin at her nape prickle.

Further along the road, a grey stone church tower stood amidst a small cluster of cottages. Plumes of smoke curled from chimneys, and the rhythmic clang of a blacksmith's hammer reached them like a distant tolling bell. The village of Stanton Drew, Helen presumed.

"Let us walk the large circle," Carlston said. He reined in Ares and dismounted smoothly. "If the power is too strong, we can revise our decision."

He led Ares to a tree that overhung the wall, the approach alarming ten or so chittering starlings from its branches. The birds swooped and scolded, echoing Helen's own irritation. They had come all this way to test Carlston's theory. They had discussed the risks. She was not going to baulk now.

She swung down from the saddle, her descent embarrassingly untidy; it had been so long since she had ridden astride that her thigh muscles trembled from the unfamiliar grip. She tethered Faro alongside his stablemate and followed Carlston over a stile and into the field. By the time they had reached the upstanding stone and walked a little way inside the circle, all strain had been stretched from her muscles, and she felt the same easing in her body as she had in the garden. A strange sensation was building around her feet too, as if she had stepped into a stream of warm water.

"I think I can sense the power," she said. "It seems quite robust."

Now that they stood within the circle, the rest of the huge mottled brown stones could be seen in formation. At least half had toppled onto their sides, but even so it was breathtaking; the circle was almost as big as the new Lord's Cricket Ground. Beyond it to the right was another circle of eight pillars linked by a straight avenue of tumbled smaller stones. Such a rigid line was anathema to the natural world, and strangely unsettling.

"What was the formation used for?" she asked.

"Some say druidical rituals. Others, ancient astronomical calendars. What I have learned through my studies is that there are energy lines, called earth currents, that crisscross every land and sea, creating a web of power around our planet. Sometimes, but not always, they pass through these stone circles."

Helen looked at her feet. "And there is one here?"

Carlston nodded. "A major one." He squinted up at the pale sun and shifted so it was to his right. "The line runs from east to west. It crosses your betrothed's estate and runs all the way here."

If it ran across Selburn's estate, then why had they ridden all this way? But Helen did not voice the question. The answer was obvious: they needed privacy to test the power.

And perhaps there was another reason too; one that neither of them wished to voice.

"It goes through that stone," Carlston pointed to an upright pillar across the circle, then drew an imaginary line past their feet, "across here, and then out via that stone towards the village." He turned and pointed to a half-buried recumbent stone behind them. "The assumption is that the line holds the greatest concentration of force."

She rubbed her gloved hands together. "So what should I do? Stand on the line in the centre of the circle?"

"I am not sure that would be the wisest course," he said dryly. "Not if you can already feel the power." He surveyed the stones again. "I think any attempt to draw it into yourself will be too risky. We should abandon the idea."

She crossed her arms, resisting the soft tone of his voice. "Lord Carlston, as much as I appreciate your concern, if I were one of the other Reclaimers – Mr Hallifax, for instance – would you be trying to dissuade me from testing this theory?"

"Jacob Hallifax has a great deal more experience than you do. I doubt he would place himself in such blatant danger."

"Experience is not in question here," she said, holding to her point. "This dyad must be made of two *Reclaimers*, Lord Carlston, not a man protecting a woman." Not William protecting Helen, she thought, but dared not say it. "I have saved your life twice. I have shot dead a Deceiver. I have absorbed the Ligatus and survived it. How many times must I prove that I am capable before you stop treating me as if I will break at the first sign of danger?" She saw the resistance in his face and added, "You protest that Selburn is holding me back, but perhaps you should look to your own behaviour."

He observed her for a stiff, silent moment, then his half-smile appeared. "A brutal cut."

"I did not mean—"

He held up his hand. "No, touché. We are the dyad; we must step forward as one into the danger." He considered the stones again. "Nevertheless, I do think the centre line holds too much risk. I suggest that you stand outside the circle first, and make an attempt to draw the energy from there."

A reasonable compromise, especially since she had made her point.

She walked outside the perimeter of the stones, focusing upon the dwindling sensation of energy beneath her feet. Carlston followed, his attention also fixed upon the ground.

"Can you feel it too?" she asked.

"No. I believe this is bound up with your particular ability to store energy." He seemed about to add something more, but shook his head and said, "You will need to remove your gloves. As I understand it, leather is one of Mr Gray's *non-electrics*."

She pulled them off, then removed her hat as well. "It will only be in the way if it is like the mesmerism power," she said, stuffing the gloves into its crown and passing the collection to him.

"Good God, I hope it is not like the mesmerism power," he said, flashing a grim smile. "We don't want to destroy an ancient monument."

He took off his own hat and gloves and placed them all in a pile a few steps away.

"Should I just crouch down and touch the earth?" she asked.

"I presume so. In this matter, I know as much, or as little, as you do."

"You should step back."

"No, I'll stay here." He settled his feet more firmly into the ground. "Just in case."

Helen gave a curt nod; indeed, anything could happen.

She crouched and, taking a deep breath, spread her fingers and placed her hands flat on the grass. The tough winter blades pricked her skin, cool from the wet remnants of the frost. Nothing else; no sensation of power. She released her breath. Perhaps she had walked too far from the circle.

She dug her fingers into the wet earth, forcing a way into the cold gritty soil. Slowly, a warm sensation collected around her hands, as if warm water lapped at them. Just like her feet.

She looked up at Carlston. "It is a little bit warm, but nothing—"

From between her hands a jagged line of lightning speared up from the earth, through the damp air, and slammed into the nearest recumbent stone with an ear-splitting crack, lighting it into a pillar of glowing red. As if joined by a fuse, the other twenty-six stones lit up too, radiating orange and red as if the circle was on fire.

Boiling power surged through Helen, rocking her back on her heels. In reflex, she rammed her hands deeper into the dirt, anchoring herself against the searing force. The energy within the linked stones exploded upward in pulsing colours – red, orange, purple, yellow, blue – illuminating a net of white lightning that flashed inside the circle as if caught in a glass dome. Lud, she had joined the earth to the heavens in a rainbow of colour!

Through the roaring in her ears, she heard the squeal of the horses and Carlston yelling, "Helen, let go!"

He lunged and grabbed her shoulder. The heat and roar of the streaming power suddenly narrowed within her as it found another path: Carlston. It was as if his hand was fused to her flesh and bones.

The connection forced him to his knees beside her, his face twisted in agony. He flung out his free hand, grasping for support, but there was nothing to hold. The energy flowed through her and into him – a thick blue stream that exploded from his palm. He screamed as the air before them seemed to bend and shimmer around the blue light, like a melting mirror, obscuring the field behind it.

Helen heard the Ligatus power within her start to gibber and scream, felt its strength claw across her consciousness towards Carlston, towards the melting air. A snapping, surging beast made of bitterness and hate and sickening images of screaming, dying people.

She wrenched her fingers out of the earth, but the power pulled her back, sucking one hand down into the hot soil again. She yanked at her wrist, hauled on it, but it would not move. She had to stop the power. It was twisting and bending the viscous air. Digging out the Ligatus.

In desperation she slammed her shoulder against Carlston's chest. He gasped under the impact, but his hand did not shift from her shoulder.

"Break my elbow!" he yelled.

"No!" She could not hurt him again.

"Helen, I cannot let go! It is killing me!"

Gathering all her strength, she rammed the heel of her hand up into the point of Carlston's elbow and heard his bones snap under the brutal force.

He screamed as his hand convulsed off her shoulder. He collapsed at her side, the roar of power suddenly silent, the melting air gone, the green field beyond it once again solid, calm and quiet.

Panting, Helen scrabbled back from the patch of turned earth that had sucked down her hand. "I'm sorry, I'm sorry."

Carlston clutched his arm to his chest, his skin ashen. He hauled himself up to a sitting position, teeth clenched, and managed a tight smile. "There was no other way we were going to separate." He surveyed the silent stones. "And we are not even *inside* the circle."

"I had no control over it." She stared at the recumbent stone, trying to sort through the order of what had just happened. "When you touched me, it was as if the power had found a pathway. It *flowed* through you."

"Like a conduit," he said.

"Did you have control of it?"

"I'm not sure control is the right word. It is possible I could have directed it, but that is about all."

"What was that thing in the air? Like melting glass."

"I don't know." He rocked forward and climbed stiffly to his feet, hissing as the movement jolted his arm. "I think I saw the rift in your mind." He grimaced. "No, *saw* is the wrong word; I felt it. A savage thing, spewing foul emotions and images and an awful sensation of threat." He shook his head. "I am sorry you have to carry such an abomination."

It was a horribly accurate description. "Do you think we have made the rift larger?"

"I cannot say. Not until I have spoken to Darby and we compare what we experienced."

It was a fair response, yet she felt a spike of fury. Why could he not just answer the question?

She looked at her hands; no sign of the searing power. And in all truth, it was not fury she felt. It was fear.

Carlston closed his eyes, his face still a ghastly shade of grey. "I feel as if everything has been stripped out of me."

"Let me help you." She rose to her feet, fluid and fast, every sense heightened: the sun brighter, the smell of the turned earth almost overwhelming, the starlings' chatter raucous in her ears.

He opened his eyes and watched her tiredly. "You are energised again, as in the garden. I can see it in your face."

She touched her cheek, feeling the heat from the blood flowing under her skin and the brush of every fine hair. "Yes, ten times more energised."

He nodded. "When I saw you come in from the garden yesterday, I made a leap of logic that I desperately hoped was wrong. But now I know I am right."

"About what?"

"The Trinitas. You have heard Pike, Benchley and myself speak of the Vis."

"Yes, the Trinitas's power source. You said it was safe from Deceiver hands."

He gave a small, pained shrug. "More or less. You are standing on it. The earth itself is the Vis. We thought it was safe because there has never been a way to access the earth currents." His mouth quirked wryly. "Until now."

"What do you mean?"

He slumped. "I think you are the Trinitas, Helen."

"What?" She stepped back from the enormity of his words. "The Trinitas is a weapon. How can that be?"

"There is a Colligat made with your hair woven into it. You hold the Ligatus in your mind. And now you can draw energy from the Vis. You are a power source. And those are the three parts of the Trinitas."

She stared at him, his logic locking together into truth. "But why? Is this part of being the Grand Reclaimer?"

"I cannot see how. The Ligatus was never meant to be inside your head. It was meant to be held in a book."

"In other words, you don't know!" She paced a few steps, then rounded back on him. "If I am the Trinitas, Carlston, then so are you. At least in terms of controlling the earth power." She clenched her fists, fighting back the panic. "I had no control, but you did. You could channel and direct it like a weapon."

"True," he said heavily. "It seems we may have found my role in our Reclaimer dyad, and perhaps in this unintended Trinitas too." He looked across at the distant collection of houses. "We need to go. Our experiment has not gone unnoticed."

A group of people had gathered on the village's main street, eyes shielded to peer at the sky. It would not be long before they overcame their fear and headed to the stone circle.

"The horses..." Carlston swung around to check.

Both beasts were shifting in agitation, but still tethered to the tree. Helen could see a gash upon Ares's shoulder – a collision with a bough perhaps, or Faro's hooves – but otherwise they seemed whole.

"It is a miracle they did not bolt," Carlston said.

Holding his injured arm close to his chest, he picked up her hat and gloves and passed them to her, then retrieved his own. The effort made him sway upon his feet.

"You will not make it across the field," she said. "Lean on me."

He placed his hat upon his head and fixed his eyes on the horses. "I will make it."

He took one shaky step across the grass, then another, the third step collapsing into a stagger.

She crossed the short distance between them. "William!"

He lifted his head, skin blanched white.

"Here, lean on my shoulder." She took his hand, the rare touch of his bare skin bringing her to a halt, her eyes meeting his in a silent, breathless rush of images – lips meeting, tongues searching, flesh pressed to flesh...

Good God. She dropped his hand. Saw the same shock in his face.

"Did you feel —"

"No," she said.

He knew it for a lie, but nodded.

She fixed her eyes upon the horses. "We must go. Now!"

She heard him breathe out. Felt his hand upon her shoulder, his weight heavy on her bones. Slowly she led him away from the circle, yet she could not look at him in case it was all still there, within her. Within him.

Chapter Eight

Back at Chenwith Hall, no one seemed to know about their early morning expedition. Helen had passed Carlston into the care of Quinn, and returned to the house in her women's clothes as planned; and it was only Carlston's injury and his absence from breakfast that required an explanation. As it turned out, the breakfast party was depleted by one more: Selburn had already left to visit a tenant by the time the others had assembled.

"As I understand it," Mr Hammond said, finishing his report of Carlston's riding "accident" as a footman poured him coffee, "it is just a sprained arm."

"Well, that is good news at least," Delia said.

"I was under the impression that Carlston was a Corinthian," Lady Georgina remarked. Her small fingers shredded a sweet roll on her plate. "I've always heard him spoken of in the same breath as Alvanley and the others in the Four-Horse Club."

Helen, her mind still set unhappily on the revelation that she and Carlston were the Trinitas, looked up from buttering a slice of bread. Lady Georgina's voice held a tone of disbelief. Was she truly suspicious or just indulging in schadenfreude? It was hard to tell, but Helen thought it best to deflect any further discussion.

Before she could intervene, however, Lord Henry answered his wife. "Carlston is a fine horseman. One of the best seats I've ever seen, and he holds the current record for the London to Worthing run. How the mighty fall, eh?" He snorted at his own joke.

Lady Margaret, considering a selection of cheeses set out on the sideboard, turned abruptly to face him. "I am sure it was an extraordinary circumstance. We must be thankful it was not more serious."

"Such vehement defence, Lady Margaret," Lady Georgina said. "He must be a *great* friend of yours." She smiled. "Although I have heard that his wife is still alive. The spy?"

"Where did you hear that?" Lady Margaret demanded.

Helen put down her butter knife. It was a very good question. Lady Georgina should not have that information. Someone had let it slip; Delia, most likely. She did have a tendency to prattle.

Lady Georgina lifted an elegant shoulder. "I don't know. It is all around town."

"Really? Around town?" Lady Margaret repeated.

She glanced at Helen with a question in her eyes: was it possible that somehow it had got out into general knowledge? Helen shook her head; the only avenue for that would be Pike, and that was unlikely.

"Of course," Lady Margaret added, "those of us who *have* friends would never repeat a vulgar rumour at their expense."

Mr Hammond coughed – a suppressed laugh – but in truth it was no laughing matter, Helen thought. Only ten people knew that Lady Elise was still alive and a spy, and one of them had spoken out of turn.

As they left the breakfast room, Helen caught Delia's arm, slowing her progress across the grand foyer until they walked alone.

"Did you tell Lady Georgina about Lord Carlston's wife?" she whispered.

Delia's brows drew together. "No. I was as surprised as you when she said that. I didn't tell her, Helen."

"Are you sure? No inadvertent slip?"

Delia's alabaster skin reddened. "I have barely spoken three words to her since we arrived. You immediately thought it was me, didn't you?"

"Someone told her," Helen said, sidestepping the accusation.

Fairwood approached. Delia pulled her arm from Helen's grasp and continued across the foyer.

"My lady," the butler said, calling Helen's attention from her friend's stiff-backed departure, "Cook would like to speak to you about tonight's menu. At your convenience."

Of course; from now on she was to have the design of dinner.

"I'll speak to her now, Fairwood. Where is she?"

"The Dowager Duchess always conferred with Cook in the green writing room, my lady."

"Then I will do the same," Helen said. She looked around inquiringly. "The room is … where?"

Fairwood bowed. "This way, my lady."

Oddly, the green writing room had hardly any green furnishings in it, the dominant hue being a bright, fashionable yellow. Perhaps it was the majestic view of the lawns that had supplied its name.

As Helen took a seat at a small satinwood writing desk near the window, she heard music: the pianoforte from the drawing room. Delia playing "The Highland Fairy Lullaby" if she were not mistaken. A sad Irish folk song about a baby stolen by fairies. Delia's rendition, however, was unusually heavy-handed, fuelled perhaps by indignation. It ended abruptly in a discordant crash just as Selburn's cook, Mrs Carroll, arrived.

The brawny, fierce-browed Mrs Carroll, Helen soon realised, had firm views upon many subjects, including the use of eels – in a pie or jellied, but never stewed – and geese – vile birds with little meat – and was scrupulously honest about her skills, confessing that she had yet to conquer the tricky three-layered Prince of Wales jelly.

"I am sure you will vanquish it, Mrs Carroll," Helen said diplomatically. "Shall we discuss tonight's menu?"

The soup and fish removes and the three courses were soon chosen, and Mrs Carroll even smiled thinly at one point as they discovered a mutual dislike of caper sauce.

"There, I think that will do us very well," Helen said, passing across the course plans. She put down her pen. Now came the trickier negotiation: the employment of Lady Margaret's precious cook and kitchen maids. "Mrs Carroll, no doubt you are aware that Lady Margaret's household arrived with us yesterday, also displaced by the gas explosion?"

The woman observed her shrewdly. So far there had been accord, but they both knew the alliance was not yet sealed. "Aye."

Helen pushed on. "Mrs Clarke has agreed to employ Lady Margaret's senior staff and her maids and footmen for the Christmas and wedding festivities, but she has informed me that you choose your own staff. Would Lady Margaret's cook and kitchen maids be of use to you during this busy time?"

Mrs Carroll squinted at the proposal. "If you forgive me, my lady, there's a saying: 'Too many cooks…'"

Lud, the woman did not want another cook in her domain. Another tactic then.

"Yes, of course," Helen said. "Although it is inevitable that more staff will be taken on for the wedding preparations. His Grace has mentioned bringing in a famous French chef, a Monsieur…" She waved her hand airily. "I cannot remember his name. An émigré. He is supposed to be very good."

Mrs Carroll sniffed. "A Frenchman, you say? From France?"

"Yes," Helen said, letting the full horror of the invented Frenchman sink in.

Mrs Carroll shook her head slowly. "I don't think we need come to that."

"Quite. Shall I tell Lady Margaret's cook and her girls to report to your kitchen?"

"Aye, I think that would be best," Mrs Carroll said, a bobbed curtsey and her thin smile sealing the deal.

Helen's own smile faded as she watched the cook depart. If all went well – if the Grand Deceiver was defeated and the dyad dissolved – this was to be her life. Of course, it was gratifying to have created a fine menu, placed Lady Margaret's staff and organised the extra help that would be required for Christmas and the wedding. A well-run house was an achievement – that was what her aunt always said.

She ran her forefinger across the sharp crenulations of her knuckles. Even so, she had battled demons and felt the earth energy burst through her body, its savage echo still humming in her bones. It was a terrifying burden, especially now that she and Carlston were most likely the Trinitas. And it was rather more *important* than choosing a sauce. After wielding such power, could she return to making morning calls and creating menus for the rest of her life?

She shook her head; that was oversimplifying such a life. There would be children – God granted – and a house and estate that supported hundreds of people. A life that was important in its own way.

She reached for the bell and rang for the butler. "Where is Lady Margaret, Fairwood?"

"I believe she and Miss Cransdon went to the library, my lady."

"Thank you."

He cleared his throat. "Lady Georgina is still in the drawing room," he volunteered.

Helen observed him narrowly. He clearly had something more to impart. "What has happened, Fairwood?"

"Lady Georgina told Miss Cransdon to 'stop playing that awful dirge and give her some peace', and there was an ... *exchange*, my lady."

"An exchange?"

"Apparently, Lady Georgina attempted to close the piano-forte lid while Miss Cransdon's fingers were still upon the keys."

"Ah." That explained the sudden cessation of music. Lady Georgina, it seemed, delighted in discord. "Thank you, Fairwood."

Her next duty as hostess was clear: she must mediate between the ladies, and bring peace back to the drawing room.

Helen stood in the doorway of the Chenwith library and took a deep, appreciative breath. The celebrated room, which ran almost the entire length of the south-wing ground floor, smelled of furniture oil, leather and that slightly mouldy perfume of foxed paper that promised hours of delight.

She walked in, hoping to find Delia and Lady Margaret in one of the elegant clusters of armchairs and sofas set out at either end of the gallery. She had tried to listen for them on her way from the morning room, but during the day the house was too noisy, and in truth she knew only one rhythm of respiration well enough to pick it out from the multitude. Carlston's. Perhaps being able to find him in such a way was part of the dyad union. Or maybe she just needed more practice to recognise individual respirations.

Delia and Lady Margaret were not to be found at the east

end, the burgundy silk sofa empty, its pale blue cushions arranged in a perfect line. She skirted the huge polished table that held a chessboard and a globe of the world, and made her way past the bookshelves and glass-fronted cabinets to the west end, where another reading nook was hidden behind a huge black marble column. They were not there either. She had missed them; or perhaps they had never arrived.

She lingered for a moment, peering into a glass cabinet where a new-bound book, *Arrivals From India*, had been arranged face-out. She had read novels by the author before – Henrietta Rouviere Mosse – and although a little too worthy, they were a pleasant diversion.

Duty called, however.

She straightened, her attention caught by a painting set on the wall above. A portrait of three youths by the magnificent hand of Lawrence, if she were any judge. One of the young men was clearly the Duke, and the other Lord Henry. The third, Helen realised, must be Oliver, Marquess of Camford, the eldest son and, until his premature death, heir apparent to the Dukedom. Like his two younger brothers, Oliver had the distinctive Annisford blond hair and fair skin, but he had sidestepped the long chin and been the most handsome of the three.

"Lady Helen!" She swung around to see Lord Henry approaching from the doorway. Lud, the last thing she needed was to be cornered by one of his monologues. "I had not pegged you as a bluestocking."

She smiled politely. "I am seeking Lady Margaret and Miss Cransdon. Have you seen them?"

"Not since breakfast."

"Well, I shall continue my search." Helen prepared to make her farewell, but Lord Henry stopped at her side, blocking the path to the door.

He looked up at the portrait. "Ah, you have found the Terrible Three." His customary joviality seemed a little too forced. "It's by Lawrence, you know, but our father consigned it to the library after Oliver died. Said he couldn't bear to see it."

Selburn had not told her a great deal about his deceased half-brother. She knew the old Duke had been married three times: the first marriage producing Oliver; the second producing Selburn and Lord Henry; and the third without issue. She had to admit she was rather curious about the tragic Oliver.

"Your brother died from an illness, I believe," she prompted.

"Yes, devil of a business." Lord Henry recollected himself and bowed. "Beg pardon. I meant, it was a sad business." He looked up at the painting again. "Consumption. A long and messy end. We were all with him, of course. I remember he coughed up so much blood at the last." He twitched his shoulders as if the memory had run a cold fingertip down his spine. "Ghastly, no way for a man to die. The hurt of it nearly killed our father too. Probably did in the end. Oliver was always his favourite, you see. Father locked himself away after that and wouldn't even let Selburn take on the Marquess title – said it was Oliver's in perpetuity. Made him take the Chenwith Viscountcy instead, until he came into the Dukedom. Oliver wouldn't have cared, you know. He was the best of us." He blinked rapidly. "The best."

"How long ago was it?" Helen asked.

"He died in 1802, during the peace with France. I remember because I had just turned sixteen, and Oliver was planning to go to Paris to celebrate his majority. I desperately wanted to go with him – the annoying younger brother. Of course, he never made it to Paris or to twenty-one. And then the truce ended."

"That was the year my parents drowned," Helen said.

"Devil of a year all round," Lord Henry said softly, and this time he did not apologise. "We shouldn't look back too often, eh?" He rallied a smile. "I am glad I have happened upon you. I have a favour to ask."

So their meeting had not been accidental at all.

"I will endeavour to oblige you, of course," she said, trying to keep the wariness from her voice.

"Lady Georgina is..." Lord Henry rubbed the back of his neck, seeming to run out of words.

Helen studied his face; had his wife told him about her disagreement with Delia?

"You and she are soon to be sisters," he finally said. "I am glad of it."

Helen smiled and waited.

He rocked back on his heels. "She only has a brother, you see."

"Yes, I am the same."

"Will you be a friend to her, Lady Helen?" he blurted out. "She does not make friends easily. It is her beauty, you see – there is always jealousy. But I think you are better than that, aren't you? She needs a friend, and I have observed that you are very kind."

Helen flushed. Thus far she had not been particularly kind towards Lady Georgina; she had even blamed her for this latest exchange with Delia without knowing the particulars. Perhaps her judgment had been too quick and too harsh. Clearly, Lady Georgina prompted her husband's devotion, so there must be something more to her than sour temper and vanity.

"As you say, we will soon be sisters," she said. "Of course, friendship requires more than a bond forged by marriage, but I think it is a good start."

"Yes, indeed," he said, the hopeful inquiry in his face broadening into a relieved smile. "Thank you. You will need to persevere

– she is used to turning people away. And you will start soon, won't you? She is in the drawing room, I believe. Alone."

His idea of "soon" was plainly "now".

"I have a few errands I must attend to, but I have no doubt I will see Lady Georgina before long," Helen said firmly. She curtseyed. "If you will excuse me."

"Yes, yes, of course." He bowed and moved aside. "But you will make it soon, won't you? I would be most grateful."

She gave him a non-committal smile and walked towards the door, an uneasy sense of burden settling upon her shoulders. Such a strange and rather presumptuous request. She looked back, half expecting to see him in pursuit. Instead, he stood staring up at the portrait, hands clasped behind his back, an expression upon his face that seemed very close to despair.

Helen walked swiftly from the library to the Great Hall, trying to put some distance between herself and Lord Henry. Why was she so rattled by their interview? Certainly, the request was odd, but his terrible sense of sadness felt far more disturbing. Perhaps it was because she had cast him as a buffoon, and finding such depth of feeling within him did not reflect well upon her charity or her ability to read the truth of people.

Her footsteps echoed in the huge empty hall. An unusual pale winter sunshine shimmered across the four immense chandeliers and cast bright squares of light onto the marquetry dance floor. Perhaps Lady Margaret and Delia had taken refuge in the gardens, drawn outside by the dry weather. She quit the Great Hall and headed through the foyer past the staircase, casting a quick glance upward at the dome. Sunlight streamed in through the small windows set around its base and lit the scene of love into vivid colours. So much brighter than it had been in yesterday's gloom.

"My lady?"

Helen whirled around. Quinn stood beside the staircase – attained, it seemed, by Terrene stealth – his expression unusually tense.

Had something happened to Carlston? Even as she thought it, she reached for their bond and found the beat, slow and heavy. He was in the deep sleep of the Reclaimer fugue to heal his arm.

"Is it not working?" she asked. "Is he all right?"

Quinn ducked his head. "He is healing well, my lady. Hammond is with him." He rubbed his mouth, as if unsure of his next words. Not his usual manner at all. "If you would, my lady, I'd speak to you in private."

"Of course." Helen glanced around, trying to determine the best place. The footmen would already be preparing the dining room for luncheon, and Lord Henry could emerge from the library and through the Great Hall at any time. Back then to the green writing room. She motioned for Quinn to follow. As they walked, she glanced at his face. Beneath his *moko* – she knew the correct name for his tattoos now – his brown skin was bleached of its normal health.

"Are you quite well yourself, Mr Quinn?" she asked.

"I am, my lady."

She led the way into the green writing room, and Quinn closed the door behind them. He had a barely contained energy about him. Not anger, but an agitation that almost rocked him upon his feet.

"Will you sit?" Helen asked, motioning to the chair placed near the desk.

"Thank you, my lady."

As he sat, she turned the chair out from under the satinwood desk and seated herself opposite him. It occurred to her that this was perhaps the first time they had conversed alone.

"What is it, Mr Quinn?"

He leaned forward. "Something is wrong with Miss Darby, my lady. She is worried, morbid worried, and she won't tell me why."

Helen met his steady, watchful gaze. Clearly he had sensed Darby's fear about the rift. And, just as clearly, he could now sense her own knowledge of it. His years with Carlston had taught him more than battle skills.

"What is troubling her, my lady?"

The flat tone of his voice demanded the truth. And surely such fierce loyalty to Darby deserved it. But how much, in all conscience, could she tell him?

"I cannot give you details, Mr Quinn, but I will say you are correct. Something is not only affecting Darby but also his lordship and myself. For now, Darby has been asked to maintain her silence. She is following my orders, not withholding information from you."

"I see." He sat back and folded his arms across his chest. "This is something to do with the Ligatus bond between you all, isn't it? I know that whatever happened in Barnes," he stretched his muscular neck to one side, as if easing the pain of that day in his mind, "whatever happened in that attic changed everything for the three of you. I know I can't be privy to it all. Even so, you and I know, my lady, that I have an interest in Miss Darby's welfare beyond friendship, and I will not abdicate that interest."

"I understand, Mr Quinn."

"Then you *must* tell me, is she in danger?" His hand flicked away the obvious. "Beyond that in which we all stand?"

She could at least tell him that unnerving truth. "Yes, she is."

He sucked in a breath. "Dire danger?"

"Possibly." No, that was not correct. "Probably," she amended.

He released the breath in a long hiss. "And you will not tell me what it is?"

"Not at present."

"I see." He bowed his head, hands clasping his knees. It was not an attitude of acceptance, Helen realised, but rather a gathering of determination. He lifted his head, his mouth set into a thin line. "I have a request. I wish to marry Miss Darby as soon as possible, if she will have me."

Helen stared at him.

"I know it is against Dark Days Club rules, but you are marrying the Duke, my lady, and I figure since that's the case, then Mr Pike can have no quarrel with me and Jen –" he cleared his throat, "I mean Miss Darby – also marrying."

Helen pressed her steepled fingers to her mouth to moderate the smile upon her face. "I would not allow Mr Pike to have any quarrel. Darby will be so happy."

Quinn did not try to moderate his own grin. "I hope so, my lady. It is my aim."

Yet through her gladness, Helen already felt the cold shadow of reality.

"But what will happen afterwards, Mr Quinn? If we defeat the Grand Deceiver, if Lord Carlston and I are no longer the dyad ... you must be with him, and Darby must be with me."

He shook his head. "I don't pretend to know what will happen in the future, my lady. I just know the present. Right now, I have a chance to belong to Jen Darby, and she to belong to me. Our own family." He touched the untattooed side of his forehead. "I got taken from my family when I was barely thirteen, just coming into manhood. Now I've lived more of my life away from my people than I have with them. I used to think

I'd find my way back one day, but my path is here now, with his lordship and the Dark Days Club. And with Miss Darby, if she says yes. I trust we will prevail in the oncoming battle, but if we do not, I want to stand beside her in the house of God, holding her hand as husband and wife. And if I am to go first…" He dug his hand into the pocket of his jacket and brought out a wad of bank notes. "I have money put aside, my lady. I don't come without means."

"I doubt that matters to Darby," Helen said.

He smiled, the expression so sweet, so fond, that it pierced Helen's heart. "She is a practical woman, my lady."

She returned his smile. "Yes, she is."

He sobered. "I do not need your permission to ask for her hand, my lady, but I know Jen – I know she would not accept without your approval. And so I ask you for it."

"You have it, Mr Quinn." Helen paused. "Have you spoken about this to his lordship?"

He shook his head. "I will when he wakes." He rubbed his forehead. "I usually know his mind, my lady, but this time I can't pick what he'll say. He's always been hard against fraternising, but then…" He stopped, a quirk of his mouth acknowledging the last few months.

Yes, *but then* … the bawdy house and *amore mio*, and the horror of Barnes Terrace: Carlston's madness, the death of Stokes at his hands, and the agonising blood bond made through the Ligatus. And, of course, her betrothal to Selburn.

"I doubt you'll have any quarrel from his lordship," Helen said, making it a promise.

Helen hugged the wonderful knowledge of Mr Quinn's intentions to herself as she continued her search for Delia and Lady Margaret. It would be hard not to tell them – she felt as if she were brimming with the news – but until Darby accepted him and they made it known to the world, she must remain silent. At least this time it was a happy secret.

Finally, she tracked her quarry to the Long Gallery. They sat on an alcove seat in one of the row of huge windows that overlooked the south lawn, heads bent together in conversation, still clad in pelisses and bonnets. Both looked up when they heard her footsteps on the polished wooden floor, and she had the distinct impression that she was facing a united front.

"I have some news regarding your staff, Lady Margaret," she said, hoping to disarm the bristling regard. She sat in a chair opposite them. "I know you were concerned about their employment, so if it suits you, I have arranged for them to take positions alongside the Chenwith staff while you are the Duke's guest."

For an instant, Helen saw refusal in Lady Margaret's face; no doubt a reflex born of her dislike of Selburn. But to her credit, she quickly put the contrariness aside. "That is generous of the Duke, Lady Helen. Thank you."

Helen shifted, unseated by an odd discordance. The Duke had played no part in the decision and yet Lady Margaret had immediately attributed the good deed to him. Of course, it was his house and therefore no surprise that Lady Margaret would acknowledge his generosity, but it was strange to be unified in people's minds already, before they were even married.

"My brother tells me that Lord Carlston's arm is broken," Lady Margaret said. "I presume he did not come off his horse as reported, so what really happened?"

"I cannot say. At least, not yet."

Lady Margaret's mouth pursed. "So we are back to that, are we?"

They all sat in a silence that was full of something unsaid.

Helen looked down the Long Gallery, aware of Lady Margaret's eyes upon her.

Delia plucked at the pink tasselled trim on her pelisse. "You do not trust me, Helen."

So now it was said.

"That is not true." Helen leaned forward. "I believe you. However, someone said something to Lady Georgina. And there are only ten of us who know Lady Elise is still alive and a spy."

"But you suspected me first," Delia said.

Helen looked away from the resentment in her friend's eyes.

"Frankly, none of us has had the time nor the inclination to tell Lady Georgina anything," Lady Margaret said. "Do you know she slammed down the pianoforte lid and almost caught Delia's fingers under it?"

Delia, not *Miss Cransdon*, Helen noted. "Really? She tried to slam it on your fingers?"

Delia nodded as Lady Margaret said, "Close enough to it." She observed Helen shrewdly. "I think it is safe to say we can discount Lord Carlston as the source of the indiscretion. Nor is it Delia, myself or my brother. Lady Georgina has had no contact with Quinn, Darby, Sir Jonathan or Mr Pike, so there is only one other feasible place it could have come from."

Helen nodded reluctantly. The Duke. She straightened, realising that she had slumped. "I know that being here is not ideal for us, nor is Lady Georgina's company. To make matters more difficult, we will soon have my aunt here as well. We must make sure we are on guard at all times."

"And will you tell His Grace that as well?" Lady Margaret asked.

"I will," Helen said. Selburn would not like being admonished – after all, who did? – but he would surely see the danger of such loose talk and agree to be more vigilant.

She looked at Delia. "I am sorry."

Her friend nodded, but Helen was not sure she had been forgiven.

Chapter Nine

The afternoon was spent in the drawing room with peace restored, mainly due to the absence of Lady Georgina who had refused luncheon and retired to her rooms. At the smaller whist table in the corner, Delia and Lady Margaret sorted packets of silk ribbons, buttons and trims – Twelfth Night gifts for Lady Margaret's staff – while Helen pretended to read the Mosse novel on the chaise longue, but in truth see-sawed between smiling about Quinn and Darby, and reliving over and over the terrifying wonder of the earth power. It was still in her bones and marrow; a more robust buzz that had joined the ever-present hum of the Ligatus. Did that mean it had forced open the rift inside her even more? The thought clenched her stomach.

At least they now knew she could draw upon the earth's energy and that Carlston could, perhaps, direct it. His lordship, as far as she could tell, was still in the deep healing sleep of the Reclaimer fugue; no anxious musings for him. It did not matter; she had enough for both of them.

At around four in the afternoon, as the light began to drop into dusk, a knock on the door brought everyone's attention from their tasks.

"Come," Helen called, thinking it was the footmen to light the candles and lamps.

Instead, Lord Carlston entered the room, his arm in a linen sling, followed by Mr Hammond. They bowed.

"Are we intruding?" Carlston asked.

"Not at all," Helen said, swinging her feet down to the carpet. "We are quite alone."

She had been so involved with her own thoughts that she had not checked his breathing for an hour and had missed his emergence from the fugue. It was ridiculous to feel guilty about it, and yet she felt as if she had somehow failed him.

"As I see."

"How is your arm, Lord Carlston?" Lady Margaret asked.

"Healed." He lifted it in the sling. "This is more for show than anything else. I cannot be seen using it yet, so Hammond and I thought we would join you here." He addressed Helen. "Considering that we are indeed unusually alone, perhaps we could take the opportunity to consider new ways to find the Bath Deceiver."

A quirk of his mouth added: *Now that finding him is even more vital.* So she was not alone in her anxiety; a reassuring thought.

His lordship took a seat in the armchair next to Helen's chaise longue. As Lady Margaret and Delia abandoned their trim sorting, and Hammond took the other armchair, Carlston leaned across to her and whispered, "It seems there will be a wedding before your own, Lady Helen. I hope that does not vex you."

"Of course it does not. I am so glad you gave your permission," Helen whispered back.

His eyebrows lifted. "Did you think I would begrudge my closest friend his happiness?"

"If I recall correctly, you supported Pike's ban upon marriage in the Dark Days Club."

"It made sense at the time, but when the matter of your marriage arose I argued to rescind it." He gave a half-smile. "So you have me to blame."

She ignored his dry whimsy. "There is also the matter of..." She touched her forehead: *the rift*.

"Is that not more of a reason for Quinn to jump at happiness? It must be taken when it comes."

She looked away from the intensity in his eyes.

"He is yet to ask the question," he continued softly, "but assuming Miss Darby accepts him, I have offered to procure a special licence. A wedding gift. As soon as that is in hand, I believe they will take their vows. They wish to keep it quiet – just you and I, and Pike, of course, to make it official with the Dark Days Club."

Helen imagined Quinn's proposal; would he go on one knee? Yes, for all his solid good sense, he had a touch of the romantic about him. Darby would be quizzical, telling him to get up before she realised what was happening. And then, of course, the bright happiness of both. Quite a long way from her own engagement to the Duke; that awful moment on the road to Barnes when they had been discovered by Pug, Lady Dunwick and her nasty, nosy companion Mrs Albridge. Selburn had announced their alliance without her formal consent – a *fait accompli* to protect her reputation. Highly honourable, of course, but not exactly romantic. To be fair, he'd had every reason to expect that consent; she had more or less accepted him once before, prior to her presentation ball. Besides, who would not want to marry the Duke of Selburn, a man of integrity and a leader of society?

"I have been thinking that maybe our assumptions about

the Bath Deceiver are incorrect," Hammond said, bringing Helen back to the room. "We are assuming that he, or she, like most other Deceivers, has risen to a genteel rank."

"I think it is a sound assumption, Michael," Lady Margaret said from the sofa. "Proportionally there are more of them in the higher ranks." She spread her hands. "With generations of life, why would they linger in poverty or without any social power?"

Helen sat forward. "But that does not mean our Bath Deceiver is not one of those in the lower ranks. That is possibly why we have failed to find him. Or her."

"From your recounting of his last moments, the Comte d'Antraigues indicated that he and the Bath Deceiver were both members of that Deceiver Society he spoke of at Lady Dunwick's rout," Carlston said.

"The Society of Sensation," Helen said. "But we have found no trace of it. He did say it was only a small number of like-minded Deceivers."

"The Comte d'Antraigues operated as one of the French nobility, and for all his early revolutionary leanings he did not in fact tolerate the lowest orders, at least not in any social setting." Carlston slid his arm out of the sling, leaning both elbows upon the chair's armrests as he contemplated the Comte's prejudices. "I am fairly certain the Deceiver we seek is genteel. Professional at the very least."

"That still leaves a lot of people at Bath," Delia said. "The proverbial needle in a haystack."

"But surely it is still safe to say the Deceiver is a resident of the town?" Hammond offered. "After all, it is called the Bath Deceiver."

"I think we must assume that, or we have no tether at all," Carlston said. "So, we have a middling to genteel or perhaps even noble Bath resident who is a member of a hidden Deceiver society." He raked his fingers through his hair. "It is clear that this society is our best way forward. Perhaps we could try to draw out another member?"

"That assumes there is another member, and one that will make itself known to Reclaimers," Hammond said.

"True, but it is clear our current methods are failing," Carlston said. "We must try as many avenues as possible."

Helen nodded. "You could wear the fob to some of the public assemblies and concerts again to see if it prompts a reaction?"

"It did not work last time," Lady Margaret said. She contemplated Helen, a slow smile dawning. "This is a strange suggestion, I know, but it would be far more effective if you wore the fob as a pendant, Lady Helen. Such an unusual decoration would certainly make an impression, whereas just another fob upon a gentleman's fob ribbon is easily overlooked."

Helen touched her throat. "As a pendant?" The idea was startling.

"That is ridiculous," Delia said.

"No, it is brilliant, Lady Margaret," Carlston said, setting a flush across that lady's pale skin. "Since your engagement, all eyes are upon you, Lady Helen. Everyone would notice such an odd—"

The clang of the grooms' bell from the stables stopped the conversation. Helen listened: the thud of hooves and grind of wheels across the gravel confirmed the arrival of a coach. She rose from the chaise longue and crossed to the window just as her aunt's mud-spattered travelling coach drew up to the front portico, escorted by Selburn on his favourite grey mare. He must have met up with the new arrivals on the road back from visiting his tenants.

As he dismounted and passed his reins to a groom, the

footman opened the coach door and Aunt, tightly grasping the young man's hand, descended the steps with the inevitable stiffness of a day spent travelling.

Helen smiled at the lush arrangement of orange and brown feathers atop her aunt's bonnet. The dear lady always wore a multitude of feathers when she was trying to make a good impression. For all the difficulty Aunt's arrival would bring, Helen realised she was very glad to see that tall, spare figure and smile so like her own.

Delia joined her at the window. "Your aunt?"

"Yes," Helen said, "and Selburn is back too. They must have met—"

She stopped as another figure emerged from the carriage. A man, fair and loose-limbed, wearing a greatcoat with eight capes. Oh no: Andrew. She shot a glance back at Carlston. This was not going to end well.

Delia peered down at the carriage. "That is your brother, Lord Hayden, is it not?"

"Yes," Helen said shortly. "Although I had not expected him until the wedding."

Andrew looked up and saw them at the window. Grinning at their undignified curiosity, he raised his hand in greeting. Helen returned the wave and forced an answering smile.

"It is starting to feel somewhat crowded here," Carlston said dryly.

Helen retreated from the window. Perhaps she could ask Carlston to vacate the room until she had informed her aunt and Andrew that he was residing here as well. She observed him as he slipped his arm back into the sling and rose from his chair, a decidedly martial glint in his eye. In essence, she would be asking him to hide, which was about as likely as Aunt greeting him with delight.

Delia and Lady Margaret set to tidying the ribbons away. By the time the knock sounded on the door, everyone had positioned themselves in a tableau of drawing room etiquette: the ladies assembled in front of the sofa, and Carlston and Hammond standing by the hearth.

"Yes?" Helen called.

The doors opened to admit Fairwood, followed by Aunt Leonore and Andrew. Selburn, it seemed, had been delayed downstairs.

"My dear girl, we are finally here," Aunt declared, her gloved hands held out. She folded Helen into a tight embrace, her report continuing between a soft kiss and a pat of Helen's cheek. "Everyone says the road from London is improved, but my old bones will tell you the opposite – so full of ruts and holes. And the inn we stayed at! I swear—" She stopped, staring at Carlston. "Good God, what are you doing here?"

Carlston bowed. "Cousin." He paused – a beat too long, Helen thought sourly – then smiled. "How pleasant to see you again."

Andrew stepped forward, chin jutting, fists clenched. "Answer my aunt. What are you doing here?"

Carlston leaned an elbow upon the mantel and observed him through narrowed eyes. "I do not answer to you or your aunt."

"He is my guest, Hayden," Selburn said from the doorway. It was a call to stand down.

Helen sent the Duke a small smile of thanks, but he did not return it. He glanced around the room, his face becoming even more grim; it was obvious that prior to the arrival of Aunt and Andrew, all of the resident Dark Days Club had gathered and he had not been included.

Andrew stared at his friend. "Carlston is your guest? Selburn, you know what this man has done to our family. How he has used my sister!"

"Perhaps you did not hear what happened, Andrew," Helen said quickly. With a squeeze to her aunt's arm – a mix of fondness and a plea for restraint – she disentangled herself from their embrace. "Lady Margaret's accommodation in Bath was destroyed by an explosion of the new gas. His Grace was kind enough to offer us refuge."

"That does not answer why Carlston is here," Aunt said, clearly in no mood for restraint. "He was not a house guest at Lady Margaret's as well, was he?" Her voice rose on the last.

"No, of course not," Lady Margaret said.

"But he was a regular visitor at your accommodation," Aunt said triumphantly. "I have had reports, you know."

"Would that have been a weekly or monthly report?" Carlston asked pleasantly.

Helen sent a hard glance his way: *Do not make this worse.*

He answered with the ghost of a half-smile: *But it is so hard to resist.*

She frowned. *Try.*

"His lordship visited us no more or less than any good friend," Lady Margaret said firmly.

"My sister and I have been acquainted with him for quite some time," Hammond added.

"Good friend?" Aunt rounded on Lady Margaret again. "I entrusted my niece's reputation to you, but it is clear you have encouraged her to fraternise with a man who not only attempted to ruin her reputation in London, but has clearly shown himself to be—"

"Carlston is here because your niece asked me to invite him," Selburn said loudly across her tirade.

Helen squeezed her eyes shut. Lud, did he think that would soothe the situation?

She opened her eyes into the heavy silence. Aunt stared at

her as if she had invited all of Byron's notorious revival of the Hellfire Club into her boudoir. Andrew, with nowhere to place his fury, stalked over to the sideboard and poured himself a tumbler of brandy from the crystal decanter.

"If that is the case, Selburn," he said savagely, "you are a fool." He tossed back the measure in one gulp.

"Andrew, you have no right to say that," Helen protested.

"I have every right! If no one else is going to protect you from yourself, Helen, I will."

"I have my betrothed's protection well in hand, Hayden," the Duke said tightly.

"Really? Then who is this cuckoo in your nest?"

The insult drew a gasp from Delia and Lady Margaret. From the corner of her eye, Helen saw both Carlston and Selburn stiffen. Hammond laid a hand on Carlston's arm.

"Hayden!" Aunt said sharply. "You are plainly not yourself." She turned to the Duke. "Your Grace, it has been a long journey. My nephew and I shall withdraw to our rooms to recover before the dinner hour."

The Duke bowed. "Of course." He crossed to the bell and rang it.

Andrew looked up from his glass, his fair skin red. "Selburn, I beg your pardon."

The Duke gave a tight smile. "It is forgotten, my friend."

Fairwood arrived in the doorway and bowed.

"Show Viscountess Pennworth and Lord Hayden to their accommodations," the Duke ordered.

Andrew strode from the room, sending one last bitter glance at Carlston.

"Helen, my dear, accompany me," Aunt said. An order, not a request. Then, with a nod to the Duke and no one else, she departed.

"I'm so sorry," Helen murmured as she passed Selburn.

He caught her hand, delaying her for a moment. "Think nothing of it," he said, raising her fingers to his lips. The kiss lingered too long for mere gallantry. "Your brother is concerned for your well-being."

Helen smiled at his generosity and, retrieving her hand, followed her aunt from the room.

Mrs Clarke led Helen and Aunt Leonore upstairs without any comment. The housekeeper clearly recognised a strained silence when she heard one; or when she didn't hear one, Helen thought with grim whimsicality. She ushered them along the north wing and stopped at a room halfway along its length, then with a curtsey opened the oak door and withdrew.

Aunt Leonore stalked into the room. Helen followed, receiving a momentary impression of pale green walls and cream furnishings in the soft candlelight before her aunt whirled around and demanded, "What in God's name are you doing, Helen?"

A thin figure clad in neat navy suddenly appeared in the doorway of the adjacent dressing room. Helen flinched, body ready for battle, then realised it was Murphett, her aunt's maid.

The woman bobbed a curtsey and bustled into the room, hands at the ready to divest her mistress of spencer and bonnet. "I've order hot water, my lady, and—"

Aunt held up her hand. "Leave us, Murphett. Go downstairs. Get your dinner or something."

The maid stopped, hands dropping to her sides. "But your spencer, my lady. It is damp, I am sure of it."

"Go!"

Murphett immediately curtseyed, sending a startled glance at Helen. They both knew that tone of voice.

Aunt wrenched one orange glove off her hand and threw it on the bed, then the other, clearly waiting until the door closed behind her retreating maid. "Well? What do you have to say?" She undid the bow of her bonnet, the confection of feathers and flowers flying after the gloves onto the bed.

"I'm not sure what you are referring to, Aunt."

"Do not be obtuse. It does not suit you. Why did you ask Carlston here?"

Straight to the nub of the matter then. "He is a friend. It is a house party."

"A friend? He nearly ruined you, my dear." Aunt closed her eyes for a moment. "Do you still have feelings for him?"

Helen felt her face stiffen. She smiled, trying to soften her expression. "Of course not."

Aunt observed her through narrowed eyes. "My dear girl, lying to me is bad enough, but lying to yourself is a fool's game." She pressed her hand to her forehead, massaging the lined skin. "I cannot believe you are jeopardising your whole future for that stupid man."

"I am not jeopardising my future."

"Helen, I have been in this house for all of ten minutes and it is jaw-droppingly plain to anyone with an ounce of intelligence that the Duke hates Carlston and does not want him here. For all of Andrew's vulgarity, he was right: Carlston is a cuckoo." Aunt shook her head. "Why are you doing this to the man you are about to marry?"

Helen stared at the floor. Because she and Carlston were the dyad, the only hope to destroy a terrible enemy – but that answer was not for Aunt's ears. Dear God, how she longed to tell the truth. Lay open the last terrifying six months, from the moment Lord Carlston had shown her the Deceiver at Vauxhall Gardens to the earth power that she had drawn at the stones. The truth;

such a selfish impulse. How could she, in all conscience, drag the woman who had been a mother to her into the dangerous world of the Deceivers just to appease her own discomfort? She could not. She must not.

"The Duke knows Carlston is a friend," she said. "Nothing else."

"Dearest girl." Aunt crossed to Helen and took her hands, her skin cool and soft. "All the Duke understands is that you have invited another man into his home. And frankly, in that drawing room I saw you look at Carlston twice as often as you did Selburn. Even worse, you were *communicating* with him, without words. Do you think that goes unnoticed by the Duke? By anyone?"

"You are mistaken. I do not *communicate* with Carlston."

Aunt sighed. "Do you know that when you avoid the truth, you stare at the floor."

Helen looked up into her aunt's astute blue eyes. "I do not have feelings for Carlston."

"I understand – I truly do," Aunt said gently. "He has a handsome face and that devilish presence, and he can out-brood our dark, dangerous Lord Byron. No one would blame you for falling under such a spell. But now it is time to wake up. Tell me, do you love the Duke?"

Helen flushed. "Yes, I believe so."

Aunt observed her for a few uncomfortable seconds. "I am glad to hear it. Good will at the start of a marriage makes things decidedly easier. But even if you did not love him, you have pledged him your duty and respect. He and your uncle have signed the contracts. You *must* tell Carlston to go."

Helen withdrew her hands. "There is no good reason to ask him to leave."

"Your betrothed's dislike of the man is reason enough," Aunt said sternly. "Get rid of Carlston tomorrow and pray that you have not damaged your account with the Duke. This match with him is your redemption. Even your uncle is beginning to unbend."

"I do not care what my uncle thinks!"

"Helen!"

She bit her lip. That was insolent and ungracious. Even so, what Aunt demanded was impossible.

"The Duke invited Carlston to stay here as his guest. I will not gainsay my betrothed's word." She curtseyed and headed to the door.

"My dear," her aunt called after her, "what hold does Carlston have over you? Is it physical? If it is, it will not last. You must walk away! Helen, promise me you will walk away."

Helen closed the door behind her and stood for a moment in the cold corridor. Was the bond between her and Carlston physical? Or alchemical? She did not know. She knew only one thing with any certainty: neither of them could walk away from it.

Chapter Ten

Helen felt the brush of fingertips against her nape as Darby unhooked the single strand of pearls around her neck. The gems slithered over her collarbone, a soft clickety-clack sounding as her maid collected them in her hand.

"Did the evening go well, my lady?" Darby asked as she stepped around to gently pull the matching pearl earrings from Helen's lobes. She tucked the set into the open jewellery box on the dressing table, then turned back to extract the pearl comb from Helen's coiffure.

Helen regarded Darby's face in the candlelight, trying to read her expression. Had Quinn proposed yet? If so, then Darby was keeping it close, for she wore a countenance of polite inquiry and seemed to be avoiding Helen's eyes. Lud, had something gone wrong?

"I heard yer table beat Lady Georgina's," Sprat said, looking up from working Helen's glove from her hand. "That's what the footmen said." She pulled the glove free, folded it over and placed it in the long mahogany glove box.

"It was not a matter of beating Lady Georgina," Helen said, holding out her other hand for the removal of its glove. Even so, she had to admit the compliments from both the Duke and Lord Henry had been rather satisfying.

Although the meal had been excellent, the conversation and atmosphere at the table and in the drawing room afterwards had been, for lack of a better word, *careful*. Selburn had been his usual congenial self, but Helen had sensed a new constraint between them. She sat with Lord Henry on one side and Hammond on the other – a seating order pointedly arranged by Aunt – and throughout the long meal had tried not to look at Lord Carlston too often. To her shame, Aunt had been correct in that judgment: her attention did tend to slide towards his lordship and the wry understanding within his eyes.

Helen had taken the ladies through to the drawing room quite late, and not surprisingly the gentlemen had joined them not long after; Selburn, Carlston and her brother would hardly want to linger with each other over the port. In the drawing room, Delia and Lady Georgina had allowed themselves to be pressed for performances upon the pianoforte, which, to Helen's ears, became a rather lengthy accomplishment war, each trying to outdo the other with the complication of her pieces. It would have been rather comical if the ill feeling behind the performances had not been so blatant.

"Would you like some warm milk before you retire, my lady?" Darby asked, drawing Helen from her thoughts.

Was that an urging note in her Terrene's voice? Helen sent a sidelong glance at Darby, but beyond that odd tone there was no other sign of collusion.

"Yes, I would."

"Sprat, you go. Make sure they heat it gentle," Darby ordered, handing the girl a night candle. "None of that awful skin on the top."

Sprat reluctantly turned towards the door. "They're gunna kick up 'cause I'm askin' for it," she said under her breath.

Helen cocked her head. "What did you say?"

The girl looked back, mouth pressed into a stubby line of silence.

Darby sighed. "The other maids have set themselves against her. And the senior staff too."

"Already? We've only been here a day." Helen fixed a stern look upon Sprat. "What have you been doing?"

"Nuffin'," Sprat protested.

"It's not all her fault," Darby said with some sympathy as she set to unlacing the back of Helen's gown. "The senior servants think she's too young and common to be a lady's maid, just like it was for me at your aunt's house. And Lady Margaret's maids have been telling them all she's a thief." Darby walked around and eased the sleeves down Helen's arms. She lowered her voice. "It doesn't help that she's making dubious wagers with them and poking her nose into places she shouldn't."

"If they don't want to give up their blunt, they shouldn't take the bet," Sprat said.

"Are you fleecing them?" Helen asked, drawing on her knowledge of cant.

Sprat looked down at her feet. "Can't help it. They're all gulls."

"You *can* help it. I want you to stop bilking them. Is that understood?"

Sprat nodded. "But I can collect on tonight's dinner wager, can't I? 'Cause you won fair and square as I heard it."

Helen shot a glance at Darby, who turned to hide a smile. "No, you may not." Helen searched for the right phrase. "From now on it is *round dealing* with them all," she said. "Off you go and get my milk."

Sprat departed with a slight drag to her feet. Helen listened to make sure the girl did indeed take the servants' stairs, then asked Darby, "How bad is it?"

"She doesn't make it easy on herself."

"Will you keep an eye on things?"

"Of course," Darby said.

She unlaced the last few eyelets of Helen's short stays and pulled the corset away. Helen drew a deep, unconstricted breath, pulling the creased chemise away from her breasts. Darby folded the corset, seemingly intent upon the task.

"So, we are alone," Helen said. "Do you perhaps have something you wish to tell me?"

Darby looked up, an odd smile on her face. "Mr Quinn has proposed, my lady."

"Oh, how marvellous, Darby. I knew he intended to do so. Did he go upon one knee? Did you say yes immediately? Tell me all."

Darby bit her lip. "He told me he spoke to you, and that you gave your blessing to the union, my lady. I want to thank you for that. But..."

"But?" Helen echoed. "Holy heaven, you have not refused him, have you?"

Darby bent her head over the folded stays, her fingers smoothing the boned linen in short strokes. "I've not yet given him my answer. Lord Carlston sent for me after you went down for dinner. He told me he too had given his blessing, but he also told me what happened at the stones with the earth energy."

"What has that to do with accepting Quinn? What did Carlston tell you?"

"That you lost control of the power and he saw the rift within you." Darby pressed her lips together; a remembered frustration. "We tried to compare what we saw, but we couldn't

164

come to any certainty. As far as we could tell, it has not unduly increased in size." She stopped, but there was plainly more to be said.

"And?" Helen prompted.

Darby eyed her intently. "Lord Carlston said the two of you are the Trinitas. Is that true, my lady?"

Helen released a held breath. "It would seem so."

"Oh, my lady," Darby whispered. "It is too much. The rift and now this."

Helen squeezed her eyes shut. Darby was right; it was too much. Yet what could she do?

"God only sends us what we can bear," she said, but there was little consolation in the words.

"Then he must think you are a colossus."

Helen smiled at the dry comment. "It is not only a burden, Darby. If we locate the Colligat again and bring together the Trinitas, it could be the way to defeat the Grand Deceiver. A way to destroy them, or open the door to the Deceiver world and send them back to where they came from. We must look at it as an opportunity."

Darby wet her lips. "But didn't Mr Pike tell you that the Trinitas destroys all Reclaimers if it is used?"

Helen paused. Darby was now upon the path of Helen's own musings; a path that had not ended in a happy conclusion. "Yes, he did say that, and I could never understand it. Why would a weapon created by Reclaimers destroy *all* Reclaimers? It never made sense. I read the archive that describes it and it certainly says that the Trinitas will destroy the Reclaimers when deployed, but it does not use the word *all*. Now we know that, as a direct inheritor, I am the third part of the Trinitas – the source of Vis energy – and, by accident, its second part; I cannot help but think that the Trinitas weapon was never going to destroy *all* the Reclaimers."

She stopped. If she continued, Darby's quickness would inevitably take her to the final and awful conclusion.

"My lady, you must tell me."

"It is not going to destroy *all* the Reclaimers, Darby. Only those it is made up of: the Grand Reclaimer dyad. Myself and his lordship."

"Ah, that makes more sense," Darby said, her face stricken. Then, as Helen had predicted, she followed the path to its end. "And me too," she said slowly, "since I was caught up in the blood bond made through the Ligatus."

They looked at one another, seeing their mortality in each other's eyes.

"It is not certain," Helen said. "I may be wrong. Or we may never find the Colligat, or even have to use the Trinitas. We may defeat them another way."

A grasping hope. And all the while, the unsaid alternative hanging between them: the Ligatus could kill them before they even faced their enemy.

Darby looked, unseeingly, at the stays in her hands. "Well, now I am certain of my decision. How can I accept Mr Quinn when he could be a widower next week? And if we survive the rift and the Grand Deceiver, what happens then? You and his lordship must walk your separate paths, and Mr Quinn and I must follow our Reclaimers." A sob broke out of her, shaking her body. "Any which way, it cannot be."

"That is not true!" Helen took the stays and tossed them on the bureau, then grasped her Terrene's cold hands in her own. "You must not base your decision upon what *might be*, Darby. Think of *what is now*. You love Mr Quinn and he clearly loves you. Would you really refuse him and break his and your own heart because of a future that might never happen? To do so would be the height of arrogance; it would be placing yourself alongside God, claiming all knowledge. We can only know the present that we live in. To presuppose a life of suffering is to bring despair into our souls before the despair is even upon us. Lord Carlston and I will find a way to manage so you can be together. I am sure of it."

Darby freed her hand, pressing her fingers against the flow of tears. "But what if I die?" She gulped, her voice a whisper. "What if he dies?"

"Do you think by refusing him you will protect him or yourself from that heartache? If you die, he will be devastated anyway. And if he dies, it will be the same for you. All you will have achieved is to deny him, and yourself, the joy of your union."

Darby gave another sob. "Can I truly claim such happiness?"

"Of course you can. You must. Happiness must be taken when it comes."

Darby crouched down, her head in her hands, gasps rocking her body. For a second, Helen thought she had said something wrong, then realised the hard, gut-wrenching sobs were from relief.

Gently, she lifted Darby from her crouch and held her shaking body as the wild tears cleaned away an imagined future of endless loss and loneliness. Eventually, the sobs eased into ratcheted breaths and then into soft sighs. Finally, with a last embrace, Darby pulled away.

"My lady, I have something to tell you," she said with a watery smile. "I believe I am to be married."

Later, in the dark warmth of her bed, something occurred to Helen as she teetered upon the cusp of sleep. Her words to Darby – *happiness must be taken when it comes* – were the same words that Lord Carlston had said to her in the drawing room. Until that moment with Darby, she had not realised she believed them.

Of course, it begged the question: how did one know what would bring happiness?

Screams wrenched Helen awake. The piercing sound shuddered through her body, pressing the air from her lungs. She levered herself upright, one thought penetrating her gasps – *again*.

A pale blue light glowed in the centre of the room, carving out the shapes of bedposts and chairs from the darkness; the shrieks were rising from it. She kicked her way out from under the bedclothes and scrabbled over the shadowy landscape of quilt and sheets towards the eerie luminescence and nerve-shredding sound.

The glowing bundle on the floor stopped her at the edge of the bed, rocking her back on her haunches. A ghostly infant, swaddled in linen, tiny body heaving against the constraint. Wisps of transparent hair, agonised opaque face, mouth a dark pit of screaming anguish.

Little Timothy Marr.

Helen grabbed hold of the bedpost, teeth clenched, as the ghost's howling fear folded her into her own screaming despair. Yet she could make no sound. There was no air. Only pain, squeezing her suffocating lungs. And his pain. His fear. Oh God, surely he had been too young to know what was coming?

The door burst open, the force slamming it against the wall.

"My lady!" Darby's voice.

"Helen!" Carlston, behind her. "I saw that baby in my dream!"

She felt Darby's hand between her shoulder blades, anchoring her back into the room. The eerie light blinked out. Darkness, the screams cut mid-howl into silence. Helen collapsed onto the bed, gulping like a landed fish, chest aching from the heaving gasps, her vision blurred into a grey mist.

"Slowly, my lady," Darby said, rubbing her back. "Breathe slowly. Count to three as you inhale."

She slowed her gulps, drew in precious air. She felt Darby withdraw her hand, the reassurance of her touch replaced by the soft weight of a wrap – Darby's blue woollen – laid across her shoulders. Her eyes cleared, adjusting to the gloom. She finally had enough breath to raise her head. To speak. "Did you see it? The infant?" The words wheezed into a cough.

"Take your time," Carlston urged.

She waved away his concern, although she was weary right to her bones. "Did you see it?"

"Yes." He pushed his fingers through hair that was already awry from sleep. "I was dreaming about the same child, and then I heard you scream."

He wore only a creased linen shirt and a pair of buckskins donned in haste, for one button had been left undone. She had never seen him so dishevelled. Or nonplussed.

"I dreamed it too, my lady," Darby said, her face ashen. She grabbed hold of the bedpost, steadying herself. "And then it was here on the floor. A ghost." She stopped, fighting back her terror. "A ghost," she repeated with a firm nod of acceptance. "How can that be?"

"It was Timothy Marr, the baby that Benchley killed for the Ligatus," Helen said. "Before, I could only hear his voice, his cries, but now we can *see* him. All of us. It must be the rift. The earth energy must have forced it open even more."

"It would seem so." Carlston stared at the floor where the apparition had been. "It is quite an escalation. The extra influx of energy must have enabled the..." He paused, searching for the right word. *"Manifestation."* He looked at Helen, his mouth a tight line of contrition. "It is my fault. I should not have taken you to the stones."

Helen shook her head. "I insisted upon drawing the energy."

"I swear I am not imagining it, Henry, I heard a child!" Lady Georgina's panicked voice rose from the room across the hallway. Helen heard a door opening. "There is a child somewhere. I swear it. I swear it. I am not imagining it!"

Oh no, Lord Henry and Lady Georgina were coming to investigate.

"I think it came from my niece's room." Aunt's voice, in the corridor, approaching fast.

Helen drew her legs around to sit on the edge of the bed and pulled Darby's wrap around to cover more of her nightgown. Had she woken everyone?

Her aunt walked into the room, a mauve dressing robe over her nightgown, her night candle held high, its soft light exaggerating the anxious hollows of her eyes and mouth. "My dear girl, are you ill? Was that you screaming like a ban—" Her voice flattened into an outraged whisper. "Carlston, what are you doing in here?"

"Like you, I heard Lady Helen screaming," he said.

"God forfend, man, you are half dressed! Are you intent on ruining my niece?"

Helen cut across her horror. "He came in with Darby." That was true at least.

Aunt looked back at the doorway. "Get out, before someone else—"

But she was too late. Lord Henry and Lady Georgina arrived in the doorway, candles in hand, with Delia and Lady Margaret close behind, their wraps clutched over their nightgowns. A commotion of male voices announced the arrival of Selburn,

Andrew and Hammond from their accommodations on the ground floor.

"For pity's sake, Carlston, get away from the bed," Aunt hissed.

He stepped back just as those gathered at the door parted to allow Selburn to stride into the room. Andrew followed, still in evening dress, stumbling from exhaustion and, Helen realised from the smell of fermented fruit, an excess of brandy. A bad combination.

"Helen, are you ill?" Selburn asked. He had managed to don a banyan robe, the rich red silk shimmering in the light of Aunt's candle. He crossed to the bed and took Helen's hand, his warm hold tight with concern.

She smiled reassuringly. "I had a nightmare. That is all."

"I'll say you did. You woke up the whole house," Delia said from the doorway.

"I am sure I heard a child shrieking," Lady Georgina insisted.

"That was me. I woke up screaming," Helen said quickly. She withdrew her hand from Selburn's and pulled the wrap more tightly around her body, as if she could cocoon herself from the questions. She wanted them all gone, even her betrothed. "I apologise for waking everyone in such a frightening manner."

"But you are recovered now?" Selburn asked.

Helen nodded. "As I said, it was just a nightmare."

He did not quite believe her – his eyes held that all too familiar resentment.

"What are *you* doing in here, Carlston?" Andrew demanded. He took a step closer to his lordship, arms too loose at his sides. "You seem to be everywhere you are not wanted."

"You are foxed, Hayden," Carlston said. "Go back to bed and sleep it off."

"You shouldn't be in here," Andrew slurred. "You're trying to compromise my sister."

Helen stiffened. She felt Aunt's hand squeeze her shoulder. Half reassurance, half warning.

"Do not be vulgar, Andrew. Lord Carlston came in with me," Aunt said crisply. "I did not know why Helen was screaming, so I thought it best to have some protection."

A blatant lie, and unexpected. Helen kept her face immobile, but reached up and touched her aunt's fingers still clasped to her shoulder.

Andrew swayed upon his feet. "Protection?" he repeated, squinting at the concept.

Selburn regarded Carlston narrowly. "It was fortunate that you were on hand so quickly."

Carlston bowed. "It was my honour to have been of service to Lady Pennworth and your betrothed."

"Quite," Selburn said flatly. He looked at the curious faces assembled at the door. "We should all return to our beds if we are to be in any fit state to attend service tomorrow." He motioned to Darby. "Stay with your mistress."

Darby bobbed a curtsey and began to straighten the bedclothes and pillows.

Without another word, Carlston strode from the room, his departure breaking up the assembly in the doorway. Helen heard Lord Henry soothing Lady Georgina as they entered their own rooms – a promise to mix her a dose of her medicine; and Hammond informing Lady Margaret that Andrew had drunk almost two bottles of brandy by himself. Not an unusual occurrence, Helen thought.

"Good night, my dear. I hope there will be no more nightmares," Aunt said, pressing a soft kiss upon her cheek.

She regarded Helen for a troubled moment – tomorrow

would, no doubt, bring another private interview to demand Carlston's removal – then took Andrew's arm and ushered him towards the door. He seemed inclined to turn back, but she deftly bore him from the room with a mix of implacable steering and murmured encouragement; tactics no doubt learned from a lifetime with Uncle Pennworth.

Selburn watched them leave, then addressed Helen. "If you do not feel well enough to go to the Abbey for service tomorrow, I will stay behind with you."

"There is no need. I am not delicate. Quite the opposite."

"I know," he said, his face sombre. "But you must let me try to look after you." With that, he bowed and departed.

Helen sighed; she could count on two interviews tomorrow.

Darby closed the door behind him. "Did you want me to stay, my lady?"

Helen nodded. "Yes, for now I think you must sleep here. Share my bed, and if it happens again, if the child manifests, you must wake me immediately. We cannot afford to disturb the house again."

"Could something else emerge from the rift?"

Helen hugged her arms around her body. During the mesmerism she had glimpsed what lurked in the Ligatus beyond little Timothy Marr, and all of it had been screaming.

"We must pray to God that does not happen."

Chapter Eleven

SUNDAY, 13 DECEMBER 1812

Helen took a sip of her coffee and observed the drawn faces around the breakfast table. Had there ever been a more awkward gathering at Chenwith in all its long history? Only the chink of cutlery against porcelain and the slosh of coffee poured by the footman sounded in the heavy silence. She put down her cup, motioning the footman to refill it. Lord knows, she needed it. The ghostly infant had not manifested again during the night, but wondering if it would make another appearance had kept her and poor Darby awake until morning. As had the terrifying likelihood that, by drawing upon the earth energy, she had opened the rift in her mind even more. She could not help but agree with Carlston's conclusion: why else would the nightmare have escalated into a manifestation? It was too much of a coincidence.

What if she never used the power again? Never drew upon the earth. Never reclaimed. Cowardly thoughts, and yet they also held a measure of relief. She stared at her dark reflection in the refilled cup; surely she was braver than that? Carlston, at least, believed she had courage. She could not let him down.

There was still no conversation around the table. It was

easy to understand why Selburn and Aunt were silent – both were still disturbed and a little angry at the events of last night. Andrew's silence looked to be the effects of those two bottles of brandy; his skin had a bilious tinge and his hand shook as he lifted his coffee cup to his mouth. Lady Georgina had shredded a brioche onto her plate without taking a bite of it, the carnage prompted by some private turmoil that clouded her fine eyes. Lord Henry's abstraction seemed to be caused only by his ham and eggs, which he was consuming with great intensity. Delia was still out of sorts, and Lady Margaret and Hammond seemed to be responding to the general malaise. That left Carlston – no longer dishevelled, and focused upon his own thoughts – but Helen was trying not to look in his direction at all.

It was time to step in and alleviate the strained atmosphere.

"Selburn, what time do we leave for Bath?" she asked, forcing a bright tone.

"In about half an hour," he said, barely looking up from his plate.

"Are we to stay after? There is the promenade at the Pump Room and, I believe, a gathering at the Upper Rooms. Perhaps we could attend?"

"If you wish."

So much for starting a conversation. She turned to Aunt, but before she could assay that lady's opinion on the Upper Rooms, the door opened to admit Fairwood. He carried his silver salver, a single packet upon it.

"Is that mail, Fairwood? But it is Sunday," Lady Georgina said.

"An express, just arrived, my lady," Fairwood replied.

But who was the recipient? The question roused everyone from their introspection, the entire company watching the butler's progress around the table.

He stopped at Lord Carlston's side and bowed. "The messenger was told not to wait for a return, my lord."

Ignoring the circle of intense interest, Carlston took the packet. "Thank you."

He turned it over and Helen caught sight of the written direction: Pike's hand. Carlston recognised it too for he glanced at her – *What does he want?* – and with a flick of his thumb broke the wax seal. Another packet was wrapped inside. Carlston slid it out onto his palm and cast an eye over his name written upon the front.

His face drained of colour. *"Mon Dieu."*

"Is it bad news, Lord Carlston?" Lady Margaret asked.

Carlston stood, his chair toppling onto its back, and strode to the door, both packets in hand. The footman just managed to open the door in time to allow his exit.

"Definitely not good news," Lord Henry remarked.

Fairwood bent and picked up the chair, setting it back into position.

"From where did the messenger come?" Selburn asked his butler.

"London, Your Grace."

Helen rose. If it was bad news from Pike, she needed to know. "If you will excuse me."

Selburn looked up. "Helen?"

She hesitated, meeting his reproachful eyes with her own resolve – *Reclaimer business* – then headed to the door.

"Why is she going after him, Selburn?" she heard Lady Georgina ask.

Silence, however, had returned to the table.

Helen found Carlston at the far end of the Long Gallery, the furthermost place from the breakfast room. He had bolted as far as he could, she realised, like an injured animal.

He stood with his back against the wall, head bowed over the opened letters in his hands, shoulders slumped.

He must have heard her footsteps on the wooden floor, but he did not look up. "It is from Elise. Sent to the Home Office and forwarded here by Pike." He finally lifted his head, a wry quirk to his lips. "No doubt after he had read it."

"You are certain it is from her? Not a counterfeit?"

"I recognise her hand. And what she says in it ... the details of our marriage – they confirm her authorship."

Helen stared at the letter; what was in it? A plea for forgiveness? A demand for scandalous divorce? God help her, how she wanted to read it – a most unworthy impulse.

"What does she want?"

He smoothed the top edge between thumb and forefinger. "It is not a letter meant for a young woman's eyes."

"I understand. Of course, it is private. Between husband and wife."

He shook his head. "No, no, it is not that." He offered the page. "If you wish to..."

Helen took it. A sprawling hand with extravagant flourishes, the salutation in French: *Guillaume, mon amour.* William, my love. She swallowed, her mouth strangely dry. *My love.*

"It looks to be intimate, Lord Carlston. Are you sure you wish me to read it?"

"As I said on the way to the stones, there is only regret now. Nothing else." His hand wiped the air. "Nothing."

Was he reassuring her or convincing himself?

She could not hand back the letter. How odd, that impulse to *know* at all cost. She began to read.

Guillaume, mon amour,
* I have heard, through those secret paths we both know*

177

exist, that you are now aware that I am alive and are looking for me with that implacable will of yours that does not brook defeat.

How you must detest me. Even so, I ask that you read this missive with the memory of our early months together, when our love was charged with that dizzying union of innocence and exploration. I still see in my dreams the column of your throat above me, the span of your shoulders, that stubborn jaw that I would kiss over and over, following its unyielding geography to the beautiful mouth and lips that brought such pleasure.

Helen stopped reading, her fingers circling her flushed throat, the memory of her mouth against Carlston's overwhelming everything for a second. She too had once followed that same unyielding geography, when they had kissed in Kate Holt's bawdy house in Brighton. Six months ago, and the sensation still haunted her; a low, aching need that brought wild thoughts. She clenched her teeth. Such heat must offend all sensibilities, especially since she was holding a letter from his wife.

I swear I did not enter our marriage with France as a third bedfellow, but my past caught up with me and I was obliged to serve my mother country or suffer the consequences. When my deceit was discovered by the Home Office, I was given less than a few hours' warning by my compatriots, and so I fled, covering my tracks as best I could.

I learned, much later, that you were accused of my murder. It was not my intention to add that dishonour to your name, but you will rightly say it has served me well. It is, I know, too late to repair that damage and yet ... je le regrette, mon chéri. Je le regrette profondément.

We are still husband and wife, Guillaume, and so I ask that you meet me in Calais, at a time of your choosing. We have, I think, a conclusion to discuss. Or perhaps a beginning.

A letter directed to the Hôtel Dessin at Calais will come to my hands.

Elise

Helen kept her eyes on the letter a moment longer – time enough to ensure no heat lingered upon her skin – then passed it back. "What does she mean *a beginning*?"

"Perhaps she thinks to ask for forgiveness with a hope to reunite." His voice was hard, the answer in his tone.

"Will you go?"

He rubbed his mouth, his fingers unconsciously tracing its shape. "I will."

"Now?" Lud, even she could hear the aggrieved note in her voice.

He gave his half-smile; he had heard it too. "No, not until we have found the Bath Deceiver and have some answers. Perhaps not even until we have faced the Grand Deceiver."

She turned away. She had no right to feel so … jealous of that inevitable reunion, nor to feel so glad that he was not rushing towards it.

Helen flexed her hands in her blue embroidered gloves, wishing she had thought to bring her velvet and fur muff for the journey. Maybe even a hot brick; her feet were beginning to cramp in her half-boots. Although the day was bright, the wind held a sharp edge exacerbated by the brisk trot of Selburn's matched bays and the open fields on either side of the road to Bath. Beside her, Selburn sat slightly forward in the leather seat, reins in hand, intent upon the road. He had insisted they drive to church together in his curricle, leaving the remainder of their party to make the journey in Aunt's coach and Lord Henry's town carriage.

Since Selburn had made no mention of the recent events at breakfast – no one had made much mention of anything, even after Helen had returned to the table – she was certain he would bring them up during the privacy of the drive. Yet so far their conversation had been limited to the frustratingly slow progress being made on the new dance pavilion. Best then to speak first.

"There is something I must ask you," she said, over the combined thud of hooves and the rumble of the three equipages upon the road.

He glanced at her. Wary. Or was she imagining it?

"Yesterday Lady Georgina made a reference at breakfast to Lord Carlston's wife being alive and a spy. Information she should not have. I thought Miss Cransdon might have inadvertently let it slip, but she swears she did not." Helen paused; there was no way to soften the next. "Did you do so?"

"That is what you want to ask me?" he demanded, his fair brows drawing together beneath the smooth grey brim of his hat. "Did I break my oath and blather about Carlston's wife?"

"There is no one else who had the opportunity to speak to Lady Georgina about the subject."

"Even so," he snapped, "I do not pass on gossip."

Helen chewed on her bottom lip, the wind chilling the wet skin. She had to take his word, yet someone had spoken out of turn.

"Carlston's letter today – it was about Lady Elise, wasn't it?" he asked.

Helen stared at him; how could he know that? "It is not for us to discuss. It is Carlston's private business."

"Why then does he discuss it with you?"

She ignored the comment and stared at the bobbing heads of the horses, her fingers finding the Comte's fob on its ribbon around her neck.

"It must have been about Elise," he continued through her silence. "Only news of her would prod Carlston out of his insolent self-regard. Has she been found? Is she in England?"

"You are eager to know her whereabouts," Helen said, the temple portrait rising to mind, all dark hair and sly eyes.

"I am eager to know when Carlston will take his leave and allow us to enjoy our wedding."

"I would not know. Sometime after we have defeated the Grand Deceiver."

His mouth compressed into a thin line. They drove for a few minutes in silence.

"I take it Lady Georgina was not forthcoming about the source of her information," he finally said. A thankful return to the immediate problem.

"She says she heard it about town."

"Do you believe her? Could she have done so?"

"If she did, we have a bigger problem. It would mean someone in the Home Office has talked."

"But Pike is the only one there who knows about Elise, and it does not seem likely he would be indiscreet. Are you sure Miss Cransdon is telling the truth? In my experience, young women do not have a close hold upon keeping secrets or their word." He saw her expression and added hurriedly, "Not you, of course, but generally."

Helen sighed and released the fob, the weight of it thumping against the top of her breastbone. Delia *was* prone to listening at doors and "blathering", as Selburn described it. But if she had blatantly lied, that was a most disquieting thought.

"It is possible, I suppose," she said. "I shall have to look into it further."

"Allow me to ask Georgina where she obtained the information. She will answer me."

"Thank you."

"You see, I do wish to help."

Helen caught the admonishing note in his voice. "I know you do. Still, it will not always be possible."

He stared ahead. "Always?"

The word hung between them. Helen glanced at him. What had she said to cause such sharpness?

"Surely when the Grand Deceiver is defeated, you will no longer wish to risk yourself and our future?" he added. "It is my fervent wish to have a family, an heir, as soon as possible."

He expected an end to her duty as a Reclaimer. Not an unreasonable expectation. After all, it was his right to expect an heir. And if she retired from the Dark Days Club, it would release dear Darby to enjoy her own married life.

"I too wish to start our family, Selburn. But it must be after the Grand Deceiver is defeated."

His lips pursed. "My dear, it may not work out that way."

"What do you mean?"

He busied himself with the reins. "Speak to your aunt. She is a married woman."

His meaning dawned on her: he was referring to marital congress.

"But surely it does not always result in a baby?" she said. It was coarse to speak of such matters, but he had brought it up. "When the stallion covers the mares on Uncle's estate, it does not always result in a foal. I am sure it cannot be so different for us?"

"This is not something we should be speaking about," he said.

"But if it does, we must abstain until the Grand Deceiver is defeated," Helen added.

"Abstain?" Selburn gave a small laugh. "The purpose of marriage is to beget children, not abstain. Besides..." He stopped.

"Besides?"

He flicked his wrist, a touch of his whip correcting the gait of the off-side horse. "It is a man's right," he said flatly.

That was true: by law Selburn could take what was his once they were married. At the seminary she had heard whispered stories of "rights" forced upon wives until they bled. Stories that were meant to be cautionary, or perhaps just preparative, but they had clenched her fists into a futile mix of rage and fear.

Except her clenched fists were not futile any more. Unlike other women, she could throw a man across the room if she chose to do so. Helen shifted on the leather seat. It was a startling possibility, and one that surely must have occurred to Selburn as well. She observed his profile: long jaw set, lips firm, steady blue eyes ahead. Did he not remember her strength, or what she had done to Carlston to stop his vestige madness escalating into murder? Or did he just believe she would never take such action against her own husband? Indeed, in the wedding ceremony she would be promising, before God, to honour and obey him, and Selburn knew she kept her word to the bitter end. Perhaps such belief was justified.

He collected the reins in one hand and reached across to gently cup her chin, his gloved forefinger tracing an arc across her cheek. "I have chosen you to be the mother of my children, Helen. Your sons will be leaders amongst men; your daughters the most sought-after pearls in society." His voice changed, softening. "I thought you wanted a family too."

"I do, but—"

He released her chin and took up the reins in both hands

again. "Then we are agreed." He gave a small shrug. "Let us not borrow difficulties. You are set upon the path of the Grand Deceiver. If God is with us, the creatures will be found and defeated before our wedding day."

Amen, Helen thought. *May God be with us.* She did not ever want to arrive at a point where she had to break a vow to the Almighty and throw her husband across a room.

They made good time to Bath, their procession of carriages drawing up at the corner of the Abbey's west entrance well before service.

The crisp dry weather and pale sunshine had gathered a good number of the congregation in the Pump Yard. As Helen stood to alight from the curricle, she took a moment to admire the way the rich winter silks and jewelled velvets matched the glimpses of colour in the huge arched stained-glass window set above the Abbey doors. The golden Bath stone frontage had been sculpted with the heavenly choir, and on the matching towers that stood either side of the window, angels climbed Jacob's ladder, some heading towards heaven and others looking nervously over their shoulders at the ground below. Of course, one was meant to be awed by them, but Helen could not help smiling at those descending angels and their all-too-human earthbound glances. Behind the angels and ladders, the central square bell tower loomed, waiting to peal the call to worship.

In a little over three weeks, Helen would emerge from that entrance as a wife, the bells announcing the nuptials of the Duke and Duchess of Selburn. In fact, the third banns were soon to be read by the vicar during the service. The final asking: *If any of you know cause of just impediment why these two persons should not be joined together in holy matrimony, ye are to declare it.* She had held her breath during each of the previous banns, but there was, of course, no impediment. Unless an alchemical bond with another man could be called so – and that bond was already blessed by God, if not quite yet by her betrothed.

"Lady Helen, are you coming?" Selburn prompted from the pavement, his hand extended.

She gathered her pelisse and gown – rust wool and cerulean blue silk, the vivid combination a pleasure in itself – and, grasping his hand, stepped onto the step and then the stone flags.

Aunt emerged from her chariot, followed by Andrew, Lady Margaret and Mr Hammond in a particularly well-fitted blue jacket. Beyond them, Helen caught sight of Lady Georgina reading the advertising placard upon one of the closed lean-to shops set against the Abbey wall, Lord Henry at her side, and Carlston handing down Delia from the coach. By the smile upon Delia's face, she seemed to be enjoying his company. Of course, he could be charming when he felt like it.

"Helen, my dear," Aunt called. "Wait for me." She bustled past Andrew and Hammond and came to Helen's side, nodding across the yard at the side entrance to the Pump Room. "After service we must take a glass of the water, and I will sign the arrivals book."

"But we are not staying at Bath."

Aunt hesitated for an odd moment, then said, "I am sure the Duke's estate is counted as being at Bath. I must sign also Mr King's subscription book, since we will no doubt wish to attend some of the balls or concerts at the Upper Rooms."

"Then you will want to sign Mr Guynette's too, for the Lower Rooms," Helen said as they walked into the yard.

"Oh yes, they are reopened," Aunt said, adjusting her

reticule upon her wrist by its gold chain. "I read there are to be some lectures on astronomy." The recollection clearly prompted another, less edifying thought. "I did not realise until I looked in my almanac this morning that your wedding ball is to be on the night before a new moon. What on earth possessed Selburn to choose a moonless night? It will be most inconvenient for everyone."

"It was not his choice, Aunt. The Palace said it was the only night that the Queen could attend."

Aunt's mouth quirked to one side. "Well then, I suppose we cannot quibble. We will have to consider how to light the driveway for the carriages, and maybe even the road for a short distance."

"Lady Pennworth!" a strident voice called. "There you are!"

Aunt looked up, instantly alert. "Ah, it is Lady Dunwick and Lady Elizabeth."

Helen heard a note of satisfaction in her aunt's voice. Strange; the advent of Lady Dunwick and her daughter usually had quite the opposite effect.

"Lady Helen!" Pug's squeal penetrated the murmur of conversation in the yard as the two ladies threaded their way through the groups of people.

Lady Dunwick, it seemed, had hurt her leg, for she limped and was leaning on a walking cane topped with a silver handle. Both had taken up the current military fad in fashion, wearing tall shako hats with front plumes, and pelisses with abundant gold braid and frogged clasps. Pug had chosen a vibrant red, her mother a more subdued navy blue.

"I am so glad to see you," Pug said, clasping Helen's hand. "Poor Mama has not been well and is only relieved by my company. We have not been out a great deal." She lowered her voice, which was not very low at all. "Not that we have missed much – Bath has been so dreary these past few weeks. Your wedding was the only thing to look forward to until we got your aunt's message this morning."

"Lady Dunwick, well met," Aunt said hurriedly across Pug's comment.

Message? Helen glanced at Aunt as they all bobbed into curtseys, but she pointedly did not look in Helen's direction.

"Elizabeth is right, it was such a pleasant surprise," Lady Dunwick added. "Of course we had heard about the gas explosion on Great Pulteney Street, and that you and your chaperone had gone to His Grace's estate, Lady Helen, and so we had quite given up the idea of you staying with us. When your letter arrived this morning, Lady Pennworth, we were delighted, weren't we, Elizabeth?" She beamed at her daughter for confirmation.

Pug nodded vigorously. "Indeed!"

Helen stared at her aunt. What had she done?

"You are welcome to stay with us as long as you like," Lady Dunwick continued. "We have a house in the Royal Crescent and plenty of room. The two of us have been rattling around it by ourselves."

Aunt, still not meeting Helen's eye, said, "You are most kind. We would not wish to impose upon you for more than a week. Helen is still to have her bride gown made and we wish to take some time choosing the cloth and maker."

"Aunt?" Helen said.

"Of course, you must take your time," Lady Dunwick said. "And while you are here, perhaps you will attend some of the balls and assemblies? I have been a sad stay-at-home with this leg of mine, only visiting the baths and taking in a concert now and then. Poor Elizabeth has been suffering for company and entertainment."

"I think some balls and assemblies would be—"

"Aunt!" Helen said, finally managing to interject herself into the conversation. She turned to Lady Dunwick. "You are very generous, but my aunt has failed to take into account that I have friends at Chenwith whom I cannot abandon."

Lady Dunwick flapped a blue-gloved hand. "No, no, my dear, your aunt informed us of your friends and we are happy to include them in the invitation. There is more than enough room for Lady Margaret and Miss Cransdon, and Lady Annisford too if she wishes to stay. We are not yet acquainted, but I am sure that can be remedied in a trice. You need not even return to Chenwith; all is ready now. Just send for your clothes and maids and we will start our happy sojourn tonight!"

"An excellent thought," Aunt said.

Helen saw Selburn still at the curricle, watching them, and a searing leap of intuition curled her fingers into fists. Aunt would never be so rude as to abandon his hospitality without his knowledge and consent; he must have agreed to it. The two of them did not want her and Carlston to be in the same house. And Selburn had made no mention of it in the curricle.

She opened her mouth to protest again, but realised she had been outmanoeuvred. Aunt had already accepted the invitation on her behalf, and any refusal now would be a grievous insult to Lady Dunwick and dear Pug.

She finally caught Aunt's eye – no contrition there. Only an adamant message: *It is for the best, my dear.*

Pug leaned in closer to peer at Helen's throat. "Is that a fob you are wearing? Is it the new fashion? Mama, do you see?"

Lady Dunwick glanced at the fob. "How interesting."

"I must procure one too!" Pug said.

Lady Dunwick, however, was more intent upon organising her house party. "Let us see if your friends will join us, Lady Helen."

She raised a hand, catching Lady Margaret's eye, and waved her and Delia over to join them.

The invitation was duly issued, and Helen had no doubt that the expression on Lady Margaret's face had been her own minutes ago: part astonishment, part hurriedly hidden horror.

"Why, that is a wonderful idea," Delia said, with enough enthusiasm to cover Lady Margaret's silence. "I would like that very much."

"Indeed, yes," Lady Margaret finally managed. She met Helen's eyes – *What is going on?* – then looked at Carlston, who was walking away from a stiff-backed Andrew near the church entrance. Her eyelids flickered; it seemed she had answered her own question.

"Well now, Lady Pennworth, perhaps you could introduce me to Lady Georgina and we will see if we have a full complement," Lady Dunwick said. "Come, Elizabeth, you must add your voice to our entreaties."

With farewell curtseys exchanged, Pug and the two older women set off to find their quarry, leaving Helen, Lady Margaret and Delia to watch their determined progress across the busy flagged yard.

"I was ambushed," Helen said.

"To be fair, your aunt does not know the events of the last six months," Lady Margaret said. "She still thinks of you as a girl needing protection."

"Besides, it is well past the time to do your bride shopping," Delia said. "And we have yet to discuss what Lady Margaret and I are to wear as your attendants."

"But a whole week with Lady Dunwick and Pug," Lady Margaret added. "There will be no peace."

"That is unkind," Helen protested. "Lady Elizabeth may be ... enthusiastic, but you must admit she is a staunch friend."

Whether or not Lady Margaret agreed was lost in the sudden glorious peal of the Abbey's famous ten bells. The Duke, on a laughing rejoinder, finished his conversation with Lord and Lady Carnarvon and made his way towards the three of them. Helen observed his approach with some sourness. He should have told her about Aunt's plan.

He bowed to her and offered his arm. "May I escort you, Lady Helen?"

She glanced at Delia and Lady Margaret – a silent request for privacy.

"If you will excuse us, Your Grace," Lady Margaret said, curtseying. She took Delia's arm and steered her towards the church doors.

Helen laid her hand upon Selburn's arm and whispered, "So I am to Lady Dunwick's now. You said nothing in the curricle."

He waited until a lady and gentleman passed, then whispered back, "Your aunt sent the messenger this morning and extracted my word that I would not mention it to anyone. Besides, Lady Dunwick may not have wanted guests and it could have come to naught."

"Why did you agree to it?"

"What would you have me do? Refuse your guardian?"

"My uncle is my guardian!"

"Do not split hairs; your aunt is your guardian by proxy." They walked towards the church entrance. "She came to me this morning, intent upon the idea. It was all dressed up as a bridal shopping trip, but…" His eyes cut to Carlston, who was escorting Lady Margaret and Delia into the church.

Helen lowered her voice, answering the unsaid accusation. "You know we are trying to control our power."

"I am aware of that, but your aunt is not," he said curtly.

"Have you not considered that a week in Bath will give you ample time to search for you-know-who?"

Helen stared at him. Lud, by giving his consent he had contrived a chance for her to search for the Bath Deceiver. Even so, he should have told her about Aunt's plan.

He smiled grimly at her astonishment. "I may not have been included in your meeting yesterday, but I do know what the priority is at the moment."

"That was indeed good forethought," she said. "I'm sorry." She was not quite sure for what she was apologising. The assumption that he would work against her perhaps; or a suspicion that he was not committed to the Dark Days Club. "The meeting was impromptu," she added lamely. "Carlston saw the opportunity."

"Carlston always sees the opportunity," Selburn said.

They had reached the Abbey doors, where a small cluster of people still waited to enter. On seeing the Duke's arrival, they parted with bows and curtseys to allow him to pass, their deference curtailing any need for Helen to reply to the edged observation.

Chapter Twelve

After the church service, it took quite a while for Helen and her aunt to make their way across the cobbled yard to the Pump Room. At least five of her aunt's acquaintances hailed them, eager to welcome Lady Pennworth to Bath and to congratulate Helen on her impending marriage.

"Angling for an invitation to your wedding ball, now the last of the banns has been read," Aunt remarked *sotto voce* as the fifth lady – a very slight acquaintance indeed – twittered a farewell at the front steps of the Pump Room. "Mind you, it is a relief to have all three read."

Helen glanced at her quizzically. "Why? Did you expect a problem?"

"I don't know any more, Helen," her aunt said with a touch of acid. "Everything seems to be unnecessarily complicated with you now."

An uncomfortably accurate statement, Helen thought as she followed her aunt across the marble foyer.

They stopped together on the threshold of the Pump Room, brought up short by the sudden press of heat, stink of minerals, and clamour of conversation that warred with the soaring music from the quartet on the small balcony gallery.

Those promenading around the room had taken to strolling in an anti-clockwise direction, a loose whirlpool of pale winter faces, luxuriously feathered bonnets, fur tippets and well-cut jackets. Helen smiled as four young ladies in white muslin drifted out of the stately circle, snagged by the handsome face of the pumper handing out tumblers of spa water from the fountain. Her amusement deepened as two elderly ladies in mourning came to an abrupt stop in the middle of the flow to loudly compare ailments: twin black-bombazine rocks standing firm amidst the stream of chattering fashionables.

She found her lorgnette upon its cord and raised the crystal lenses to her eyes. Blue energy sprang up around every figure in the room; all of it pale blue – human – except for one brighter blue signature near the anteroom. A Deceiver! She peered more intently. Ah, it was only Mr Thomas, one of the fifteen Deceivers – no, sixteen now, including Mrs Knoll – they had already located at Bath.

She lowered the glasses and saw Miss Chatham near the windows lift her own pair to view the promenade. Good heavens, Helen thought, it seemed her use of the lorgnette in company had prompted some other young ladies to carry a pair of the old-fashioned spectacles as decoration. Not only that, but Pug was amongst a number of ladies at church who had been taken by the idea of wearing a fob pendant. Helen touched the gold disc hanging from its riband. Was she to be a leader of fashion, then? An alarming thought, but at least her use of the lorgnette would not be so particular now.

"Where is the arrivals book, my dear?" Aunt asked.

"Over there, beneath the Beau," Helen said, indicating a table set under a marble statue of Beau Nash, the Master of Ceremonies who had reigned supreme in Bath last century. She took her aunt's arm and together they skirted the edge of the promenade circle, dodging a group of young officers to arrive at the table.

As her aunt tapped out the quill and bent to sign the book, Helen considered the statue of the Beau standing above them. It was not a particularly well-carved tribute to the man who had set down for all time the rules of civil behaviour that allowed the current congenial mix of nobility, gentry, professionals and even middlings at the resort. The sculptor seemed to have taken more pains with the Beau's clothes – including a marvellously chiselled cravat, and well-shaped buttons and fobs – than with his countenance, which seemed somewhat clumsy in comparison. Perhaps that was how it should be for a leader of fashion, Helen thought.

Fobs? She leaned closer. One of them was the same oval shape as the Comte's disc. She rose onto her toes, trying to see if there was a tiny image carved upon its surface. Something was inscribed there, but it was a rough impression rather than a precise rendition.

She caught up her gold fob and peered at the figure etched upon it. They might be similar, if one stretched a point. A frisson of possibility shivered across her scalp. Could the Beau have been a Deceiver? The man was long dead, of course, but perhaps the same Deceiver could still be at Bath, living within the body of one of its children. If the Beau had fathered any children.

"Aunt, does Beau Nash have any descendants at Bath?"

Her aunt looked up from signing the book. "Lud, how should I know? He is rather before my time." She placed the pen back onto its rest and stepped aside to make way for a lady and gentleman waiting their turn to sign the book. "Mind you," she added, leaning in to whisper in Helen's ear, "I do know that on his death, his mistress, Juliana Popjoy, was so distraught that she took up living in the hollow of a tree for forty years."

"In a tree?" Helen echoed.

"I swear it. For forty years." She looked at the Beau. "He must have had a great deal of charm to elicit such a response. He certainly did not have much in the way of looks. I have a vague memory that he never married."

If that were the case, Helen thought, any children would be by-blows. She peered at the fob again. A similar shape carved upon the stone watch-chain of a statue was a specious connection at the very best, but even so, she would write to Sir Jonathan and ask him to trace Beau Nash's line. Just in case.

"Why are you wearing a man's fob?" Aunt demanded. "It is so big and clumsy. Where on earth did you get it?"

"Selburn gave it to me," Helen lied.

"Odd gift for a girl. And why you would even think to wear it as a pendant ... most eccentric." Her attention shifted to someone across the room. "Ah, dear Lady Porchester is here." She waved to a stately lady. "I have not seen her these past three months. Come, let us join her."

"If you don't mind, I will go to Lady Margaret and Miss Cransdon," Helen said hurriedly; she did not want to get caught in one of her aunt's conversations. "They are just over there." She nodded to where her friends stood with Mr Hammond beside the row of tall windows that looked over the Pump Yard.

"Of course, dearest. Just remember," Aunt patted Helen's arm, "eccentricity is charming in a Duchess, but not so delightful in an unmarried girl." With that sage warning, she set off towards Lady Porchester.

Stifling her amusement, Helen took a moment to locate Carlston. He was somewhere in the room – their shared pulse had intensified as she had walked across the yard – but she could not see the familiar set of his shoulders or tilt of his dark head amongst those promenading. Instead, she found Andrew, seated in glowering silence beside a fair young lady in rose-pink muslin whose mama stood at a protective but hopeful distance. Poor Andrew; his head plainly still ached like the devil. A direct route would take her past him, and he would no doubt leap at the chance to escape, but she did not want to deal with his ill temper. She skirted around the Roman Bath edge of the room, drawing up to Mr Hammond's side with a smile of greeting.

"I hear we are to lose your company at Chenwith," he said.

"Does his lordship know yet?" she asked.

"I told him as we went into the church," Lady Margaret said. She glanced irritably at the two elderly ladies in black who had taken a position beside her to watch the promenade. "As you can imagine, he is not pleased about it."

"Has anyone seen the Duke?" Helen asked, realising she had rather lost track of her betrothed.

"He is over there, in conversation with Miss Serendill." Delia indicated the direction with a lift of her chin. "Has he introduced her to you? She is the Jamaican sugar heiress."

The Duke stood near the water fountain in conversation with two ladies: a dignified older woman in lavender crepe, and a young brown-skinned woman dressed in a handsome red pelisse laced with gold cord. Miss Serendill, Helen presumed.

"Close on twenty thousand," Delia added, lowering her voice. "Her mother was her father's *slave* housekeeper until he freed her and they married. That is what I have heard anyway. Although one never knows if these stories are just jealous hum. She has a most lively countenance, don't you think?"

Helen glanced at her friend. "Do you know that for the truth?"

Delia shrugged. "It is what I heard."

"You should not pass on that kind of gossip, Delia. Surely

your own experience with Mr Trent taught you that."

Delia reddened. "I did not think…"

Lady Margaret glared at Helen. "Really, did you have to bring up Mr Trent? Besides, gathering intelligence, listening to gossip, is why we come to the Pump Room. Why are you so determined to put Delia in the wrong?"

Helen stood her ground, although it suddenly felt a little unsteady. "Because the Duke has sworn he did not speak to Lady Georgina."

"Well, it was not I," Delia protested.

Lady Margaret clicked her tongue. "This again? What makes Delia's word less than the Duke's?"

"Margaret!" Mr Hammond said, calling his sister to order.

Even so, it was a fair point, Helen conceded. It seemed a woman's word was always suspect. Unyielding honour was the province of men. At least that was what the world said, and the world was definitely the province of men.

"Lady Helen, will you take a turn with me?" Mr Hammond said. "I have something I wish to discuss in private."

She took his arm, keen to move away from the united – and righteously resentful – front. "With pleasure."

"Margaret, will you follow? Miss Cransdon?" It was more an order than a request.

The women nodded and linked arms, falling in behind at a discreet distance for the sake of propriety.

"I cannot see Carlston," Helen said. If anyone knew where he was, it would be Hammond.

"Over there." Hammond nodded towards the foyer door where his lordship stood with his back to them. "Your brother is in a particularly belligerent mood this morning. He attempted to provoke his lordship into an argument, so Carlston thought it best not to approach you. Thus, I am his emissary."

Helen closed her eyes briefly. Andrew was proving as trouble-some as predicted.

She allowed Hammond to steer her towards a pair of vacant chairs set almost beneath the small orchestra gallery. The music was loud enough to obscure anything they said. They sat, Lady Margaret and Delia taking up position a few steps away. The pretty Irish air played by the band came to an end and the company stopped in their procession to clap. Helen and Hammond joined in the polite, glove-muffled applause, waiting until the next song started: a folk tune with a good amount of trumpet.

"We will not be able to sit together long before it is noticed," Hammond said. "His lordship wants you to continue the search for the Bath Deceiver."

"He is not going to remain at Chenwith, is he?" She could see no happy conclusion to that arrangement.

"No, we intend to make our excuses and return to his rooms to continue the search as well. He thinks it would be prudent, however, for him to stay away from you in case your brother decides to do something stupid, or your aunt takes it into her head to do something even more obstructive."

They both looked at the lady in question. She was already peering across the room at them, lips pursed in disapproval, no doubt suspecting that Hammond was Carlston's messenger. Which he was, although not delivering the kind of message Aunt had in mind.

"Send word to us by Darby if you discover anything," Hammond added.

Helen nodded, her fingers finding the hard shape of the fob upon its ribbon. "Do you know anything about Beau Nash?"

"Only that he brought Bath into fashion. Why?"

"There is a carved fob upon the fob ribbon on his statue over there, the same oval shape as the Comte's. I thought there could be a connection."

Hammond eyed the statue. "It is too far away for me to make a judgment. Does it have the same decoration?"

"There is not enough detail. I am probably making too much of it – there are many oval fobs in the world – but…"

"Best to follow up all leads," Hammond finished. "I will tell his lordship. He may know more about the Beau."

"I intend to write to Sir Jonathan for a trace too." She looked at Carlston, his back still turned to them. He must be so aggravated. "Will you please tell his lordship that I am sorry my brother and Aunt are causing so much difficulty."

"It would be much easier if they knew the truth about us."

"No!" Her vehemence drew the attention of a passing couple. She shifted, turning her face away from the promenade. "They are the only real family I have left. I cannot put them in danger … I could not bear it if something happened to them. Once the wedding is over they will leave, and all will be as it once was. Besides, we could never trust Andrew to keep such a secret. He is too—"

"Volatile?" Hammond supplied. "Yes, I have seen him in his cups. Even so, they may be safer if they did know."

Helen shook her head. "Andrew has no discretion and would be forever trying to save me from danger. Aunt's actions today tell me she would do the same."

"I suppose you are right." Hammond paused. "His lordship told us about the letter from Lady Elise. How are you faring?"

"What do you mean?"

He tilted his head, eyes soft with sympathy. "I was there when you came out of the salon in Brighton, Lady Helen. I know what he said to you. *Amore mio*. And I know that it is returned. This letter … it is proof she is alive and well … it must cause you pain."

She shook her head. She had no right to feel such pain. "I am betrothed to the Duke, Mr Hammond, and it is a true attachment." She held his eyes with her own; he must see her sincerity. "True and *right*."

"Nevertheless, I know the signs of suffering, Lady Helen; I see them in the mirror every day. And across the table." He looked at Lady Margaret, who was whispering something in Delia's ear. "My sister, at least, has found some distraction in mentoring Miss Cransdon."

"I do not doubt the truth of your pain, Mr Hammond, or your sister's. I do, however, doubt my own. I cannot help but think this other 'attachment' is caused by alchemy. Nothing more." Or was it that she *hoped* it was nothing more?

Hammond leaned forward, as much emphasis as propriety would allow. "Of course it is alchemy. Love is God's own alchemy – an unknowable mix of circumstance and soul."

"No, I mean the alchemy of the Grand Reclaimer bond. A trick of the Old Arts to strengthen the union."

He frowned. "You truly believe that?"

"Yes." She shook her head. "Maybe. I cannot tell." She tightened her hand around her reticule. "How do you know if what you feel for someone is real or not?"

He watched the promenade; holding back his answer, Helen realised, until there was a safe gap in the procession.

"I have had a lifetime of almost everyone around me – my acquaintances, my church, society – telling me that what I feel is not real," he finally said. "Worse, that it is an abomination. A sickness of the soul that will eventually see me in hell. Yet what I have learned is that love is a leap of faith. A leap that not only takes you towards the person you love but also towards the truth of yourself. Whom you love and how you love them will tell you more about yourself than anything else in this world."

They both looked across the room at Carlston. He had turned, intent upon the parade of fashionables, but must have felt their gaze for his attention suddenly shifted to where they sat.

His eyes found Helen's: *Is everything all right?*

She gave a nod: *All is well.*

She turned back to Hammond to find him watching her silently, mouth quirked up at the corner. Helen felt her skin warm into a flush.

"What is it?" she demanded. "Why do you look at me in such a way?"

"God's own alchemy."

She shook her head. "There is nothing divine in it, Mr Hammond. It is all alchemy and no God."

"Could it not be the other way around?"

"In what way?"

"Rather than the Reclaimer bond creating your feelings, it is your feelings that have allowed such a strong bond?"

His words flared across her heart into sudden fury. "I did not bring this upon myself, Mr Hammond. This awful power is not of my making."

"I did not mean to imply—"

She leaned in, trying to keep her vehemence contained to a whisper. "You do not understand the terror of the Ligatus. No one with an ounce of self-preservation would wish this vicious force into being. It is insanity woven into words and power. An incessant buzz in my head. Every day, every minute, I feel as if I may lose myself within its blood-soaked screams if I do not hold myself tight. Do you know what that is like?"

Hammond drew back. "Not about such power, but I know the feeling of holding tight every day."

Helen nodded. Of course he did. She touched his hand in grim camaraderie. "There is no love in this power, Mr Hammond. Only death."

"Forgive me, my friend. I did not realise."

She shook her head. "No, forgive me; of course you did not know. No one can. Not even Lord Carlston."

Across the room, the Duke had bowed to Miss Serendill and her chaperone and was now searching the company, clearly looking for his betrothed.

Helen gathered up her reticule and rose from the chair. "I believe my absence has been noted. Time to rejoin the parade."

Chapter Thirteen

WEDNESDAY, 16 DECEMBER 1812

Helen turned her head on the pillow to look at the little white enamel clock set on the bedside table. Six o'clock. *Finally.* She sat up, her eyes dry from lack of sleep.

It was no fault of Lady Dunwick's excellent arrangements: the guest room was sizable enough and the mahogany bed was comfortable, if a little cramped at present. No, it was all the fault of the Ligatus buzzing in her bones like angry bees, and the possibility that little Timothy Marr could manifest again.

She drew the bedclothes up to her chest to ward off the morning chill and watched Darby, curled beside her, open her eyes and yawn. The maid awoke at exactly six every morning, precise as an automaton.

"Good morning, Darby."

"Good morning, my lady." Darby blinked in the morning gloom and rose onto one elbow to study Helen through narrowed eyes. "Did you sleep?"

"A little."

Darby bunched her lips at the patent lie and threw off the bedclothes. "You will do yourself a harm, my lady," she said, pulling one of Helen's old dressing robes over her flannel nightgown.

"You must sleep, or you will be useless to yourself and to everyone else. It's been three nights now and the child hasn't appeared. His lordship must be right: it was just a peculiarity brought on by the stone energy."

"We cannot be sure though, can we? And Lady Dunwick's house is a lot smaller than Chenwith. If it happens again, everyone will be upon us in a minute."

Darby straightened from reordering the bedclothes. "If you do not trust me to guard against the ghosts and stop anyone from entering, I may as well sleep in the dressing room in my own bed."

"I do trust you," Helen protested.

"Then for goodness' sake, sleep. Please!" Darby's vehemence settled into the thick silence. She twitched the already straight quilt. "Forgive me, my lady, I should not have spoken so."

Poor Darby. Helen's wakefulness, it seemed, was wearing upon both of them. And no doubt some of her ill humour came from being parted from Quinn. They had barely had a day to enjoy their secret engagement before Darby had been obliged to come to Bath and Lady Dunwick's house.

"You need not apologise," Helen said.

Darby gave a tired smile and peered at the cold fireplace. "I'll tell Mary to do your room first."

As she closed the door behind her, Helen wriggled down into the warmth of the bed again. Darby was right about one thing: if she did not sleep soon, she would be of no use to anyone. It seemed even a Reclaimer constitution infused with earth energy could not do without sleep for four nights.

With some effort, she ignored the relentless hum in her body and focused upon the deeper beat of the Reclaimer bond, trying to find some ease. And perhaps to determine if Lord Carlston had decamped from Chenwith. They had not seen him at all in the last three days. Were he and Mr Quinn even at Bath? It was hard to make such fine distinctions within the rhythm, especially in regard to mid-distances. When Carlston was far away, like Paris, it was faint. Close, in the next room, it was strong. But everywhere else in between was ... in between. She breathed deeply, trying to distinguish the sensation. There ... something had changed – a slight deepening of the pulse. Did that mean he was closer? And if it did, how was she to determine how close? She sighed. No answers, only questions.

Around her, the routine of the waking house unfolded. Mary, the housemaid, entered and stoked the fire, the warmth creeping across the chilled room. Sprat, whose services had been lent to Delia for the week, came in to open Helen's shutters and deliver a cup of chocolate, all in careful silence. Darby must have threatened death to achieve such quiet attendance.

In glorious solitude, Helen drank her chocolate and watched the foggy view of Lansdown Crescent, set higher on the hill, sharpen into a pale yellow semicircle of townhouses. There was something exceptionally soothing about John Wood's graceful, orderly architecture. She closed her eyes, the warmth of her bed dragging her down into a soft, dark sense of...

Screaming! A stabbing howl of misery. Helen lurched upright. The infant again, writhing on the floor. This time a woman stood over him, shrieking, her terror piercing the air, slicing through Helen's mind. Dear God, his poor mother. Her pale hands reached towards her sobbing ghost child.

Helen lunged forward, wrenching her way out of the bedclothes. She must stop them – they would bring the whole house into her room.

The opaque woman turned, her face a screaming maw of darkness. Helen collapsed under a wave of pain and anguish, chest slamming against knees, face pressed against the quilted silk. Crushed under the agonised despair. She clawed at the quilt, fighting to breathe. No air! She had no air!

"My lady!" A blur of blue. Firm hands on her shoulders, pulling her up.

The screaming mother and child – in her head, in the room – folded in upon themselves, disappearing into silence. And air. Sweet air.

Darby's face, still blurred, filled her vision. "Into bed, my lady. Quick! Before someone comes."

She felt herself thrust back against the pillows, bedcovers yanked across her body. Her vision cleared to see Darby stoop to pick up something white from the floor – a letter? – and grab the washstand as if to steady herself.

"Helen! Is something wrong?" Aunt's voice demanded. The door opened and she peered into the room, still clad in her nightgown. "My dear girl, was that you screaming again? Did you have another nightmare?"

Helen managed a smile. "No, it wasn't me. I think it came from next door."

Aunt frowned at the adjoining wall as if she could divine the activity beyond it. "I hardly think so. Sir Roger Bancroft lives there and he is a magistrate."

Behind her, Pug peered in, her hair half dressed in tight curls. "Maybe it came from outside," she said. "Could have been cats. When they fight, it sounds an awful lot like people screaming."

"Well, cats or no, it is entirely inconsiderate – it is not yet struck nine o'clock." Aunt pulled the door closed, saying, "I will see you at breakfast, my dear."

"Of course," Helen called.

She listened as the two sets of footsteps retreated; Aunt's

heavier tread pausing as she passed Lady Georgina's room. "It was cats," her aunt's muffled voice said. "Nothing to be so distressed by, Lady Georgina. Do calm yourself."

"Did you see?" Helen said to Darby. "A woman ghost as well. Poor Mrs Marr, I think. Another escalation. It cannot just be the earth energy."

"My lady, I am..." Darby took an unsteady step towards the bed, then staggered back into the washstand, sending the porcelain clinking. The letter fell from her grip. "I feel..." She collapsed heavily to the floor.

"Darby!" Helen kicked off the bedclothes and scrabbled over the end of the bed, landing on her knees beside her Terrene's limp form. Senseless. She pressed her hand on Darby's bodice. Still breathing, thank God, but her face was a ghastly shade of white.

"Darby, can you hear me?"

No response. Helen patted her cheek – her soft skin was so cold. Was this the work of the ghosts? She took Darby's freezing hand in her own. What was she to do?

First get her off the floor and onto the bed.

Helen shifted into a crouch, edged her hands beneath her maid's broad back and braced herself. A heave and a thrust upward with all the strength in her legs and she was standing, Darby cradled in her arms. Not too difficult – the advantage of Reclaimer strength.

She manoeuvred past the bedposts and eased Darby onto the bed, pulling her rucked-up gown back over her ankles. Still so pale. Smelling salts? She had none. But in London, when she had nearly fainted next to the rotting corpse of Berta, the Deceiver maid, Carlston had pushed her head down over her knees and it had helped.

She sat on the bed and slid her hand under Darby's back

to pull her upright, then dragged her legs over the edge of the bed. Darby slumped against her shoulder, head lolling forward. With a hand on Darby's damp forehead, and the other against her chest, she gently bent her over, chest against knees, and held her in the odd position.

Darby's breath seemed ominously light, and her skin still had no bloom of colour. Maybe it was the wrong thing to do.

"Darby?"

No response. Perhaps smelling salts would be more effective. Aunt did not use them, but Lady Dunwick might have some.

Helen peered into the ashen face again. Was that a flickering of eyelids?

"My dear? Can you hear me?"

"Mmm?" Darby slowly opened her eyes.

"You fainted," Helen said. "Stay down for the moment, until you recover."

Darby grimaced. "I feel all weak, like after you blew up the house." Her voice seemed faraway, but some pink had returned to her cheeks. She drew in a steadying breath, then frowned. "My lady, did you carry me to the bed? You should not have done so. I'm sorry."

"I was hardly going to leave you on the floor."

"Kind of you." Her voice was still a little dreamy. She briefly touched Helen's hand upon her chest. "I think I can sit up now, thank you."

Although not convinced, Helen drew back her hands.

Darby grabbed the edge of the bed and slowly levered herself upright. "There!"

"You should really lie down. Rest."

Darby shook her head, wincing. "No, I think I may be ill if I lie down. What happened, my lady?"

"I think it was the ghosts. You stopped them."

"*I* stopped them? I thought I was just waking you up."

"No, when you touched me I felt all their energy go back into the Ligatus." Helen rubbed her forehead, remembering the strange sensation of the ghosts folding in upon themselves. "I think they escape my mind when I sleep, yet I am definitely awake when they start screaming."

"But how did I stop them? I did nothing."

"This will sound strange, I know, but I think you are like one of Mr Gray's non-electrics. The ghosts' energy cannot flow through you, and somehow that stops it."

"Is that why there has been no sign of the ghosts for three nights?" Darby gasped, her eyes opening wide. "Oh my! Do you think this is what I am supposed to do as your Terrene? Instead of helping you rid yourself of Deceiver energy, I do the opposite. I stop the energy you have stored from escaping?"

Helen nodded. "That is exactly what I think."

"Just by touch?" She lifted her hand as if seeing it for the first time. Fierce hope narrowed her face. "Do you think I could hold back all the rift energy?"

So clever and brave. Still, Helen thought, it did not change the terrifying fact of this power.

"Those two ghosts sent you into a dead faint when you stopped them," she said slowly. "Yet they are nothing compared to the full Ligatus energy in me. If it breaks through, I do not think you could dam all its power. It would kill you before you could do so."

"You don't know that for certain."

"I know what is in me, Darby. I feel its strength every day. You would not stand a chance." Helen smiled to take the edge from her words. "At least we know that, for now, you can hold back the ghosts."

Darby sighed. "I'm sorry I was not here to stop them this time.

I was coming back up the stairs when I felt a terrible pressure in my head – the same as when the baby first manifested." She squinted, clearly trying to remember something. "Ah, the letter, for you." She pointed to the packet on the carpet. "That is why I was downstairs. Mr Quinn delivered it." Just saying his name brought a smile to her wan face. "He and his lordship are in Bath again." The smile widened. "We have a marriage licence, my lady!"

Carlston was back in town. Helen could not help her own smile. "That is wonderful news."

"We are to be married tomorrow morning, if you are amenable." Darby's hands curled under her chin, almost as if in prayer. "I was hoping you would consent to witness our vows? We would be most honoured. Mr Quinn has asked his lordship to stand for him."

"Of course." Helen's face warmed with the pleasure of the invitation. "It is I who would be honoured!"

"Then it is set." Darby gave a small laugh. "Tomorrow!"

"That being the case, you must now rest," Helen ordered. "We cannot have a bride who is pasty and weak."

Darby smiled. "I think I *will* rest, if you do not mind. Just for a few minutes."

She leaned back against the bedhead, closing her eyes with a ragged sigh. Helen watched her for a moment. Darby was not one for taking to bed, even when she was ill. The manifestation had affected her more than she was willing to admit.

As silently as she could, Helen rose from the bed and retrieved the packet from the floor. Nothing inscribed upon the front. She turned it over. A blank red wax seal; no doubt a precaution in case her aunt intercepted the delivery. She split the wax with her thumb and spread out the page, her heart quickening.

7 Green Park, Bath, Wednesday, 16th December, 1812

Lady Helen,

At Mr Pike's request, I quit Chenwith for London on the day you left for Bath. The reason for my swift visit to the capital was a troubling one: Mrs Pike's condition worsened appreciably last week and her insane outbursts could not be contained by normal human intervention. At least two Reclaimers were required to subdue the savagery of her vestige violence. Mr Hallifax was already in London and so I joined him in an effort to assist the poor woman. After two days of anguish and struggle, she finally returned to a precarious sense of sanity.

Pike knows there is only one cure – for you and I to reclaim her – but until he makes that decision, her physician has recommended a course of hot baths to help calm the attacks. The hot water does seem to have some positive effect, and I cannot help but think the vestige within her is also somehow connected to water. It is, after all, a form of Deceiver energy, and we now know that their energy uses water as a conduit.

To expedite Mrs Pike's comfort I offered Mr Pike the use of my rooms near the Queen's Bath, which he has gladly taken. They are now in residence at Bath, and Mr Hammond and I have found rooms at a lodging house in Green Park. Mr Pike knows you are currently visiting with Lady Dunwick at the Royal Crescent, and I think he finds great comfort in the idea that two Reclaimers are on hand in case his wife's condition deteriorates again. In all truth, the poor lady needs to be reclaimed now, but Pike still cannot bring himself to risk her life. I am grieved to say it, but for now that is a godsend since we dare not risk using our power.

Sir Jonathan has asked me to inform you that he traced

Beau Nash as you requested, and the man has no recorded
Deceiver history nor any legitimate or illegitimate offspring.
Alas, another failed path of inquiry, but it was a good
thought. Sir Jonathan has not yet discovered a safer way
to mesmerise you and so has elected to stay in London
over Christmas with his books and archives in case we have
more trace requests.

In happier news, I have procured a special licence for
Mr Quinn and Miss Darby from the Archbishop. His
Grace is aware of our calling and thus has granted them
the special dispensation. I suspect we shall be witnessing the
nuptials in the next day or so, for Mr Quinn is most eager
to solemnise his regard.

Send word if you have news of your own – any sense of
progress would be most welcome. Otherwise Mr Hammond
and I will happen upon you at the Pump Room today, or
if that does not transpire, tonight at the Upper Rooms.

Yrs etc,
Carlston

It was clear that he hoped they had made some headway in his
absence, but so far there had been naught. Not from lack of
effort, Helen thought. Last night, she had attended the card
assembly at the Upper Rooms with Lady Margaret and Delia,
and they must have played cards with everyone in the room,
both young and old. A few of the younger ladies had commented
upon the fob around her neck, but none of the gentlemen had
mentioned it, nor had any carried one that was its match.

She read the note again. It was a great kindness for Carlston
to offer his rooms to Pike, even if it did bring the problem of
Mrs Pike closer to them. For now, while Pike hesitated, they
could keep the existence of the rift secret from him and the Dark

Days Club. But when he decided it was time to risk reclaiming Isabella – and from Carlston's description of her suffering, that decision must come soon – they would be forced to admit that any use of their power would rip apart not only Isabella, but themselves too. And poor Darby as well, forever caught in their Grand Reclaimer bond.

The words on the paper blurred, the room around her bleached into grey haze. Helen closed her eyes, fighting an overwhelming crash of terror that swept her along in its freezing current.

"My lady?" Darby said. "I have had a thought." Her voice held a heavy note.

Helen drew a deep breath and opened her eyes, forcing her way through the bone-chilling fear and back into the room. Allowing her terror to gather so much momentum was not going to help at all.

"What thought?"

Darby's hands were bunched into the bedclothes. "If I stop the ghosts from manifesting when you sleep, then I must not leave you at night."

For a moment, the statement did not seem to warrant such wretchedness in her voice. Then Helen realised what she meant.

"Oh, you will not be able to…" She paused, feeling her face heat. "Spend the nights with your husband."

"But it is not only Mr Quinn and me, is it? It will affect you and His Grace too. When you are married."

"I will have to tell him about the rift," Helen whispered.

She imagined the Duke's anger; yet another secret between her and Lord Carlston, deliberately kept from him.

"I've never felt easy keeping it from Mr Quinn, my lady," Darby said. "Perhaps it is best that those we love know the truth of what we face?"

"Perhaps."

"In case we do not…" Darby trailed off.

Helen swiftly crossed the room, and sat on the bed beside her Terrene. "We will find a way to close it," she promised. "We will. We must."

They both reached across, hands meeting halfway, soft skin against calloused. A fragile link holding fast against the future.

"Here is some interesting news, my dear," Aunt remarked from behind the *Bath and Cheltenham Gazette*. "The shop of the late Madame Simeon on Milsom Street is selling all its stock. I think we should look in for gloves and lace tomorrow. Slack's Warehouse has new stock as well – a shipment of satins and imperial nets. It is time to decide upon the cloth for your wedding gown. You have waited far too long as it is."

"As you wish," Helen murmured, all her attention upon the rain-washed view of Bath from Lady Dunwick's drawing room window. The city lay spread to the south-east, a golden-hued map of her frustration. The Bath Deceiver was out there somewhere, eluding their search. The vital information that could close the rift and help them control their power: so close yet still so unreachable. Helen could just make out Queen Square; did he or she live in one of the townhouses? Or perhaps along Princess Street, or even in the lower quarter?

She touched the fob strung on a blue ribbon around her neck, her aunt's words finally penetrating her introspection. "Oh, were you thinking of going today? I thought we were already engaged this afternoon?" She had resigned herself to waiting until evening to see Lord Carlston at the Upper Rooms, but perhaps they would be able to visit the Pump Room after all.

Aunt lowered the paper. "Do stop wool-gathering, Helen. I said we will go to Milsom Street *tomorrow*. We are to drink tea with Lady Carnarvon this afternoon, when Lady Dunwick returns from her treatment at the baths."

"Mother said Lady Carnarvon particularly invited you, Lady Helen," Pug offered. "She has a distant connection to the Duke, you know. A third cousin or something." She held up the black paper silhouette of Helen she was cutting, her head tilted in appraisal. "Noses are so difficult."

Lady Margaret looked up from the latest edition of *The Lady's Magazine* that she and Delia were flicking through together on the sofa. "The invitation this afternoon does not include us, does it, Lady Pennworth? Miss Cransdon and I are set upon completing some errands."

"Twelfth Night shopping," Delia added.

"Of course it includes you and Miss Cransdon," Aunt said. "I'm sure you would not wish to embarrass your hostess, Lady Margaret, and refuse the plan. As I said, we can all go shopping tomorrow." She smiled, steel within the brief expression.

Lady Margaret glanced accusingly at Helen. She did not appreciate being under another woman's direction, and plainly it was Helen's fault. She returned, pointedly, to the magazine.

"We don't exchange Twelfth Night gifts," Lady Georgina said from the armchair opposite Aunt. She pulled a thread through in her embroidery. "We give the servants their due, of course, but we certainly don't give each other gifts."

"Really, do you not?" Pug paused mid-cut, the idea of no gifts patently appalling. "How ... frugal."

"Oh dear." Lady Margaret looked up from the magazine, gathering Delia and Helen into her consternation. "There is a notice in here about your friend Miss Gardwell."

"What do you mean?"

"It reports that Miss Millicent Gardwell, of Mayfair, has ended her engagement to Lord Holbridge only four weeks from the wedding, on the grounds of the lady finding love elsewhere.

The family has retired to Ireland." Lady Margaret looked up again. "Did you know of it?"

Helen shook her head, aghast. She'd had no letter from Millicent. Then again, she had sadly neglected her own correspondence to her friend. Poor Delia – this must surely bring back her own dreadful elopement with Mr Trent – although she did not seem to have yet made the correlation. Perhaps the horror of that encounter was finally beginning to diminish.

"Finding love elsewhere?" Lady Georgina said, wrinkling her nose. "How sordid. She will branded a jilt. No one of consequence will invite her anywhere."

Helen glared at the dire prediction, although it was true. Poor dear Millicent, carted away to Ireland, just like Caro Lamb. "I cannot believe it."

Aunt cleared her throat. "I fear it is true. I had a letter from Lady Gardwell declining the invitation to your wedding ball. Apparently Millicent decided she was in love with a much lesser man. She always was a flirt, Helen, you have to admit it. The match with Holbridge was far better than I had thought she would ever make. And now it is all gone. What is wrong with you modern girls? Always on this silly quest for love. It has very little to do with a good match and as far as I can see only brings heartache for all concerned." She sighed. "We do not even know if the other man intends to marry Millicent."

"When were you going to tell me?" Helen demanded. Her aunt did not answer, but it was clear in the expression upon her face: not until after Helen's own wedding, in case she was inspired by her friend's scandalous behaviour.

"I must write to her," Helen said.

"No, my dear, best to hold off until the heat of it dies down," Aunt cautioned. "I have no forwarding address." She eyed Helen's mutinous face. "Think on it, my dear. You will be of much more use to Millicent as the Duchess of Selburn. Wait until after your wedding to write. That way, when she receives an invitation to stay with Her Grace, the Duchess of Selburn, no one will dare snub her. Until then, I am afraid she is rather ruined goods."

"Why don't you write, Miss Cransdon?" Lady Margaret said, glancing sideways at Aunt. "She is your school friend as well, is she not?"

"Yes, of course." Delia nodded. "I shall write on both our behalf, Helen."

"Thank you, Delia," Helen said.

With a sniff, Aunt returned to her reading. Helen rubbed tiredly at her eyes. She had thought Millicent and Lord Holbridge to be so well suited. It had not been a violent love, of course, but Millicent had held him in some regard and it had certainly been an excellent match considering the Gardwells' pecuniary situation. And while it was true Millicent did like to flirt, she only did so in a light-hearted way, and never beyond propriety. Whom had she met to inspire such reckless abandonment of her duty and her reputation?

"Now infants murdered. It is too, too horrid," Aunt commented, shaking her head over the paper.

Lady Georgina lowered her embroidery. "Infants?"

Aunt commenced to read: *"As the coachman of Mr Alderman Walf, of Bristol, was passing on Wednesday morning last through a field of his master's near Remison bath, he was attracted by some ravens hovering over a hedge, where he was much shocked by discovering the bodies of two infant children and part of a third, supposed to be two or three days old! – An inquest has been held on the bodies, and a verdict of wilful murder has been given against some person or persons unknown."*

Lady Margaret straightened in her seat. Was she thinking

the same as Helen? One infant's death might be placed at the hands of a desperate housemaid or tavern girl. But three? Was it the work of a Deceiver?

"Were there any marks upon the bodies?" Lady Margaret asked, her eyes meeting Helen's.

"That is a rather ghoulish question," Aunt said. "There is nothing more about it than this report."

"Lady Georgina, are you quite well?" Pug asked.

The answer was clearly no, for Lady Georgina sat with her hands clasped into fists in her lap, tears silently streaming down her cheeks. "If you will excuse me," she gasped and rose from her chair. She was across the room and out before anyone could utter anything else.

"Lud," Delia said as the footman closed the door. "I did not think she *could* cry."

"I will see what is wrong," Helen said.

Out in the foyer, she caught sight of a swirl of Lady Georgina's primrose-yellow hem through the banister of the staircase. She was heading, it would seem, to her bedchamber on the second floor. Helen gathered her own skirts and followed, carefully containing her speed to give Lady Georgina enough time to find sanctuary.

She listened as she climbed: wet sobs, a door opening, and Lady Georgina's voice, congested and nasty, "Get out. Now!"

"Please, my lady, allow me to mix you some medicine."

Lord Henry had said something about medicine on the night of the manifestation. Was Lady Georgina ill?

"No," Lady Georgina snapped. "It solves nothing. Get out!"

Helen arrived on the landing just as Lady Georgina's maid – a small, dark woman with a quiet air of elegance – backed out of the room and closed the door, her neat profile set into an anxious frown at the sound of sobbing behind it.

"Your mistress is in her room?"

The maid whirled around startled, then bobbed a curtsey. "Lady Helen ... I do not think she wishes to be disturbed."

"What is your name?"

"Wainwright, my lady."

"Is your mistress ill, Wainwright? Does she need a physician?"

"I do not think so, my lady."

"This has happened before, hasn't it?"

A rather unfair question – any answer would be disloyal – yet the woman was clearly concerned about her mistress.

"I could not say, my lady," she whispered, her true answer in the slight press of her lips and soft pity in her eyes.

"I understand. You may go." Helen watched as Wainwright descended the staircase, then considered the firmly closed door. By all rights she should respect Lady Georgina's privacy. Still, the woman was clearly in great distress, and it was a chance to keep her promise to Lord Henry.

She knocked and said loudly, "It is Lady Helen. May I enter?" Without waiting for an answer, she pushed open the door.

"No ... I..." Lady Georgina sat hunched on the large bed, a black leather-bound Bible under one hand, the other wound into the pale green covers as if anchoring herself against the violence of her sobs. She drew in a deep breath. "You must not have heard me. I wish to be alone."

"Are you unwell?" Helen asked. "We are all very concerned."

Lady Georgina's mouth twisted into disbelief. "Thank you. I am quite well."

"As I see," Helen said.

"Please go. I will return to the drawing room in a few minutes."

Although it went against all good manners, Helen closed the door and crossed to the bed. The room, like her own, was one of the larger chambers, with a view to Lansdown Crescent behind them. There was a medicinal scent to the room, no doubt from the collection of brown glass bottles arranged on the table by the bed, a mixing glass amongst them. Helen caught a name upon a label: laudanum.

"What are you doing?" Lady Georgina demanded.

Helen sat on the edge of the bed. She did not quite dare take Lady Georgina's hand, but placed her own near the one that rested upon the Bible. "We are to be sisters before long, and sisters share their troubles. Will you not tell me what grieves you?"

"Nothing is grieving me." She picked up the Bible and placed it on her lap as if it were a shield.

"I heard you crying once before, at Chenwith, when I had my nightmare." Helen cocked her head, the two instances coming together in a rush of revelation: little Timothy Marr and now the murdered babies. "This is about infants, isn't it?"

It was as if a giant hand slammed down upon Lady Georgina. She collapsed inward, Bible clutched to her chest, body shaking, her beautiful mouth wide in a silent agonised howl and tears streaming from her eyes.

Helen grabbed her shoulders. A liberty, but surely the poor woman would shake apart if she did not. "Lady Georgina, what is wrong? Tell me what is wrong."

"My fifth. My fifth." The words were barely more than sobs. A trail of spittle spooled from her mouth, her shoulders heaving under Helen's hands. "All of them lost."

Ah, now it was clear. Lady Georgina had conceived five times and not held the babies. Helen tightened her grip in sympathy. For all her inexperience, she knew such losses were common and dangerous. Aunt had suffered one just after Helen and Andrew had first arrived at the Pennworth estate – a late desperate hope, dashed. The blame always seemed to rest upon the woman: an excess of worry, or a foul mood, or too much education. In Aunt's case, all the blame had been placed upon her vigorous walks, and none of it, Helen had silently observed, on her uncle's frequent violent tempers.

"How long ago?" she asked gently.

"A month." Lady Georgina slowly straightened and wiped her mouth. "Five in two years. My sole purpose is to provide an heir, yet I cannot keep a baby. I am useless!" She balled her fist, bringing it down hard into her stomach. "Useless!"

Shocked, Helen caught the fist on another upswing, barely remembering to constrain her own strength. "You must not do that. You will hurt yourself."

Lady Georgina wrenched her hand away. "What does it matter? If I cannot have children, I have no use in this world."

"That is not true! Besides, there is still time."

"And what if time runs out? What then? I will be resented by my husband. Scorned by society."

"Lord Henry does not resent you, Lady Georgina. Quite the contrary." Helen paused; would the truth alleviate the woman's pain or add to it? "He asked me to befriend you. He knows you are suffering."

She gave a bitter laugh. "Is that why you are here? Because he asked you?"

"In part," Helen admitted. "But I would have come anyway."

Lady Georgina studied her quizzically. "Yes, I believe you would have." She drew a deep, steadying breath and spread her hand across the Bible on her lap. "I have been married five years now, Lady Helen, without issue. I have prayed, I have rested, I have taken a cooling diet, and now I have consulted the best *accoucheur*, Sir Richard Croft. He suggested I take the waters here at Bath, but if they do not help, I do not know what I will do. Or, indeed, what Lord Henry will do."

"He would not abandon you."

"Of course not. Yet he, like every other man, wants – needs – a son and heir. If I cannot provide that, all I am is a burden. A barren ornament. My marriage will become poisoned by blame and resentment. I have seen it happen."

Helen had no answer to such a dire prediction. She too had seen such disappointment curdle her aunt and uncle's marriage.

Lady Georgina gave a grim, watery smile. "Do not look so solemn, Lady Helen, it is not your predicament. No doubt you will do your duty to the Duke with great expedience, over and over, and all will be as it should." She looked down at the Bible. "God willing."

A generous benediction under the circumstances. And yet Helen rose from the bed, needing to move away from the invocation of such a successful future.

"I will go back downstairs," she said, walking to the door. "Shall I send Wainwright to you?"

Lady Georgina nodded. "I must tidy myself. Tears do not belong in a drawing room."

Helen paused on the threshold and looked back. She could not leave without offering some kind of hope. "I will pray for you."

"Thank you." Lady Georgina drew the Bible against her belly. "I will pray for you too."

Chapter Fourteen

Darby, tongue held between her teeth, eased out the hot tong from Helen's hair. They both surveyed the result in the mirror.

Darby gave a huff of relief. "I thought that one would never sit in place. It really is time you had your hair cut, my lady."

"The Duke does not like the fashion for short hair." Helen picked up one of the curls clustered around her face then let it bounce back into place. Soon it would be too long to brush into a man's style. "I will have it cut again after the wedding."

In the mirror, she watched Darby place the tong back upon its little silver box of coals to heat for the next curl. Perhaps it was the effect of the candlelight, but Darby's eyes had blueish hollows beneath them, even though she claimed to be fully recovered from the dramatic events of the morning.

"Do not wait up for me tonight," Helen said. "You do not want dark circles for your wedding day. Sprat can undress me after she has seen to Delia."

Darby snorted. "You will never get to bed in that case. No, I will undress you, my lady."

Helen met her eyes in the mirror. "I want you to rest."

Darby's round face set into obstinacy. "I am quite well, my

lady. I will wait up for you. I doubt I will sleep tonight anyway."

It was clear Helen was not going to win this battle. "Then I will be back as soon as the concert ends."

Darby nodded and bent to rotate the heating tong. "Will his lordship be there?"

"Yes." Helen turned in the chair. "Are you sure you only wish the two of us at your wedding?"

Darby looked up. "Just you and his lordship, my lady, and Mr Pike too. Mr Quinn and I want it to be quiet, and Mr Pike has offered to host the ceremony at his lodgings. We don't want to take away from your celebrations."

Helen waved away the consideration. "I would not have you deny yourself friends at your wedding just because mine approaches. What about your family? Your mother and father?"

"They don't like the idea of Mr Quinn." Darby's chin jutted. "But I'm of age now so they don't have a say in it."

"I see. I am sorry."

She smiled. "Be assured, my lady, what is planned tomorrow is exactly how I would wish it."

She bent to the curling tong again, and Helen turned back to the mirror. She found Darby's pronouncement somewhat unsettling. Was her own wedding how she would wish it? She had never been one to rehearse the day in her mind, unlike poor Millicent who had been planning her wedding since she was ten. Now it seemed unlikely her friend would ever have one, or if she did it would be a very quiet affair. The Duke, on the other hand, had very firm ideas of how his nuptials should proceed, and she – for good or ill – had made no objection to them. Perhaps she should be more involved, but in truth she had other, rather more urgent matters to plan: namely, their deliverance from the Ligatus and the destruction of the Grand Deceiver.

* * *

It was decided that the evening was dry and mild enough for the company to walk to the subscription concert at the nearby Upper Assembly Rooms, under the escort of two footmen. Much to Helen's surprise, Lady Margaret insisted on taking her arm. The bracing night air pressed them into a quick pace along Brock Street, and by the time they started across the cobbled expanse of King's Circus – John Wood's showcase circle of townhouses – they were a good six yards ahead of Pug and Delia, with the others lagging further behind.

"Those infants," Lady Margaret said, her voice low. "Did you have the same thought as I did?"

"A Deceiver glut?" Helen replied. "I thought it might be, but on further reflection it does not seem likely. An infant's life energy would not be enough to build a weapon. Even three little lives would probably not add up to one whip."

"It could be a sustaining feed though." Lady Margaret's mouth set into grim distaste. "It could be infanticide, I suppose. Then again, it is very strange. *Three* of them."

"Killing infants is guaranteed to ignite all our resources to destroy such a perpetrator. Why risk it when they can skim within the agreement of the Pact?"

"If the creature…" Lady Margaret paused as a gentleman strode past, nodding politely to him. "If it was embedded within its human life and determined to keep its identity hidden, it might not want to take the chance of skimming and being discovered. Especially if it is aware that two Reclaimers are in town looking for it."

"You think this may be the work of the Bath Deceiver?"

"Possibly."

"Lady Helen!"

She and Lady Margaret turned. Pug, Delia and one of the footmen were coming up fast upon them.

"You are walking at such a pace," Pug said. "Your aunt asks you to wait so that we may all enter together."

Their discussion was clearly at an end. To Helen, it seemed quite a leap to connect the tragic murder of the infants with the Bath Deceiver, but Lady Margaret was right about one thing: the circumstances were indeed strange.

The Upper Assembly Rooms were already busy with arrivals. A line of sedan chairs discharged their single passengers at the west entrance doors set between Doric columns while town carriages rumbled across the cobbles to the north-west entrance. One handsome equipage made the mistake of turning towards the west doors and a group of chairmen met its intrusion with loud yells, startling the two carriage horses into stamping agitation. Words were exchanged, the haughty coachman refusing to turn, the chairmen's insults quickly deteriorating into language unsuitable for gentle ears.

Aunt and Lady Dunwick quickly shepherded their charges up the steps and into the Rooms, leaving the footmen outside to enjoy the fracas and await the end of the concert.

"What does 'bollocks' mean?" Pug whispered to Helen as they joined the throng in the entrance hall.

Helen, who had used the word with great relish as Mr Amberley, shrugged. "I think it is something to do with oxen."

"Ah, of course," Pug said.

Hiding her smile, Helen focused upon the Reclaimer bond and found, to her delight, a beat that held the strength of proximity. She rocked onto her toes and peered across the crowd, finding Miss Serendill and her chaperone near the corridor, and Lord and Lady Carnarvon beside the marble columns. No sign, however, of Carlston's tall figure. He must not yet be in the building.

She raised her lorgnette to search the room for any skimming

Deceivers. Oddly, there were none. Or at least none that were making themselves known by feeding upon the chattering arrivals. Perhaps they were already in the concert room, skimming the anticipation buzzing through the audience.

"Well, this is a crush," Aunt said as they slowly made their way further into the foyer. "It must be for Mr Elliot. It is his only appearance at Bath."

Lady Dunwick pointed her fan across the foyer. "The cloak-rooms," she said, raising her voice to reach her daughter, Lady Georgina and Lady Margaret, who were caught behind an elderly lady and gentleman. "Let us divest and take our seats."

They were waiting their turn to enter the tea room, converted for the evening into the concert hall, when Helen heard her name called. She turned to see an officer in blue, bowing.

For a second, she did not recognise the dark-skinned young man, then her memory supplied an image – dancing in Brighton – and thankfully a name.

"Mr Nesbitt, how do you do!"

"Very well, my lady." He smiled beneath his rather dashing moustache – all the Hussars wore them – clearly pleased to have been remembered.

"Aunt, may I introduce Mr Nesbitt of the 10th Light Dragoons."

Aunt nodded graciously to his smart bow.

"What do you do at Bath?" Helen asked. "Are you not stationed in Brighton?"

His smile became a grin. "We are here for your wedding, my lady. Well, to be more precise, we are here to serve Her Majesty when she arrives for your wedding ball."

Of course, they were the Prince Regent's own regiment.

"Well then, I will send you and your comrades some wedding cake for such gallant service," she said.

"We would be most obliged, my lady."

Aunt turned away to acknowledge another acquaintance, and Mr Nesbitt leaned closer. "Forgive me for being so bold, my lady," he said, his voice barely above a whisper, "but I also wished to say that His Royal Highness has instructed all of us in the 10th Light Dragoons that if ever you or Lord Carlston are in need of assistance, we are to do your bidding."

Helen met his earnest eyes. Did he know of the Deceivers? "I see. Did His Highness say why?"

"No, my lady. The order is enough. Be assured we stand by."

"Thank you, Mr Nesbitt."

He gave another bow and withdrew.

"That is a rather strange acquaintance, Helen," Aunt said, watching the young man weave his way through the crowd to his friends.

"I danced with him at Lady Dunwick's ball in Brighton." Lud, that dance seemed an age ago, before Stokes and the Comte had died and the awful events at Barnes Terrace. "He grew up in India and has the most fascinating stories. Did you know that elephants—"

Her aunt, however, had turned to acknowledge a gentleman hovering with some purpose nearby. "Ah, Mr King. How do you do?"

The Master of Ceremonies of the Upper Assembly Rooms bowed. "Very well, Lady Pennworth, and may I say how marvellous it is to see you at Bath again."

For an older gentleman, Mr King was rather attractive, with dark, silver-streaked hair swept into a Brutus, and classic features softened a little by good living and a perpetual, sincere smile. It seemed that Aunt had also noticed his charms, for she touched her coiffure, the colour in her cheeks deepening.

Mr King turned to Helen. "It is always a great pleasure to

see you too, Lady Helen. Does the Duke accompany you?"

"Alas, no, he is at Chenwith."

"We do not see him here often. I do hope your good influence will change that situation."

Helen smiled; she doubted it. Selburn did not like public assemblies. A distaste, he said, built from too many years being the prime catch upon the marriage mart and the target of designing mamas.

"You have a sad crush tonight, Mr King," Aunt said. "Congratulations."

He laughed. "I cannot claim the triumph, my lady. This is Mr Ashe's doing. He organises the concerts."

"But I hear you have made a great success of your role," Aunt said. "All whom I meet say that it has been a seamless transition from Mr Tyson's rule to your own. Particularly with the balls."

Mr King bowed. "I am glad to hear it. I have made it my mission to carry on his excellent program." His smile angled into droll self-interest. "And since the subject has been raised, I do hope you and your niece will attend our fancy ball tomorrow night. We would be most honoured if Lady Helen would consent to lead our dancing."

Aunt laughed. "I am sure my niece will be most eager to don a costume and dance. Is it not so, Helen?"

Helen nodded. "I would be very pleased to lead." A fancy ball would be a good place to display the fob.

She reached up to touch it upon its ribbon again, drawing Mr King's eyes. He frowned. Was it in disapproval or *recognition*?

Helen's heart quickened. "I see you have marked my pendant, sir."

"Forgive me, it is a most curious decoration for a young

lady." He smiled to soften the observation. "Is that an etching upon it?"

"Yes, of Bacchus." Helen watched his face; there was definitely something behind his bonhomie.

"Ah, yes. I thought I recognised it."

She stared at him. "You recognise it?"

"Certainly. It looks to be the same design that is on Captain Wade's fob."

It felt as if everything around her had stopped, the whole world fixed upon Mr King. "Captain Wade? Is he here tonight? Can you point out the gentleman?"

"He is always here, Lady Helen," Mr King said. He glanced at Aunt, who smiled in some kind of collusion, then motioned to the Octagon Room behind them. "Come, allow me to introduce you to him. I can then show you to your seats. There is a far less crowded doorway that will take us into the tea room."

Helen followed Aunt and Mr King through the crowd, which parted with curtseys and bows before the elegant Master of Ceremonies. A glance behind still did not find Lord Carlston, yet she could feel the beat between them, strong and close. The Octagon Room was, as promised, less populated. During balls, it was set up for cards for those who did not wish to dance, but tonight it was bare of baize-covered tables, and chairs were set around its perimeter. The room's four handsome marble chimney pieces burned with good fires, each surrounded by ladies seeking an antidote to the lightness of their muslin gowns, and the gentlemen who, by duty or design, accompanied them. None of the men, however, wore an officer's red or a navy man's blue. Where was this Captain Wade?

Mr King led the way across the room to stand at one of the walls. "Lady Helen, allow me to introduce Captain Wade." He motioned to a large, full-length portrait of a handsome man bewigged in the old-fashioned way and clad in red coat and breeches.

"It is a portrait," Helen said, rather unnecessarily.

"Painted by Mr Gainsborough no less, in 1771," Mr King said. "Captain Wade was the first Master of Ceremonies of the Upper Rooms when it opened, and held the position until 1777 when..." He glanced at Aunt, as if seeking guidance upon his next words.

"When he was obliged to leave Bath and take up residence in Brighton," Aunt said. She observed Helen for a moment, then added, "Well, you are almost a married woman so I shall tell you the truth. He was named in a divorce case. I was only about fifteen at the time and it was quite the scandal."

"He was called the Bath Adonis for good reason," Mr King said.

Helen looked back at the portrait; the captain's face did have a most knowing look upon it.

Mr King pointed to the lapel of Wade's jacket. "Do you see? There is the gold decoration similar to your own."

Helen stepped closer. Indeed, a gold disc attached to the captain's lapel held an etched figure of Bacchus exactly the same as the one on the Comte's fob. The painting of it was astonishingly detailed for an artist like Gainsborough, whose style was usually more loose. But what did it mean? The man in the portrait was at least in his fourth decade, and it had been painted over forty years ago.

"Is Captain Wade still alive?" Helen asked.

Mr King shook his head. "Sadly, he passed away three years ago."

Lud, would she never find a solid path to this Bath Deceiver? "Did he have any children?"

Mr King gave a small, self-conscious laugh. "I have never

been asked that before. I am not certain, but I believe he had children with his first wife."

"But none with Elizabeth Campbell," Aunt said. She lowered her voice again. "They married, you know, after his first wife died."

Mr King nodded. "A happy ending."

"Not for the first wife, one would presume," Aunt said dryly.

"Do any of his children live here at Bath?" Helen asked.

"I am sure Mr King has not memorised the whereabouts of Captain Wade's connections, Helen," Aunt said.

"I'm afraid Lady Pennworth is correct, Lady Helen. May I ask your interest in the captain's history?"

"I am interested in all of Bath history," she said, the statement lame even to her own ears. She ignored her aunt's stare of disbelief.

Mr King smiled kindly. "Then I will endeavour to find out more for you." He bowed. "I believe the concert will start soon. Shall we make our way to our seats?"

Lady Dunwick and Pug had managed to secure a line of chairs at the front of the tea room, close to the orchestra. Pug waved them over vigorously, pointing to the two empty seats between herself and Lady Margaret. With nods of farewell to Mr King, Helen and her aunt made their way through the company to join their companions.

The fireplaces had been lit here as well, and with the huge cut-glass chandeliers blazing with candles, and the large audience, the room was edging towards hot. Most ladies had unfurled their fans, and the fluttering silk and ivory shifted the warm, pungent air against Helen's skin as she passed the rows of gilt-edged chairs.

"Where have you been?" Pug whispered. "You missed the most delightful officers from the 10th Light. They will be at the ball tomorrow and have reserved dances with myself and Miss Cransdon."

"Elizabeth!" her mother whispered, waving her quiet.

As Mr Ashe welcomed the audience and outlined the concert program, Helen lifted her lorgnette to her eyes, twisting in her seat to scan the settling audience. Pale blue energy surrounded every figure: all human, not one skimming Deceiver. Very odd. Perhaps another gathering in town held more energy potential for the creatures. Even so, there should be at least one or two Hedons feeding amongst Bath's music lovers.

She lowered her glasses, her attention caught by a tall figure at the corner of her eye. Carlston. She felt her heart lurch, the beat of their bond thundering in her chest.

He met her eyes, his mouth tensing: *Are you all right?*

She gave a small nod and lifted her brows: *And you?*

He touched his forehead, a wry quirk of his mouth answering: *I am now.* He had felt the manifestations too. A knit of his brow asked: *What happened?*

"Helen, the concert is about to start," Aunt whispered. "What are you doing?"

Helen jerked back to face the orchestra, sending her aunt an apologetic smile. "Such a large audience," she murmured.

Had Aunt noticed Carlston in the corner? It seemed not, for she settled back, eyeing Helen with only mild irritation.

Helen dared not look around again. If she wished to speak to Carlston, she must wait for the intermission and find some way of escaping her aunt's watchful eye.

The orchestra struck up the start of the Haydn grand sinfonia, but Helen only half listened, her body too aware of Carlston in the room, her mind set upon the conundrum of Captain Wade. It was exciting to find evidence of another fob existing – but what did the captain's ownership of it mean? Could he have been the

Bath Deceiver? Possibly, but he was dead now, and his life had been built in Brighton, not Bath. Could he have passed into one of his children and now be living in Bath? Maybe – Sir Jonathan would need to trace his progeny. And then there was Beau Nash. Was he in any way related to Captain Wade? Yet, Sir Jonathan had found no evidence that the Beau had been a Deceiver, or indeed had any progeny. Had she been entirely mistaken about the fob on his statue?

The frustrating questions played over and over in her mind, her attention only briefly caught by the need to clap at the end of each performance. Finally, intermission was called. Helen glanced over her shoulder. Carlston still stood near the back, this time with Hammond at his side. Both men were looking her way.

She tilted her head to the door that led to the antechamber. It would be a risk to meet amongst so many acquaintances, but she had to tell him about the ghosts. Carlston nodded, and both men turned to join the mass of people heading out of the tea room.

Helen leaned forward in her seat to catch Lady Margaret's eye – *Follow my lead* – then stood and said, "It is so hot in here. I believe I will seek some fresher air in the entrance hall."

"You cannot go out alone, Helen," Aunt said. "I will come—"

"Allow me, Lady Pennworth," Lady Margaret said, standing abruptly and ushering Helen along the row. "I will be happy to accompany her. We shall not be long."

One advantage of her impending marriage, Helen thought as they forged a way through the throng, would be an end to such assiduous chaperonage. A married woman had so much more freedom. She would even be able to drive out with Carlston if she felt like it, which would make things a great deal easier as one half of the Grand Reclaimer. Mind you, she could not see Selburn embracing the idea. Well, he must – at least until they defeated the Grand Deceiver. *If* they defeated the Grand Deceiver. She twitched her shoulders, trying to shake off the dread that accompanied the dark qualification.

"Will you keep an eye out for my aunt or Lady Dunwick?" she said close to Lady Margaret's ear. "I need to speak to Carlston."

"Of course." Lady Margaret nodded towards one of the columns that marked the entrance to the Octagon Room. "He is over there, with Michael."

It took them a good five minutes to work their way through the chattering crowd, most of the delay caused by Mrs Osgood, an acquaintance of Lady Margaret's, who had a great deal to impart about purchasing Chippendale dining chairs. Finally, they made the columns and curtseyed.

"Lord Carlston, how do you do," Helen said. "And Mr Hammond. I had not expected to see you here."

The two men bowed.

"It is a great pleasure to see you again," Carlston said formally.

Although the antechamber was crowded, a small circle of space had formed around Lord Carlston. The elderly Viscount Glanwis had even pointedly turned his back. Bath, it seemed, was abuzz with the possibility that Lord Carlston's wife was still alive and, in fact, a spy whom he had helped escape back to France. It certainly gave credence to Lady Georgina's claim that she had heard about Lady Elise in town.

Carlston leaned one hand upon the column, the relaxed stance giving every indication that he had not noticed the *cut direct*, but Helen could see the hard set of his jaw. It must be galling, she thought, to move from murderer to traitor and once again be tried in the court of gossip.

She pitched her voice in the soft tone reserved for Reclaimer ears and spoke in Italian, doubting any of those nearby would be fluent in the language. "*Sono venuti due fantasmi questa mattina.*" Two ghosts came this morning. "*Darby li fermò, ma era sbalordita inconscia dal loro potere.*" Darby stopped them, but she was stunned unconscious by their power.

Carlston frowned. "*È recuperata?*" Is she recovered?

"*Fortunatamente si è recuperata rapidamente, ma è stato un crollo spaventoso. Peggio ancora prima.*" Thankfully she recovered quickly, but it was a frightening collapse. Worse than before.

Carlston rubbed his fingers across his mouth, considering her words. He continued in Italian. "It is escalating. We must not use our power until we can close the rift."

A relief to hear him say it. Even so, it begged another question. "What if we find the Grand Deceiver? We must be able to use this power to defeat them."

"You said it before: we cannot risk killing ourselves before we even face them." Carlston touched his forehead. "I felt the ghosts manifest too. At least, I felt the power leaking out from the—" He stopped.

Ligatus, Helen supplied silently. Yes, best not to say the word in company, even amidst a conversation in Italian.

He gave a grim smile. "I was out of my lodgings and halfway to the Royal Crescent before I knew it. Then I felt the power stop. That must have been when Darby was stunned."

"You were coming?" She bit her lip. Too much gladness in her voice, and quite the wrong detail to focus upon.

"I had little choice. It was as if I was being drawn by the power."

"Ah, I see." The alchemical bond. "I have found another fob," she said abruptly. "In the portrait of Captain Wade in the Octagon Room. On his lapel."

Carlston drew his mouth down. "But if I recall correctly, he is dead these past few years?"

She nodded. "It does not make sense to me either, but I will write to Sir Jonathan to trace his progeny."

Lady Margaret tugged Helen's sleeve, a glance gathering Carlston into the warning. "Your aunt."

Helen looked over her shoulder. Aunt had just emerged from the concert room with Pug and Lady Dunwick in tow, the older ladies searching the crowd with some intent.

"Hammond, I will see you back at the lodgings," Carlston said in English. He bowed to Helen. *"Almeno domani avremo qualcosa di reale per festeggiare."* At least tomorrow we will have something real to celebrate.

Helen watched him weave deftly through the crowd and into the Octagon Room then, with a bright smile, she turned to greet her aunt.

Chapter Fifteen

THURSDAY, 17 DECEMBER 1812

Helen and Darby stood on the wet pavement outside Number 20 Queen's Square, formerly the lodging of Lord Carlston and now that of Mr and Mrs Pike. The Square was no longer one of the fashionable addresses in Bath, but it still held the majesty of John Wood's design. The uniform colonnaded frontages of the townhouses made it seem as if they were all one magnificent palace; and the pleasure garden at the centre of the square, designed around an imposing obelisk dedicated to Frederick, Prince of Wales, brought a touch of nature into the busy town setting.

"Are you ready to go in?" Helen asked over the grind of a colliers cart passing behind them. Even at eight thirty on a misty December morning, a steady stream of carriages, wagons, sedan chairs and pedestrians hurried through the square.

Darby gave a nod and pulled her new Norwich shawl tighter around her shoulders. The rich brown and gold weave suited her, Helen thought, pleased with her choice of wedding gift. She had also gifted, from her own wardrobe, the hastily altered navy-blue silk gown that Darby wore – a good colour for her too, although the fit was a little rushed – and one guinea, an amount that had brought tears to Darby's eyes when she had opened the hand-knitted purse.

They climbed the stone steps, the door opening as they approached it. Mr Pike stood holding it, a thin smile upon his lips. Probably as welcoming as the man could get, Helen thought.

He gave a small bow. "The vicar is already here," he said in way of greeting. "We are ready to proceed."

Helen felt Darby's hand clutch hers in a moment of exquisite excitement.

They followed Pike into the slightly worn but still handsome hallway, their boots leaving a wet track upon the black-and-white tiled floor.

"Mrs Pike and I have the first-floor lodgings," he explained, leading the way up the staircase. "A most comfortable situation. It has been a boon for Mrs Pike to have such easy access to her treatments."

"How does she fare?" Helen asked.

Pike's shoulders lifted. Not so well, Helen thought.

"The baths are very beneficial," he said firmly. "We are holding the ceremony in the parlour so as not to disturb her rest. The breakfast will be in the dining room."

"The breakfast?" Darby echoed as they turned the first landing.

"Lord Carlston has ordered a repast from Molland's."

"Molland's," Darby breathed. "How kind!"

Helen smiled. Kindness indeed. She had not known that was part of the plan.

They reached the Pikes' lodgings. The smell of the repast – fresh bread, a spiced meat dish and newly brewed coffee, if Helen was not mistaken – scented the air. She drew in a deep breath; she had fasted in solidarity with Darby and felt the sharp pang of it.

Pike opened the door to a front room and stepped back as they entered. The room had once been the townhouse's drawing room: a large, elegant apartment with a classically inspired marble mantelpiece set now with a generous fire, and two tall windows that overlooked the garden. That was all Helen registered, for standing in a group near the window were Carlston, Quinn and a gentleman in sober black, presumably the vicar.

"The bride has arrived," Lord Carlston said, bowing, but his eyes were upon Helen, not Darby. A look of worried assessment. *Any more ghosts?*

She gave a small shake of her head. He must already know, for he would have felt them, but she was glad of the concern.

Darby curtseyed, her smile broadening as she found Quinn, resplendent in his freshly brushed blue Sunday jacket, a red Belcher kerchief and buckskins.

He crossed the room and took her hand; everyone else, it seemed, quite forgotten. "You look so fine, Jen."

She gave a little skip of excitement. "My lady gave me the dress and the shawl." She placed a hand upon his arm and whispered, "And a whole guinea, Nathaniel. Can you warrant it?"

"Lady Helen," Carlston said, calling her attention away from the couple, "may I present Mr Redmond. He will be officiating today."

The vicar, a rather spare, mid-aged man with greying hair, bowed with considerable dignity. "My lady, may I offer my felicitations on your own betrothal."

"Thank you," Helen said.

He turned to Darby and Quinn. "Lord Carlston has supplied the special licence, so we are ready to proceed. If you will step aside with me, I shall explain the service." He drew them away, murmuring instructions.

Carlston leaned in closer to Helen. "So, no manifestations last night."

She smelled a faint, pleasant scent of cologne upon his navy-blue jacket. He had, she noticed, switched his usual immaculate cravat for a neatly tied blue Belcher, in keeping with Quinn's dress. It suited him.

"I am sure it is because Darby slept beside me," she answered.

"I think so too, which means she must continue to do so, at least for the time being. A rather unfortunate situation, considering what we are about to witness." He smoothed down the back of his hair, uncharacteristic awkwardness in his bearing. "Forgive me for mentioning this, but if you are amenable, I thought we could relieve Darby and Quinn of their duties tonight while we attend the fancy ball at the Upper Rooms. Give them, at least, that time together."

Helen felt heat rise through her body, settling in her cheeks. Lud, she must be scarlet all over. "Of course."

"Shall we begin?" Mr Redmond said, ushering Quinn and Darby to stand before the hearth. "Lady Helen, if you stand beside Miss Darby; and Lord Carlston and Mr Pike, beside Mr Quinn."

Everyone took their positions. The vicar opened his *Book of Common Prayer* and, with one last inquiring look at the bride and groom, began.

"Dearly beloved, we are gathered together here in the sight of God, and in the face of this congregation..." He paused, eyeing Helen, Carlston and Pike. "This congregation," he repeated a little dryly, "to join together this Man and this Woman in holy Matrimony; which is an honourable estate, instituted of God in the time of man's innocency, signifying unto us the mystical union..."

Helen closed her eyes to settle the hot discomfort that still lingered in her cheeks, and to listen to the solemn and beautiful words that were binding Quinn and Darby together. They were like music, and the Reclaimer beat in her body pulsed beneath them like a joyous counterpoint.

"Nathaniel Quinn, wilt thou have this Woman to thy wedded Wife, to live together after God's ordinance in the holy estate of Matrimony? Wilt thou love her, comfort her, honour, and keep her in sickness and in health; and, forsaking all other, keep thee only unto her, so long as ye both shall live?"

"I will," Quinn said. So much elation in those two simple words.

In just a few weeks, Helen thought, she would be saying the same vow before a congregation in the Abbey. A rather unnerving prospect. And she too must think of her wedding night. How was she to explain to Selburn that Darby must sleep in the same bed?

She opened her eyes as the vicar turned to Darby. "Jennifer Rose Darby, wilt thou have this Man to thy wedded Husband, to live together after God's ordinance in the holy estate of Matrimony? Wilt thou obey him, and serve him, love, honour, and keep him in sickness and in health; and, forsaking all other, keep thee only unto him, so long as ye both shall live?"

Please, let it be a long life, Helen prayed. *They deserve happiness.*

"I will," Darby said.

Helen felt the Reclaimer beat within her deepen, and glanced at Carlston. Their eyes connected for an unexpected, breathless second, and Darby's words melded into the beat that thundered through her body: *I will, I will, I will.* Did he feel it too? Could he hear the vow singing in his blood, drumming through his heart?

Helen wrenched her eyes back to the ceremony.

"The ring, please," the vicar said, holding out his prayer book. "Now, place the ring upon her finger and repeat after me..."

With gentle delicacy, Quinn slid the gold circlet onto Darby's finger, and held it between his finger and thumb as he echoed the vicar's words. "With this Ring I thee wed, with my Body I thee worship, and with all my worldly Goods I thee endow: In the Name of the Father, and of the Son, and of the Holy Ghost. Amen."

Mr Redmond began the final blessing, but Helen hardly heard the words, all her attention fixed upon resisting the draw of Carlston's eyes. She clenched her teeth, forcing back the overwhelming thud of the Reclaimer bond. So hard to restrain it. What would happen if she just let go – let loose the wild, alchemical force? She'd had a taste of it in Kate Holt's bawdy house: that dizzying, glorious kiss, all restraint gone for a few frenzied moments until she could contain the fire. But what if she did let go again and could not pull it back? What would happen beyond that immediate soaring release?

She drew a shaking breath, dread squeezing her chest. It would be a betrayal of everything she held sacred: honour, family, duty, her word. A selfish betrayal of a good man's heart, and a step forever out of all that was respectable and modest. For what? A bond that was built from death and destruction. A mere physical attraction that any decent person would hold in contempt.

The vicar placed Darby's hand into Quinn's, uniting them before the Almighty. "Those whom God hath joined together let no man put asunder," he intoned, then turned to Helen, Carlston and Pike. "Forasmuch as Nathaniel Quinn and Jennifer Rose Darby have consented together in holy Wedlock, and have witnessed the same before God and this company, and thereto have given and pledged their troth either to other, and have declared the same by giving and receiving of a Ring, and by joining of hands; I pronounce that they be Man and Wife together, In the Name of the Father, and of the Son, and of the Holy Ghost. Amen."

"Amen," Helen said. Amen to a bond of decency and faithfulness.

The vicar closed the prayer book and smiled. "Congratulations, Mr and Mrs Quinn."

For a second, there was silence, and then Darby laughed, the sound bubbling with delight. "I am Mrs Quinn!"

This was not the time for dark thoughts. Helen took Darby's gloved hands in her own, and pulled her into a hug. "Congratulations, my dear Mrs Quinn. And to you, Mr Quinn." She drew back. "Lud, am I to call you Quinn now, Darby? That will rather let the cat out of the bag."

Darby shook her head. "I shall remain Jen Darby for now, my lady, until after your wedding." She looked up at her new husband with a tender smile. "Then we shall tell everyone."

Quinn nodded, returning the sweet smile. "It is what we have agreed, my lady."

Helen stepped aside to allow Carlston to offer his congratulations. As if by mutual consent they were keeping a careful distance from one another, eyes skipping past any connection, all attention upon the newlyweds. Yet she felt as if her treacherous body reached towards him, tracking his every move.

She turned to Pike. "It is good of you to allow them to marry here."

His wintry smile appeared. "I could hardly refuse his lordship, could I? Not after he gave up these lodgings for Isabella." He observed the Quinns, his smile fading. "I was just as happy at my own wedding, you know."

"Is Isabella very ill?" Helen asked softly.

"She no longer knows who I am." So much pain in his voice.

Helen touched his arm. "I am sorry."

"Not a subject for a wedding breakfast, I think." He turned to the company and motioned to the doorway. "Shall we go through to the dining room? I have readied the documents there to sign, and then we may toast the bride and groom. Mr and Mrs Quinn, if you will lead us?"

Quinn, with a bow, offered his arm to his new wife. Darby, with a great air, placed her hand upon the crook of his elbow, then added a small poke to his ribs that set him laughing.

Helen smiled. It was indeed a good match.

"Lady Helen?"

"Lord Carlston," she said, finally looking into his face again. There, she could meet his eyes, ignore the fullness within them. She could walk this path of control.

"May I escort you?"

She tucked her hand into the crook of his arm and walked by his side into the dining room, ignoring the beat in her body that still whispered, *I will, I will, I will*.

Later that afternoon, after a light luncheon, the ladies at the Royal Crescent repaired upstairs to ready themselves for their shopping trip to Milsom Street.

"I am sorry you cannot be with Mr Quinn until tonight," Helen said with what she thought was excellent composure, as Darby worked a glove onto her hand. "You should be on your wedding tour, not standing outside shops at Bath."

Darby glanced up with a wry smile. "People like me and Mr Quinn don't go on wedding tours, my lady. I remember in my village, one of the farmers got married and he and his new wife were back milking the cows two hours later. Mr Quinn and I are blessed by what we have, my lady. You and his lord-ship have been so kind." She picked up the second glove with a frown. "I am not convinced this shade of yellow goes well with your olive spencer, my lady. What do you think?"

Finally, with gloves, spencer and bonnet suitably matched, Helen and Darby joined the rest of the shopping party in the foyer. The dispersal of the rain clouds prompted the more intrepid members to declare a desire for exercise. Thus it was only Lady Dunwick, Aunt and Lady Georgina who took the carriage. Helen, Delia, Lady Margaret and Pug – in the company of a footman and Darby – set off on foot, wrapped in scarves and shawls, with the goal of meeting the other ladies in Slack's Warehouse at two o'clock.

As they turned the corner into George Street, they saw that some kind of spectacle was in progress at the top of Milsom Street. A large crowd had gathered, stopping all thoroughfare on both roads.

"We should go around the other way," Lady Margaret said, but Pug, ever curious, forged ahead into the outer circle of spectators.

"What is happening?" she asked, rising on her toes in an effort to see past a broad lady sporting a very tall shako hat.

"Some kind of acrobatic act," Helen reported, her height bringing the advantage. Over the bobbing expanse of beaver hats and feathered bonnets she found a board propped against the streetlamp. "They are advertising a holiday spectacle next week at the Theatre Royal: *The Knight and the Wood Daemon.*"

A girl in a green costume trailing diaphanous scarves suddenly spun up into the air above the crowd, the astonishing height prompting a draw of collective breath. Her partner, a sturdy young man, caught her deftly by her feet, holding her upright without a tremble in his arms. Laughs of relief rose from the audience.

"Oh, how thrilling!" Pug said, clapping along with the thud-thud-thud of gloved applause. "Did you see that?"

"Lady Helen, over here," Delia called from the doorway of Godwin's circulating library, which was set at an angle on the corner. Helen shuffled back in the crowd and felt Delia grab her arm, steering her up onto the step. "We thought it best to get out of the way." She motioned vigorously to Pug. "Lady Elizabeth!"

"Darby?" Helen called.

"Here, my lady!" She had tucked herself against the wall, beside Lady Dunwick's footman.

"Watch your belongings," Lady Margaret said, moving back to allow Pug onto the step. "The pickpockets will make the most of this opportunity."

Not only the pickpockets, Helen thought. Deceivers too. She hooked her finger around her lorgnette cord and pulled out the spectacles from beneath her pelisse. Raising them to her eyes, she saw pale blue energy spring up around every figure in the crowd. There, just as she had thought: a thick, grey feeder tentacle reached like a huge blindworm across oblivious shoulders and backs, pulsating as it sucked upon the life forces of those it caressed. Through the glasses, she followed its foul, undulating length back to the vibrant blue energy of the feeding Deceiver, but the creature itself was hidden from view by two footmen watching the impromptu show from behind burdens of hatboxes and parcels. Helen lowered the lorgnette. Was it one of the sixteen Deceivers already identified, or a new one?

The acrobat girl was spinning in the air again, her feet landing in the steady grip of her partner to more applause. Just as she bent into a handstand upon his shoulders, a woman in the crowd pointed to two men striding down George Street with an air of stern authority. Someone, it seemed, had alerted the constables.

Whispers and nudges rippled through the audience, and Helen noticed a few smoky types slipping back into shops and disappearing into the deepening winter shadows. The two footmen exchanged glances – time for a prudent return to their post – and edged towards Milsom Street, leaving the back of the Deceiver in clear view. A woman, in a stylish navy-blue bonnet and burgundy pelisse.

As if she felt Helen's regard, she turned. Mrs Knoll. Again.

She boldly held Helen's gaze, her navy-gloved hand pressed to her mouth as if stifling a laugh, eyes bright with such an expression of disdain that Helen felt herself rock onto her toes, fists clenched for battle. Two encounters now. Surely that could not be a coincidence.

"Is that the Deceiver from Molland's?" Delia asked, close to her ear. "She has a most insolent look upon her face."

"I am sure I know her from somewhere."

"London?"

"I don't know. Perhaps. It is not her face I recognise, but..." Helen shook her head. The memory was just out of reach. "I am going to confront her."

"I think you have missed the opportunity," Delia said.

Indeed, Mrs Knoll was pushing past her fellow spectators, making for the far side of Milsom Street. Helen gauged the crowd between them: too densely packed to make it across with normal speed, and no good reason to move at Reclaimer speed. Damn. She watched as the Deceiver emerged from the throng, then walked rapidly beyond the corner buildings and out of sight. Not even a backward glance.

"What a fine display," Pug said as the constables sent the

acrobats on their way and waved their audience back into the business of the day. "We should take tickets for the spectacle."

"I am sure we will have returned to Chenwith by then," Lady Margaret said. A rather ungracious rejoinder to a good-natured suggestion, Helen thought.

They abandoned the step and made their way around the corner into Milsom Street. The sudden slap of freezing wind tucked Helen's chin into the folds of her scarf. She strode ahead, Reclaimer sight attuned to any flash of blue bonnet or burgundy pelisse amongst the pedestrians, carriages and sedan chairs in motion upon the street. But of course there was none; the Deceiver was well and truly gone.

Delia caught up to walk at her side. "Do you think she is following you?"

"She was in the crowd before us, so it is unlikely."

"Even so, she seemed awfully interested in you."

True, and it was a troubling thought. Helen rubbed her forehead; why could she not remember the woman?

In the distance, the clock in the Abbey tower showed five past two. They were late to meet Aunt and Lady Dunwick.

Helen quickened her pace past Mr Evill's Auction Rooms – a sign at the doorway advertising crockery meant for America but now stranded in Bath by the war. On the busy road beside them, a gap opened up between a jaunty gig and a slow-moving cart. With a wave to the others, Helen gathered up the hem of her gown and led the way across the dung-strewn road. On the other side, Lady Margaret and Delia were immediately drawn to the display of new hats in Spornberg's window. Pug stopped to listen to a hawker crying out the benefits of the *wondrous Egyptian Elixir, guaranteed to reduce inches from all areas of the body* until Helen back-tracked and took her arm.

"It is all hum," Helen said as she steered Pug firmly towards the others still viewing the hats. "Probably nothing more than water with a bit of colour."

"Still," Pug sighed. "It would be lovely to just drink away one's excess flesh."

Although it was early afternoon, Spornberg's had already placed evening lamps in their window to combat the wintry closing in of the day, the soft yellow light catching a gleam of gold braid on a cap and the sheen on a red velvet bonnet. Further along the street, Slack's Warehouse, too, had illuminated their display of gold-and-blue cashmere saris with clusters of exotic Moorish brass lamps.

Helen pushed open the drapery's door, the bell above it swinging into a tinny peal. The smell of cloth – a mix of dye and dust, wool oil and fresh cotton – came in a rush of warmer air.

"You may come inside too," Helen told Darby and the footman. No one should have to wait on the street in such inclement weather.

They all filed into the shop. A slim young man in a well-fitted brown jacket and professional smile immediately emerged from behind one of the two long wooden counters set on either side of the shop. Huge rolls of vivid velvets, diaphanous white muslins, sprigged cambrics and fine merino wools were stacked up against each wall, and silk saris hung from a row of rods to show their intricate borders.

"Are Lady Pennworth and Lady Dunwick here?" Helen asked.

"Ah, I thought I heard your voice, my dear." Aunt emerged from behind a stand of rich brocades in the inner reaches of the shop. She beckoned. "I have found a number of satins and French nets that you should look at, and a rather pretty blue moire silk that might do for a wedding trip spencer."

Delia leaned closer to Helen. "Lady Margaret and I are going to view the muslins," she whispered. "Good luck."

"Cowards," Helen hissed back, earning a giggle from Delia.

Helen and Pug followed the young shop assistant further into the shop, where Aunt, Lady Dunwick and Lady Georgina perused the satin display.

"Oh my," Pug breathed, craning her neck to view the rolls of gleaming satins stacked high on the shelves. "Look at that blue! And the pink. Oh, that pink is magnificent."

"Do you think so?" Lady Georgina asked. "Is it not a trifle overblown?"

"It won't do for Helen's colouring," Aunt said briskly. She pointed to a roll of mid-green at shoulder height. "Now this would do very well."

The young man deftly drew it from its home and offered the bolt for inspection. "It is called Willow, my lady. Just in."

Helen touched the cloth; stiffer than expected, but with a luxurious smoothness to it. "It would hold the sleeve shape well."

"And slashed with gold it would be most striking," Lady Dunwick offered.

They all considered the possibility.

"Too dark perhaps?" Aunt conceded. She waved it away and pointed to a cream satin. "This is very like the cloth we had for your presentation ball gown, but with silver net over it." As they waited for the young man to slot back the green bolt and pull out the cream, Aunt added, "That reminds me, Helen, you will never guess whom I saw on the street."

"Bonaparte?"

Aunt raised her eyebrows at the quip. "No, that footman who ran off the night of your ball. What was his name? He had the temerity to bow and address me as if we were acquaintances."

Helen's breathing locked. "Philip?" she managed. Dear God,

the harbinger of the Grand Deceiver, in Bath. The encounter with Aunt could not have been chance – he wanted them to know he was in town. But why?

"Yes, that's him. Such a scoundrel," Aunt continued. "He said he hoped you would meet soon. The insolence. I have half a mind to report him to—"

"Meet me?" Helen said. Was it an attempt at a trap? Possibly, but Philip had seemed to be under instruction not to harm her. Unless that had changed since Brighton. Either way, it was the first sign of action from the Grand Deceiver in over five months, and Philip had been the last one in possession of the Colligat set inside her mother's miniature. If she could retrieve it, the Trinitas would be complete.

Helen grabbed her aunt's arm. "Where did you see him? When?"

"Just before we came in here. On the corner of Quiet Street. Why?"

He had probably already gone, but she had to be certain. Hitching up her hems, she ran, boot soles thudding on the wooden floors.

"Helen, what are you doing?" Aunt's voice was shrill. "Where are you going?"

Out of the corner of her eye, Helen saw Lady Margaret and Delia peer out from between bolts of velvet, and then she was passing the long counters, another shop assistant gaping at her unseemly sprint.

Darby stepped out of an alcove. "My lady, what's wrong?"

Helen wrenched open the door, the bell tinkling maniacally. "Philip!"

Darby thrust the basket she carried into the footman's hands and followed Helen through the door, Lady Margaret and Delia a few steps behind. They all stopped in the middle of the pavement, the flow of pedestrians parting around them. Helen looked wildly down the busy thoroughfare, wincing as the noise roared in her Reclaimer ears. A misty rain wet the air, the fall of fine droplets caught in the lamplight from Slack's doorway.

"Philip is here?" Lady Margaret asked over the rumble and grind of the carriages and carts.

"My aunt saw him. He said he wanted to meet."

"A trap, surely, my lady?" Darby protested.

"My thought too, but I am no longer the half-trained girl he saw in Brighton." Lud, she could not get her bearings. "Which one is Quiet Street?"

"Down there, to the right." Delia pointed across the road.

A loaded cart blocked the view. Helen rose on her toes as it trundled past, but the gap between it and the coach following offered only a glimpse of the opposite corner. The angle was wrong; only the Milsom Street side was in view.

A larger space had opened up between the coach and a handcart being pushed laboriously up the hill. Reclaimer speed was out of the question; too many witnesses. Human speed then. Helen launched herself between the two vehicles, slipping on wet dung. She recovered in the next step, and heard Darby's grunt of disgust behind as she stepped in the same mess. They made the opposite pavement together, their unseemly dash spinning a delighted gentleman around to watch. Helen ducked between three matronly shoppers, their gasps following her, and almost collided with the edge of the undertaker's bow window, only a wild skipping sidestep saving her from impact.

She looked over her shoulder. Darby was trapped behind the three women, her warm breath rising in puffs of apology as she backtracked and skirted around them.

Across the road, Delia dodged between pedestrians, her neck craned to keep sight of Helen beyond the vehicles. Lady

Margaret ran behind, gown and pelisse caught up in her hand, clearly trying to stop her friend's headlong dash.

Delia should know by now that a face-to-face confrontation with a Deceiver was no place for an aide, Helen thought.

The Quiet Street corner was only three shops away, the lamps above the doorways of Molland's Pastry shop and White's Instruments casting yellow glows that lit the drizzling rain and painted a moment of gold upon passing faces. She sorted through the male shadowy figures hurrying about their business – too short, too fat, too hunched – and then a frisson shivered across her scalp. There, beside the streetlamp.

Philip watched her approach, his arms crossed nonchalantly over his greatcoat, the light illuminating the curl of red hair beneath his grey hat and the gleam of his satisfied smile. And beside him, an older woman. Burgundy pelisse and blue bonnet. Mrs Knoll.

Helen felt the Reclaimer beat within her quicken, hammering alarm. Could Carlston feel it? Would he know what it meant? The call to battle rolled through her body like a fireball, her fast breath misting before her face. Yet she could not just launch herself at them. Not in the street. And certainly not with the Ligatus power untamed and primed to explode.

She slowed, groping for her lorgnette, and raised the spectacles to her eyes. Mrs Knoll, in league with Philip. Who was this woman? The tantalising memory hovered at the edge of her mind, but she could not grab hold of it.

Pale blue light blossomed around every person on the street, almost blinding her with its intensity in the gloom. She blinked to adjust her eyes, then focused on the vivid ultramarine light that surrounded the two Deceivers. They each had a whip – a thick tentacle of dark blue energy rooted between their shoulder blades and curling above their heads, like raised scorpion tails.

Somewhere, two innocent people were dead; killed to make those weapons.

Helen bit down on her fury and stopped a few yards from the brightly lit pair. The itch of their energy crawled across her skin. Their whips were a plain message of violent intent, but surely they would not use them in a busy street?

She shrugged off the speculation. She had trained for this moment for the last six months. They only had one whip each; and even without the Ligatus power, she had her Reclaimer combat skills. If they did dare to attack, she was ready: every sense primed, her mind clear and focused.

Behind her, she felt the arrival of her Terrene's solid presence, heard her breath coming in short huffs. At the corner of her eye, the pale blue forms of Delia and Lady Margaret crossed the road towards them. She waved them back, but dared not shift her attention from the Deceivers.

"Lady Helen, how pleasant to see you again," Philip said, unfolding his arms, the vivid blue around him leaving a momentary trail in the damp air.

"How did you know my aunt would tell me you were here?"

"I worked in her house for six months. The woman could not keep anything to herself."

Helen narrowed her eyes at his insolence. "So now I am here. What do you want?" She nodded towards Mrs Knoll, whose disdainful smile was still in place. "Who is she? Another minion?"

Philip cocked his head, the light catching upon the sharp plane of his freckled cheekbone. "Do you not recognise her?" He gave a soft laugh, and Mrs Knoll joined in with a lighter feminine trill, her gloved hand covering her mouth. "But then, I suppose you wouldn't."

Helen heard Darby gasp – a sound of recognition – just as

Delia and Lady Margaret stepped onto the pavement.

"Go back to the shop," Helen hissed at them.

Too late. Mrs Knoll took a few sauntering steps across the pavement to stand beside the two women, her ultramarine whip slightly weaving from side to side like the tail of an irritated cat.

Although they could not see it, both Delia and Lady Margaret stiffened. They knew enough to understand they had made a strategic mistake.

"We have business to attend to," Philip said, straightening from his lounge against the streetlamp. His whip drew back further into a menacing curl.

Was he still under instruction to avoid all combat with her, Helen wondered. She could not rely upon it.

She risked a glance at White's side window. In its reflection, the pale blue forms of Lady Margaret and Delia stepped closer together, uncertainty writ on their faces. Nearby, the glowing forms of two chairmen carrying an empty sedan chair stopped to watch the strange tableau of a lady of quality in some kind of stand-off with a smoky cove. A servant girl stopped as well, her curiosity drawing a nearby muffin seller and a few beggar children into the circle. Already too many innocent bystanders.

"We want the journal," Philip said. "We know you and Carlston have it."

Helen clenched her hand on the lorgnette handle. They did not know she was the Ligatus. Surely that must be counted as a victory?

"You know we will never give it to you."

Philip hooked his forefinger around his watch chain and drew out a familiar shape from his fob pocket – a gold filigree frame set with a miniature portrait. Was that what she thought it was? He held it up, dangling from the chain. The portrait spun, her mother's face flashing past. Good God, he had brought the

Colligat! Finally, a chance to redress her failure in London.

In the next instant, the air seemed to contract like a closing fist as a future certainty played out in her mind's eye: Philip lunging forward, his whip slicing through the cold air, its lethal edge aimed at Lady Margaret. The forewarning burned through Helen's veins, bunching her muscles into readiness. Why attack Lady Margaret?

The thought was lost in a roaring rush of energy. She dropped the lorgnette upon its cord – both hands needed now – and all the blue light snapped back to dull normality. Every sense reached towards Philip, searching for a narrowing of eyes, a pop of speed, the buzzing itch of power, or the fresh-air smell of spent lightning.

She heard it first – a whoosh of air, then the displacement of it rolling across her skin – a warm, damp tactile map of the whip's trajectory. She spun and leaped in front of Lady Margaret, the action imprinted in mind's eye and muscle, her hands grabbing for the invisible whip as it snapped towards her face. Her fingers brushed its tip, groped for purchase, and closed around the pulsing weapon. Its glorious power slammed through her, charging her flesh and bones, setting the meat of her mind alight. She felt the Ligatus rise, a hum of intent, and suddenly she could see the ultramarine energy of Philip and Mrs Knoll, and the paler blue around Delia, Lady Margaret and the chairmen. All visible without her lens.

"She is taking my energy!" Philip yelled. He strained back from her hold, eyes bulging, jaw set hard with the effort to free himself.

"Release him!" Mrs Knoll cried. She lunged across the space between them, her fist slamming into Helen's shoulder.

The blow jarred Helen's arm, convulsing her hand open. Philip wrenched the glowing whip from her hand and the blue energy around him – around everyone – vanished.

The whip was no longer visible, but Helen felt the end of it snap past her face, a fresh metallic smell in its wake. She grabbed for it again, its trail visible for a second through the misty rain, but missed by a hair's-breadth.

Lady Margaret grabbed Helen's arm. "What is happening?"

Philip spun on his heel and ran at human speed, dodging around the gaping chairmen. Mrs Knoll pushed past Delia to follow her comrade. Why were they running? It did not make sense. Still, they were taking the Colligat. That was all that mattered.

Helen launched herself after them, hitching her hems and angling her body into speed. She heard familiar footsteps following – Darby, at full pelt – and rough male voices hooting and calling at the sight.

Philip looked over his shoulder, oily smile back in place. Taunting her. He called something to Mrs Knoll, running at his side. Not English. Something like Prussian?

Behind her, Darby gasped, "My lady?"

"He has the Colligat!" Helen said between breaths.

Both Deceivers looked back, still grinning, and then Mrs Knoll veered left, away from Philip, heading towards the corner of Queen Street. Her blue pelisse flapped behind her like a sail as she dodged around a slow-moving cart, ignoring the yell from the driver, then turned the corner. Gone from view, only the receding thwack of her boots charting her path.

Philip turned right into John Street. There was no question whom to follow: Philip had the Colligat. Yet this all had the flavour of a trap.

Helen took the turn into John Street, the cold biting through her glove as she pushed off the freezing stone wall into greater speed.

She heard Darby's grunt as she took the hill behind her. "Careful, my lady, it could be an ambush!"

Helen slowed and lifted her lorgnette. John Street was almost deserted: only a matted brown dog sniffing a pile of refuse, and the pale blue figure of a man in a leather apron manoeuvring a wooden keg through a doorway. Not an ambush then. The man looked up as the ultramarine figure of Philip ran past, surprise shifting into suspicion.

Philip glanced over his shoulder again, then turned to face her, slowing into a backward walk. What was he doing? He watched her approach, a faint smile on his lips. Too confident. Was he preparing to attack?

Helen matched his pace, keeping the distance between them. His vivid blue whip pulsed with energy, still raised over his head, weaving, but not drawn back. If anything, defensive. She could attack, try to retrieve the Colligat … except she would be drawing on the Grand Reclaimer power.

Deep within her, as though called upon her thought, the Ligatus shifted. A humming swarm rising upward, the voices of the dead whispering, cackling, softly howling their destructive force. She gritted her teeth. Carlston was right: after the recent ghostly manifestations, she could not let it loose and risk widening the rift. Possibly killing him and herself, and Darby too, before they had destroyed the Grand Deceiver. She drew a breath, and another, willing the swarm to settle.

"Why has he stopped, my lady?" Darby whispered, a pace behind.

"Oy, what you playing at?" the keg man called to Philip.

Helen glanced across at him. He had jammed the keg against the doorframe for support, and his shoulders were set into sturdy gallantry.

"Go inside," she ordered.

"Has he picked your purse, my lady?"

"He is my servant. Go!"

He ducked his head – never step in between a mistress and her servant – and hauled his keg into the building, the door slapping shut behind him.

Philip bent in a slight, ironic bow. "Your servant, my lady."

Joking now; what was his game? She stopped a few yards from him, Darby at her shoulder.

"You will not attack me," she said with as much confidence as she could muster. "Give me my mother's miniature."

"I will not kill you," he amended. He tilted his head, as if listening. "Not until it is time. But really, you should not leave your friends unprotected."

A frisson of danger tightened Helen's spine. Lady Margaret and Delia. And her aunt could be with them by now too.

"You would not dare!"

He took a step back, and another. "We will take them, Lady Helen, one by one, until you give us the Ligatus. Tell Lord Carlston. Tell Pike. It will not stop until we have what we want."

A distant scream ripped through the wet air, a rolling howl of horror that splintered into more screaming voices, more shouts.

Helen spun around, locating the sound. Back from where they had come. Whose voice was it? Delia's? Lady Margaret's? God forfend – Aunt's?

"Only the beginning," Philip said. "We will send word for the exchange."

She launched herself downhill, past Darby, the screaming stretching into slower, deeper howls as her speed blurred the buildings into dirty yellow smears.

She gripped the wall edge as she took the turn into Quiet

Street, a hunk of stone coming off in her hand. She staggered, unbalanced, her speed checked into a human run. Ahead, a circle of spectators on the corner, the screams rising from its centre. Through the mill of shouting men and sobbing women, she caught a flash of a woman holding a slumped body in her arms. Who was it?

Behind her, two sets of steps, one at uncanny speed. Was Philip daring to follow?

She looked back. A blur, but it was not Philip – the hair too dark, the body athletic and broad. The figure slowed. Carlston! No hat, his greatcoat undone. Behind him, Quinn, head bare too.

"What has happened?" Carlston asked, reaching her side. "I felt your alarm."

She had no words to explain, only a soft keen of dread in her throat.

They reached the edge of the spectators. Carlston's authority opened a path through the gawping shop boys, sobbing ladies, bedraggled children and silent chairmen.

Helen caught sight of Pug and Lady Georgina, faces white with shock, ominous dark patches on their shoes and hems. But safe, thank God. And no sign of Aunt or Lady Dunwick. They must have stayed in the shop.

Then she saw the blood. A semicircle spray of dark red on the paving, smeared at the outer edges by feet, but as neat as a draftsman's drawing around the two figures on the ground. Lady Margaret cradled Delia's limp, still body across her lap, her gloved hands blood-sodden and pressed against the savage slash that had opened Delia's pale throat into a gaping red crescent.

Helen staggered, falling to her knees beside the ghastly pietà. Delia's blank eyes stared at the grey sky, her face slack, its alabaster contours already turning ashen beneath the fine sheen of rain. Her dear life, gone.

"Sweet mercy," she heard Carlston say. Then, "What happened? You, chairman, tell me what you saw."

"We was just standin' here, my lord," a gruff male voice answered. "Her ladyship took off after that young cove she was talkin' to, and then before we knew it, the young lady—" He stopped, collected himself. "God rest her soul, the young lady's throat was just cut and sprayin' blood all over us, and she dropped to the ground. There was no one about – we didn't see no one with a knife or nothin', did we?"

His appeal brought a murmur of agreement from around the circle. No one had seen a knife. No one had seen the killer.

Lady Margaret lifted her head, tears tracking through an arc of blood across her cheeks. "The woman who was with Philip," she whispered to Helen. "I saw her walk by."

Mrs Knoll, doubling back for the kill. She would have used her whip, invisible to the eye, to slash Delia's throat. Dear God, the pain and terror Delia must have felt in those last moments.

Helen bowed her head. It was all her fault. She had fallen for their trap. Failed to protect her aide. Failed to protect her friend.

Failed as a Reclaimer.

Chapter Sixteen

Carlston closed the door of Pike's parlour and motioned for everyone to take seats. "We do not have much time. Your aunt is, of course, demanding to see you, Lady Helen, and the constables will be here soon."

Helen felt Darby's hand upon her arm, firmly guiding her towards an armchair beside the hearth. Hammond stood working an iron poker through the glowing embers to bring them back to flame. The firelight cast his face into a pale mask of sorrow.

"Warm yourself, my lady," Darby said, adjusting the cushion on the chair with an odd intensity. Her eyes were swollen from tears.

Helen sat, but could not feel the fire's heat. She was frozen inside and out, her mind still in the cold reality of Quiet Street, still kneeling beside Delia's fallen body.

Opposite, Lady Margaret sat hunched on the sofa, hands loose in her lap, the quicks of her fingernails stained rusty red. Her brother had peeled off her blood-soaked gloves, but the brim of her bonnet, her pelisse and gown still held the dark spray of Delia's death upon them.

So many arcs of blood, Helen thought. On the ground, on people, on White's wall.

Hammond placed the poker back into its rack. Lady Margaret flinched at the clang of iron against iron. "Sorry," he said.

"Where is Delia now?" Lady Margaret asked. Her voice held an almost feverish quality.

No wonder, Helen thought: she had seen Delia's throat sliced open, caught her friend's body in her arms, watched her die.

Pike crossed the room to stand at the hearth, his hands tucked beneath the fold of his arms. "Mr Sheppard, the under-taker on Milsom Street, has moved her to his premises to await the coroner."

"I thought you were going to take her to the White Hart," Carlston said.

Pike nodded, the harsh lines between his nose and mouth deepening. "It was my intention, but the inn is full at this time of year, and they are not over careful with access to their cool store. Too many people would pay to see the—" He stopped.

Helen supplied the final, awful word in her mind: *corpse*.

Pike cleared his throat. "Sheppard offered his basement. He has daughters of his own, and said he couldn't bear to think of a young lady being on public display."

"My aunt!" Helen said, half rising from the chair. "Philip said they were coming for everyone!"

"Quinn has my pistols, and he is escorting Lady Pennworth back to the Royal Crescent with Lady Georgina, Lady Dunwick and her daughter," Carlston said. "They will be safe for now."

Helen sank back into the chair. *For now.* It had an ominous ring. "And the Duke?"

"I have sent a message to Chenwith," Pike said. He turned to Carlston. "I know you want all the other Reclaimers here, but I cannot divert Mr Ball at the moment. I have sent for Mr Hallifax – he was in Bristol, and will be here in the next hour or so – and Mr Dunn and Mr Dempsey. They should be able to provide adequate protection."

"I have not seen Dunn since Stokes's death," Carlston said. Helen heard the question in the statement.

"Like Hallifax, he has accepted the circumstances," Pike said. "He knows you were not in your right mind."

Carlston scrubbed at his eyes, squeezing them shut for a moment. "Generous."

He walked across to the fireplace and crouched before Helen. She could see the dark reminder of Stokes's death in his eyes; he was, perhaps, the only person in the world who could know how she felt. The crushing guilt. She was to blame for Delia's death, and from now on she would carry the hollow anguish of it. A constant companion in lieu of her friend.

"It was a trap," she whispered. "I walked straight into it. So, so stupid."

"You did what I would have done," he said.

She drew a broken breath, finding a moment of comfort in the wet wool and warm skin smell of him. He reached for her hand, but hesitated, and gripped the chair arm instead. He was right to do so, but she was not so strong. She laid her chilled fingers upon the back of his hand, needing the anchor, the reassurance, of his touch. He turned his hand and locked his warm fingers into her own.

"I know you want to take the time to mourn Miss Cransdon," he said, "but we cannot stand still. Philip and this Mrs Knoll creature have made a declaration of war. They have not only broken the Pact, they have done so in the most inflammatory way possible. Tell us what Philip said to you, exactly as you remember it. I want Mr Pike to hear what they said."

Helen fought back the rise of grief that clogged her lungs and dragged upon her chest until she could barely breathe. "He said they wanted the Ligatus. They did not seem to know it is within me." She tightened her hand in his. "That is an advantage, isn't it? That is something we can use."

"Yes, it is," he said. "Go on."

"They said they would..." She had no air, no voice. She gulped, then forced out the final words. "Take all our friends until we gave it to them. He told me to tell you and Mr Pike. And that they would send word for the exchange."

Carlston glanced up at Darby. "Is that what you heard too?"

"It is, my lord." She took a step closer to Helen's chair. "Also, when my lady challenged him, he said he would not kill her until it was *time*."

"Time for what?" Carlston looked at Pike. "It would seem they do have a plan, and it has a schedule."

The Second Secretary gave a grim nod of acknowledgment. "You were right."

"I think they will not strike again, for now," Carlston added. "They have made their point. We must now play our card."

Lady Margaret leaned forward, her reddened, swollen eyes intent beneath the brim of her bonnet. "Are Philip and this woman the Grand Deceiver?" Hammond placed his hand upon her stiff shoulder, but she did not seem to notice, all her focus upon Carlston. "Are they?"

The silence stretched. No one was eager to pronounce the arrival of their enemy.

"Possibly," Carlston said. "We have no record of Mrs Knoll."

"Yet I have a strange feeling that I know her from somewhere," Helen said.

"I do too, my lady," Darby said. "And I think I know from where, although it doesn't make any sense to me. It was her and

266

Philip standing together, you see, and the way she covered her mouth when she laughed." Darby demonstrated the gesture. "It was what Berta used to do, my lady. She reminds me of Berta."

Helen gasped, the memory finally locking into place. Berta and Philip in her uncle's house: maid and footman. "Yes, that is who she reminds me of too."

Carlston frowned. "Berta? You mean the Deceiver maid who slit her own throat in London?"

Pike shook his head. "It cannot be her. Mrs Knoll is older than that maid by a good ten years. She could not be her progeny."

True, Helen thought. On the death of a Deceiver's human body, the creature could only survive by moving into the body of one of its human children imbued with a spark of its energy – the vestige. It was a physical impossibility for Mrs Knoll to be Berta's child. Yet Philip had asked if Helen recognised Mrs Knoll. And there was another oddity too.

"Do I remember correctly that Berta was Bavarian?" Helen asked Darby.

"Yes, a new émigré, my lady. At least that is what she said."

"When we were running, I heard Philip call something to her in another language. I thought it was Prussian, but maybe it was Bavarian."

Darby nodded. "I heard it too, my lady."

"Even so," Pike persisted, "it is impossible."

"Perhaps they are related in some way?" Darby said.

"Deceivers are not *related*," Pike said. "They go out of their way to isolate themselves from each other. Besides, a Deceiver cannot breed with another, nor can their children interbreed. The vestiges within them go to war and they are rendered impotent."

"That is how we understand the process for normal Deceivers,"

Carlston said. "However, if Philip and Mrs Knoll are the Grand Deceiver, then we must consider anything possible. The Comte d'Antraigues said the Grand Deceiver has abilities far beyond the norm. Is that not so, Lady Helen?"

"He said they were *Lusus Naturae*. Like no other."

"But it seems unlikely, don't you think?" Hammond said.

"What do you mean?" Carlston asked.

"Those two being the Grand Deceiver. They don't seem too grand to me."

Carlston smiled bleakly. "The clue is in the name."

It was clearly an old shared joke for Hammond's grim smile flashed back. "Deception is their game."

"Still, it is a good point," Carlston said. "We do not know if these two are the Grand Deceiver or not. I have no sense of whether they have the charm that the archives note as being a trait of the Grand Deceiver."

He looked to Helen, but she shook her head. She would not call either of them charming.

"And Philip," he continued, "has not risen in society in one lifetime. Another sign."

"They do, however, have the requisite ruthlessness and cunning," Pike said.

"Quite," Carlston said grimly. "And the archives are unreliable at best."

"Philip had the Colligat," Helen said, relieved to focus upon something other than the howling ache in her chest. "And he spoke as if he and Mrs Knoll were a pair. He told me in London that he served the Grand Deceiver, and yet I saw him in Brighton with Lawrence. And we know that Lawrence was in the employ of the Grand Deceiver."

"That does not necessarily mean Lawrence was serving Philip," Pike said, "but to be safe, I believe we must go ahead on the supposition that they are the Grand Deceiver. And if that is the case, we must find a way to destroy them. Preferably away from Bath in the height of the winter Season."

"We know so little about them," Hammond said. "I think—"

A knock on the door stopped him voicing his thought.

"Come," Pike said.

The door opened to admit a stocky maid, her face tense. "Excuse me, sir, but Mrs Pike is awake and she's a bit bothered."

Pike looked at the back wall, as if he could spy his wife through the painted plaster. "How bothered?"

"She's muttering, sir, and crying." It was said with some authority.

A nurse, then, not a maid, Helen thought.

Pike's shoulders tensed. "Thank you, Mrs Taylor. I will be there directly."

The woman nodded and withdrew.

"Do you need assistance?" Carlston asked.

Pike shook his head. "She just needs to be calmed." He cast a glance around the assembled company. "Hunt down and destroy these two Deceivers. Whether they are the Grand Deceiver or not, they have killed one of our own and broken the Pact. We must show the Deceiver world that this will not be tolerated."

The door closed behind him.

Helen glanced at Carlston. *We must tell Pike about the rift.*

He gave a slight nod. *It is time.*

"Mrs Knoll's address would be in the arrivals book," Hammond said.

"I doubt she would remain in the same lodgings," Carlston said. "Still, it is worth investigating." He tightened his hand around Helen's. "Since we will never give them the Ligatus, our priorities, as I see them, are to protect you all, and to hunt down Philip and Mrs Knoll before they strike again. As Pike said, we must also move this situation away from Bath and its inhabitants. Too many people witnessed Miss Cransdon's murder. We cannot have these two attempt another strike and potentially kill innocents—"

"Delia was innocent," Helen said, the hollow in her chest opening up again.

Carlston nodded. "Do not fear, we will have our revenge. When Mr Hallifax arrives, you and he must escort Mr Hammond, Lady Margaret and your family to Chenwith for protection. Perhaps even Pike and his wife. Mr Dunn and I will search for Philip and Mrs Knoll."

"That does not make sense," Helen protested. "If Philip and Mrs Knoll are the Grand Deceiver, you and Mr Dunn cannot destroy them. It must be you and I together. It must be the Grand Reclaimer."

"She is right, Carlston," Hammond said. "You have spent the last six months preparing her for this very battle. You cannot baulk now, just because you..." He stopped.

Ignoring him, Carlston stood up and addressed Helen. "You are the Ligatus. We must protect you." His eyes held the even more awful truth: *You are the Trinitas, the weapon, and it is breaking apart.*

Helen shook her head: *If it is breaking apart, then we must use it before it kills us.*

He stared at her, clearly trying to find a way around that terrible truth, then drew a resigned breath. *You are right.*

"*We* are the way to destroy this threat," she said for the benefit of the others. "I will stay at Bath and search for Philip and Mrs Knoll with you."

"I will stay too," Lady Margaret said. "Lady Helen cannot stay alone, and I will be part of this revenge."

"If you are staying, Margaret, then I stay too," Hammond said, placing his hand upon his sister's shoulder.

"If the Duke allows it, then we will *all* return to Chenwith," Carlston said. "It is containable, and sufficiently away from Bath to protect the populace. We will draw Philip and Mrs Knoll there and—"

A vicious scream on the landing outside the room whirled everyone around. Helen sprang to her feet as the door burst inward and slammed against the wall.

"Isabella, no!" cried Pike.

A woman stood in the doorway, long hair tangled, her face a sharp triangle of white skin stretched over bones. Good God, was that Isabella Pike? Helen glimpsed Pike's face behind her, bright blood streaming from his nose.

"Evil!" Isabella screamed, lunging into the room. She stumbled over a tea table, and wrenched it aside. "Evil!"

"Watch out, she is strong!" Pike yelled. "Vestige strong!"

Carlston grabbed for her, but she dodged, her momentum carrying her into the side of the sofa. She leaped onto it, her eyes locking with Helen's. Such insanity within them. Helen had seen it before in young Jeremiah's eyes in London, and Mad Lester's too. And, of course, in Carlston's eyes.

"Darby, get Hammond and Lady Margaret out!" Helen yelled as Isabella launched herself across the space between them.

The impact of the woman's bony body was harder than Helen expected. She staggered back, locking her arms around Isabella's skeletal frame.

She glimpsed Carlston pushing Pike out of the room. "Get the laudanum," he ordered.

"Evil!" Isabella screamed, spittle spraying Helen's face on a gust of rotting breath. She clawed at Helen's hands, writhing in the tight grip around her middle. "Deceiver evil!"

Could she feel the Ligatus energy?

The woman's elbows slammed into Helen's ribs, loosening her hold for a second. It was enough. Isabella lunged at Darby and Lady Margaret as they ducked past, pulling Helen off-balance.

"Evil!" she screamed and grabbed Mr Hammond's jacket. Helen saw the horrified pity in his eyes. He prised her fingers from his lapel.

"Go!" Helen yelled, tightening her hold. She dragged Isabella back towards the wall, gritting her teeth as the woman's head slammed into her chest bones, over and over. "Carlston!"

"Coming!" Carlston said. He grabbed Darby's shoulder, pushing her out the door. "Pike's getting her laudanum. You bring it in." He slammed the door behind her and ran across the room.

"Take her legs," Helen ordered.

He grabbed for Isabella's flailing legs, fighting to keep hold.

"We are surrounded by pure evil!" she shrieked and rammed her foot into his stomach.

"God's blood," he gasped, but doggedly hung on to her pale, thrashing limbs.

"I think I am making her worse," Helen said, panting. "I think she can feel the Ligatus."

The door opened and Darby ran in holding a brown glass bottle, Pike and the nurse a step behind.

"How much, Mr Pike?" she demanded. "How much?"

"A quarter of it, God help her."

"Hold her still, my lady," Darby said.

"We are trying," Carlston said as Isabella bucked against their hold.

For a second, Helen met his grim gaze: *We must reclaim her soon or she'll die.* And yet the rift. She saw it in his eyes too. A deadly stalemate.

Darby grabbed Isabella's jaw. "Someone hold her nose. We must make her open her mouth!"

The nurse pinched Isabella's nose closed. "You'll need to be quick," she told Darby. "And we must hold her mouth shut – she spits."

Isabella thrashed against them. Her mouth opened to gulp for air, and Darby deftly tipped a large measure of the bottle's contents into it, then forced her jaw shut with an unyielding hand, the nurse doubling the effort with a hand locked around Isabella's chin. She bucked against the constraint, eyes wild.

"Steady, Mrs Pike," the nurse said. "Let the medicine work."

It did not take long. No wonder with the amount administered, Helen thought. Isabella slumped in her arms, head lolling to one side, spittle and laudanum oozing from her mouth and collecting in the tangle of her long hair.

"May I carry her to her bedchamber?" Carlston gently asked Pike.

"Yes, thank you ... I ... yes," he said, his eyes fixed upon his wife's slack face.

"Ready her bed," Carlston told the nurse. "I will bring her in shortly."

The nurse bobbed a curtsey and hurried from the room.

Hammond and Lady Margaret peered in through the door, their entrance halted by a shake of Carlston's head. Helen helped him shift his grip to take Isabella's lax body in his arms, cradled like a child. Darby hurried forward to adjust her nightgown over her legs.

"Poor lady," she whispered.

Carlston observed Isabella's pale face, pity tensing his mouth. "I think you are right," he said to Helen. "She can feel the Ligatus in you, like Jeremiah felt the Deceiver energy in the Colligat. Hammond and I will settle things here. I want you and Darby to escort Lady Margaret to Lady Dunwick's. Send Quinn back to me."

"And Delia?" Helen whispered. Sorrow and guilt returned with heart-crushing pain, and she pressed her hand to her chest.

"For now, we must keep everyone else safe," he reminded her.

Isabella stirred in his arms, her head shifting against his chest. "Evil," she muttered.

"You had best leave," Carlston said. "Before she wakes up again."

Helen hesitated, everything welling up inside her: Delia, Isabella, the rift, the Grand Deceiver … all of it wrapped in despair.

"I know," he said, reading her face. He freed his hand from holding Isabella and gripped Helen's arm. "We are the Grand Reclaimer. We will find a way."

We. It was enough, for now.

Helen stood for a moment outside Lady Dunwick's drawing room. The struggle with Isabella still hummed through her blood and muscle, the shock of it barely dampened by her swift walk to the Royal Crescent. Poor Isabella had recognised the Ligatus within her and named it for what it was: evil. Helen shuddered, remembering her attempt to buy the Ligatus from Benchley's Terrene, Lowry, in the tavern at Lewes. A repulsive man, all yellowed teeth and foul breath, who had casually told her, "Benchley said you was just the bringer of evil."

Finally, she nodded to the waiting footman. He opened the door and stepped back as she entered the chamber, his air of curiosity barely contained. The news of Delia's murder had travelled fast.

Inside the drawing room, the night candles and lamps had been lit against the winter evening and, Helen thought grimly, the all too immediate darkness in the world beyond. Pug stood at the table, staring down at the remains of her silhouette cuttings. Lady Dunwick half reclined upon the sofa with her eyes closed and a stack of cushions at her back, a tiny bottle of smelling salts clutched in her hand. Aunt sat in the armchair opposite, a shawl clasped tightly around her shoulders, the lines upon her face dug deeper than usual.

Helen bit back an exclamation of relief as she saw two men in drab coats standing at the hearth. One was instantly recognisable: Mr Hallifax, Reclaimer. Helen had made his acquaintance in London at a meeting of the Dark Days Club; a craggy-faced, loose-limbed man from the west who had staunchly supported Carlston after the death of Stokes. The other man – big and broad with a ginger moustache – was most likely his Terrene. They must have ridden hard to make such good time from Bristol.

Both bowed at her entrance, Mr Hallifax's polite expression carefully free of their prior association.

"Oh, my dear girl." Aunt rose from the sofa and crossed the room with her hands outstretched. "My dear, dear girl."

Helen leaned into her embrace, the smell of her perfume and the warmth of her body a momentary comfort.

Aunt stepped back, still clasping Helen's hand, and motioned to the two newcomers. "Allow me to introduce Mr Hallifax and Mr Lennox. They have just arrived; sent by the Bath constables to reassure us."

Helen curtseyed and murmured, "Mr Hallifax. Mr Lennox."

Hallifax bowed again. "A tragedy, Lady Helen. We will discover the perpetrator."

She met his grave blue eyes. Indeed they would.

"I cannot believe it ... we were only here together this morning," Pug said.

"I know." Helen squeezed her aunt's hands, then crossed to her friend. "Come, sit down." She led Pug to the other armchair and gently guided her onto its cushions.

"All the blood," Pug whispered.

Helen took her hand. "You must think of something else," she said, although in truth she too could not rid herself of the memory of that red crescent on the pavement.

"Why were you gone so long?" Aunt asked. "No one would tell me where you were. I could not get a straight answer out of anyone." She glanced narrowly at Mr Hallifax.

"Lady Margaret and I were witnesses," Helen said, letting that stand as an explanation.

"Where is Lady Margaret?" Lady Dunwick demanded.

"She has gone straight upstairs. Her clothes..."

"Yes, of course. Poor Lady Margaret. She must order a bath. I will arrange it now," Lady Dunwick said, preparing to rise from the sofa.

"I took the liberty and ordered one," Helen said. "For myself as well. I hope that was not presumptuous." She looked down at the dark patch upon her pelisse where she had kneeled in Delia's blood.

Lady Dunwick sat back, her eyes flitting past the stain. "Whatever you need, my dear."

"Where is Lady Georgina?" Helen asked.

"She has gone upstairs too. Quite shaken, of course, seeing the—" Lady Dunwick stopped.

"Lady Margaret will need to write to Miss Cransdon's parents today," Aunt said into the heavy silence. "The poor girl was in her care, so the sad duty falls to her."

Helen bit her lip. No, Delia had been in *her* care.

"Her mother and father will no doubt want to take her back to her own church for burial," Aunt continued. "Although

I suspect they will have to wait for the coroner." She glanced at Hallifax, clearly accepting him as the authority. He nodded confirmation. Aunt sighed. "They will want to know the circumstances, I'm sure. But how to tell them about such a brutal and random attack?"

Lady Dunwick raised the smelling salts to her nose. "Do you think it is another madman, like the Ratcliffe Highway killer?"

"That happened in Town, Lady Dunwick," Aunt said, as if London held all of England's iniquity.

"They have caught the man who was responsible for that heinous crime, my lady," Mr Hallifax added. "John Williams. He hanged himself in his cell."

The wrong man. Helen remembered Benchley's mad, whiptail eyes.

"It could be another maniac on the loose," Lady Dunwick said, a shrill edge to her voice. "Who else would kill an innocent girl in the middle of the street? Bath is not safe any more!"

A truer statement than she knew, Helen thought. And if Lady Dunwick was thinking that way, others would be as well. Such fear could quickly build into the same kind of terror that had reigned over London last Christmas after the Ratcliffe murders. She glanced at Mr Hallifax. A warning must be sent to the Home Office. The government would want to do everything in its power to avoid another outbreak of panic amongst its populace.

"We must procure some black ribbon," Aunt said, as if she had not heard Lady Dunwick's dire pronouncement. A tactic, Helen realised, to defuse her friend's excitability. "One's impulse is to wear black, of course, to register the horror of it, but Miss Cransdon was not a relation, so I think black armbands would be more appropriate."

"Or white," Lady Dunwick said, diverted by the intricacies of mourning attire. "Since she was unmarried."

Unmarried. A life barely lived. Helen squeezed shut her eyes. A pressure was building inside her – a compulsion to scream and cry and roar. If she did not move now, she may burst with rage and grief. And guilt.

"My dear, do you need my salts?" Lady Dunwick said, holding them out. "You are looking very odd."

"No, thank you," Helen said. "But if you will excuse me, I will go upstairs."

"Of course. I will have tea sent up to you," Lady Dunwick said.

"Thank you," Helen managed.

"My dear, shall I come with you?" Aunt asked. "I do not like to think of you alone at such a distressing time."

Helen shook her head. "I just need some time to compose myself, Aunt. I will take a bath, and return directly."

Aunt observed her for a worried moment, then nodded. "As you wish."

"Thank you, Mr Hallifax, for coming to reassure us," Helen said politely, knowing the Reclaimer would read her true, deep gratitude for his swift arrival. "And you, Mr Lennox."

The two men bowed.

"It is our honour," Mr Hallifax said, his heavy brows angled in concern. Clearly he could also read her rage and guilt. His mouth quirked with grim sympathy, but he did not say any more. Not in their present company.

"It is my opinion that white gloves rather than black would be more appropriate for you and your niece," Lady Dunwick said to Aunt. "And maybe white scarves."

Helen fixed her eyes upon the door and walked stiffly away from the discussion of gloves and scarves and ribbons. In the dim hallway, she ignored the silent presence of the footman and took the stairs at a run, pulling herself up by the balustrade, trying to work the turmoil from her body. She arrived at the third floor with hands clenched, heartbeat barely raised, the weight on her chest still unbearable. She wanted to rip Mrs Knoll apart. Rip everything apart. She closed her hands around the wooden railing, feeling it creak beneath her grip.

"Lady Helen. I am glad you are here."

She swung around. Lady Georgina stood under the wall lamp in the hallway, holding Sprat by her arm. The girl pulled against the constraint, her face set into narrow-eyed defiance.

"Your maid – I found her going through Miss Cransdon's belongings."

Helen rocked back, trying to focus beyond her rage. "Belongings?" she repeated.

"Yes." Lady Georgina held out a ring set with seed pearls, the gold glinting in the lamplight. "I saw her slip this into her apron pocket."

Helen took the ring, cupping it in her palm. This was well beyond normal theft; it was stealing from the dead. "Sprat, is it true? You stole this from Miss Cransdon?"

The girl stopped straining in her captor's grip and stood with her head bowed, her dull brown topknot skewed to one side. "I dunno."

"Of course it is true," Lady Georgina said, clearly offended. "I am not in the habit of making up stories about maids. You must cast her out." She released Sprat with an unkind push towards Helen. "Today, and without a character. I am sure Lady Dunwick does not want a thief in her house. And I certainly do not wish to be in the same house as a foul creature who steals from the dead."

Sprat's head jerked up. She opened her mouth to say something, but Helen gripped her shoulder in warning.

"My dear Lady Georgina," Helen said, "Sprat is still very young, little more than a child. She has had little moral teaching in her life, and less kindness. To cast her out would seal a terrible fate."

Lady Georgina eyed Helen, her beautiful lips pursed. "A fate she has brought upon herself."

"Surely we must show her the path to virtue through forgiveness and example?"

"I would say she is already set in her delinquency."

Helen widened her eyes at Sprat: *Step wisely*. "Tell me, do you wish to improve?"

"I do, my lady." It was said meekly and with a solemn nod. The girl at least recognised the danger.

Helen turned to Lady Georgina. "See? She wants to improve, and I believe she can be redeemed. She is but a child. It would be a great favour to me – a *great* favour – if you could forget about this incident, and not mention it to anyone, particularly Lady Dunwick and the Duke."

"His Grace would certainly throw her into the street," Lady Georgina said. She drew in a ruminative breath, its expulsion a long sigh of agreement. "Very well … sister." She met Helen's eyes in a moment of shy connection. "I will not mention it."

Sister. Helen bowed her head in gratitude. "Thank you."

"I intend to send for Lord Henry tomorrow," Lady Georgina added. "I think we should return to Chenwith as soon as possible. To stay any longer would be most inconsiderate to Lady Dunwick."

"You are probably right," Helen said. "Let us discuss it later."

She tightened her grip on Sprat's shoulder and marched her back along the corridor to Delia's bedchamber. The girl must return the ring and understand the seriousness of the crime.

They both paused on the threshold of the small, cold room. A candle in its silver holder stood on the bedside table, casting a flickering light across the neatly made narrow bed. A travelling trunk was set at the bed's end, and four somewhat battered hat boxes stood in a row against the wall. The clothes press was open, one shelf of linen neatly arranged, the other higgledy-piggledy. Helen caught a faint scent of rose upon the air – Delia's perfume. She swallowed past the hard tightening of her throat.

"I was tidyin' Miss Cransdon's things when one of the house-maids came in and told me," Sprat whispered. "Said she'd had her throat cut in the street."

"And so in response you decided to steal Miss Cransdon's ring?"

Sprat shook her head. "It weren't a decision, my lady. I just did it."

Helen sat down on the bed. "Come, sit with me."

Sprat's shoulders hunched at the unorthodox invitation, but she sat on the very edge of the mattress, her reddened hands tucked between her knees.

"Why did you take the ring? You know it is wrong. You promised me that if you felt the impulse to steal, you would come to me first."

Sprat looked up squarely. "You weren't here."

Helen wet her lips. She had failed in her duty again. "Even so, you must know that stealing from the dead is despicable."

Sprat bowed her head. "I wasn't gunna sell it or nuthin'. Just keep it."

"You wanted it as a keepsake?"

She shrugged. "I dunno." She dragged her fingernails along the quilted bedcover. "I liked Miss Cransdon, my lady. We got along. She said I had po-tensh…" She frowned. "Po-tensh…"

"Potential?"

"That's it, my lady, potential. She was gunna ask you if she could keep me as her maid." She pointed to the small dressing table, jumbled with hairpins and bottles. "She was just sitting

281

there this mornin', laughin' at one of my stories while I did her hair. She liked to hear about the bawdy house. She wasn't like you, my lady. She wasn't that bothered about bein' good."

Helen blinked. "Sprat, you should not speak ill of the dead."

The girl shook her head vigorously. "I'm not disrespectin' her, my lady. She weren't bad or nuthin'. I'm just sayin', I been around a lot of folk who ain't that bothered and Miss Cransdon was one of 'em."

In all fairness, she was probably right. Delia did have – Helen caught herself with a pang of pain – Delia *had* a habit of listening at doors and revelling in gossip.

Sprat lowered her voice. "Them Deceivers killed her, didn't they?"

Helen nodded.

"You gunna kill 'em back?"

"Yes," Helen said. *Oh, yes.*

Sprat nodded in grim satisfaction, then wiped her knuckles across her eyes, smearing a trail of wet across her cheeks. "I liked her, my lady."

"So did I," Helen said. She pushed her palm hard against her forehead, pressing back her own tears. If she started to weep now, she may never stop.

"I'm sorry I took her fawney," Sprat said.

"I know. You must try harder to resist."

The girl nodded, her face so forlorn that Helen put her arm around her thin body. Sprat stiffened, the jut of her shoulder blades sharp against Helen's hold, then slowly she leaned into the embrace, her breath cracking into a sob.

"I hope you kill 'em real good."

Chapter Seventeen

Helen sent Sprat to the kitchen to collect the ordered tea, mainly to keep the girl occupied, and made her way to her own bedchamber. Now that she had the time and solitude to think upon what had happened in Quiet Street, an uneasy conviction was pushing its way into her mind; that Mrs Knoll had, indeed, once been Berta.

She opened the door to find Darby standing at the window, staring at Lansdown Crescent beneath the rising full moon, her arms crossed over her chest. She turned at the sound of the door and dipped a curtsey. Her eyes were red, the skin around them damp and swollen. "Your bath is almost prepared, my lady."

"You have been crying," Helen said. "I am so sorry. This is not the wedding day I would wish for you."

Darby quit the window, waving away the consideration. "My tears are for poor Miss Cransdon, my lady, not for myself. I am wed to Mr Quinn and that is all I need. Right now, we must focus upon the Grand Deceiver." She took Helen's scarf and placed it on the bed. "I had not thought Mrs Pike so far gone though. She is all but skin and bone. And no sense at all, poor lady."

"I am not so certain about her sense." Helen lifted her chin as Darby undid the frogged clasps on her pelisse. "I am sure she felt the Ligatus in me. Maybe even the rift."

She turned and angled her arms behind herself to allow Darby to ease the coat off. Her maid held it up, staring at the wide seep of blood that had dried into the wool.

"I do not think we will be able to clean this," she remarked.

"You may have it, if you wish, or do what you will with it," Helen said. "I could never wear it again."

"Nor me." Darby folded the pelisse and placed it on the bed, her head bowed. "I must confess to such feelings of hatred towards Philip and Mrs Knoll, my lady. To take Miss Cransdon's life in order to send a message... It is beyond heinous."

"I know." Helen's own rage crawled hot beneath her skin. "Tell me, are you certain you recognised Berta within Mrs Knoll?"

Darby looked up. "That is bothering you too, my lady? I know it is impossible, but I really did think it was Berta."

"I do too," Helen said. "I have been thinking upon it. If we are correct and Berta somehow moved into Mrs Knoll's body, then it must follow that she is different. Could she be one half of a Grand Deceiver?"

"But we had already come to that, my lady," Darby said. "At least, Lord Carlston and Mr Pike are making our plans upon the belief of it."

"Yes, but not via the idea of Berta being Mrs Knoll. Think further. If that is the case, could it be that a Deceiver that is part of a Grand Deceiver does not need to move into its own progeny, like all other Deceivers? Perhaps it might move into whatever body, whatever living person, it wants."

Darby stepped back. "Anyone?"

Helen nodded at her Terrene's horror. "It could be anyone at any time."

"Oh, my lady. That is…" Darby shook her head. "But how?"

Helen frowned. Anyone. *Any time.* She drew in a sharp breath. Beau Nash and Captain Wade … no connection to each other but wearing the same fob. *Possibly* the same fob, she amended. It was a leap, but could one Deceiver be the Bath Master of Ceremonies over a hundred years? Of course it could, if a Grand Deceiver had the ability to shift into a body that was not its progeny. Such maintenance of the role would certainly earn the creature the title of the Bath Deceiver. And if that were the case, it would lead, by logic, to the current Master of Ceremonies. But there were two at present: Mr King of the Upper Rooms, and Mr Guynette of the Lower. Holy star, could they together form another Grand Deceiver?

Helen swallowed past a sudden dryness in her throat. It was likely a mad idea, all built upon her and Darby's intuition about Berta, but it warranted investigation. And she needed something to ameliorate her feeling of failure.

"Darby, get my cloak," she said. "We are going to the Upper Rooms."

Helen peered in the front doorway of the Assembly Rooms with Darby at her back staunchly blocking the worst of the cold wind that gusted along Alfred Street. The establishment was in that mid-time between the departure of card players and tea drinkers, and preparation for the evening's subscription Fancy Ball. The ball she had promised Mr King she would lead.

Not now. She was in mourning. It felt wrong that the dance was still going ahead, but there was little in the world that would stop a Bath subscription ball.

A waiter carrying a silver tray full of glasses paused in his trajectory across the foyer and bowed. "My lady, may I be of assistance?"

"I am seeking Mr King," Helen said.

"I fear you have just missed him."

"Do you know where he has gone?"

The man's round, pasty face froze into the polite mask of service. "My apologies, my lady, I do not know."

It was a lie. Helen opened her reticule and drew out a sixpence. "Are you sure?"

The waiter eyed the coin. "He's gone to look at the girl who was murdered. At Sheppard's on Milsom Street."

Helen closed her fist around the bribe. How dare King go to gawk at Delia. Deceiver or not, it was disgusting.

"How long ago did he leave?" she managed to ask.

"Ten minutes, my lady. No more."

Helen placed the coin on the silver tray. "Thank you."

She and Darby retreated to the freezing portico. The wind tugged and snarled their cloaks, flattening the straw brim of Darby's bonnet and lifting Helen's buckram silk upon its ribbons tied under her chin. She clamped her hand upon the hard flat top and pushed it more firmly on her head. A moment to steady her fury.

"Find Lord Carlston," she ordered. "He is most probably still at Mr Pike's, but if not, try his rooms. Tell him to meet me at Mr Sheppard's, the undertaker."

Darby leaned in, her voice low and urgent. "My lady, if you truly think Mr King is the Bath Deceiver, you must wait for his lordship to arrive. Please do not face the creature by yourself."

"I will not allow another Deceiver to go near Delia," Helen said forcefully. "If you are swift about your task I will not be alone. Now go!"

Darby curtseyed and, with a last worried glance, bent into the wind to cross the Circus again, the quickest route to Queen's Square.

Helen clutched the edges of her cloak more firmly together and walked briskly to the steep decline of Bartlett Street. Every fibre of her body wanted to launch into Reclaimer speed, but too many fellow pedestrians, carriages and sedan chairs progressed along the lamp-lit road. Besides, if she continued into town on her own without a maid or footman, she would attract too much attention. She peered at a sedan chair on the other side of the street, most probably making its way to the public stand under the Assembly Rooms' colonnade.

"Chair! Are you free?" she called to the lead man.

"Aye, my lady."

The two men waited for a wagon to pass, then crossed the road at a quick pace, pitching the chair to the ground beside Helen in a well-practised move.

The lead rolled his shoulders in his regulation dark blue greatcoat and asked, "Where to, my lady?"

"The start of Milsom Street, near Quiet."

He exchanged a glance with his partner. "Are you aware of the trouble down there, my lady? A poor young lady was murdered most cruel there two hours past, and there still be a crowd gawpin' at the site. If I may be so bold, it's not the time to be travellin' alone. Not with this full moon an' all."

Helen gripped her reticule more tightly. "It was my friend, sir, who was so cruelly taken. I go to Mr Sheppard's, the undertaker, where she lies."

"Are you sure, my lady? It's said she's kept at the White Hart."

"No, Sheppard's. Can you deliver me there quickly?"

His weathered face softened with pity. "We can, my lady, and right swift." He took off his black hat. "My condolences to you. The two chairmen who was standin' nearby be known to us. They are sworn to the peace of our city, like we are – special constables – an' they be right mortified to have missed catchin' the rogue who done it."

"I suppose everyone is talking about it," Helen said. If there was anyone who knew the current disposition of the public, it would be the chairmen.

"Aye, it's got the gentle folk and common all in a twitter."

With a smart bow, he opened the front door of the black painted cabin and lifted the roof upon its hinge. Helen stepped in and turned to sit upon the bench seat, which was upholstered in thick brocade. With a swift professional glance, the chairman gauged the height of her bonnet, then, satisfied, lowered the roof and shut the front of the cabin with a click of the snib.

The two chairmen took to the pavements, calling "Have a care," and "Make way," as they carried Helen down Bartlett Street into George, past the handsome Edgar Buildings and then into Milsom Street. Through the cabin windows, she caught glimpses of Bath as it hurried about its business; a man and woman clamping their headwear against the wind, a boy's laughing face under a street lamp, a ribbon seller turning to shield his box from a spray of coach-wheel mud. Helen held her gloved fists in her lap, silently urging on the pace. What if she were wrong about Mr King? She shook her head; that did not matter. A mistake would require only an apology and an excuse of duress. No, the true difficulties came if she were right.

A small crowd still lingered around the corner of Quiet Street. Helen turned her face away as they drew up to Mr Sheppard's shop; she could not bear to look at the stained pavement where Delia had died.

The chair was lowered to the ground and the lead man opened the front door and lifted the roof. "That be a shilling, my lady," he said with a bow. He eyed the gawkers exchanging loud views upon the murder a few yards away. "Would you like us to wait for you?"

Helen stepped out and passed the fare into his heavily gloved hand. "No, thank you."

The front of the shop was emblazoned with the sign *Mr T. Sheppard, Woollen-draper, Hatter and Undertaker.* Three night lamps had already been lit within the window, which showed a fine display of gentlemen's and ladies' hats upon wicker stands. Through the glass, she made out the angular figure of a man measuring a length of woollen cloth upon a side bench.

Helen pushed open the door, the tinkling bell announcing her entrance. The man looked up over his wire spectacles, a smile upon his long-boned face. He bowed.

Helen nodded. "Good evening. Are you Mr Sheppard?"

"I am indeed. How may I help you?"

There was no use in trying a silent approach. If Mr King was a Deceiver and already in the shop, he would have heard her arrival.

"I am Lady Helen Wrexhall. Miss Cransdon was my friend." *My responsibility.* She drew a breath through the suffocating guilt.

Mr Sheppard's professional smile faltered. "Ah, my condolences, my lady. Such a horrid occurrence."

"Where is she?"

"You wish to view the deceased. Now?" His eyes darted to a staircase that led downward.

To the basement, Helen realised. It stood to reason: the stone underpinnings would be the coldest part of the building. She headed to the stairs.

"My lady! She is not ready!" Mr Sheppard skirted the bench, following her along the aisle.

She eyed him coolly. "Mr King is downstairs, is he not?"

He stopped, pushing back his spectacles. "He said he knew

the young lady and wished to sit vigil. I had no reason to refuse him. He is *Mr King*, after all."

What did Mr King want with Delia?

"Lord Carlston will be here in a few minutes," Helen said. "Show him the way down when he arrives. You need not accompany me."

He took her at her word for she did not hear him behind her as she made her way down the creaking wooden stairs. She did, however, hear footsteps below. A confident tread, pacing.

She paused on the second-last step. A narrow corridor stretched to her left, painted white and frugally lit with one candle in a wall sconce made for three. Halfway along, a brighter light from an open doorway cast a rectangle upon the scrubbed floorboards. The sound of breathing within pinpointed the location of Mr King.

Should she wait for Carlston? She frowned at her own trepidation. Was she not as strong and as skilled as he? More to the point, would he wait for her? She allowed herself an inner snort, a moment of bravado that pushed her down the last two steps.

"Mr King?" she called.

A beat of silence, then came, "Lady Helen." Yet he did not come to the doorway.

She walked down the corridor listening, the colder air bringing a shiver across her shoulders. He had stopped pacing. All she heard was his breathing ... a little quicker than before. Anticipation? Or was he afraid?

The thought took her to the doorway. She found her lorgnette on its neck-cord and raised the spectacles to her eyes. Cautiously, she peered around the door jamb.

Mr King stood by a bench that was covered by a calico cloth, the shape of a body beneath it. The lorgnette lenses showed the blue energy around him. He had fed recently – skimmed, no doubt, from the card players at the Assembly Rooms – but he had not built a whip.

Helen's eyes were drawn down to the bench, brutally lit by four oil lamps set around it. The cloth had been pulled back to show Delia's ashen face, drained of all animation, and the terrible wound at her neck crusted with thick dried blood. Not one speck of blue energy around her. So final.

Helen swayed and grabbed the doorframe, the lorgnette falling to the end of its cord. In all the anticipation of meeting Mr King, she had quite suppressed the fact that the room also held Delia.

"I am sorry for the death of your friend," Mr King said with a bow. He had taken off his beaver hat and held it in his gloved hands. A mark of respect. "Losing a friend in such a violent way is heartbreaking. I know."

He took a step forward that stiffened Helen's back. He stopped, hand held up in truce.

"Tell me, did you kill *my* friend, the Comte d'Antraigues?" he asked. "The reports of it in the papers were, to say the least, rather odd. A mad valet intent upon revenge? So very Gothic. I saw the hand of the Dark Days Club in it. Not to mention the fact that you have his fob – a possession I do not believe he would have willingly given up."

His voice held no threat. Still, she did not trust his mildness, especially since he had just proclaimed himself heartbroken at the loss of his friend.

"The Comte gave me the fob as he was dying," Helen said, taking a careful step into the room, trying to resist the ghastly draw of her friend's face. "The valet – Lawrence – fatally stabbed him and the Comtesse. It was an assassination."

"But *Mors Ultima*?"

"It was his choice. He did not want to live without the Comtesse."

Mr King's mouth quirked. "Now that I believe."

"Before the Comte died, he told me to find the Bath Deceiver. That is you, is it not? You inhabited Beau Nash and Captain Wade."

He bent his head in acknowledgment. "Webster too, and a few others."

He hooked his finger under his fob ribbon and drew out a gold disc from his pocket. She caught the etching of Bacchus upon it: an exact match for the Comte's fob.

"I thought to muddy the waters with the Wade portrait and my sojourn in Brighton," he added, "but I underestimated you. Louis said you were clever."

Helen tensed, muscles ready. "He told me you would know about the Grand Deceiver. But it is my thought that you *are* a Grand Deceiver. Half of one, at least. That is why you can move into bodies other than your own progeny."

The tinkle of the bell above the shop door made them both look up. The snip-snip-tear of Mr Sheppard's cloth cutting stopped. Helen recognised the firm tread across the floorboards and the curt request for direction. Carlston. She felt her heartbeat quicken, the rhythm of their bond loud in her ears.

"Ah, the Grand Reclaimer complete," Mr King announced. He raised his brows at her surprise. "Louis wagered it was so before he was killed. He would have been pleased to have won the bet."

His lordship made no attempt at stealth. Only his set of footsteps moved through the shop and down the stairs. No doubt he had left Quinn and Darby behind to protect the Pikes and Mr Hammond.

"We are in here, Lord Carlston," Mr King called.

Carlston appeared at the doorway; greatcoat and hat patterned by fresh raindrops, boots splashed with mud, dark eyes sweeping the room in quick evaluation. His face was composed, but Helen saw the tight line of his mouth: thunderous.

Mr King bowed. "Good evening."

Carlston nodded. "An unusual place to meet, sir."

A savage glance in Helen's direction made her lift her chin: *You would have done the same.*

"Your Reclaimer partner has been informing me that I am half of a Grand Deceiver," Mr King said pleasantly.

It took Carlston only an instant to catch up. He braced himself. "And is my partner correct?"

"Quite," Mr King said. He waved a reassuring hand. "No, no, my lord, stand down. The other half of my power was destroyed, *Mors Ultima*, a long time ago."

Helen saw Carlston's eyelids flutter and understood his thought: a Grand Deceiver killed *Mors Ultima*; the relief to know it could be done.

"I have no desire to attack you," Mr King continued. "And since I have not transgressed the Pact, I sincerely hope you will not attack me."

"What are you doing here then?" Carlston asked.

Mr King looked at the shrouded figure on the bench. "I wished to see whether this young lady was killed by a Deceiver."

"She was," Helen said. Why would he be investigating that?

"Indeed. The wound and circumstances – as I heard them from one of my staff – tell the story."

"We think it is the – or should I say *a* – Grand Deceiver," Carlston said. "They are targeting us, and our friends and family. Louis told Lady Helen that you would help us."

Mr King's perpetual smile faded. "I am not in the habit of helping Reclaimers, Lord Carlston, despite my friend's promise."

"Louis told us that you have information about the Grand

Deceiver that is essential to our cause," Carlston said.

Mr King's eyes narrowed. "I never understood his odd trust in you."

Carlston rocked forward on his toes. Helen felt the beat of their bond quicken. "All you need to understand, Mr King, is that I want information about this Grand Deceiver and I am willing to use any method to get it. I have neither the time nor the temper for refusal."

"Are you threatening me in my own city, Lord Carlston?"

His city, Helen noted.

Carlston stepped further into the room. "I am, Mr King."

"Gentlemen! Stop!" Helen lifted her hand to punctuate the command, ignoring Carlston's glare. "If you help us, Mr King, I believe we can offer you something you want."

He wrenched his eyes from Carlston's looming figure. "What is it you think I want, Lady Helen?"

"To rid your city of the biggest threat since the riots. You are the *Bath* Deceiver, Mr King, and if this Grand Deceiver keeps killing people in Bath in such a brutal manner – Miss Cransdon and before that, I believe, those poor infants – everyone will abandon the Season. You will be Master of Ceremonies of an empty Assembly Room in a failed spa town, and your easy feeding ground will be ruined."

Mr King walked to the end of the bench, the harsh lamplight casting half his face in shadow. "You do me a disservice, Lady Helen. I am not only concerned with self-preservation. As you say, Bath is *my* city. I have been its Master of Ceremonies, off and on, for over one hundred years, as Webster and then Nash. I have nurtured it into the glory it is today. I will not have it destroyed by this battle."

"We can shift the battle to another ground," Helen said. "With your help."

He stroked the brim of his hat between his fingers, considering the proposal. "And if I refuse, you will stay and put my city at more risk. Is that it?"

She had offered in good faith, but of course there was that darker underside. "Yes."

She glanced at Carlston. Did he agree with her offer and her bluff? A tiny lift of his lips gave the answer: *Well played*.

Mr King gave a dry laugh. "So the question is: will my love of this city outweigh my natural distrust of you and your partner?" He looked back at Delia's face, a trace of pity in the draw of his mouth. "I rather believe it does. I do, however, require a guarantee that there will be no more murders like this in the bounds of my city."

"If you supply us with the information we require, we will return to Chenwith Hall tomorrow," Carlston said. "All those who are at risk from the Grand Deceiver's threat will be under Dark Days Club protection until that time."

Mr King tapped his finger upon the top of his hat. "That is not a guarantee, and I doubt you will be able to protect them all."

"It is what we offer," Carlston said. "And it is on my word."

For a long moment, the two men stared at one another, then King nodded. "I hear that your word, once given, is set in stone." He placed his hat upon the corner of a worktable. "What is it you wish to know?"

Helen suppressed a sigh of relief. The first hurdle completed.

"Do you know who the two halves of the Grand Deceiver are?" Carlston asked.

King shook his head. "I can, like all others of my kind, recognise some inner energies through skin touch." He held up his gloved hands. "But as you aware, that kind of intimacy does not occur often in public arenas. My incumbency as Master of Ceremonies is not unknown amongst my kind and very few would enter the Upper Rooms to invade my territory. Having said that, there is a newcomer in the city who has prompted some whispering. A woman by the name of Knoll. And by all accounts, she was present when your friend was killed."

Helen shot a glance at Carlston. "We think that Deceiver was once a maid of mine and has since shifted into Mrs Knoll."

She could not help but look at Delia again. There was a ghastly symmetry to it all: the body of Berta had lain on such a bench, throat cut by her own hand, and now here lay Delia, most probably killed by the same hand.

It seemed disrespectful to be talking over her body. Helen crossed to the bench, her advance pushing Mr King back a step.

"I think my friend has shown us enough," she said and gently pulled the calico over Delia's face.

"If Mrs Knoll is half of a Grand Deceiver, she has probably been many more women between your maid and this current identity," Mr King said. "In this world, a Grand Deceiver is a male–female pair, just as you are a male–female pair. And like you, they are more powerful as a dyad than as individuals."

He stopped and cleared his throat. He had said more than he wished, Helen thought.

"I do not know who her male partner would be," he added quickly. "Do you have any idea?"

"How can she shift into a body without her vestige in it?" Carlston asked, ignoring the query.

Mr King gave a small shrug. "It is, like all things in the physical world, a transference of energy. However, unlike transference via a vestige, which can be achieved over great distances, the new body chosen by a Grand Deceiver must be in close proximity. The medium through which it is done is individual to the Grand Deceiver pair. I use touch. Some use bodily fluids; others can do so through the air itself."

"Through the water in the air?" Helen asked. "Like the way your electrical whips are manipulated?"

A nod of his head confirmed what she had learned from the Ligatus.

"But you still kill the person's soul when you take over their body, like the others of your kind?" she added. "They are still dead."

"I have only ever done so to ensure my own survival, Lady Helen. Never with malignant intention."

A lack of malignancy did not temper the fact that all those men's souls, their essential being, had been obliterated to make way for his existence.

"Are you unable to shift into a Reclaimer?" she asked. "It seems the obvious thing to do."

Mr King smiled thinly. "A Reclaimer is built to drain Deceiver energy through his body and return it to the earth. We cannot maintain a … *foothold*, if you like, within a Reclaimer soul and body. It would be immediate *Mors Ultima*."

It might be different in her own case, Helen thought, since she could store energy. She had dragged power from both Lawrence and Philip, clearly devouring their energy, not the other way round. But she was not going to mention that to a Deceiver.

Carlston had moved on to another subject. "Is Bonaparte one half of a Grand Deceiver? Are the people of France under a similar threat to us?"

Mr King snorted. "Hardly. Bonaparte is a very ambitious Cruor whose aim is the aim of all Cruors: bloodshed and power. That is not the aim of a Grand Deceiver."

"What *is* the aim of a Grand Deceiver?" Carlston asked quickly.

Mr King crossed his arms. "You demand a great deal."

"If you expect us to keep our part of the bargain, then you must keep yours," Carlston said.

King studied them both in a sidelong glance, as if gauging their ability to comprehend what was to come. "The majority of my kind exist in another realm from this one, and it is dying. There are too many of us, stripping it bare like locusts. It cannot continue for much longer. This decay has created weaknesses in the walls between our realm and the *many other* realms that exist."

"Many other realms?" Helen echoed. "As in other worlds?"

They had always known that the Deceivers came from an otherworld, but the idea of more than one such world existing was all at once bewildering, exciting and appalling.

"In a sense," Mr King said. "Suffice to say that the walls between them cannot be seen, but they exist just as light and air exist."

Helen glanced at Carlston. "At the stones. That strange effect in the air."

He nodded, his eyes still fixed upon King. "Go on."

"On occasion, a number of my kind can unite to fracture a wall for a brief time. It takes an enormous expenditure of energy to do so, but when these fractures are created, those of us who survive the process pour through the opening before it closes, hoping that the new realm beyond will support our energy."

A cold shiver of recognition crawled across Helen's scalp. The macabre verse in the records about the Grand Deceiver: *When the earth fractures and the poison pours forth...*

"And if we are able to survive in the new realm," Mr King continued, "it is the mission of the Grand Deceivers to create a larger fracture that will enable the remainder of us to migrate through to the new realm and so survive."

"And the Deceivers living here, in this realm?" Helen asked. "What is their role?"

"When the time comes, those already in this world and physically near the fracture will become part of the energy expenditure required to widen it."

"They sacrifice themselves?"

"It is not a choice. It is a compulsion."

So brutal, Helen thought. But then it all sounded desperate. A fight for survival.

"But how do you fracture the wall from this side?" Carlston asked.

"It is the Grand Deceiver's mission to build an artefact that mixes the energies of both realms: Deceiver and human energy together in three parts. A triad of power."

Helen crossed her arms, hugging her body. He was describing the Trinitas. "What will it do?" To her surprise her voice sounded normal.

"It will break open a fracture in the wall, and hold it open long enough for millions of my kind to overrun this realm."

Helen felt her mouth dry with fear. Their records had been right: the Trinitas could open a doorway to *millions* of Deceivers. She looked at Carlston. He was endeavouring to hide his shock, but she saw the flinch of it in his eyes. If they could not stop this fracture, they would have no chance of saving England. And, indeed, every country beyond.

"Does this world only connect to yours?" Carlston asked.

Mr King smiled, clearly impressed by the question. "No, all the realms are connected, and there are countless numbers of them. However, while our initial rupture into a realm is by chance, any triad mechanism made with Deceiver energy will force open a rupture back into my home realm. Do you understand?"

Carlston nodded. "The triad mechanism is keyed to your realm, like a musical instrument. It will always open a pathway to your realm."

"Exactly."

"How is it activated?" Helen asked.

"It is the task of a Grand Deceiver to create the triad according to the physical laws of the realm they are in."

"So how do we stop it?" Carlston demanded. "How do we stop the Grand Deceiver?"

Mr King flourished a hand. "Isn't it obvious? Destroy the three artefacts. Or at least one of them."

Carlston glanced at Helen, the unintended Ligatus. "That is not possible," he said flatly. "How do we defeat the Grand Deceiver before they put this plan into action?"

"Isn't that the calling of the Grand Reclaimer? Do you not have your own mechanism to stop the triad?"

Carlston's jaw shifted. They had no mechanism.

King gave a small shrug. "Then I do not know. Your predecessors must have achieved it at some points in your history, otherwise we would not be standing here. Besides, while I may be desirous of protecting my existence here at Bath, I do not wish to do so at the expense of my entire kind. There are limits." He drew out his fob watch and consulted it with a frown. "Are we finished? I have a Fancy Ball to organise."

"No, we are not," Carlston said. He angled a glance at Helen: *The rift in your mind?*

Can we trust him with the knowledge of it?

He tilted his head: *I think we must.*

Helen considered. If Mr King knew about the Trinitas, or the triad as he called it, perhaps he would know how to close the rift caused by the Ligatus. That was if he recognised it.

She stepped forward, working off her glove, and extended

her hand. "Would you do me the favour of reading the energy within me?"

He stared at her hand as if it were a venomous creature. "You wish me to touch you?"

"Yes."

He addressed Carlston. "What is this about?"

"There is no trick to it," Carlston said. "Lady Helen wishes you to sense her energy."

Still cautious, Mr King drew off his own glove and fastidiously placed it in his upturned hat. With one last glance at Carlston – a chance, it would seem, for the Earl to halt the unseemly proceedings – he reached across and placed his fingers upon Helen's outstretched hand. His skin was cool against her own, the press of his fingers firm.

He looked into her eyes, head to one side as if he listened. Could he hear the beat of her bond with Carlston, the relentless hum of power in her bones, the chorus that howled their deaths in ghastly whispers?

The wariness upon his face shifted into a frown, and then his eyes darted to her face, his skin draining of colour. "Good God!" He snatched his hand back. "You are part of a triad. How can that be? How did it happen?"

"We do not know," Helen said. "But we believe it has prised open a rift and it is forcing its way out of me."

"You are right." Mr King stepped back, and for an instant she saw sharp fear. A rare, unguarded glimpse, quickly hidden. "You seem to be holding the power back by sheer will, but from what I sensed that will not work much longer. You need to anchor it now – before it overwhelms your control!"

"What do you mean? Anchor it how?"

"You have never reclaimed – I did not sense any of the immovable energy in you. That is why that blood and death power is not tethered to your soul, why it is forcing its way out." He pulled on his glove again, working his fingers into it with a feverish intensity. "Lady Helen, it is repugnant to me to recommend this, but you need to reclaim a vestige as soon as possible. The amount of death power in you could level this world to the ground."

A vestige – that spark of darkness planted within a human at conception by its Deceiver parent. It was the only kind of Deceiver energy that stayed, immovable, within a Reclaimer's body.

Helen looked at Carlston. They had decided it would be best if she did not reclaim any progeny and absorb their vestige. Had that been a mistake? For a dizzying second, she saw an image of Isabella Pike in the parlour, straining against her hold. A vestige ready to reclaim nearby.

"If I open myself to the power, I may not be able to control it," she said to Mr King.

"That is indeed the risk. But I swear it is the lesser risk compared to what will happen if you do not anchor all that energy. You will need to be swift and brutal. This will not be about saving the progeny, Lady Helen. This will be about ripping out as much immovable vestige energy as you can and absorbing it into your soul to tie down the power – before it overwhelms you."

Carlston frowned at the savage instruction. Was he too thinking of Isabella? Surely the risk was too high: to her and to themselves? Besides, it could be a Deceiver trick. And yet also a chance to control the power.

Mr King donned his hat. "I have answered your questions and kept my part of the agreement, Lord Carlston. I trust you will keep your word and leave Bath tomorrow. Even a vestige tether will not hold forever." He bowed. "I bid you good night, and good luck."

Helen listened as he climbed the stairs, his swift footsteps beating a rhythm of alarm. They waited until the tinkle of the bell sounded, the door shut, and only the sound of Mr Sheppard at his cutting could be heard.

"Do you believe him?" Carlston asked.

"What he said about the fracture and his kind pouring through tallies with the records we have. And we both saw the melting air at the stones."

"Indeed. I certainly want to believe him about the *Mors Ultima*. He said his own power was halved by the death of his dyad partner. If that is truly the case, we can disable our Grand Deceiver if we can kill one of them *Mors Ultima*."

"A difficult task if they can jump into any body at any time," Helen said. "We cannot just reclaim their progeny and leave them no place to go like a normal Deceiver."

"Still, it is a better alternative than destroying the Trinitas." He gave her a wry smile. "We do not hold the Colligat, and I would rather not destroy the earth or kill the Ligatus."

"Thank you," she said, matching his wryness.

"I believe him about the Grand Deceiver, but I'm not so sure about reclaiming the vestige. It could be a very clever way to destroy us."

"To me, his fear of the Ligatus power was real," Helen said. "And he does want to protect Bath."

"The fear struck me as genuine too." He rubbed the back of his neck, considering. "When all is said and done, we must come back to the fact that the manifestations are increasing in number and intensity. The Ligatus power is breaking through. I think we must take the chance."

"I think so too," Helen said. Was it the right decision? The doubt hardened in her innards like cold stone.

"We must tell Pike about this interview," Carlston added.

"Isabella is the closest known progeny, and you saw her state. Reclaiming her will not only save her life, but also ours." He paused. "Possibly."

"But do we have any hair from her Deceiver sire for the Elixir of the Soul?"

"No."

She spread her hands in mystification. "Then how are we to do the ritual? We need the elixir to help us travel the pathway to her soul."

"We do in a normal reclaiming, but this is far from normal." Carlston rubbed his eyes wearily. Whatever was coming next was not good news. "I think your hair and hers will be enough to create the link. After that, I believe the Ligatus power will rip a pathway into Isabella's soul. The Deceiver energy will seek its own."

"Just like it did with Mad Lester," Helen whispered, remembering the ravening, boiling force from the journal that had fused her and the boy together as it stripped the vestige from him. The power had nearly destroyed her mind, and buried her in a Reclaimer fugue for hours. "The risk will be enormous."

"I know. To you as well. There is not only the reclaiming itself, but what comes after. The ague."

Helen nodded. She had seen Carlston suffer the ague – the inevitable result of taking in the toxic vestige energy – after he had reclaimed Jeremiah. His body had shaken so violently that Quinn had been forced to hold him down.

"At least I know what is coming," she said. "But Isabella has not agreed to any of this. We must tell Mr Pike everything and abide by his decision."

Carlston stood silent, his jaw set.

"Do you not agree?" she pressed.

"In principle I agree, but in practice I fear we may not have the time for such niceties." He looked at Delia's covered body. "The gloves are off now, and we are fighting for our lives."

Chapter Eighteen

At the Queen's Square lodgings, the little brown-haired maid who served Mr and Mrs Pike bobbed a curtsey, her anxious gaze fixed on Carlston. "My master, Mrs Taylor and the two other gentlemen took the mistress to the Cross Bath, my lord," she said, her hands twisting into her apron.

"Your mistress is awake *already*?" Helen asked. By the amount of laudanum they had poured down Isabella's throat, she should have been senseless for the whole night.

"She woke but an hour after her medicine, my lady, and was crying and screaming and beating at herself. Mrs Taylor said they must take her to the mineral baths to calm her down. My mistress can have it to herself after six, you see. Mr Pike arranged it so with the serjeant and cloth-women."

"Did they leave any message for us?" Carlston asked.

"The big man with the heathen drawings," she touched her cheek, "said if you were to come by to direct you to the bath, and to say Miss Darby has gone back to the Royal Crescent with Mr Hammond."

No doubt to help Hallifax protect those at the townhouse and to ensure Aunt did not become alarmed at her absence,

Helen thought. Poor Darby; it was an awful way to spend her wedding night.

"Thank you," Carlston said and led the way back down the staircase to the foyer. "It is perhaps fortuitous," he added to Helen. "According to Pike, the warm waters bring almost immediate tranquillity to his wife, even moments of lucidity. It will be easier to reclaim her if she has some measure of calm."

If Pike agrees, Helen silently added. Or even better, if Isabella was lucid enough to agree.

She frowned as the implication of Carlston's words became clear. "Do you mean I should reclaim her in the water?"

He opened the front door and stood aside. "I think you will have a better chance if you do. She will be calm, and you know the process requires meditation on your part. That will also be helped by the warm mineral waters."

Helen paused upon the porch to look out over the shadowy gardens set in the middle of the square, the obelisk a dark arrow pointing to the night sky and the round, bright moon. Reclaimer power was at its height at the full moon.

"What about the possibility that the water will amplify the Ligatus?" she said, the harsh cold chilling her breath into white steam. "Mr King confirmed the relationship between Deceiver power and water. With that and the full moon, I might blow up this entire city."

"The water might also work in your favour. We do not know." He offered his arm and they descended the steps. "I will be there too, instructing you. We will save Isabella, and we will save ourselves."

He said it so confidently that Helen allowed herself to believe him.

The Cross Bath – so named for the stone cross that had once stood within it, but had long since been removed – was situated at the end of Bath Street. Helen studied the building as they approached: a handsome, somewhat triangular design made of the local golden stone, with a rounded wing on each side and a tall frontage that housed the chimney and its name in crisply carved gold lettering: *Cross Bath Pump Room*. She had never been inside; this bath, along with the King's, Queen's and Hot Baths, was more for the invalid patients of the hospital and the lower orders. People of condition attended the Private Baths on Stall Street.

Lord Carlston opened the door and Helen stepped from the freezing night into the damp warmth of the Pump Room, the difference of temperature and air thick in her nose and throat. An old woman, dressed in a plain blue gown with her hair bound into a linen turban, rose from a chair beside the pump and curtseyed. The folded linen stacked in easy reach marked her as the cloth-woman.

Quinn, lounging against the wall, straightened. "My lord! Is all well?"

"Not entirely," Carlston said. "Where is Pike?"

"In the pool with his wife. She is calmer with him at her side."

"Tell him we need to speak."

Quinn bowed and departed throughout the Pump Room door.

"The dressing rooms and slips have their doors outside, my lord. Mighty inconvenient," the cloth-woman explained. "Would you care for a glass of the waters?"

Carlston waved away the offer.

Quinn returned, closing the door behind him. "He says he dare not leave Mrs Pike while she's in the bath, my lord. And it takes some time to remove her from it."

Carlston glanced at Helen. "We will join him."

He beckoned to the cloth-woman. "Help Lady Helen ready

herself for the pool." He pulled a coin from his fob pocket and passed it to her, his voice a command. "Then you shall leave. Understood?"

"Yes, my lord." She took the coin, then gathered up a wad of the drying sheets and passed them to him. "For after, my lord, but I have no men's jackets left. None that are clean anyways. I could bring one from the Hot Baths across the street."

He shook his head. "It is not important."

The woman collected another pile of linens, then bobbed a curtsey towards Helen. "This way, my lady."

They went back into the night, the cold air sending a shiver along Helen's shoulders, and cut through the columns of the portico to a door set into the Bath Street frontage. The cloth-woman opened it and stood back with a curtsey.

Inside was a small dressing room, bare of all furniture except for one wooden bench, with a doorway that clearly led to the bath – Helen could hear muffled voices beyond it – and a hearth in which embers still glowed. She hurried over to the modest warmth.

The cloth-woman placed the stack of drying sheets upon the bench and closed the door. She curtseyed. "Your cloak, my lady?"

It was duly handed over and the woman folded it neatly, then received Helen's bonnet and reticule.

"I do not have my bathing dress with me," Helen said.

The cloth-woman looked up, her face solemn. "Forgive me for asking, my lady, but is this," she waved in the direction of the bath, "your own choosing? I have a granddaughter, you see, about your age. You could leave this chamber right now, if you wish. I could dally to give you time."

"No, I am here of my own volition," Helen said, touched by the woman's concern. "Thank you."

She nodded. "As to your dress, a bathing jacket be included in the fee, my lady. You can wear it over your chemise. I would take off your stays though. Hard to undo when the ties be wet." She risked a small smile. "And they can tighten something awful."

Helen took her advice, and a little while later stood in just her chemise and the long brown bathing jacket, her hair wrapped in the same turban style as her attendant. Her gown, petticoat, stays and hose had been piled neatly atop her cloak.

"Now, there be plenty of sheets here," the woman said, patting the pile. "Make sure you be full dry before you go out again into the night air." She cocked her head. "That nurse in there, will she help you dress? I can stay if you want, coin or no coin."

"Thank you, but Mrs Taylor will help me," Helen said, her arms wrapped over her breasts. An image rose in her mind: blue fire exploding through the Great Pulteney Street house. The rift had not even been open then and she had destroyed most of the building. "Do you live nearby?"

"Not really, my lady. Near the Great Road."

Helen nodded. If the worst were to happen, maybe this kind woman would be far enough away to survive.

The cloth-woman curtseyed. "Good night then, my lady."

Helen watched her depart, then drew a steadying breath, shaking off the ghastly fantasy. It was at least pleasant to breathe deeply without the constriction of stays. She looked down at her chest. The air was warm, but what if the double layer of cloth did not hide... She shook her head. The water would be warm too, and such physical mortifications were nothing compared to the prospect of reclaiming Isabella.

She pushed through the bath-side door, and followed the gentle decline of the slip-walk made for those who could not manage steps or needed to be carried by sedan chair into the pool. The stone chilled her bare feet, but all her attention was drawn upward. The Cross Bath was open to the heavens and the cloudless night sky stretched overhead, bright with stars, the huge moon casting the buildings beyond the walls into silvery relief.

"Oh my," she breathed.

"Lady Helen," Carlston called softly.

She turned to look down into the oblong pool. He was already standing in the water, and must have submerged his whole body on entry, for his white linen shirt clung wetly to his chest and outlined the muscles of his shoulders and arms. Lud, the linen was almost transparent.

She quickly shifted her attention to Mr Pike and Isabella. Mr Pike was mostly submerged and supporting his wife's head and shoulders as she floated on her back, eyes closed, her pale, sharp features serene above the dark wet linen of her bathing jacket.

Mrs Taylor, the nurse, was not in the bath, but stood upon its edge, hands on hips, watching her patient. The stone wall behind her was lit gold by oil lamps, which brought the large carving of a man upon it into sharp relief – Bladud, Helen recalled from the guidebook, the eighth king of Briton and founder of the hot springs.

"Tell me what has happened, Lord Carlston. I insist," Pike said. He kept his voice low and calm, but Helen heard the misgiving deep within it.

Carlston turned to the nurse. "You are relieved of your duty for now, Mrs Taylor. Go back to Queen's Square."

"She has taken the oath," Pike said.

"Even so."

Pike nodded confirmation of the order to the nurse, his face tense. With a curtsey, the woman retreated through the other slip doorway. Helen listened, following her footsteps out of the dressing room.

Carlston was clearly listening too, for as soon as Mrs Taylor reached Bath Street, he addressed Pike. "Lady Helen has found the Bath Deceiver. It is Mr King."

Pike raised his brows at Helen. "Mr King? Well, that is oddly suitable." He gave a dour smile. "Did you find out what you needed to know?"

"Lady Helen, would you be so kind as to join us?" Carlston said, ignoring the question.

Helen walked down the stone slip, the hot mineral waters soft around her toes, then her ankles. Her steps slowed as the rising water gathered her hems around her calves, but she pulled the wet cloth away from her legs and forged further into the steaming bath. Thighs, hips, belly, breasts, the heat seeping into her chilled skin and loosening her muscles.

"Lord Carlston, did you find out what you needed to know?" Pike repeated, his voice hardening.

Isabella's eyelids fluttered and she gave a groan, as if she felt his suspicion through the cradle of his arms.

"Shh, my darling, nothing to worry about," Pike whispered against her ear.

"There have been some events you are not yet aware of," Carlston said, "which now have a bearing upon what we must do next to defeat the Grand Deceiver."

"Events I am not aware of?" Pike echoed, struggling to keep the volume and edge from his voice.

Helen slowly waded across to them as Carlston told Pike about the emergence of the rift inside her caused by the mesmerism session, their visit to the stone circle, the subsequent manifestations, Mr King's information and his solution to the rift's danger. She dipped lower in the hot water until it covered her shoulders, only her cheeks feeling the bite of the night air, listening to Carlston's soft, firm voice lay down the terrible choice before Pike. She could not look at the anguish dawning on the man's face, and so kept her eyes upon Carlston, watching the strong line of his throat, the gleam of his wet skin, the sympathy in his eyes. She could not fully forgive nor forget the pain and anguish that Pike had inflicted upon Mr Hammond and herself at Brighton, the coercion and brutality, but even he did not deserve such a punishment. Isabella certainly did not, for all that she had killed a Reclaimer and destroyed her husband's calling as the man's Terrene. The poor woman had been insane at the time, just as Carlston had been insane when he killed Stokes. Surely God must forgive such unknowing crimes.

"You should have told me about the rift well before this," Pike said quietly, his fury evident in the clench of his jaw. "You truly believe that reclaiming Isabella will tether this power?"

"I do," Carlston said. "And possibly save her sanity and her life. Our lives as well."

"But there is just as much possibility it will kill her," Pike said. He smoothed a curled lock of wet hair from Isabella's forehead, his attention fixed fiercely upon it. "You are asking me to offer up my wife as a potential sacrifice."

"I am," Carlston said unflinchingly. "I will not soften the truth, Pike. Saving Isabella cannot be our first priority. Lady Helen and I sincerely hope we can reclaim her, but if we do not tether the Ligatus power, it will destroy us and any chance of stopping the Grand Deceiver."

"And the Grand Deceiver is here," Pike said, almost to himself. He squeezed shut his eyes. "I know you have both lost people you love – or at least thought you had. But how can I possibly do this to my wife?"

Carlston's eyes flickered at the tactless remark. It had not been intentional, Helen thought, just gracelessness made from misery.

"You have given your oath to the King to protect England," he said. "As we have."

"And I have given my oath to protect Isabella," Pike snapped.

The violence of his words opened Isabella's eyes again. Her cracked lips moved. "Ignatious?" It was barely audible.

"Here I am, my love," he said.

Her sweet smile appeared for a moment, then her eyes closed again. "So tired." The words were as soft as a breath.

"The bath is strengthening the effect of the laudanum." He bent his head closer, resting his cheek against her wrapped hair. "That is the first time she has recognised me in three days."

"It will only get worse," Carlston said. "We all know I would be dead by now if Lady Helen had not intervened at Barnes Terrace. This kind of vestige madness can only be cured by alchemy, and I do not think Isabella has much more time."

The sound of the dressing room door opening and approaching footsteps turned Helen in the pool, her movement slowed by the drag of her wet chemise and jacket. Mr Quinn appeared at the left slip, carrying a leather saddlebag. He bowed his head in greeting, then placed the bag on the stone floor beside the pool. Helen heard the soft, tinny clink of metal against metal. She knew that sound: the silver bowls to combine the alchemical elixirs.

Pike observed Quinn for a long, pained moment, then addressed Carlston. "Are those the supplies necessary for reclaiming?"

"Yes," Carlston said. A clipped confirmation, but heavy with expectation.

From outside the bounds of the bath walls came the muffled

sound of a carriage, the clack of hooves beating out the silent seconds.

Finally Pike said, "Do it then. Take the vestige while you still can. May God help us and protect us." He pressed a fierce kiss upon his wife's head.

"We will need to cut a piece of Isabella's hair, dry if possible," Carlston said. "Yours as well, Lady Helen. And we should all position ourselves closer to the edge of the pool – to make and administer the elixirs."

And for ease of exit if the reclaiming went awry, Helen thought grimly. Her stomach clenched at the thought of what was to come. The Ligatus power only ever brought chaos, and here they were, adding the very element that seemed to amplify it.

She swam an awkward stroke towards Quinn and the silver bowls, creating a small wave that slapped over the stone lip. "Do you think Isabella would be calm enough to come out of the water?" she asked Pike. "I think it would be safer if we were not in it."

She shot a glance at Carlston. He conceded with a nod.

"She does not like to leave the water," Pike said, slowly towing his wife towards the edge. "But she may stay calm – I cannot be sure. She is unpredictable, especially with Reclaimers."

"Nonetheless, I think we should try," Helen said.

"Mr Quinn, will you assist me to lift her from the pool?" Pike inquired.

"Of course."

Quinn positioned himself to help, but as soon as Pike moved away from Isabella in preparation, she howled and thrashed against the unfamiliar hands that tried to grip her under her arms. Her flailing limbs sent waves of water slapping onto the stone surrounds, drenching Quinn's breeches and washing the metal bowls into a clanging collision against the wall.

"Leave her!" Carlston said. "She will have the whole city down upon us."

Pike gathered Isabella once more into his arms, holding her head above the surface. Immediately, she quieted.

"We must stay in the pool," Carlston said. "Bring her closer, Pike, so we may take a piece of hair." He turned to Helen. "Do you wish me to see the vestige too? If so, the elixir will need my hair as well."

"Yes, in case something goes wrong," Helen said. She wet her lips, tasting the earthy minerals of the water upon her tongue. "Will you give me your word that you will stop the reclaiming if the power becomes uncontrollable, as it did at the stone circle and the house?"

"I will," he said.

She met his eyes. *I will. I will. I will.* The beat of their bond.

Quinn retrieved the bowls, dried them upon one of the sheets, then produced scissors from the saddlebag and handed them to Carlston.

"Hold Isabella still," Carlston ordered Pike. Gently, he found a dry curl under her hair wrap, carefully snipped, and dropped it into the bowl. "Lady Helen?"

She turned her back, lifting her turban, and closed her eyes at the touch of Carlston's fingers in her hair, the warmth of his breath on her neck. It was a disturbing and oddly reassuring sensation.

He placed the lock into the silver bowl, and handed the scissors to Helen. "My turn."

She dried her hands upon the sheet and waded a step closer to him. She drew his hair between her fingers and thumb. His head was turned towards her, dark eyes following the gentle trajectory of her fingers.

"The ends are probably too wet," he said.

She pushed her fingertips through the short, drier layer of hair, feeling the beautiful shape of skull meeting spine beneath, and heard the sharp draw of his breath.

"There," she said, ignoring the leap within her own body. A snip and a black lock was harvested. She dropped it into the bowl atop her own brown curl and Isabella's fairer offering.

Carlston turned to Quinn, avoiding her gaze. "Light the taper."

Quinn drew the thin candle from the saddlebag and disappeared into the dressing room, returning swiftly with the wick alight, his palm cupped protectively around the flame. He offered it to Carlston.

"No, Lady Helen must cast out the devil," Carlston said. "She is the one who will be reclaiming Mrs Pike."

Helen had never performed the ritual herself, although she had watched Carlston reclaim Jeremiah. When she had reclaimed Mad Lester, it had been unintentional, caused by the Ligatus power written into the pages of Benchley's journal in blood ink. Her mouth dried at the memory. Even when it was still bound inside the book, the power had almost dragged her into insanity. Now she held it *inside* her mind. Was it even possible to control it long enough to reclaim Isabella's vestige and tether the squirming hell of it?

She waded to the edge of the pool, fighting the hot-bath lassitude that weighed down her limbs, and took the taper. A touch of the tiny flame to the hair and it hissed, sending up foul smoke that smelled of sulphur. Helen coughed and turned her face, waiting for it to dissipate. She waved the last of it away, then checked the bowl. Dark ash powdered its base.

"Do you have the seawater and milk?" she asked Quinn.

The bottle was already out of the saddlebag. Quinn drew the silver stopper and passed the odd mixture across. Helen carefully poured it into the bowl, swirling the ash and the liquid together.

"The Elixir of the Soul," she announced.

She passed the bottle back to Quinn, then raised the bowl to her lips, trying to block the repulsive smell. Bad eggs and soured milk. She took a swig, throwing back her head to wash it past her gag of disgust.

"I had forgotten just how bad it is," she said, grimacing at the acidic aftertaste. She passed the bowl to Carlston.

He looked at the mixture with misgiving. *"Salut."* He took a large mouthful, squeezing his eyes shut as he swallowed, then returned the bowl to Helen.

He could have passed it on to Pike himself, Helen thought, then realised it was a courtesy. She was the Reclaimer. The leader.

She passed the elixir to Pike. "Isabella needs to swallow a good mouthful. It will help to establish the link between us."

Pike deftly opened his wife's mouth and tipped the bowl, holding her close as her eyes fluttered open and her throat muscles contracted from the passage of the foul liquid. Her hand slapped the water in protest, sending a spray over them both.

"I'm sorry, I'm sorry. All done now, no more," Pike said gently, his face haggard in the yellow lamplight.

"No more," she murmured, eyes closing again.

Helen waded closer to them. "We need to place our hands upon her."

He nodded, wiping water spray – or was it tears? – from his cheek.

Helen laid her hand upon Isabella's chest. Through the wet cloth, she felt the hard V-shape of Isabella's breastbone and the slow beat of her heart. The gateway to the soul.

"Your hand must be on top," Carlston instructed softly.

Of course; this time she was not the observer. She must be free to grab the vestige.

She withdrew her hand and met his eyes – *Not the best start* – but found only a smile of reassurance as he spread his fingers to make the connection to Isabella's soul. With a deep breath, Helen placed her left hand over his, feeling the warmth of his fingers under her palm. She cradled one side of Isabella's head with her right hand, fingers finding the stark angle of cheekbone and jaw.

Carlston did the same at the other side, pausing as Isabella groaned. He studied her for a moment, then pressed the span of his fingertips across her forehead, temple and cheek.

Helen glanced at him: *Is she ready? Are you ready?*

The barest of nods: *Ready.*

"Mr Pike, please remain as quiet as possible so that Lord Carlston and I can find the path to Isabella's soul," Helen said.

"I understand."

She saw the prayer in his eyes – *Save her!* – and the weight of his fear spiked her own doubt. *Holy Father, help me,* she prayed.

The warmth of the water had already brought a softness into her mind, a malleability that had allowed the hum in her bones to come to the fore. She focused past the resonance and found the beat of her Reclaimer bond, strong and sure. It would help to establish the pathway. She closed her eyes, drawing in the warm steamy air and releasing it slowly and carefully. Carlston, she knew, would already be following her rhythm, matching his breath to hers, merging their pulses into one beat like their bond. Beneath her hand, she felt the rise and fall of Isabella's chest, the rhythm slowly melding with her own ebb and flow of air. Inhale, exhale, over and over, drawing all three of them beyond the limits of flesh.

She found a sound within herself – a sweet note, somehow

319

sustained. The key to the soul. The pressure of the song built inside her, through her, drawing Isabella and Carlston deeper and deeper into the connection. They were on the brink, balancing between flesh and soul. And then they drew a breath so deep and full of harmony that it snapped something open, deep and bright and joyous.

She opened her eyes. A bilious yellow glow surrounded Isabella. Helen had seen this before: the sickened soul light. In contrast, the light around Carlston's and her own hands and arms shone bright and dense.

Carlston glanced at her, his breathing still in concert with her own, an odd expression in his eyes: resignation. Ah, he did not expect to save Isabella and no wonder – the vestige was huge. A pudding-sized mass of darkness set into the sickly light above her head, squirming with black tentacles rooted deep in her soul, smothering it into a bare flicker of light.

A familiar whispering howl shivered down Helen's spine. The Ligatus; it was rising.

She saw Carlston register it too, through the link, the steady rhythm of his breath breaking for a moment. "Quick! We don't have long," he said.

Helen drew back her fist. Where was the flaw? For all the vestige's size, there must be a weakness in the heaving labyrinth of tentacles. Some kind of laxness in the tangle. She searched the squirming monstrosity. There!

She punched into the outer layers, forcing a way up to her knuckles. Beyond the soul plane, she saw Pike flinch in the water as if the blow had been for him. The tentacles contracted at the assault, then slithered across her hand, blocking her passage and wrapping her fingers in an oily muscular web that ground her bones together. She felt – no, heard – a child's sob in her mind. Little Timothy, coming closer.

She gritted her teeth and rammed her hand deeper into the dark mass, groping, trying to hook her fingers into its centre. The inner tentacles slithered and seethed, an unyielding wall. She could not get through. Heat flashed through her body, a searing herald of the howling, screaming, sobbing power. Around them the water swirled, the steam misting upward, dense and hot.

"Take it!" Carlston yelled. "For Christ's sake, take it."

A dank metallic taste flooded her mouth. A boiling sensation tightened her skin, and then the gibbering, ravening force of the Ligatus rose in a seething chaotic sweep of power, called towards the foul dark energy. Helen felt her mind seize beneath the onslaught, all control slipping. Around her the pool heaved, loosening her foothold, the slapping waves knocking her into Carlston. She felt his hands brace her against the roiling water. Desperately she fixed upon the wild energy breaking over them. So much power!

In her mind she grabbed for it, finding a momentary hold in the terrifying turmoil. She bent her head against the driving force within and focused upon one thought: *save her*. Channelling as much of the power as she could, she slammed her fist into the vestige again. For a terrible second, the wall of tentacles held, and then it collapsed, her fingers digging into the slimy mass behind. She wrenched her hand back, ripping the vestige from its roots, the tentacles spreading wide then wrapping around her wrist. She glimpsed Isabella's soul. A flicker. Then tasted blood, death, ash as the dark mass melted into her own bright light.

She staggered in the water, the link broken with Isabella and Carlston as the foul energy anchored itself into her soul, a vein of darkness within the glow of grace. She felt the vestige wrap itself around the gibbering power of the Ligatus like a noose, anchoring the howling blood power into her mind and heart.

She heard Carlston yell, "Quinn, get Mrs Pike out!", and then she collapsed under the water, its heat burning her eyes and filling her nose, her mouth. She floundered, trying to stand, her chemise caught around her legs. A hand closed around her arm, pulling her up, and propped her against the side of the pool. She gasped for air, eyes stinging, everything a blur.

"Did it work?" Carlston demanded, a bleary pale face beside her, his dark hair slicked wet against his head. "Is the power tethered?"

Panting, she rubbed her eyes, trying to focus inward. Had it worked? Yes, there was a new sense of stability. Of control. She had done it.

"It worked!" The relief brought a gasping laugh that cracked into a wet cough.

She glimpsed Carlston's broad smile, and then she collapsed into a heaving spasm of coughing that doubled her over the side of the pool. She felt his hand upon her back, his touch almost an embrace, steadying her until she found her breath.

"The ague is starting," he said. He pulled himself out of the pool and crouched beside her, offering his hand, his shirt and breeches streaming with water. "You need to get out and get dressed. Now! You'll only have about twenty minutes before it really hits you."

Helen grabbed the stone edge, ready to haul herself out of the water, then saw Pike and Quinn crouched over Isabella. Her arms and legs were splayed on the wet stone floor, her sodden hair loose and spread like a sea creature.

"She's not breathing, my lord," Quinn said.

Carlston lunged across to her, landing on his knees to peer into her face. "Damn it."

He rolled Isabella onto her side and slapped her back, over and over, each heavy blow shifting her across the stone, closer to Helen. Her eyes were open, dilated pupils fixed upon the wall beyond, her face slack. A trickle of water ran from her mouth as her body lurched forward again.

"Stop!" Pike pulled at Carlston's shoulder. "Stop, you will hurt her."

Quinn wrenched Pike back. "God's blood, man, he is just trying to help her."

"She didn't go under the water, I'm sure of it," Carlston said between slaps.

Quinn leaned over Isabella and cupped his hand beneath her nose. "Still nothing, my lord, but I don't think she drowned. She ain't got the blue in her skin."

"But I saved her," Helen said. "I got the vestige."

"I saw you pull it out of her, but there was no answering bloom of soul light," Carlston said heavily.

"I'll keep trying, my lord," Quinn said. He rolled Isabella onto her back and lifted her flaccid arms above her head.

"Get off her!" Pike screamed. He crawled over to his wife and pulled her shoulders onto his lap, cradling her head. "Isabella? My darling?"

In silence, they all watched the body in his arms. No rise of chest, no fluttering of eyelids, no blessed fit of coughing.

"I'm sorry, Pike," Carlston said gently. "I have never seen a vestige that big. It was too much for her, too far embedded in her soul. She did well to hold against it this long."

Pike cupped his dead wife's face. "No. You are wrong. Isabella?" Her eyes stared sightlessly up at him. "Oh, dear God, no," he whispered.

He looked at Helen, his mouth drawing into a snarl of accusation. "Did you even try to save her?"

Helen stepped back, the water rippling around her retreat. "I did, Mr Pike. I swear it upon God's word." She looked to

Carlston for confirmation. "You saw me take the vestige."

"Lady Helen and I did everything possible," Carlston said. "It was a risk. We all knew it."

"A risk," Pike whispered. He cradled Isabella's head to his chest, his face tightening into anguish as he laid his cheek against her sodden hair. "God forgive me, my darling, for letting them near you." He looked up, his voice fierce through his choking tears. "Get away from us. You had no intention of saving her!"

Carlston touched Quinn's shoulder, and the two men rose and retreated a few steps. Helen heard Carlston issue a quiet order to his Terrene.

"Mrs Pike must be found in her own bed, not here. Go to Queen's Square and bring back Mrs Taylor and one of the chairs we can trust."

"Yes, my lord." Quinn dipped his head and, with a last pitying look at the husband and wife, departed.

"Lady Helen, you and I must return to the Royal Crescent with expediency," Carlston said. "You need your Terrene and a safe place to ride out the ague."

Helen shook her head. "I must do something. I must —"

She had no idea what she must do, but she could not leave the Pikes. She squeezed her eyes shut. First Delia dead, and now Isabella too.

"You can do nothing now except get out of the pool and get dressed," Carlston said. It was a command.

"I tried to save her," she whispered. "I tried."

"I know."

She waded back to the other slip to exit the pool, her body unbearably heavy. She had failed again. She could not save anyone.

Chapter Nineteen

The first spasm overtook Helen on Brock Street. She gripped the cold paling of an iron fence, gasping for breath as a wave of nausea and searing pain rocked her on her feet.

Carlston took her other arm, holding her upright. "We are nearly at Lady Dunwick's house," he said.

She drew a deeper breath, relieved to find it did not hold hot pain at the end of it. A blessing. She straightened and took a tentative step. "How long will this last?" She was not sure she could bear so much pain.

"I'm afraid it is going to be an hour or so at least. It is a baptism of sorts – we all go through it after our first reclaim." The bright moonlight caught the sympathy in his eyes.

God forfend, an hour?

The next spasm came at the front door of Lady Dunwick's townhouse. Helen stumbled up the last step, her legs losing the battle against the violent convulsion that shook her body. She doubled over, spine on fire, and grabbed the front of Carlston's coat, the shirt beneath sodden and cold. He wrapped his arm around her, hauling her back to her feet.

She blinked away tears as the butler opened the door, his

face blurring into a pale oval of reproach. No one arrived at this hour.

"My lord!" He stared at Helen in Carlston's embrace. "My lady? Is that you?"

"For God's sake, man, get out of the way. Lady Helen is unwell."

The butler stood aside, his face rigid.

"I cannot walk," Helen said through panting breaths.

Carlston scooped one arm around her waist and the other under her legs and hoisted her up against his chest, holding her tight against the bone-shaking seizure. He addressed the butler. "Which room still has a high-stoked fire?"

"Drawing room, my lord," the butler said quickly.

Carlston strode into the foyer and took the staircase, the butler trailing behind. Through her squint of pain, Helen could see the man's anxious assessment of her condition.

"Shall I call for a doctor, my lord?"

"Absolutely not. Who is in the drawing room?" Carlston demanded.

"His Grace the Duke of Selburn, Lord Hayden, Lady Pennworth, Mr Hammond, and the constable, Hallifax."

Carlston gave a short, abrupt curse. Helen missed the sense of it, but the butler flinched.

"Your brother and your betrothed – just what we need," Carlston said to her, then addressed the butler again. "Where are your mistress and Lady Elizabeth?" He paused, clearly sorting out who should be where. "And Ladies Georgina and Margaret?"

"Lady Dunwick retired, my lord, unwell. Lady Elizabeth went up with her to help her settle. Neither Lady Georgina or Lady Margaret have come down since the ... incident."

"And Lord Henry? Did he not arrive with Selburn?"

"Only Lord Hayden accompanied His Grace, my lord."

"Well, that is something at least."

They reached the first floor, the warmth of the house easing the chill on Helen's skin but not the pain that wrenched her muscles and tore at her innards. The footman waiting outside the drawing room doors straightened at their arrival, his professional demeanour rapidly shifting into shock.

Helen could not stop a groan rising past her lips. Carlston's arms tightened again around her shaking body.

"Get Miss Darby," he ordered the butler. "Tell her to bring two blankets, a clean scrap of cloth and a piece of wood."

"A piece of wood, my lord?"

"About so big." Carlston awkwardly shifted his hand from under Helen's back and measured three inches between finger and thumb. "And bring brandy when you've done that."

The butler nodded and hurried up the next flight of stairs.

"You!" Carlston said to the footman. "Stop gawping like a fool and open the door."

Inside the drawing room, the noise of their approach had not gone unnoticed. Mr Hallifax waited just inside the door, and Helen saw that her aunt and Andrew had risen from the sofa. The Duke stood at the sideboard, claret decanter still in his hand, his attention upon the door.

"Heaven forbid," Aunt said. "Is that Helen?"

Selburn's face darkened. He slammed down the decanter. "What the hell have you done now, Carlston?"

Ignoring them both, Carlston addressed Mr Hallifax. "Jacob, my thanks for coming so promptly. Is Lennox outside?" At the other Reclaimer's nod, Carlston added, "Would you secure the perimeter?"

"Of course," Mr Hallifax said. He leaned closer to Helen and said with gruff kindness, "This first ague will feel like you're dying, my lady, but it will pass. We all go through it to become what we truly are." He departed, closing the door behind him.

"What the devil are you doing?" Andrew demanded, lunging at Carlston. "Unhand my sister."

"Don't be a fool, Hayden," Carlston snapped. "Clearly Lady Helen is unwell. Hammond, if you would?"

Helen saw Mr Hammond come into view, hand outstretched to intercept Andrew.

"It will be better if you are on the floor," Carlston murmured close to her ear as he carried her to the hearth. "I have fallen from chairs and sofas mid-ague, and I do not recommend it."

She gave a barely controlled nod, her teeth clenched as a new wave of pain rolled through her body. He crouched to lie her gently on the carpet beside the fireplace, then gripped her hand briefly. A silent message of solidarity.

"Take a seat, Hayden," she heard Hammond say. "You'll only get in the way."

Selburn stalked over to face Carlston, both of them looming over her. "Tell me what is wrong with her! What did Hallifax mean by first ague?"

"It's something to do with this Reclaimer business, isn't it?" Andrew said, pushing past Hammond to range himself beside the Duke. "Selburn told me what it was all about."

Helen closed her eyes. Lud, Andrew knew?

Carlston rounded on the Duke. "You told Hayden? In violation of your oath?" Helen could not see his face, but whatever expression was on it made Selburn step back.

"Told him what? What is going on?" Aunt asked. She crouched beside Helen, cupping her face with cool, soft hands. "My dear girl, you are burning with fever."

The convulsion suddenly eased. Helen took a deep breath.

"It is not as bad as it looks," she whispered. A blatant lie, but she could not bear the fear in her aunt's face.

"As I see it, Hayden deserves to know what is going on," Selburn said. "He is her brother after all."

"Know about what?" Aunt asked again, looking over her shoulder. "If Hayden knows, I should too."

"That decision is not yours to make, Selburn," Carlston said. "You do not have the authority."

The Duke shrugged. "He was with me when the message came to Chenwith about Miss Cransdon's murder. What was I to say?"

"Anything else would have been preferable," Carlston snapped. He took off his hat and set it on the side table, then began to unbutton his greatcoat. "Lady Pennworth, would you please help Lady Helen out of her bonnet? She would be far more comfortable."

"Lord Carlston, what is wrong with my niece?" Aunt demanded. She undid the ribbons beneath Helen's chin and took off the bonnet. "Sweet heavens, child, your hair is soaked! You need a doctor. Who is the best here in Bath, Duke? I will send a man immediately."

Helen grasped her aunt's arm, gathering the strength to make the words. "No doctor."

"My dearest, you are very ill." Aunt stood, beckoning to Andrew and the Duke. "We must get her off the floor onto the sofa."

"No," Carlston said. "She must stay where she is. It will be safer. Trust me."

"Trust you? I do not trust you!" Aunt's voice rose into a shriek. "What is wrong with my niece?" She paused for a heavy moment. "Why are your clothes wet, Lord Carlston?"

The door opened to admit the butler carrying a silver tray

set with a brandy decanter and a number of glasses. "My lord, Miss Darby is on her way."

"Good. Pour me two measures," Carlston ordered. "Make them big." He crouched beside Helen again. "I believe it is time to inform your aunt of the truth," he said softly.

"I did not want her to know," Helen managed through the rising wave of pain. "Or Andrew."

"A pity your betrothed was not aware of that," he said with an unfriendly glance in Selburn's direction.

Helen tried to lift her head closer. "Not the bawdy house or Amberley," she whispered. "Not the baths."

Carlston gripped her arm briefly. "Only what they need to know."

The butler arrived with the two measures of brandy.

Carlston slotted one glass into Helen's shaking hand, and lifted his own in salute. "Drink. It will help." He drained the liquor in one mouthful.

Helen pressed her lips to the edge of the glass, her teeth clicking against it, and gulped the whole measure. She felt it burn its way through her chest, the fruity heat rising into her nose. It did seem to ease the shaking and the parched rawness of her throat.

Aunt stood over them, her voice quavering with rage. "Lord Carlston, I will not be ignored."

He stood, eyeing her with some sympathy. "Lady Pennworth, I fully intend to offer an explanation, but you will need to wait until I ensure your niece's safety."

"Her safety?"

"She is about to go into a rolling sequence of seizures, and I know how best to prevent any injury."

"Seizures?" she echoed, and sank down upon the sofa.

"Lady Pennworth, Lord Carlston knows what he is doing,"

Hammond said. "Allow me to pour you a glass of brandy."

The door opened again, this time to admit Darby carrying the requested blanket, wood and cloth. She bobbed a curtsey to the general company.

"Over here," Carlston called. "Quickly."

Darby hurried across the room, her eyes fixed upon Helen. "My lady?"

Helen nodded, trying to smile some reassurance through the new onslaught of fire through her body.

"Lady Helen has reclaimed Mrs Pike," Carlston said.

Darby's drawn face lightened into a smile. "At last. I'm so glad."

Carlston shook his head. "Mrs Pike did not survive the removal of the vestige."

"She died?" At Carlston's grim nod, Darby dropped to her knees beside Helen and gripped her hand. "Oh, my lady. I'm so sorry."

Helen felt the sting of tears in her eyes – Darby understood the horror of it, so close upon the heels of Delia's death – but she could not make any answer to her Terrene's sweet sympathy. The new spasm had clamped her jaw shut. The searing pain, like molten metal through her veins, dragged her knees up to her chest. She closed her eyes. God forfend, surely her teeth would break under the clenching force.

She heard Carlston say, "The rift has been dealt with, for now, Darby. Right now, your duty is to get Lady Helen through this first ague. The vestige was far larger than I expected. Her reaction is going to be severe."

The pain eased slightly. Panting, Helen opened her eyes to see Darby wrapping the cloth tightly around the length of wood.

"Mr Quinn taught me what to do, my lord."

"It may take both of us to hold her down," Carlston said.

"Let me know if you cannot manage." He took one of the blankets and wrapped it around himself.

Were the convulsions truly going to get worse?

Darby spread the other blanket over Helen, then crawled around to her back. "It will be all right, my lady," she said, and Helen felt Darby's strong hands find a grip beneath her armpits to pull her onto her lap. "Bite on this."

Deft fingers slid the cloth-wrapped wood between Helen's teeth, the fatty taste of laundry soap on it. She bit down. At least her teeth would not break. Darby's arms locked over her shoulders and stomach, and almost immediately Helen felt an influx of strength, of inner resilience. A godsend, delivered through their Reclaimer–Terrene bond.

"I will be here, holding you the whole time, my lady," Darby said. "You'll be..."

But Helen did not hear the rest of Darby's reassurance. A new wave of agony rolled over her, twisting her against her Terrene's tight hold, her teeth grinding into the cloth-covered bite, her whole body suspended in bone-wrenching, blood-pounding, endless shuddering waves.

She finally surfaced through the layers of pain to hear Carlston say, "What I am about to tell you is vital to the safety of England. Both of you must agree to take an oath to King and country before God..."

His voice faded as the pain rose into another peak. It felt as if she rode upward upon the excruciating crest for hours, yet when she opened her eyes again, Carlston was still talking and Darby's tight hold had not shifted.

"Like me, your sister, your niece, is a Reclaimer. In fact she is a direct inheritor, the most rare of our kind. She inherited her gifts from the late Countess Hayden."

"Are you saying my sister was one of these things too?"

Aunt's voice, horrified. "Is that why she and her husband died?"

"Possibly." Carlston, patient, calm. "Lord Hayden was his wife's Terrene."

"But I am their *son*. Why am I not one of these Reclaimers?" Andrew's voice.

Idiot! Does he want this? Helen managed to think before she was dragged into the fiery torment again. Her fury helped her ride the pain, the tethered Ligatus howling and gibbering as every convulsion anchored the vestige more and more deeply in her soul.

Time passed; she could feel it at the ebb of each rolling wave, the agony softening briefly to gather momentum. She heard snatches of words and phrases: generations old, progeny, skimming energy, the Grand Deceiver.

She surfaced again, her gulping breaths momentarily free from pain. Darby's arms were still locked around her, keeping her from shaking apart. She squinted, trying to focus on the tear-blurred figures bending over her. When would it stop? She had to know. But the only sound she could make was a low animal groan.

"... almost an hour!" The Duke's voice, sharp.

"It is brutal, I know." Carlston. "The vestige she reclaimed is becoming part of her, and there is nothing we can do except keep her safe until it is incorporated." His tall figure bent and his hand rested for a second upon her forehead. A warm, reassuring pressure. "The process is running its normal course."

"Normal?" Selburn's tone was savage. For an instant, Helen's vision cleared and she saw his face: mouth a tight line, fair skin red with fury. "There is nothing normal about my betrothed convulsing on the floor! You have brought this on her, Carlston, and by God, when her duty is done, she will take no part in it ever again. Once this Grand Deceiver is defeated, it is over.

I want you and your damned Dark Days Club as far away from her as possible."

"If that is what Lady Helen wants, I will go," Carlston said flatly. "But right now I don't have time for your ultimatums." He addressed Darby. "Are you managing? Do you need help?"

Helen felt the soft rumble of Darby's voice through her back. "I can feel an echo of the pain. Is that normal?"

"Yes, it is your bond."

Darby's arms tightened a little. "She is so strong. So brave. I do not know if I could bear so much." Strong? Brave? No, no, she just wanted it to stop. She tried to say so, but the fireball rolled over her again, arching her back against Darby's arms, sweeping her into agony.

She woke. Body stretched out on the soft support of a mattress, warm covers, the delicate chain moulding along the edge of the ceiling just visible in the candlelight. Her bedchamber. She blinked. Eyes dry, mouth parched, and no pain – a blessed absence that made her feel as if she was floating.

An image of Delia's throat crusted with blood; and Isabella, her hair spread upon the stone – the last day arrived like a cold weight in her heart.

The tether: was it still in place? She focused inward. The hum was still in her bones, and, of course, the steady beat of her bond with Carlston. The Ligatus felt different. Restrained. Still present, and as dark as ever, but clearly held back by the vestige. She closed her eyes in a brief prayer of thanks. All that pain had been worth it. And yet it had cost Isabella her life.

She cleared her throat, the sound harsh in the silence. A rustle of silk beside the bed. She turned her head upon the pillow.

"Helen, my dear. How do you feel?" Aunt Leonore asked, rising from a chair. The candlelight caught the red rims of her eyes. Poor Aunt; exhausted, and recently weeping.

"How long?" Helen's voice cracked, barely a whisper. "The ague? How long was it?"

"Over two hours." The shock was still in Aunt's voice. "You have been asleep a few hours as well. It is just past two in the morning." A reassuring smile, held a moment too long. "Lord Carlston said that when you awake you must drink. Shall I help you sit up?"

"I can do it," Helen said, rising up on her elbow. "Where is he?" From the beat of their bond he was not close by. She felt a tiny grab of disappointment.

"He said he had business to complete with Mr Pike. I am to tell you that Mr Hallifax will be protecting the house, along with his man, Lennox." Her aunt slid a hand in behind Helen to shift the pillow against the headboard. "Not constables at all, it seems, but..."

"Reclaimer and Terrene, like Lord Carlston and Quinn." Helen dragged herself up to lean on the pillow and added cautiously, "Like myself and Darby."

Aunt tucked her chin against her chest. "Quite. You and Darby. She is very devoted. Even after the seizures were over she stayed with you, holding your hand. I had to order her to take some rest herself."

Darby must have been worried still about the rift and manifestations, Helen thought. Ever cautious. Ever loyal.

"The Duke stayed too, until we put you to bed." A note of reproof in Aunt's voice: she had not asked after her betrothed. "Here, my dear, drink."

Helen was glad the Duke had not been disgusted by what he had seen. She grasped the glass and sipped the tepid cordial, the smooth liquid easing the dusty ache in her throat. Her aunt retreated back to the chair.

"So now you know," Helen said, watching her over the rim. "I have ... abilities."

Aunt nodded. "Lord Carlston demonstrated most convincingly," she said with a wan smile. "The speed. The strength." She shook her head. "I must believe they are gifts from God."

The lost look in her eyes showed her doubt. Or perhaps it was just bewilderment.

"He told me there is alchemy involved too. He called it the Old Arts." She dropped her voice. "Helen, it makes me very uneasy. Alchemy is heathen nonsense. Heretical."

"It is not nonsense, Aunt. At least not all of it. Besides, it is all in the service of England. The Dark Days Club protects the country from the Deceivers. The Queen knows about us, and the Prince Regent too. They approve."

"So I understand. But why you? Why our family?" Her hands closed into tight knots.

"To fight the Grand Deceiver," Helen said. "Did not Lord Carlston explain it?"

"He did. Together you are the Grand Reclaimer dyad, and you are a direct inheritor. But it is a lot to take in." She looked down at her fists as if they were not her own. "I know you could not tell me about your ... *abilities*. You took an oath to the Crown and God – Lord Carlston made that clear. But..." She seemed unable to go on.

"I did not want you involved, Aunt. Or Andrew. You are both too dear to me, and it is all so dangerous."

Aunt looked up, her mouth tight. "Do you think I do not understand that? Miss Cransdon murdered; you convulsing for hours on end; your mother and father killed. Yes, Lord Carlston told me the truth of that too. Not traitors at all. That was a relief to know at least." She did not sound relieved. She sounded angry. "My beloved sister and brother-in-law died for this Dark

Days Club. I could not bear it if you were killed too, Helen. I lost one daughter at birth; I could not bear to lose another."

Daughter. Indeed, Aunt Leonore was as much her mother as the long-departed Lady Catherine.

Helen reached across and placed her hand over her aunt's bunched fists. There was nothing she could say to answer her fear. Any reassurance would ring false. Aunt had lost family, seen Delia's blood, witnessed the ague. The inherent violence of the Reclaimer world could not be hidden.

Aunt bent her head, her shoulders heaving once in a stifled sob. "Forgive me," she whispered. "I am tired." She grasped Helen's hand between both of her own. "My dear girl, I thought you were going to die. Those convulsions."

"All Reclaimers must go through it," Helen said.

The words seemed familiar. *We must all go through it to become what we truly are.* A Reclaimer. A killer.

"Your uncle knows, doesn't he?"

"I never told him anything," Helen said. She remembered facing Uncle Pennworth in her bedchamber at her ill-fated ball; the fear in his eyes as she had wrenched his vicious grip off her arm using Reclaimer force. "Even so, I think he knows something is different about me. My strength at least."

"It would explain why he refuses to see you." Aunt's lip curled. "He has always been a coward."

Helen lowered her glass, surprised.

"Of course I know what he is," Aunt said flatly. She patted Helen's hand. "At least your husband-to-be is a man of true worth. The Duke tells me he has known about the Dark Days Club since you were in Brighton, and took his oath immediately."

Helen nodded. "I did not want him to get involved either."

"But he did so without hesitation, Helen. To stand by you in such … *unusual* circumstances shows a great deal of devotion.

You were not even betrothed at the time. Do not let him slip through your fingers."

"I am not about to let him *slip through my fingers*."

"Really? He told me about this connection you have with Lord Carlston—"

"It is the Grand Reclaimer bond," Helen said quickly.

Aunt raised her brows, as if the fact of the interjection meant something. Helen withdrew her hand and took a sip of the barley water. Perhaps she had sounded a little defensive.

"This *'Grand Reclaimer bond'* troubles the Duke greatly, my dear. Should it?"

Helen put down the glass on the bedside table; a few extra moments to gather her composure. "It is an alchemical bond, Aunt, forced upon us." Perhaps that was not entirely true – she had sought the bond to cure Carlston of his madness – but in a general sense it had been thrust upon them. "It is what creates the Grand Reclaimer dyad. It gives us more power and makes us stronger so we can do our duty to defeat the Grand Deceiver." Perhaps the last would curtail any more discussion.

"Yes, your duty. Lord Carlston spoke a great deal about that too. The Duke and I both understand the importance of duty, Helen. We know you have given your oath and that you stand by your word." She paused. "The Duke told me that he has asked you to walk away from the Dark Days Club and this *alchemical* bond that you have with Lord Carlston as soon as you defeat the Grand Deceiver."

"Yes."

"He also said you have not really answered him. You must do so. You must promise to walk away."

"It is not that simple, Aunt. Even if we do defeat the Grand Deceiver, there will still be other Deceivers in England preying upon mankind. There will still be the Pact. I have been given these abilities, and you say yourself that they must be from God. Surely I have a duty to use them."

"You will have other duties, as a wife and, if God wills it, a mother." Aunt took her hand again, the grip tight. "If you love me at all, if you love the Duke, promise me that you will walk away once this Grand Deceiver duty is done. I could not bear to lose you, especially not in the service of the same men who let my sister – your dear mother – die. Who allowed our family name to be tainted forever." Her eyes were bright with tears. "How dare they place a man's duty upon a girl. How dare they let you take the burden of death and destruction. They will not have another one of us to throw upon the fire of their duty. Promise me, Helen. Please!"

Helen saw ten years of anguish, anger and humiliation in her aunt's tear-tracked face. But also ten years of protection and care, and a mother's ferocious love that still shone bright. There was only one answer she could make. Besides, it was what she wanted too, wasn't it? A good husband, a life of safety, a family. To be done with fear and the crushing guilt that dogged her every breath.

"I promise I will walk away, Aunt," she said.

And yet the whisper of another vow – another *I will* – was still entwined into the steady Reclaimer beat under her heart.

Chapter Twenty

FRIDAY, 18 DECEMBER 1812

Lady Dunwick peered worriedly at Helen across the breakfast table. "Are you sure you are quite well, my dear? Gossard tells me you were in a very bad way last night. He wanted to send for the doctor, but *Lord Carlston* said it was not needed."

Helen stiffened at the slightly scandalised tone in Lady Dunwick's voice.

"A *fuga*, Lady Dunwick," Aunt said quickly. "Brought on by the tragedy of Miss Cransdon's death. Lord Carlston was kind enough to return my niece to us when he saw her out in the Crescent. It was most fortunate."

Helen eyed her aunt with respect. She was lying with great aplomb.

"Out in the Crescent? Goodness me!" Lady Dunwick dabbed carefully at her mouth with her napkin. "Then we can assume it is nothing contagious?"

"Absolutely not," Aunt said.

"Well, that is good news." Lady Dunwick smiled around the table. "After I have been to the baths for my treatment, perhaps we could all take a turn around the Pump Room." She caught Helen's flinch at the word *baths*. "Of course, only if you are feeling up to it, Lady Helen."

"I beg you to leave me out of such plans," Lady Georgina said, placing her coffee cup on its saucer with care. "After the upset of the last few days, I cannot intrude upon your kindness any longer, Lady Dunwick. I have decided to return to Chenwith. I have sent for Lord Henry and he will be arriving soon. I thank you, sincerely, for your hospitality."

"Oh, of course," Lady Dunwick managed to say through a large bite of buttered bread. She chewed vigorously and swallowed. "Although I assure you, Lady Georgina, that you are in no way intruding."

"Even so, I cannot help but feel that remaining at Bath would be *de trop.*" Lady Georgina picked up her coffee cup again and took a neat sip.

Helen sipped at her own cup. This was a way for them all to return to Chenwith without offence.

"It is probably time for us to leave too, is it not, Aunt?" she said.

Aunt took the hint. "Yes, after the events of the last few days Bath has too many sad associations. And we do not wish to be a burden upon you, Lady Dunwick."

"The Duke has given me leave to invite you and Lady Elizabeth to Chenwith for Christmas, however," Helen added. "We could all travel together today, if that suits you. As you said yesterday, none of us feel completely safe at Bath any more."

In fact, Selburn was probably not yet aware of Carlston's plan to decamp to Chenwith, but there could be no other course of action. She and Carlston had to leave Bath, and they had to protect those who were at risk from the Grand Deceiver's ghastly threat. To Helen's mind, that now included Pug and Lady Dunwick.

"Really?" Pug squealed. "A Christmas house party at Chenwith! Do say we may go, Mother. We have no other pressing engagements, do we?"

Lady Dunwick straightened in her chair. She did, after all, have an unmarried daughter. "The Duke has invited us, you say? Well, we should be most delighted."

It was decided that the party would move to Chenwith that afternoon, and a note was sent to the mews to ready Lady Dunwick's coach for a two o'clock departure. Orders were issued for maids to pack travelling trunks – the sad duty of packing Delia's belongings falling to Darby.

Lord Henry arrived amongst all the preparation to collect his wife and, apprised of the plan, promised to carry a message to Chenwith's housekeeper that two extra rooms were required. It was at this point that Helen realised they faced a dangerous lack of Reclaimer and Terrene protection to cover all those she deemed at risk.

She searched for Mr Hallifax, and found him in the rear yard keeping watch upon the back alley, his arms crossed over his buttoned greatcoat, hands tucked under his armpits to ward off the cold. The morning light was unusually gloomy. They would have snow by afternoon, Helen thought.

"Mr Hallifax, we have a problem," she said in way of greeting.

He gave a grim smile. "I'd say we had a few, my lady. Which one in particular?"

"Providing protection for Lady Dunwick and her daughter when they go to the baths, as well as protecting Lady Georgina and Lord Henry on their return to Chenwith."

Hallifax pushed back the brim of his hat. "Who do you deem more at risk?"

Helen hesitated. Would the enemy think an old friend a more

valuable ransom than a potential in-law? By the attack upon Delia, it seemed the former would be the greater target.

"I think Lady Dunwick and Lady Elizabeth," she said.

"Then I'll go with them, and Lennox can follow Lady Georgina." He rubbed his jaw, which was rough with bristle. "I know it is not ideal."

Far from ideal, Helen thought. Although Lennox was an experienced Terrene, he had little chance of combating a Deceiver by himself.

"It is the best we can do until Mr Dunn and Mr Dempsey arrive with their men," she said.

"We need to keep everyone together," Hallifax said.

"I know. I am working on the problem."

He glanced at her and gave a nod. From one Reclaimer to another, Helen realised. No condescension. No wonderment that she could think rationally. Just a nod to an equal. She nodded back.

Ten minutes after Hallifax and Lennox had departed to follow their charges, Helen sent two footmen out into the gloom. The first to Carlston and Hammond at Green Park, and the second to Selburn and Andrew at the York Hotel, both with urgent messages to gather at the the Royal Crescent townhouse for a Dark Days Club meeting. The agenda: to plan their answer to the Grand Deceiver's threat, including the problem of protection.

Helen decided against sending a third message to Mr Pike. She had no words that could possibly communicate her sorrow at what had happened, and a brief note to attend a meeting without any reference to Isabella would be insupportable. Instead, she had included a sentence to Carlston to ask that he inform Pike. A rather shameful passing of responsibility.

* * *

Helen, Darby, Aunt and Lady Margaret waited in the drawing room for the arrival of the men. Lady Margaret had taken one of the armchairs, her eyes still puffy from weeping, the pallor of her skin accentuated by her black bombazine mourning gown. Delia's death had struck her hard. Helen looked down at the sprig of rosemary tied with black ribbon she had pinned upon her cream muslin dress; in contrast, a rather poor showing of grief for her dear friend and Isabella. But that did not mean she was not mourning just as hard. Delia's absence was a sharp, unforgiving blade constantly twisting into her heart. Everywhere she went – the breakfast table, the drawing room, the stairs – Delia's laugh, her eagerness, her bright curiosity had all once lived. Now those places were empty of her vitality: a ceaseless reminder of her loss.

Helen crossed to the window to watch the Royal Crescent, already busy with morning deliveries and fashionables making their way to the Pump Room despite the threatening sky.

"How long have you been a part of all this, Lady Margaret?" she heard Aunt ask.

"A number of years," Lady Margaret said curtly. "It is a privilege to know about the Dark Days Club, Lady Pennworth. I hope you are aware of that."

Helen inwardly winced. Lady Margaret's grief was making her even more irascible.

"I am quite aware of it, thank you, Lady Margaret," Aunt snapped back. "I am also aware of the danger it has placed my niece in and the ridiculous level of responsibility she has been expected to shoulder."

Two familiar figures appeared at the top of Brock Street, making their way around the curve of the Crescent.

"Your brother is here, Lady Margaret," Helen said loudly, hoping to interrupt the hostilities, "and Lord Carlston." But no Mr Pike, she noted. Had he refused to come?

The question was answered by Carlston once the usual courtesies had been exchanged and he had joined her at the window.

"Pike is sitting vigil and will not give up the duty to anyone," he said, his voice pitched for privacy. "Dunn and his man Pollack have arrived and I have bid them protect him."

"I am glad to hear Mr Dunn has arrived." Helen hesitated. "Does Pike blame me?"

Carlston rubbed at his eyes. He had clearly not slept – Helen could almost feel the hum of exhaustion in him – nor had he shaved, and his hair held the odd stiffness that came from the mineral waters. She touched her own hair, feeling the same dryness that Darby had not been able to brush out.

"It is little more than twelve hours since Isabella died. All Pike can think of is his own pain," Carlston said. "I know what he is feeling. Devastation, anger, guilt that he could do nothing to save the woman he loved. He will blame himself." He touched her arm: a brief brush of reassurance. "The vestige was too large, too embedded into her soul. Even a seasoned Reclaimer could not have saved her life."

Helen fought back the rise of tears, the tight knot in her innards unravelling a little under the kindness of his words.

They both looked down at movement upon the street: Selburn and Andrew walking swiftly around the curve of the Royal Crescent, their heads together in conversation.

"I certainly hope Selburn can keep your brother in check," Carlston said.

"I would think so. He does whatever the Duke says." She smoothed down the knot of rosemary and ribbons upon her bodice. "It would be more prudent if I asked the Duke about our return to Chenwith."

He sent her a droll sidelong glance. "A wife's methods already?"

She glared at him; answer enough. His irritating half-smile appeared, but he made no other comment.

By the time the Duke and Andrew made their bows in the drawing room, Carlston had left Helen's side to stand at the hearth. Even so, the invisible link of their Reclaimer bond pulsed between them.

Selburn crossed the room and took her hands in his – the privilege of betrothal. She felt the cold morning on his skin. "I am so pleased to see you upright and so … so vibrant." He raised one hand to his lips. "I was beside myself with worry. I have to admit I was ready to throttle Carlston with all his calm reassurances that such terrible seizures are normal."

"As you can see, I am without effect," Helen said.

He kept hold of her hand, watching her closely as if she might suddenly drop to the floor, convulsing, again.

She lowered her voice. "Truly, Gerard, I am fully recovered. You know I am made of stern stuff. Are you aware that Miss Cransdon's death was a foul threat from the Grand Deceiver?"

He nodded.

"Will you allow us all to return to Chenwith? It is the best place to protect everyone. I believe the final confrontation is upon us."

"And then we will be done with this madness?"

"All being well," she said dryly.

He smiled. "You are made of stern stuff. I have faith in you."

He turned to the assembled company, drawing everyone's attention by just the lift of his hand. "At Lady Helen's request, I am inviting you all back to Chenwith. It will be our fortress. A place to stand strong, avenge Miss Cransdon, and rid England of the Deceiver scourge."

"Hear, hear," Andrew called, although the smile he directed at Helen had a strained quality. She knew her brother's expressions. Although he was trying to hide it, what he had heard and seen last night had frightened him.

"Thank you, Duke," Carlston said with a polite bow. "Chenwith is without a doubt the best place for Lady Helen, myself and the other Reclaimers to protect you all."

"I have invited Lady Dunwick and Lady Elizabeth as well," Helen said with an apologetic glance at her betrothed. "I am aware it will make things more difficult as they do not know about the Dark Days Club, but I believe that by hosting us here they have been placed at risk too."

"Why not just tell them, as you did us?" Aunt asked.

"No," Carlston said. "There have already been far too many unwarranted additions to our membership." He stared at Selburn, who crossed his arms at the silent condemnation.

"Lord Henry and Lady Georgina are not aware of our true purpose either," Lady Margaret said. "Not to mention the Duke's staff."

"I do not believe the staff will be targets," Carlston said. "The Grand Deceiver has threatened our inner circle and that is where they will strike. As Lady Helen has pointed out, by the fact of Lady Dunwick hosting you, that circle now includes her and her daughter, and Lady Georgina. It also includes Mr Pike, who will join us after his wife's funeral."

Helen bowed her head. She could not, of course, attend the funeral or burial – they were not the province of women of her rank – but perhaps she could sit vigil with Pike. A good thought, except she could not be spared from the protection of her friends and family. And it was unlikely she would be welcomed by Pike anyway.

"Lady Pennworth, I am placing you in charge of ensuring

those three ladies do not stray from the house or the protected parts of the grounds," Carlston said. Aunt nodded her acquiescence. He addressed Andrew. "Hayden, you must keep Lord Henry within the same bounds."

"For how long?" Andrew asked.

"I suspect it will not be long at all. Mr Hammond has discovered that the inquest into Miss Cransdon's death has been scheduled for Tuesday. It is to be held at the White Hart."

"Four days hence?" the Duke said. "That is a fair wait."

"They could not get the coroner until then," Hammond said. "At least they will be able to release Miss Cransdon's body to her family before Christmas." He turned to his sister. "You are to be called as a witness, Margaret."

"Am I not called as well?" Helen asked.

"No, you were not there at the actual…"

"Murder," Lady Margaret finished bleakly.

"Obviously you cannot testify," Selburn said to Lady Margaret. "I will have a word in the right ear to excuse you."

"No!" She sat forward in her chair, a flush of colour across her cheeks. "That will not be necessary, Your Grace. I wish to go."

Hammond laid his hand upon her shoulder. "It will be too dangerous, Margaret. That is where his lordship thinks the Grand Deceiver will strike, isn't it?"

Carlston turned from his contemplation of the fire. "I believe so. Not at the inquest itself – that would be too hard to control – but on the way in or out. You are right that it will be dangerous, Hammond, but I still think Lady Margaret should attend."

Selburn released an irritated breath. "You have just finished telling us that we must all return to Chenwith for protection. Surely—"

Carlston held up his hand, stopping the Duke. "Our problem is locating Philip and Mrs Knoll. I have people searching for them, but they are masters of concealment. They have already established that they will kill for the Ligatus. I believe their next step will be to take a hostage in order to make an exchange for it. Preferably someone of high value to us. They will be looking for a chance to strike again and the inquest will provide it."

"You want to use my sister as bait?" Hammond stared at Carlston, aghast. "No, I will not allow it. If she is taken, she will be at the mercy of those barbaric creatures. They will have methods of coercion that we cannot even imagine." He looked at his sister. "Margaret, you must not do this."

"It is my decision, Michael." She touched his hand still on her shoulder. "I took my oath to the Dark Days Club with the same knowledge of danger as you. We are here to defeat the Grand Deceiver, are we not?"

"Yes, but—"

"Besides, I want to testify at the inquest. It is the least I can do for Delia and her poor parents. She died in my arms, looking up at me." She pressed her lips together, pushing back, it seemed, the relentless horror of that moment. "I know we cannot tell them the whole truth, but we must give them the solace of seeing how well she was regarded by her friends."

"Lady Helen and I will be there too, along with Hallifax and Dunn," Carlston said to the still-seething Hammond. "Four Reclaimers. It will be dangerous, I will not deny it, but if we barricade ourselves inside Chenwith with no other plan than protection, the Deceivers are controlling the situation. We must *act*. We must stop their attack and turn it back upon them, and, God willing, end their threat forever."

"How do you plan to do that?" Selburn asked.

"The Grand Reclaimer will cut down one half of the Grand Deceiver dyad," he said.

"Why only one?" Selburn demanded. "Why not both?"

"We only need to kill one to destroy the dyad," Carlston said. "And we have four days to plan how to do it."

Helen met Carlston's eyes across the room. Four days to work out how they could use their power, their bond, to kill either Philip or Mrs Knoll *Mors Ultima*.

Chapter Twenty-One

At two o'clock, they left Bath for Chenwith Hall. The sky was still dark and heavy, but not yet producing rain or snow; a blessing for those on horseback. Carlston and Quinn, armed with pistols, rode ahead of Lady Dunwick's coach, Selburn's curricle and the luggage cart, watching for any approach by a Deceiver. Even a creature at uncanny speed could be stopped by a lead ball if they did not see it coming. Hallifax brought up the rear, a rifle at the ready. Helen had wanted to ride alongside him – another pair of eyes attuned to Deceiver speed – but Carlston insisted she take her place in the coach, pistol primed, with Darby up beside the driver armed with a blunderbuss. They would be the last line of defence for the ladies.

They arrived at Chenwith without incident. Helen waited until Aunt, Lady Margaret, Lady Dunwick and an awestruck Pug had climbed out of the coach and were heading up the sweep of stone steps, then carefully drew out the half-cocked pistol she had held under the rug on her lap for the entire journey. She stretched the tension from her neck, sighing a relieved breath. For now, they were all safe.

"Are you coming out, sprite?" Andrew's voice asked. He

leaned in the open door, offering his hand. "I thought we might take a turn before we go inside."

He wished to speak to her, alone; she recognised the subdued lilt in his voice.

She threw off the rug and took his hand. "Is Quinn still out there?"

He scanned the drive. "Yes. Do you want him?" At her nod, he called Quinn over.

Helen descended the coach steps and looked up at the Hall's majestic honey-stone front. The last time she had arrived, Sir Jonathan's mesmerism had opened the rift in her mind and the Ligatus had begun to force its way out. Now it was tethered at the cost of Isabella's life. Sir Jonathan had warned her that, like him, she would make mistakes and choices that would kill innocents, their deaths forever branded upon her soul. She had thought she knew what he meant, but the deaths of Lowry and Lawrence had been only glancing blows to her heart. Now, she truly understood why Sir Jonathan had touched his chest as if the pain still burned within him. Delia and Isabella – one mistake, and one choice – were hot coals of guilt in her own heart. Their deaths must be made to count. Yet even then, Helen thought, the pain within her would not be eased.

Quinn arrived in front of her. "What is it, my lady?"

Helen handed him the pistol. "It is still loaded. Could you take care of it, please?"

"Certainly, my lady." He nodded towards the Hall. "Lord Carlston has gone up, but he asked that you and Miss Darby meet him at the temple of Venus at four o'clock. I've already passed the message to Miss Darby, my lady. His lordship wishes to start planning the campaign."

The temple was an odd choice of meeting place. Clearly Carlston wanted some distance from the house, no doubt to test the tether. The thought brought a sick clench of fear to her innards. What if it did not hold?

"His lordship also wanted you to know that Mr Dempsey and his man, Young, have arrived," Quinn added.

So, four Reclaimers and their Terrenes here at Chenwith. And Dunn and his man still with Pike. Not a very large army.

"Thank you, Quinn."

With a bow, he withdrew.

"Campaign?" Andrew said, shaking his head. "It is like you are a soldier."

"I am a soldier," Helen said. The disbelief in his face stopped her from adding that she was, in fact, a general in this war. It would be too much. He was still becoming accustomed to the idea of the Reclaimer world, and her place in it.

She gestured to the end of the immense front lawn, its gentle slope hiding the sunken recessed wall that kept the sheep in the lower field. "Shall we walk to the ha-ha?"

"Will I get my boots wet?" Andrew said. "I have just got a good shine on them."

"Your boots will be safe," Helen assured him.

They walked off the gravel drive onto the grass, which was only a little damp from the morning frost. The slight hum in Helen's bones increased – earth energy. She bunched her toes and released them in her half-boots, enjoying the gentle wash of renewal. It was like stepping into warm sunshine after weeks of rain. Surely that boded well for the test.

"So all this time you have known that Mother was not a traitor at all," Andrew said, pulling her from her communion. She opened her mouth to explain her secrecy, but he waved it away. "No, I understand why you could not say anything. It is just a relief to know that she was, in fact, loyal. I never really thought she could have betrayed England."

Helen sent him a sidelong glance. "You said she was probably mad and we should deny her."

He frowned. "I don't remember that. It was Uncle who said she was mad." He squinted into the distance. "But all her seemingly irrational behaviour – she was really concealing the truth that she was a Reclaimer, and Father, her Terrene. Selburn told me that they did not drown accidentally." He rubbed his mouth with the back of his hand, as if the words were like spikes. "Is it true, sprite? Do you think they were murdered?"

"I do," Helen said soberly. "From what I have discovered, it seems their deaths were orchestrated by someone with the initials VC. Do you remember anyone in their lives who had those initials?"

"VC?" he repeated, head tilted. "The only VC I know is Venetia Cavendish, Lord Lekie's sister, and she would have been ten when they died."

"I cannot think of anyone either."

"Would Aunt know?"

"She cannot recall anyone of those initials." Helen squeezed his arm. "I will find whoever it is, and I will make them pay."

He stared at her, drawing back from her hand. "*You* will make them pay? You sound like a man."

"No, I sound like a Reclaimer, Drew. I am a Reclaimer."

"Well, that is just it, isn't it ... this thing you are..."

Helen stopped walking. "Thing?"

"You know what I mean – it is not natural, is it? No woman should be stronger than a man, or faster, or have such feelings of revenge and violence. Surely if someone in our family was to be a Reclaimer, it should have been me." He jabbed his finger into his chest. "I am the son and heir. I should be the one with the abilities. I am the head of the family now. I should be the one protecting you."

"It doesn't work like that," Helen said. She had to be patient. It had taken her a long time to understand it all too. "A direct inheritor, such as I am, is very rare and only exists to create a Grand Reclaimer dyad to fight the Grand Deceiver."

"Even so, it is not the duty of a girl. Females should not – cannot – fight. You do not have enough control of yourself and your emotions. I know Selburn thinks the same."

Helen pulled her hand from his arm. "Selburn thinks I do not have enough control? Did he say that to you?" Andrew had to be mistaken. Just that morning the Duke had said he had faith in her ability; that she was made of stern stuff.

"He told me about the house at Bath and how you blew it up. He is gravely concerned." Her brother's face held only sincerity. "I am too. Helen, I saw the seizures last night. It is clear this is all too much for you."

"The seizures last night were normal. Part of being a Reclaimer."

"There was nothing normal about them, sprite. Besides, even Carlston said they were more severe than he had ever seen."

"That was because of the size of the vestige."

He looked blankly at her. Why was she even trying to explain it to him?

"Lord Carlston believes I can control my emotions and my power," she said stiffly. "He believes I can fight the Grand Deceiver. He is counting on it!"

"It doesn't matter what Carlston thinks." Andrew crossed his arms. "Do you believe you can fight and defeat these creatures? Truly?"

Helen felt herself hesitate. Two damning seconds of silence. "Why are you doing this?" she demanded.

"I'm just trying to make you see the truth. This is not something you should be expected to do."

"You have known about this world for *one day*, Drew. You think you know the truth?" Helen stepped back. "You know nothing. When you have fought Deceivers, watched friends die, ripped dark energy from souls, come back to me and talk about truth and the control of emotions!"

She turned and strode across the grass, back to the Hall, throat thick with fury.

Behind her, she heard Andrew call, "You have just proved my point, Helen."

She kept walking. He was wrong. She had just proved her point.

Inside the entrance hall, she found Pug and Lady Dunwick still admiring the dome, their heads craned back as Mrs Clarke answered their questions. They all turned at the quick clack of her boots upon the tiles. Damn, she had hoped everyone would have dispersed by now. It was already half past three, and it would take twenty minutes to walk to the Venus temple.

"I say, Lady Helen, this is the most beautiful dome I have ever seen," Pug said, her round face aglow. "So romantic."

Helen forced a smile to her lips as she waved away the waiting maid. No reason to take off her gloves and bonnet since she would soon be walking across the grounds. "Very romantic. You must be tired from the journey. Would you like to go up to your rooms, or take some tea in the drawing room?"

"I think we should rest before dinner," Lady Dunwick said.

"But, Mama—"

"Rest, my dear," Lady Dunwick said, her tone stopping any further objection.

"We keep town hours here," Helen added, "so we will be dining at eight o'clock, but the gong will sound at seven." She addressed Mrs Clarke. "Show Lady Dunwick and Lady Elizabeth to their rooms, please."

The housekeeper bobbed a curtsey. "Yes, my lady." She stepped closer. "His Grace has asked that you meet him upstairs in the Queen's Room."

Helen hesitated. She did not know the whereabouts of the Queen's Room.

"First floor, my lady, just past the breakfast room," Mrs Clarke whispered. "You can take the south stairs."

Ah, she knew the south stairs; set at the east end of the library, through the Great Hall. She waited until Lady Dunwick and Pug had turned the first landing on the grand staircase, then cut through the Great Hall, her mind still too roiled from her encounter with Andrew to admire the outlook through the tall windows. She could see no footmen or maids near the smaller staircase, so she took the steps two at a time, finding some relief from her anger in the stretching of muscle and the unladylike speed. A pity it was only one flight.

The Queen's Room, it turned out, was the last set of suites at the east end of the Grand Corridor. The double doors stood open, a faint smell of fresh paint in the air. She peered in. A huge mahogany bed dominated the room, its blue velvet canopy topped by an extravagant display of ostrich feathers. Beyond it, Selburn stood at the damask-swagged windows, the late afternoon light casting him in silhouette. In the distance, light glinted on the glass walls of the new dance pavilion. His wedding gift, almost completed it seemed. Although she longed to view it in full, she averted her eyes. A promise, after all, was a promise.

He turned. "You are still wearing your bonnet. I did not mean for you to come *so* directly."

"I have a walk ahead of me. Lord Carlston has called a meeting of the Reclaimers at the Venus temple."

"Ah, I see." He spread his arms. "What do you think?

Somewhat plain, I know, but unlike her son, the Queen does not like anything too elaborate."

"Is that another state bed?" Two in one house – surely such a thing had never been seen before.

"I had it brought down from my York seat."

"You should have used the one in my room."

"Not at all. That is yours." He turned around, inspecting the room, an expression of satisfaction upon his face. "The pale blue is pretty on the walls, is it not? And the carpet is new, from Westminster. Her Majesty is, I think, partial to roses."

Helen looked down at the beautiful roses and vines creating an elegant pattern across the thick pile, then ran her eyes over the rest of the room. A Chippendale secretaire and chair, a deep blue velvet chaise longue. A glimpse through the adjoining doorway showed a large dressing room, and through that another bedroom for the ladies-in-waiting.

"I think she will be very pleased," she said.

"But are you pleased?"

"I am."

"You don't sound particularly pleased."

His tone of satisfaction had disappeared. She had not meant to spoil his pleasure.

"It is not the room," she said, rubbing her gloved hands together. "I have just been with my brother." Was she really going to repeat Andrew's ridiculous claim? It seemed so. "He said you do not think I have enough control to fight the Grand Deceiver. Is that true?"

His brows lifted in bemusement. "I never said such a thing. I have seen you train, Helen. You are completely in control. Your brother does have the rather odd idea that all women are prone to mania. It is why I told him about the Dark Days Club – he was convincing himself that you were following your mother into madness and was making plans to wrest you back to Lansdale." He gave a huff of dry laughter. "In one respect he is right: you are following your mother. But into heroism, not madness."

Heroism. She felt the stiff breath in her body soften, her scalp and skin heat under such approbation.

"It is no wonder Andrew has that view of women," she said. "Our uncle was forever telling us that our mother was mad."

Selburn walked across and took her hands, pressing them between his own. "I have every expectation that you will defeat the Grand Deceiver with great expediency, and we will be married on New Year's Day." She watched the almost-dimple at one side of his smile that only appeared with a certain roguish mood. "Do you think I would go to all the trouble to have a second state bed hauled from York if I thought otherwise?"

She laughed, still watching his mouth, still with her hands enclosed in the warmth of his clasp. They were standing so close together and, for once, completely alone. Would he kiss her? He had done so only twice since their betrothal: swift, sweet tokens of regard. She often saw heat in his eyes, but would it flare within a proper kiss? An image flashed into her mind: the bawdy house and the wild, all-consuming heat that had blazed between her and Carlston, their bodies locked together. A shameful, illicit comparison, and yet...

Selburn plainly saw her fixation upon his lips, for he said softly, "It would be most ungentlemanly of me to steal a kiss while you are a guest under my roof."

She felt her cheeks burn; she had been too brazen. It was difficult sometimes to return to propriety after the freedoms she had tasted as the Grand Reclaimer. "Of course, I know you would never take advantage..."

He drew her hands to his chest, placing them upon his heart, the action pulling her a step closer. Through kid leather, satin and linen, she felt the beat of his heart under her palms. Steady, calm. She looked up into his eyes. Ah, yes, there was the heat, but kept in check, his intense gaze watching for her agreement. She angled her face upward.

It started sweetly: a brush of lips, an intermingling of breath. He drew back slightly – not an end but a search for a more commanding angle – and then his mouth caught her lips, just as her hands were caught in his embrace. She swayed closer, a warm sweep of energy tightening her innards and yet loosening them too. She felt the quickening beat of her heart in her ears, her blood singing with desire, and another pulse beneath it. The dyad bond. She ignored it, focusing upon the steady heartbeat beneath her palms, the fresh-air-cologne smell of his skin, the hard press of lips and tongue against her own, and the sound of their breathing, quick and mixed with soft croons of pleasure.

Her mind clouded with sensation. She stepped closer, tried to move her hands to touch more of him – his face, his hair, the broad length of shoulder – but he pulled away, resting his forehead against her own.

"Little temptress," he said. "I am not made of stone."

She gave a small, gasping laugh. Nor was she.

He stepped back, releasing her hands.

From the corner of her eye, Helen caught the swirl of a gown hem at the doorway. Someone had seen them.

Selburn had seen the flash of gown too for he demanded, "Who is it?"

Darby stepped into view. She curtseyed. "Forgive me, Your Grace, I was seeking my lady."

"Ah, your Reclaimer duties call," he said to Helen.

She hesitated, loath to leave such an intense moment.

Perhaps, also, to show him that she did not always run to Lord Carlston's bidding.

He nodded as if he understood, his smile of farewell still holding the hard press of their lips.

Helen and Darby were walking across the lawns before Helen ventured a comment. "The Queen's suite is very elegant, is it not?" she said, her voice prim even to her own ears.

"I am sure Her Majesty will approve," Darby said, her voice equally prim.

They looked at one another, eyes meeting in silent laughter, no other words needed.

They forged on through the damp grass, the cold air hunching Helen's shoulders in her woollen pelisse. The moon was rising in the dark grey winter dusk. Two tiny lights in the distance flickered then caught: someone lighting lamps at the temple.

"It's a cold place to be meeting," Darby said, rubbing her gloved hands together.

"Yes, but it is also sufficiently far from the house," Helen said. "I am sure Lord Carlston wants to test the Ligatus tether."

The thought of it clamped her innards with dread again. She looked up at the full moon. Their Reclaimer powers would be at their peak.

"Of course," Darby said. "That is why he has called me too, in case the Ligatus is not properly tethered." She gave a lift of her broad shoulders. "Even so, it seems it is well held. There were no manifestations while you slept last night." It was half reassurance, half question.

"It is definitely in place, there is no doubt about that. Now we must be sure it is strong enough to restrain the Ligatus so his lordship and I can use the earth power."

"Do you think it will?"

"It must." Helen did not voice her true terror: what if all was in place and she still could not draw the power and control it?

They walked another minute or so, their breath puffing into the dusk gloom.

"Of course, all being well," she added, sending a sidelong smile across the anxious silence, "you will not need to sleep in my bed any more, Mrs Quinn."

"That being the most important part to all this," Darby said, the droll slant in her voice broadening Helen's smile.

They climbed the gentle slope to the temple, passing a stuffed hessian sack lying on the grass. One of the kind they used for training. In the lamplight, Helen saw the figure of Lord Carlston standing with his back turned to the fresco portrait of Lady Elise. Mr Hallifax and Mr Dempsey were conversing at the temple's entrance, the taller figure of Hallifax stamping his feet against the cold. What were they doing here? Surely Carlston did not intend to test the Ligatus tether with an audience.

The two men bowed as she approached.

"Good evening, Lady Helen," Dempsey said. "Mr Hallifax has just been telling me that you went through a punishing first ague last night."

"I was saying how well you handled it, Lady Helen." Hallifax shot a savage look at his colleague.

Helen observed Dempsey warily. He and the absent Mr Ball were the two Reclaimers who had refused to believe that she, a young noblewoman, could be the warrior sent to destroy the Grand Deceiver. Had he changed his mind since Mr Pike had confirmed she and Lord Carlston were the Grand Reclaimer?

Dempsey eyed her with a small smile on his face. He was not a prepossessing man like Hallifax beside him, although he had the Reclaimer height – at least six foot tall – and the customary lean build. His shoulders, however, sloped and his big-jawed face held an unattractive high colour like her uncle. It could not be from the effects of liquor, Helen decided, since it was near impossible for a Reclaimer to become inebriated. More likely to be an excess of choler. His smile, certainly, held more bile than warmth.

"Lady Helen, come in," Carlston called. "Hallifax, Dempsey, we shall make a start."

With a nod of acknowledgment to the other two Reclaimers, Helen led the way into the temple. In the lamplight, the painted eyes of Lady Elise followed her across the room. No wonder Carlston stood with his back to it.

The three of them ranged before him, Darby a little further back in the shadows behind Helen.

"I thought this was Reclaimers only," Dempsey said. "Should Young be here?"

"No, just Miss Darby," Carlston replied.

What was going on? Helen shifted, hoping to draw his attention, but he did not look her way. It felt rather deliberate.

"I believe Mr Hallifax has been informing you of what has occurred over the last few days?" Carlston added.

Dempsey nodded. "You think this pair – Philip and Mrs Knoll – are the Grand Deceiver, and that they'll strike again at the inquest. Try and grab a hostage to exchange for the Ligatus."

"Correct," Carlston said. "We also discovered the identity of the Bath Deceiver – Mr King. He gave us a great deal of information, the most disturbing fact being that the creatures that make up a Grand Deceiver can move into any body, not just their own progeny."

The two Reclaimers stared at him.

"Impossible," Dempsey said.

Hallifax rubbed his mouth. "I don't understand. How can they do it without any vestige to pull them into their new body?"

"Unlike a normal vestige transfer, they have to be near their victim. The transfer is made through water or blood, or sometimes even touch or air."

"Christ," Dempsey muttered.

"Watch your mouth," Hallifax said. He glanced at Helen, thick brows drawn together. "It's just the shock of it, my lady."

Dempsey sniffed, his shoulders hiking higher.

"It is a shock, but it is also the way in which we will defeat them," Carlston said. "They cannot transfer into a Reclaimer body. We are built to discharge Deceiver energy into the earth and so they cannot exist in our flesh, thus resulting in their *Mors Ultima*."

"I am not built to discharge their energy," Helen said, voicing her concern. "I absorb it."

"True." Carlston smiled, ignoring the astonishment of the other two men. "You absorb it and use it; I think that would be an equally bad outcome for the Deceiver."

"But is taking them into *our* bodies how we are to destroy them?" Dempsey demanded, his lips drawing back in yellow-toothed disgust. He looked at Hallifax. "You willing to do that, Jacob?"

Hallifax straightened, clearly ready to take on the challenge.

Carlston, however, answered in his stead. "That is not how we are going to destroy them." He paced across the black-and-white tiled floor. Helen saw his eyes flick to the portrait of Lady Elise, then he turned his back on it again. "We will go to the inquest and offer the Grand Deceiver a chance to obtain their hostage. Lady Ridgewell has bravely agreed to act as bait. As soon as they appear, we strike. Four Reclaimers to corral at least one of the Grand Deceiver dyad. My preference would be Mrs Knoll, but in the end it is the one we can catch and then isolate from the normal citizens of Bath. It can only be

Reclaimers who are involved. Even Terrenes will be at risk of their bodies being invaded by the Grand Deceiver."

"It makes sense," Hallifax said. He spread his hands. "But what do we do once we have it corralled and isolated? Can it be killed in a normal way?"

"We do not know how this pair shifts into their new bodies," Carlston said, shrugging. "Water, air – who knows. I do not want to take any chance that it escapes *Mors Ultima*. My intention—" He corrected himself with a gesture to Helen. "*Our* intention is to obliterate it."

It did not take a great leap to know what he meant. Helen closed her fingers into fists.

"Obliterate it how?" Dempsey asked.

Carlston nodded to Helen. "Shall we show them, Lady Helen?"

She glared at him: *What if it does not work?*

He crossed his arms, head tilted: *Have faith in yourself.* His eyes flicked to Darby: *Your Terrene is here.*

Even so, Helen thought, what if she blew up everyone? She looked down at the neat tiling. With both her boots and the marble between her and the ground, she could not feel the earth power. Too many non-electrics. What if she could not even access the power?

"Lady Helen," Carlston repeated, "shall we go outside?"

Clearly, he was set upon it. "As you wish, Lord Carlston."

The three men and Darby followed her onto the grass. Beyond the halo of warm yellow light from the lamps, the bright glow of the full moon cast nearby branches and leaves into stark silvered relief, and lit the distant Hall into eerie majesty.

Helen stripped off her gloves and passed them to Darby, then crouched and placed her hands upon the damp grass, pushing her fingers into the earth. Cold and grainy. She waited, her heart beating hard in her chest. Ah, there it was, a thrum of energy humming through her hand bones. Building. Almost as strong as the power at the stones. Carlston had said Chenwith Hall was built upon a ley line, or at least near one.

Dempsey crossed his arms over his chest. "What are we doing out here?"

"Lady Helen can draw energy from the Vis," Carlston said. "She can draw upon the earth energy."

"What?" Hallifax rocked back on his feet. "Well now, that is *something*." He addressed Dempsey, triumph in his voice. "What do you say to that? Surely you cannot deny her ladyship now."

"I haven't seen it yet," Dempsey said.

Helen stood up. Now she knew what Carlston was doing: using her pride to push her past the doubt that had crept like poison into her mind over the last two days. He knew she would not allow herself to fail in front of a man like Dempsey, or disillusion Hallifax.

She crossed to Darby. "Would you help me remove my boots, please?"

Under Darby's deft management, her boots were quickly removed, leaving Helen standing on the cold ground in her silk hose. Hallifax looked away, but Dempsey's eyes were fixed upon her slender feet. Ignoring him, she paced back to where she had crouched and worked her feet into the earth, digging in her heels.

The power pooled around her toes, warming her soles. The hum intensified, a hundred bees suddenly rising into a thousand, shifting through her body. She closed her eyes and concentrated inward, pulling the thrum into the muscles and sinews of her legs, filling her bones and marrow with heat, calling it along the winding paths of her body. She stretched out her arms and closed her fists, drawing the burning power into her blood, into the pulse of her heart and the beat of her dyad bond, melding them both into the humming force. Beneath it all, the Ligatus writhed, held firmly back by the dark tether of Isabella's vestige, a soft poisonous whisper hissing its rage, drowned out by the glorious throbbing song in her veins. She tasted wet earth and green life, felt the energy gathering in her hands, a reservoir of hot glorious power.

She unfurled her fists and spread her fingers, two blue flames igniting upon her palms. Although she could feel their heat radiating into the cold air, they did not burn her. It took concentration to keep the flow going, but she found a rhythm to it. With every beat of her heart, with every counter-beat of the Reclaimer bond, she could pull the power through her body into her hands. A constant flow. She smiled. No, a *controlled* flow.

"Holy God," Hallifax whispered.

She opened her eyes. Carlston stood before her, hand outstretched, a question in his eyes. *Ready?* She could see the other question behind it: would the power fuse them together, as it had at the stones?

"Ready," she said. Her voice sounded full, rich, crackling with heat.

She took his hand in both of hers, the blue flames engulfing their grasp. *Please, keep the fire alive,* she prayed. To God. To herself.

She heard Carlston draw a sharp breath as the power flowed into his body. Did he hear the soft howl of the leashed Ligatus?

"It is holding!" he said.

"Yes."

Slowly, he raised his other hand. A blue flame blossomed in his palm, curling into a sphere of swirling blue energy. "My turn then."

He drew back his hand, fierce hope in his eyes, and flung the flaming ball at the hessian sack. It hissed through the cold air, a trail of blue vapour in an arc behind it, the grass and ground lit by an eerie sweep of blue light. The ball slammed into the sack, ultramarine flames erupting across the cloth. The blaze heaved and reached to the sky, consuming the sack in a rush of roaring blue heat.

"Yes!" Hallifax yelled, shaking both fists in the air. He swung around to face Dempsey, jabbing his finger at him. "Admit you were wrong, John. Admit it – she's the one!"

Dempsey stepped back. "I'll admit I've not seen power like that before."

Helen let go of Carlston's hand, her concentration gone. The blue flame died in his hands, then guttered in hers, the power draining back through her body, back to the earth, in a sudden release of warmth and strength. She staggered, her breath catching at the loss.

Carlston grabbed her arms, steadying her. "Is it the tether?" he asked.

"No, that is holding fast. It is just the speed of the energy leaving me." Yet a glorious sense of renewal remained. She felt lit from within.

"Thank God. Then we have control of the earth power?"

"Yes," Helen said. She met his jubilant smile. "Yes!"

He seized her hands in a tight clasp of triumph. *You did it. We did it.* He pressed a mad kiss upon her knuckles, their shared exultation pounding through their bond like the beat of one heart. She was, for an instant, lost in the joy in his dark eyes, the soaring sense of unity, the wonderment of so much power between them. It was as if her body shook with it.

"Enter, the Grand Reclaimer!" Hallifax yelled, his words wrenching them back to the hillside. He walked in a small circle, arms outstretched, his craggy face tilted to the night sky. "Thank you, God Almighty."

Carlston released her hands and stepped back. "Do you always pray so loudly, Jacob?"

Helen heard the slight shake in his voice, felt his eyes upon her, the beat of their bond still singing between them.

"I do when my prayers are answered," Hallifax said.

Chapter Twenty-Two

TUESDAY, 22 DECEMBER 1812

Mr Hammond, clad in his grey greatcoat and hat, stood beside Helen on the gravel drive, his chin lifted in challenge. The morning was unusually dark, and he seemed to merge into the gloom.

"I do not care if it will place me in danger, my lord," he said, looking up at Carlston astride Ares. "If my sister goes, I go too."

Lady Margaret eyed her twin through the open door of the coach. She had restrained her grief into a dove grey carriage gown and lavender wool pelisse, as befitted a friend of the deceased, but had covered her dark hair with a black veil. "We have already settled that I go alone, Michael." She gestured to Helen, waiting to climb aboard the coach. "Lady Helen will be in here with me, and we both have pistols; and Lord Carlston and Mr Hallifax ride fore and aft. Three Reclaimers, and a fourth meeting us at the White Hart. I shall be well protected all the way."

Hammond pressed his hand to his chest. "I have an uneasy feeling."

"We all have an uneasy feeling, Hammond. It is a normal response to a mission like this," Carlston said, indulging Ares's sideways dance for a few steps, then bringing the horse back into line. "It is what keeps us primed."

Helen nodded. She certainly felt uneasy too, especially about the danger to Lady Margaret. She could not bear to lose anyone else.

"You may not care about the danger to yourself, Mr Hammond," she told him, "but we do, and if you come with us you will divide our attention. We would need to protect you as well as your sister."

"I can protect myself," he said.

Selburn stepped forward. "Do you think I do not wish to go as well, Hammond, to protect my betrothed? Of course I do, but we must let the Reclaimers finish this. You have seen how Lady Helen and Lord Carlston can now manipulate the earth power. They are a formidable weapon."

Hammond glared at the Duke. "My sister does not have any weapons against a Grand Deceiver."

"She has our protection," Carlston said. "Stay here with Dempsey, as we discussed, and help him and the Terrenes protect Chenwith in case there is an attack. It is not a request, Hammond, it is an order."

There was steel in his voice, his brows drawn into stern command. It was not often he gave direct orders, Helen thought. A sign of more than unease.

Hammond's jaw shifted, but he nodded. "I obey, but under protest." He turned to Helen and offered his hand into the coach. "Please, look after her," he whispered fiercely as she climbed the step.

"You know we will." She pressed home the promise with a squeeze of his hand, then ducked into the coach and took the bodkin seat, opposite Lady Margaret.

Through the open door, she glimpsed a small, thin figure

hugging the stone wall at the corner of the north wing. Sprat. Helen lifted her hand in farewell, hoping the girl could see it.

Hammond shut the coach door.

"Helen!" Selburn looked in at her, his smile a little strained. "When you return, we must discuss the white soup for the ball."

She laughed at the odd farewell. He knew how to lighten her mood. "Of course. When I return."

She looked at Darby, who was standing with Mr Dempsey on the front portico of the Hall. Her Terrene replied with a sober nod.

Darby and Quinn had both been unhappy about staying behind – their duty was beside their Reclaimers they had argued – but Carlston remained adamant. Philip and Mrs Knoll would not be given any chance to shift into a Terrene body. Besides, Helen had told Darby she relied upon her to protect her family and the other house guests.

She had said her farewell to Aunt and Andrew the previous night, asking that neither come down in the morning to bid the battle party on their way. It would, Helen had decided, be too distressing to see her aunt's fear and her brother's doubt.

"Move on," Carlston called, urging Ares forward.

The coach lurched into motion, the figures of Selburn and Hammond and Darby dwindling in size as it rounded the curve of the driveway and rumbled along the Grand Avenue. Lady Margaret did not look back, but stared fixedly at the oncoming view. Perhaps she too did not want to see her brother's doubt.

Helen watched the grounds pass by the window: the elegant copses and created hills of Capability Brown's landscape were barely discernible in the strange morning twilight. When the two lines of old winter-bare oaks came into view – the sentinels at the estate gates – she drew the pistol from its holster fixed to the cabin wall. They would be on the open road in a minute or so.

The pistol's mate on the opposite wall had already been removed. Seeing Helen's attention upon it, Lady Margaret gave a tense smile and drew back a fold of her gown to show the gun clasped in her hand. Helen set her own to half-cock, and rested it on her lap as they passed the stone gatehouse. The iron gates flashed by, Quinn on horseback beside them, his hand lifted as if in benediction.

"It is not likely the Deceivers will strike on the road, is it?" Lady Margaret asked. She pressed down upon her black cottage hat, adjusting its fit over the veil. They had both decided to wear the new-style cap rather than bonnets, to ensure they had unobstructed side vision.

"Lord Carlston does not think so, but better to be ready," Helen said.

"Do you know what frightens me most?"

Helen shook her head, a little taken aback. Lady Margaret did not usually share her feelings, particularly about what she feared.

"Facing Delia's parents." Lady Margaret sighed. "It is my fault their daughter is dead. I do not know what to say to them."

"What makes you think it is your fault?" Helen asked. If it was anyone's fault, it was her own.

"When you ran from the draper's, I should have stopped Delia following you; and I should have stopped her crossing the road to join you and Darby. Protocol demands that we aides retreat from any chance of confrontation with Deceivers." She bowed her head. "Yet I did not stop her. I too wanted to see what was happening. And when you and Darby pursued the Deceivers, I did not take her back to safety. I stood there, like an idiot, and ... and..." Her breath caught into a sob.

There was some truth in what she said, Helen thought. Even so, the majority of fault had to rest upon her own shoulders.

"It was all so fast," she said. "You did not know what was happening. I did, and I still left you by yourselves. The blame is mine, Lady Margaret." She felt her own grief gathering momentum, the image of Delia's body bright in her mind. She cleared her throat. Right now, neither of them needed the distraction of guilt. "We should not dwell on it. Not when we are about to face our enemy."

"I cannot help it," Lady Margaret said. "Delia is on my mind, always. Did you know she tried to say something before she died?"

"No, I did not." Helen's mouth dried. "What did she say?"

"I could not understand it … through the blood…" Lady Margaret shook her head.

Helen looked out the window, all sense of calm gone. Had Delia prayed at the moment of her death? Called for her mother? Or had it been a stifled scream of terror?

They reached the city safely and well in time for the inquest, making the turn into Stall Street where the White Hart Inn stood as the Abbey clock struck ten. The coach clattered across the cobbled yard, drawing up behind a mud-splattered carriage. The darkness of the day had compelled the innkeeper to keep his lamps lit, and above the inn's front doorway, the huge white sculpture of its namesake stood bathed in yellow light, its antlered head raised as if scenting danger. Four other coaches stood in the yard: one being loaded with luggage; the other three with doors open and passengers alighting under the escort of well-dressed footmen wearing powdered hair.

Helen released the hammer on her gun and pushed it back into its holster upon the wall. "Leave yours here too," she said

374

to Lady Margaret. "We cannot draw them inside the inn and risk shooting an innocent."

Lady Margaret returned the pistol to the holster just as one of the White Hart's footmen opened the coach door. Helen raised her lorgnette and peered at him, then swept a glance across the gloomy yard for any sign of a Deceiver. Pale blue energy surrounded everyone – all human. Nor was there any sign of Philip's quick walk or the tilt of Mrs Knoll's head.

"We are here for the inquest," she said, lowering the spectacles.

"Certainly, my lady. It is being held in one of our private rooms."

Helen took his hand and stepped down, watching for any untoward movement in the cobbled yard. If it came to it, she would not be able to draw much earth energy through the stone.

Ahead, Carlston dismounted and passed his reins to the liveried groom, his eyes scanning the yard too. The lamps created circles of light; beyond them, the shadows could hold anything.

Hallifax had already handed his horse to a second boy and was surreptitiously viewing the street at their backs through one of Mr Brewster's older-style glasses – Helen recognised the thick three-part lens.

He lowered it and cupped it in his hand, then ambled past Helen as Lady Margaret descended the coach step. "Street is clear," he murmured, heading between the waiting coaches to the front entrance.

Carlston joined them, seemingly at ease, but Helen could sense the coiled tension in him. "Shall we go in?" he said.

"This way, my lord," the footman said, holding up his lamp. "My ladies."

Carlston glanced at Helen: *Be ready.*

An unnecessary instruction – she had been ready since Chenwith. She took Lady Margaret's arm and they followed the footman to the front door.

Hallifax stood outside it, his attention ranging across the busy yard. Helen lifted her lorgnette for another sweep – pale blue energy walking, stacking luggage, leading horses, delivering refreshments. No sign of any Deceivers. Surely if they were going to attack they would build weapons, which would show bright blue through the lenses, or at least glut themselves full of lethal power.

She swept the yard again. Nothing. She listened – people talking, dogs barking, the grind of wheels, the squeals of children, Lady Margaret's brave, steady heartbeat beside her – nothing out of the ordinary. Her nose gave her no warnings either: roasting chestnuts, horse dung, hot mutton fat, coffee, smoke, sweat, and the omnipresent smell of human piss. No fresh-air scent of Deceiver whips.

The footman opened the door with another bow, and Helen entered first, lorgnette still raised. Twenty or so people milled around the well-lit foyer, all with the pale blue energy of humans, all engaged in activities that gave no cause for alarm. Yet Helen felt the nape of her neck crawl with dread.

"The inquest is in the room to your left, my ladies, my lord," the footman said. "Please follow me."

Carlston waved away the attention. "We will make our own way, thank you."

"There is Dunn," Hallifax said, nodding across the foyer. "And Mr Pike."

Helen searched the direction and found the two men, still clad in their greatcoats, beside the doorway into the inquest room. Dunn stood a good head above Pike, his Reclaimer height and athletic build also setting him apart from most of the other patrons of the inn. Helen had met him a few times in London; a self-contained man who had made it clear he did not support either her or Carlston. Beside him, Pike looked like an old, gaunt man, despite them being around the same age. Grief had hollowed his cheeks and drawn all vitality from his eyes.

Did he blame her for Isabella's death? The thought brought a stark image of Isabella dead upon the wet stones.

They walked across the foyer, Lady Margaret safely between her and Carlston, Hallifax bringing up the rear. Dunn saw them first, and bent to whisper in Pike's ear. The Second Secretary drew himself up as if forcing some energy into his bones and muscles.

"This gloom is no friend to us, but we have seen no activity," he said in way of greeting after the exchange of bows and curtseys. Helen noted his eyes flicked over her face.

"Nor have we," Carlston said. He cast a glance around the foyer. "Do you know your role, Dunn? You are to take charge of Lady Margaret's and Mr Pike's safety if Philip or Mrs Knoll appear. Get them away from any danger."

Dunn nodded. "I understand."

"The room is almost full, but there are seats at the front for Lady Margaret and Lady Helen, near Miss Cransdon's parents." Pike's glance finally rested upon her for a moment, no expression within it.

"I had wanted…" Helen stopped. "I wish I had been able to it vigil with you, Mr Pike." His face held no acknowledgment. "May I ask when Mrs Pike's funeral will be held?"

"My wife is already buried, Lady Helen," he said and headed into the room.

"Ah, he did not tell me," Carlston said. "I would have attended otherwise."

Dunn sucked at his front teeth. "I'd say you and Lady Helen

were the last people he wanted there." He removed his hat and followed Pike into the room.

Helen drew a shaking breath. So, she had her answer. Perhaps it should not matter that he held her to blame. He had never been a friend. Even so, she did not want him to think she did not honour Isabella's memory, or that the taking of a life – even one by misadventure – was a callously disregarded event.

"Focus on what is at hand," Carlston said, but his voice was gentle. He removed his own hat and stood aside, ushering them into the room.

Helen raised her lorgnette as she entered, scanning the crowd. Again, pale blue energy surrounded everybody. No sign of Philip or Mrs Knoll.

The room – usually an assembly or ballroom judging by the orchestra mezzanine above – had been set with two banks of wooden chairs, the chandeliers above alight with an abundance of candles. Most of the places were already filled – almost all men – their hum of conversation suitably muted for the sombre occasion. The coroner had not yet taken his place beneath the mezzanine, but the jury was complete, the twelve men seated in two rows of six at the right of the room.

Helen followed Lady Margaret up the central aisle. Dunn and Pike took a position along one wall, Hallifax on the other, with Carlston on watch at the back of the room. A few seats remained empty at the front, set beside two silent, stiffly upright figures dressed in black. Delia's mother and father.

They stood as Helen and Lady Margaret approached, their faces puffed and pale with sorrow. Helen had met them a few times when she and Delia had been at the seminary together, but her memory provided only a vague sense of their disappointment in their daughter. Delia had always said they did not hold much hope for her prospects.

"Lady Helen, it is good of you to come," Mr Cransdon said, bowing.

His wife tried to smile, her mouth trembling. With a small gasp, she pressed her grief into a white handkerchief.

"Not at all," Helen murmured. She bit down on her own rise of tears and turned to Lady Margaret. "May I introduce Mr and Mrs Cransdon to you, Lady Ridgewell."

Bows and curtseys were exchanged.

"We understand that you..." Mr Cransdon swallowed hard. "You were there with our daughter?"

Mrs Cransdon bunched the handkerchief in her hand. "Did she suffer?" Her voice stuttered into a whisper. "Did ... did she say anything? At the last?"

"My dear, please," her husband said.

Mrs Cransdon blinked at the admonishment, but kept her eyes upon Lady Margaret, fierce for an answer.

"It was very fast, Mrs Cransdon." Lady Margaret glanced at Helen. "She said nothing. We are all so shocked. So sorry. She was in our care."

Mr Cransdon held the back of his hand against his mouth for a moment. "No, not true," he managed. "How could anyone know ... this world now." He shook his head. "Lady Helen, do you know to whom we should apply to take our daughter back home with us? She should be buried at home."

Helen did not get a chance to answer. The murmur in the room changed tenor, hardening into expectation. The coroner had arrived; his clerk called the inquest to order. Helen and Lady Margaret took their seats.

It was a heart-wrenching hour. Lady Margaret, the two chairmen and the young maid who had been present at the attack gave their testimonies. Lady Margaret's story was a masterful mix of truth and omission, her rank and calm demeanour lending authority to the eerie conclusion that ended all the eyewitness accounts: they had not seen who had wielded the blade.

The coroner and the jury brought the verdict: wilful murder by a person unknown.

Not so unknown, Helen thought, wishing she could tell Mr and Mrs Cransdon the truth. Their daughter had bravely taken a vow to serve England, and had died in that service.

"The inquest into the death of Miss Delia Cransdon, lately of Chenwith Hall at Bath, is officially closed," the coroner said. "Thank you, jury. You are dismissed."

He stood, preparing to leave, and the silence in the room was gradually overtaken by the low hum of conversation. Mr and Mrs Cransdon rose from their chairs, both hunched smaller by the verdict, and approached him. No doubt to arrange Delia's return home.

A smell of smoke and hot fat hung in the air – the inn's luncheon preparations. Helen stood to watch the slow departure of the back rows. The subdued hum of conversation rose to a normal pitch. Still no Philip or Mrs Knoll. Had Carlston been mistaken?

"Any sign?" Lady Margaret asked, rising from her seat.

"No."

Helen caught Carlston's eye. He nodded to the doorway, and headed towards it. Dunn ushered Pike along the side aisle. Hallifax hung back, waiting for Helen and Lady Margaret to depart so he could take up a position behind. All as planned.

Helen took Lady Margaret's arm, steering her down the central aisle. Men stepped aside politely, bowing, as they reached the doorway. Almost all of the room had spilled out into the foyer, the crowd filling the space. Helen saw Carlston's tall figure moving deeper into the throng. She glanced behind. Dunn and Pike were nearby; Hallifax was caught behind a knot of men in the doorway.

Carlston stopped, his searching stance suddenly coiling into predator finding prey. Her eyes followed the direction of his gaze. Red hair. Was it Philip?

A loud voice suddenly rang out. "Fire!"

For a second, everything stopped in the foyer – conversation, movement, breathing – and then the cry came again: "Fire!"

Black smoke billowed from the stairs leading to the kitchens. A scream from below, and then the crowd was surging towards the front entrance, women shrieking, men yelling instructions, footmen pushing people forward.

Carlston turned, pointing to the front doors. The flash of red hair again, heading outside.

"Stay still!" Helen yelled to Lady Margaret over the cacophony, holding up her hand. Where was Dunn? She searched the faces behind, and found him and Pike pushing their way towards them.

"Go!" Dunn yelled, as if reading her mind.

Helen waited a second more to see him reach Lady Margaret's side, then ducked between two men, using her shoulders and elbows to forge her way into the mass of panicked, coughing people closer to the doorway. At the corner of her sight she saw Hallifax: he had found a clearer route along the wall and was making good progress towards the exit, his glass up to his eye. Through the window, she saw Carlston outside, head moving as he searched the crowded yard.

She heard the sound of smashing glass, yells of "Through here!" and then she reached the door. The way was blocked by the sheer number of men and women clambering to get out.

"Let Lady Helen through!" Hallifax bawled at her side.

A number of men stepped back, creating a clear path.

She and Hallifax broke out into the cold gloomy air, their momentum taking them into the centre of the crowded yard. A carriage rolled forward, the two horses in the harness shrieking and rearing at the sudden influx of panicked people around them. The driver struggled to hold them; a new hazard that sent people running towards the street.

Helen found Carlston again, heading towards them at speed. All was in motion. She could barely distinguish a single face, let alone find Philip.

"Do you see him?" Carlston yelled across the throng.

She shook her head, still searching the faces that streamed past her and Hallifax. It was too dark, too many people running.

"It is extinguished!" a voice yelled from the doorway. A man in livery. "The fire is extinguished! Be calm. It was only a kitchen flare!"

The call rippled through the crowd.

Helen looked in through the window. The foyer was still smoky, but she could make out two figures sprawled on the carpet. A man kneeled between them, clearly looking for signs of life. Helen felt a frisson of dread.

"Inside!" she shouted to Hallifax.

She gathered her skirts and ran back to the doorway, ducking past a few staff still making their way clear of the smoke.

A girl in a maid's apron tried to catch her arm. "Miss, don't go back in!" Helen wrenched herself free from the girl's hand. She heard Hallifax call to Carlston, the two men following her into the foyer.

She pressed her arm across her mouth against the smoke and stepped over the detritus of panic spread upon the carpet: a shoe, a dropped book, a gentleman's hat upon its side. She raised her lorgnette. Pale blue energy surrounded the kneeling man and the two prone men. Alive, whoever they were.

The young man looked up, his mild brown eyes widening. He raised a hand to warn her away. "There is some blood, miss. I don't think you should come near."

Helen stared down at the sprawled figures of Dunn and Pike. Dunn lay face down upon the carpet, blood oozing from a gash at the back of his head. Pike was on his back, face pale, eyes closed. She looked frantically around the foyer. No Lady Margaret.

"Do you know these men, miss?"

"You are speaking to Lady Helen Wrexhall," Carlston said as he and Hallifax arrived, "and these men are friends of ours."

The young man clearly recognised Carlston. "I am Doctor Madison, my lord." He nodded politely to Helen. "My pardon, my lady. I was at the inquest too. Your friends are both alive, just senseless. It looks as if someone has hit them from behind."

Helen turned in a circle. The foyer was empty. Dear God, Lady Margaret was gone. She turned again, and the enormity of it doubled her over. She tried to take a breath, but had no air, her chest solid from smoke. Her vision hazed into grey.

"Helen!" Carlston's voice. She felt a supporting hand at her elbow, and then the acrid stink of smelling salts beneath her nose, forcing her to suck in a breath.

"Good. Take another one, my lady, deeper this time," said the young physician's soft voice. Her vision cleared to see his worried blue eyes peering into her face. "You should sit down, preferably outside, away from this smoke."

She shook her head. "Please, see to my friends." She pulled in a deeper breath, pushing past the clutching reflex in her lungs, and straightened. "See? I am quite well."

He watched her for a moment, his lean, tired face set into professional evaluation. "If you feel heavy again here," he touched his chest, "please do tell me." He looked at Carlston. "Are you missing someone?"

"We have it under control," Carlston said, his voice clipped.

"I see," the doctor said, recognising a dismissal when he heard one. He crouched again beside his patients.

Hallifax stood by the stairwell, peering down towards the kitchens. "We don't even know where to start looking. Or what direction they took." He slapped the sides of his thighs in frustration. "I fear they are long gone. How did it happen? Dunn was with her, and Pike, and I saw no one in the foyer. Did you?"

"No," Carlston said. He pushed his hand through his hair. "I saw Philip. I was sure of it. Damn!"

"I'll search upstairs," Hallifax said.

"Don't waste your time," Carlston said. "They will not have gone up. Down perhaps, to a basement door."

"Excuse me, my lord, there is a note here," the young physician interjected, glancing over his shoulder. "Addressed to you, Lady Helen." He pulled out a packet that had been half pushed into Mr Pike's waistcoat.

Helen took the letter, her jaw clenching, and turned it over: one sheet, folded and sealed with a wafer, her name written boldly upon the front. She glanced at Carlston: not a hand she recognised.

The doctor sat back from examining Dunn again. "This gentleman has sustained a far harder blow than the other and may be senseless for quite a while. The other gentleman is coming around. He should be awake soon."

Indeed, Pike had begun to stir, eyelids fluttering against his ashen cheeks.

"Perhaps a shot of brandy would be beneficial to him, doctor," Carlston said. "Would you get some from the taproom?

Tell them I will pay. You may also send your charges to me."

The young doctor stood, eyeing him for a cool moment. "As you wish, my lord."

Carlston waited for him to cross the foyer then beckoned to Hallifax. "Jacob, we have a message."

Hallifax jogged back to them as Helen ripped through the wafer and unfolded the page, her hand trembling. She held out the missive for the three of them to read.

Stanton Drew stones at midnight. Grand Reclaimer only. Bring the Ligatus. We will bring Lady Ridgewell.

"It implies Lady Margaret is alive, thanks be to God," Hallifax said. "Still, it is obviously a trap to kill you and obtain the Ligatus. They must think they can access the Vis power at the Stanton Drew stones."

"Yes, obviously a trap," Carlston said. He looked at Helen: *Our stones, our power.* "But it will be a trap for them, not for us."

Chapter Twenty-Three

In the Chenwith Hall billiard room, Mr Hammond gripped the baize edge of the table, his knuckles white.

"How could you have let this happen?" he hissed at Helen and Carlston. "You promised me you would look after her."

Helen bowed her head. She had promised and she had failed. Again. She felt Darby's hand upon her shoulder – a gesture of reassurance and protection.

Hammond moved, as if towards them. Quinn and Lennox immediately stepped in, keeping their distance but nonetheless blocking him on either side of the large billiard table. He looked from one to the other, his usual bonhomie replaced by flushed rage. Helen could not blame him. On their return from Bath, Carlston had bundled Hammond into the billiard room to contain his fury, allowing only the other Reclaimers, their Terrenes and Mr Pike to follow them inside. She glanced across at the Earl. His mouth was slightly swollen on the left side from Hammond's fist.

"There is no good explanation, Michael," Carlston said quietly. "That is what worries me. The Grand Deceiver—"

"Don't you dare move this conversation away from my

sister!" Hammond leaned over the table, spittle spraying across the green baize. "Don't you dare! I deserve to know how she ended up in the hands..." His voice caught in the fury in his throat. "In the hands of the Grand Deceiver. God knows what they are doing to her."

"Lord Carlston is correct, Hammond," Mr Pike said. He touched the bandage around his head. "Neither Mr Dunn nor I saw Philip or Mrs Knoll nearby. It was all panic and smoke. I believe we both heard a woman scream, the sound cut off – presumably Lady Margaret." He looked at Dunn, who nodded. "And then we were hit from behind."

Hammond pushed himself away from the table and turned his back, as if trying to collect himself. He swung around again, the candlelight catching his sneer. "How can a Reclaimer get hit from behind? Tell me, was it just incompetence?"

Dunn stood up, swaying on his feet, the bandage on his head stained with blood. He clutched the nearby cue rack. "No one calls me incompetent!"

Carlston held up his hand for calm. "As I said, that is what worries me. As far as we know, what happened should have been impossible." He waved Dunn back into his chair. "Mr Dunn is experienced and capable, and Mr Pike was once a Terrene with a number of years of experience. Yet Lady Margaret was snatched with, it seemed, apparent ease. None of us saw anything, nor did anyone in that foyer." He tilted his head, considering. "Admittedly it was not a comprehensive questioning of witnesses – most who had fled the fire did not dally in the yard."

"Your point?" Hammond demanded.

"Either the Grand Deceiver knew of our plan," Carlston looked around the room, "which seems unlikely since the details of it were kept between those involved, and no one else left the estate between then and now. Or the Grand Deceiver has an ability that enabled them to move through that panicked crowd unseen, or at least unremarked, by a Reclaimer. An ability that has not been recorded and could be one of many. That is my concern."

Helen nodded. "Even so, we have only one path we can take." She looked directly at Hammond. "We must retrieve Lady Margaret. You have all seen the note. They want the Ligatus and still think it is contained within Benchley's journal, which we have in our possession. Lord Carlston and I will go to this midnight meeting. We will hand over the journal and receive Lady Margaret in return. As soon as Lady Margaret is safely away, we will end this once and for all."

"What makes you think this meeting will end any differently from the inquest?" Hammond asked harshly.

"Because I am the Ligatus, and Lord Carlston and I are the Grand Reclaimer," Helen said, trying to infuse her words with authority. For Hammond and for herself. "We can draw upon the earth power at the Stanton Drew stones."

"Perhaps the Grand Deceiver can too." Hammond turned to Carlston. "You just said they might have other abilities. I do not trust you with my sister's life any more. I will go too."

"That is not possible," Carlston said flatly. "The same reasons apply. You will be at too much risk and you will divide our attention. Besides—"

"I do not care," Hammond interjected. "You have used my sister as a pawn, Lord Carlston. Used her devotion to you. She deserves to have someone with her interests at heart at this exchange."

He was not only speaking of Lady Margaret's devotion, Helen thought.

"I cannot allow you to come with us," Carlston said, stepping forward. "That is final, even if Quinn and Lennox have to hold you down. I will not put you at risk as well."

Helen saw the two Terrenes exchange glances. Quinn wiped his mouth; he was not comfortable restraining one of their own.

"So *now* you are concerned for our safety," Hammond said.

"You idiot. I am always concerned for everyone's safety!"

"Lord Carlston," Helen said forcibly.

He turned, his face dark with anger. "What?"

Helen glared at him: *Do you want to lose Hammond's friendship and loyalty forever?*

His mouth tightened.

Helen frowned: *We have failed him. He needs to be part of it.*

Carlston's jaw clenched, but he turned back to Hammond. "So be it. You will ride to the stones with us with a horse for Lady Margaret. When she is released, you and she must come directly back here."

Helen held her breath.

Hammond gave one stiff nod. For now, his anger had been appeased, but it was not gone.

No one, it seemed, was convinced by the strategy for the battle ahead.

Quinn stopped Helen and Carlston as they were departing the billiard room.

"You have said yourself it is a trap, my lord," he said quietly. "You two are our most powerful pieces on the board. If it comes to it, you must be able to withdraw to fight another day."

It was true: together they were the lynchpin of England's – perhaps the world's – defence against this Grand Deceiver. And Helen herself was the real Ligatus. In effect, they would be bringing together two parts of the Trinitas in a place of incredible power. As far as they knew, the Grand Deceiver was not aware that the Ligatus was held in her mind. Then again, perhaps they did, and all of this was a ruse to bring together the Trinitas and open the doorway to the Deceivers' dying realm. Even so, she and Carlston were the only ones who could face this enemy with any chance of victory. They could ignore the challenge – abandon Lady Margaret and wait for another opportunity that they had contrived themselves – but Helen knew Carlston's honour, or indeed her own, would never allow it.

"I doubt it will come to retreat," Carlston said. "We will either win or be dead."

He glanced at Helen – an apology for the blunt statement – but she already knew those were the only likely outcomes of the night ahead.

Quinn shook his head. "At least take another Reclaimer with you, my lord. You know it is good strategy. And you must take me as well. I know how you fight. I'll know if you need to retreat."

Carlston rubbed his eyes. "I want to leave Chenwith with as much protection as possible. I believe this is a true attempt by the Grand Deceiver to obtain the Ligatus and destroy us in the process. Our plan is to attack before they realise it is no longer contained in the journal, but if we do not prevail, they will attack Chenwith in search of the true Ligatus. Everyone must be ready."

Helen glanced at Quinn. From the uneasy look upon his face, he had also noted Carlston's hesitation. Lady Margaret's abduction had rattled everyone.

"We could take Hallifax," she said. He was the only one of the other Reclaimers she truly trusted. "It still leaves Dunn and Dempsey here. And Quinn is right. He should come too."

Carlston nodded. "Yes, it is a good team, and still leaves

protection here. You and Hallifax leave now," he told Quinn. "Do not dig in too close to the stones – we do not want to allow any opportunity for one of the creatures to jump into another body. And do not break your concealment until either Lady Helen or I give you the sign to approach."

"I understand, my lord."

"God be with you then."

"With all of us," Quinn replied.

The Duke, apprised of the battle plan by Helen in his private study, was appalled.

"Just the four of you?" he demanded, pacing across the room. "That is beyond foolhardy. Surely you need an army against this foe."

"Carlston and I *are* the army," Helen said, following him. She had guessed this would be his reaction; it was why she had elected to tell him alone. "You knew this battle was coming, Gerard – Grand Reclaimer against Grand Deceiver."

"That does not make it any easier to sit by while you run headlong into danger." Selburn crossed his arms. "You place a great deal of faith in Carlston."

"I do," she said firmly. "He and I have trained for this and we are ready."

Selburn eyed her for a long moment. "I cannot bear to think..." He shook his head, as if dislodging the images in his mind.

"It is what Carlston and I were born to do." She grasped his arm, trying to press home her resolve. "You have seen our power now; the weapon it has become."

He nodded: a grudging acknowledgment of their new might.

"We will prevail," she said.

"I know you will," he said, covering her hand with his own. "And I know you will return to me safe and victorious."

She found Andrew in the vacated billiard room aimlessly shooting balls around the table. He stood silently as she outlined the plan, bewilderment still in his eyes, but when she had finished he gave her an awkward, fierce hug. "This whole thing is mad," he said.

Aunt did not say much either, and cried a great deal. Terrified tears that tore at Helen as they sat together on the chaise longue in her aunt's room, their hands tightly clasped together.

"You should not have to do this," Aunt said over and over, although both of them knew she did.

Finally, when the tears had eased into weary acceptance, Aunt picked up a small black jewellery case she had laid upon the table at her side. "I have something for you. Something of your mother's that I was saving for your wedding day, but I think..." She passed the box across.

Helen unhooked the tiny clasp and opened the lid. Inside, a small gold cross studded with rubies lay upon a swirl of white satin, its chain set at intervals with pearls.

"Now your mother can be with you tonight," Aunt said. "She and God will protect you."

"It is beautiful," Helen said, drawing her fingertip across the gold that must have once touched her mother's skin. "Thank you."

She smiled and did not have the heart to tell her aunt that she could not wear gold, or any metal, into this battle.

Darby argued her case as she helped Helen change from her carriage gown into her gentleman's breeches and coat.

"What if the tether does not hold, my lady? I should go with you, just in case."

"You know the tether is strong, Darby. You saw it in action." Helen shrugged her shoulders – the men's braces needed to be loosened so she could move more easily.

"Even so, my lady, I have a feeling that I should be at the stones too." Darby touched her chest, her heart. "A feeling here."

"I know. That is our bond speaking." Helen turned around, tears in her eyes. "And your immeasurable courage. Mr Quinn will be with us, and I know that will be hard, but you must stay here at Lord Carlston's order. You must guard everyone at Chenwith. I will be easier in my mind if I know you are here protecting them."

"Of course, my lady."

"And if … will you look after Sprat if I do not return?"

Darby swallowed hard, then mustered a watery smile. "You will have to return, my lady. Sprat only ever listens to you."

They rode out under a waning gibbous moon mostly hidden behind cloud, the wrap of freezing darkness adding to Helen's disquiet. It was not the gloom; her Reclaimer eyes adjusted quickly to it. No, it was more the fact of the moon's phase. Reclaimer power was at its most potent at the full and new moons, but tonight it would be weaker. Was that a deliberate tactic by the Grand Deceiver? She could not see how – the date of the inquest had been chosen by the coroner. She must stop attributing all circumstances to their enemy.

Helen glanced over her shoulder to where Hammond rode behind with an extra horse, seeing the puff of the beasts' breath and his tense seat in the saddle. He had not said anything in the courtyard as they had mounted, his focus intensely inward as if a concentration of will could ensure the safe return of his sister. His earlier words kept rising in Helen's mind: the Grand Deceiver would have methods of coercion they could not even imagine. What would Lady Margaret be suffering at their hands? She had glimpsed terrible illustrations in her uncle's books about the Crusades and the Spanish Inquisition. The brutality of men.

What would be the brutality of creatures that had no native thought of mercy or compassion?

She turned back to face the shadowy road, the steady gait of Faro lending her some calm. Beside her, Carlston rode Ares, his profile set into determination under the brim of his hat. The beat of their bond felt especially strong. Perhaps a response to the proximity of their enemy or the expectation of battle.

Was she ready for it?

He must have felt her focus upon him for he looked across, inquiry in the shift of his eyes. She did not need to voice what was on her mind; he answered as if he had heard the question.

"I have always found there is a point before battle when one must trust in one's training, trust in one's comrades-in-arms, trust in God, and let events unfold as they will."

"And are you at that point?" she asked.

He gave a grim smile. "Almost."

She touched the hilt of her glass knife in its boot scabbard – another precious gift from him – then circled her right hand over her left forearm, and the opposite, checking the fit of her leather armguards beneath her sleeves. She had done the same checks only a few miles back yet found the repetition reassuring. She pressed her hand against the hard shape of Benchley's journal wedged into the front of her woollen waistcoat. Had Philip or Mrs Knoll ever seen it? She had to assume they would know if it was the true artefact when she brought it out.

"As soon as they touch the journal, they will know it is not the Ligatus," she said. They had been through this five times already, but it was now like a catechism.

"That is the point of strike," Carlston said. "You must try to delay passing it to them so Lady Margaret can get to Hammond."

"You will draw their attack while I summon the earth

energy, and we will join together to form the dyad," Helen said, an image in her mind of the blast of power that they had conjured last time at the stones.

"And we will kill them," Carlston finished.

Would it work? *Dear God, let it work.*

They rode on, the thud of their horses' hooves on the hard-packed road drumming their way to the battle ahead. The clouds had dissipated and the moon cast cold light upon the road, touching the trees and grasses with silver and shadow. The cold air bit at Helen's nose and dried her lips. She felt a low hum deep in her bones. The stone circle?

As if the thought had brought the stones into being, a huge rectangular boulder rose into view. Helen's innards tightened into a sick knot. Before long, she saw the monolith's recumbent neighbours, and then the other standing stones beyond them. The moonlight gave their surfaces an eerie sense of animation, as if the stones watched the approach of these small creatures with their fleeting lives. As if they knew what was to come.

Helen drew her lorgnette on its cord from under her greatcoat and studied the monument. An ultramarine energy emanated from behind one of the far stones. Its uncanny brilliance could only mean one thing. Whips.

"They are here," she said. "And they have built weapons."

Hammond leaned forward on his horse. "Can you see Lady Margaret?"

"I can only see the glow of Deceiver energy at the moment. We are not close enough."

Carlston surveyed the huge stones in the field and with a slight nod indicated a line of fir trees between the stone-circle field and the next. "Over there," he said. "If I know Jacob, that is where he and Quinn will be concealed."

About two hundred yards from the circle, they reined in the

horses at a tree beside the low drystone wall and dismounted. The position had a good view of the circle and the village beyond it, the windows of the huddled cottages dark and blank. Stanton Drew was asleep. Probably not for much longer, Helen thought.

"Wait here," Carlston told Hammond as he secured Ares to the tree, making way for Helen to tie Faro's reins. "As soon as you have Lady Margaret, go."

Hammond nodded. He drew a shaking breath. "I know you could have ignored their demand—"

"No, we would never have ignored it," Carlston said firmly. He laid his hand briefly upon Hammond's shoulder. "We do not abandon our own."

He looked at Helen, the skin around his eyes tense. "Ready?"

Their Reclaimer beat hammered in her chest under the pounding rhythm of her heart. No, she thought. And yes.

They walked side by side along the rutted road, breath puffing into steam before them. The tassels on Helen's hessian boots slapped against the leather, the regular sound marking their march. They came to the overhanging tree where they had tied Ares and Faro ten days ago – *only ten* – finding the stile that bridged the wall around the field of stones.

As Helen stepped down onto the grass, three people emerged from behind one of the upright stones across the circle – dark figures without feature. She lifted the lorgnette again. The silhouette in the middle was surrounded by the pale blue energy of humanity: Lady Margaret. The other two, on either side of her, pulsed with the bright blue charge of fully glutted Deceivers. Both had built three huge energy whips, the undulating weapons rising over their shoulders and drawn back like angry scorpions ready to attack.

"They have three whips each. Double the length and width of normal Deceiver whips," she reported, forcing steadiness into her voice. Six whips meant at least six people dead somewhere, drained of their life force. Probably more by the size of the whips. "Lady Margaret's energy is unaltered. She seems unhurt."

"Show me," Carlston said as he stepped down from the stile.

She took off her hat and dragged the lorgnette cord over her head, passing the spectacles across.

He peered through, his jaw tensing. "They are holding her up." He lowered the lorgnette. "We must assume that they have forced some of our secrets from her. She and I spoke of this possibility before we went to the inquest. There is no use trying to withstand violent coercion. Best to decide upon the most important secret you wish to keep, and give all the others over."

Helen swallowed, her mouth dry. "What was she to keep?"

Carlston passed back the lorgnette. He glanced at the three silhouetted figures, then leaned over and pressed his hand upon the journal: *You are the Trinitas.*

She nodded. Only the Colligat was missing from the triad of destruction.

He had not moved, his hand still pressed over the journal. "Helen…" He stopped, all the possibilities of the night – success, failure, life, death – in the dark fix of his eyes. It was just the two of them now. Was their bond God's own alchemy or just alchemy? She still had no answer.

She pressed her hand over his, their pulses, their union, beating through bones and sinew and skin as if their hands were their hearts. She should step back, but here by the stone circle, the real world did not exist. Only their uncanny world. Their Grand Reclaimer world. This was where they were supposed to be, the two of them, bound into a throbbing beat that thundered through their bodies.

She stepped closer, felt his hand shift to her cheek, trace the curve of her jaw to her lips. His mouth followed the soft caress of his fingertip, the clean sandalwood smell of him, his touch filling her mind and body.

"*Amore mio.*" He breathed it against her lips, the words wrapping around her heart.

It was perhaps the last time she would hear them. She had never given them in return, never crossed the line of propriety. Yet this past week she knew she had only survived the failures, the despair, the pain, by the steadfastness of his belief, by the gossamer thread of hope and faith and, yes, love that bound them together. He had never heard the words from her lips, although her heart had whispered them every time he had pressed them into her skin. Now they faced the Grand Deceiver, and that line of propriety no longer existed.

"*Amore mio,*" she whispered. The first time, and perhaps the last, he would hear it.

For a heartbeat, he was still, and then his breath released in a sigh, as if it had been held soul-deep for centuries.

"I'm sorry," Helen whispered. Sorry she had withheld the words for so long.

"I know ... the two of us ... it is impossible. We are impossible."

"Yes," she said. "Impossible."

He caught her pained laugh with his lips, their kiss sealing the words. *Amore mio.*

How did such a kiss end? It did not, Helen realised, even though they stepped apart, the darkness and cold between them again. She forced her shaking hands to loop the lorgnette cord back over her head and replace her hat. What would happen when they returned to the real world? She could not abandon Selburn. And Carlston was still married to Lady Elise.

She drew a resolute breath. First, they had to make it back to that world. She stripped off her gloves and pushed them into her greatcoat pocket.

Carlston did the same, then reached across to clasp her hand. One last touch, and then to the battle ahead.

"Time to trust," he said.

"Time to trust," she repeated as if it were a prayer. Perhaps it was.

They walked across the damp grass side by side, bare hands brushing against one another, once, twice. The hum in Helen's bones deepened – the earth power emanating from the ley line. It pooled around each step she took, warming her feet through the leather soles of her boots. Stronger than before, but she was stronger too. No need to dig her hands into the earth.

They passed between two huge recumbent stones and crossed into the middle of the circle. Philip and Mrs Knoll stood before the huge upright monolith, the moonlight illuminating their faces into silvered masks of blankness. No attempt at human expression. Lady Margaret sagged between them.

Helen and Carlston stopped a few yards away. Helen shifted her feet, digging the heels of her boots into the ground, the warm power under her soles intensifying into heat.

Lady Margaret's head lifted. One eye was swollen shut, her beautiful mouth cut and crusted. Helen sensed Carlston's body coil with outrage.

Philip pushed back his hat by the brim. "You did not come alone."

"Lady Margaret's brother," Carlston said, his voice clipped.

The Deceivers glanced at one another.

"A lady cannot go abroad unescorted," Mrs Knoll said, her blankness shifting into snide primness.

"Can you walk, Margaret?" Carlston asked gently.

She nodded.

"A happy reunion," Mrs Knoll said. "Now, where is the Ligatus?"

"Here," Helen said.

She reached into her waistcoat and withdrew the journal, its green leather cover the deep colour of moss in the moonlight. The heat from the earth had taken hold in her body: a shifting, buzzing rise of power; her army of bees lifting through her bones and muscles and veins. She blinked as her vision warped, the three figures before her shimmering into energy: pale blue around Lady Margaret; violent blue for the Deceivers, their long pulsing whips snaking above their heads. She stifled a gasp, holding it in her throat. She could see the whips without the lorgnette. She glanced at Carlston, but all of his attention was upon the Deceivers.

"Is that the journal?" Mrs Knoll asked Philip.

He nodded. "Looks like it."

Helen flexed her fingers. He did not know the journal was false. Lady Margaret had kept their secret.

"Shall we make this exchange?" Carlston drawled. "The cold is quite inhospitable."

Philip stepped forward, his hand out. Helen watched the trail of ultramarine energy as he moved. "Give it to me."

"Release Lady Margaret first," Carlston said. "You have my word of honour that we will pass over the book."

"Honour." Philip drew the word out mockingly. "No, I don't think so. We will have to swap our treasures at the same time, Lord Carlston." He smiled. "I do believe I've played this game in one of my many childhoods." He gripped Lady Margaret's arm and pulled her forward. "If you step back, Lord Carlston, Mrs Knoll shall too. Lady Helen and I shall make the exchange."

"Agreed," Carlston said.

He stepped back and nodded to Mrs Knoll. With an amused smile, she retreated.

Helen held out the journal and reached for Lady Margaret, every sense extended through the hum of earth energy. She saw Philip's three vibrant whips draw back as he reached for the book, felt the displacement of cold air, smelled the odd, fresh scent of spent lightning thick in the air. From the corner of her eye, she saw Carlston's nostrils flare – he smelled it too. Ever so slightly he tensed. Ready.

She closed her hand around Lady Margaret's forearm and yanked her across the small space as Philip snatched the useless journal from her grasp.

"Run!" Carlston yelled to Lady Margaret as Philip opened the book.

Helen shoved Lady Margaret in the direction where Hammond waited, then whirled back to face Philip.

Everything suddenly stilled, detail flooding her mind: the white lichen on the stone behind Philip, the nap on the grey felt of his hat, the line of grime upon his collar. Time stretched, the present clawing into the future then ripping back into the now. In one second, he would realise the journal was empty, in two he would yell his outrage, and in three he would attack. Three seconds.

She glanced at Carlston, the warning on her lips, but Lady Margaret had stumbled to her knees and he had bent to haul her upright. One second gone.

Time to trust. She closed her eyes and focused inward, calling the thrum of earth energy around her feet, drawing the heat up into muscle and marrow and bone. It roared along the pathways of her body, her heart and pulse hammering with its momentum, the power driving through her blood, pounding its song through her heart, through their Reclaimer bond. Would the power light up the stones like before?

The Ligatus writhed upon its tether, its savage howls and

screams a distant hiss of hate beneath the glorious soaring song of the earth. On her tongue she tasted thick spring grass and wet earth. She lifted her hands, singing the power into her palms.

Two seconds.

Power cupped in her hands. Blue flames that curled along the channels of moisture in the air, swirling into balls that held no heat on her skin but promised devastation. She heard Philip howl his realisation that the Ligatus was false, and opened her eyes. The stones were still dark.

Philip dropped the book.

Three seconds: strike moment.

A whip like liquid silver sliced towards her head. She ducked under its crackling energy, her hands encased in flame.

"Carlston!" She reached for him, their Reclaimer bond pounding with the frantic beat of her heart.

He reached for her, but a whip slammed down between them, then flicked towards Carlston, catching him in the chest. He staggered back, his coat cut open, the shirt beneath blooming red with blood. Mrs Knoll advanced upon him.

Philip's middle whip snapped round. Helen recoiled, the tip of it skimming past her ear, knocking off her hat and searing a deep raw gash across her cheek. Pain exploded across her face. Her vision hazed into an agonised starburst that dissolved into the earth power humming in her mind. Good God, she had just absorbed the flick of Philip's energy.

The third whip followed fast: a one–two punch. She rolled away from the driving blow. The whip slammed into the ground at her side, dirt and grass flying into the air and pelting her retreat.

The power was ebbing from her hands, the blues flames guttering. Gone. The bright energy around Philip and Mrs Knoll and Carlston disappeared from her vision. Damn, she could not fight and maintain enough power to see the whips.

Keep moving. *A still body is an easy target.*

Helen rolled again, drawing her glass dagger from her boot. From the corner of her eye, she saw Lady Margaret stumbling towards the edge of the stone circle at slow human speed, and Carlston, at Reclaimer speed, dodging the hammering barrage of Mrs Knoll's whips.

She pushed herself upright, dagger held out ready to strike. Should she try to grab Philip's whips? Would the burning power destroy her flesh before her mind and soul could absorb it? She had taken Lawrence's energy in the alley in Brighton, but that had been just one whip, and he had not been a Grand Deceiver.

Philip ran at her, mouth drawn back into a snarl. "Where is the Ligatus?"

She stretched her other four senses: his whips were fanned out, the energy at each tip denser and thicker, formed into a club. From the air displacement and the fast-approaching smell of lightning, they were coming at her all at once.

In reflex, she levered herself backward, away from the first club, but the second hammered into her shoulder, its invisible weight searing through her heavy coat. The third caught her on the hip, slamming her against one of the stones. The impact crushed the air from her lungs.

Gasping, she scrabbled across the grass, catching sight of Carlston on the other side of the circle. Mrs Knoll was herding him back, blocking his path. Behind him, Lady Margaret finally crossed between the stones to her brother.

Carlston lunged at Mrs Knoll and twisted, stabbing, a whip's trajectory clear in the sudden spray of dirt and grass beside him. His glass blade connected, its blade disappearing for a moment into the invisible whip, then reappearing. The momentum of the blow carried him into a roll across the grass as Mrs Knoll screamed and staggered.

Helen sucked in cold air and hauled herself upright, lunging into a run. Philip and Mrs Knoll were keeping her and Carlston apart. They must know about the dyad connection. Probably tortured from Lady Margaret.

Something wrapped around Helen's ankle, yanking her off her feet. She landed heavily on the grass, the boot leather around her ankle disintegrating. She twisted around. It was now or never. She blindly grabbed at where the whip should be, her hands locking around the invisible pulsing weapon. Philip's bright blue energy burst across her sight.

The whip heaved against her hold, burning into her ankle. Gritting her teeth, she hung on to its writhing tip. Philip hissed with fear, trying to wrench it back. Too late! The power flowed into Helen's body, a rush of sublime savagery that rolled through her flesh and bones, flooding her mind with Deceiver power. The torrent of dark energy swirled within her, around the Ligatus, and its hissing power howled with delight. It heaved against its tether, slamming the vestige with growing weight and surging strength.

She gasped: Philip's energy was feeding the Ligatus. She let go of the whip, screaming with the sudden searing loss of power.

Philip staggered back, his mouth drawn into a snarl of confusion, his whips no longer visible. "What was that?"

He had felt the Ligatus, but didn't know what it was!

Still reeling from the influx of whip energy, Helen levered herself upright and ran, all senses extended for Philip's next attack. She had to get to Carlston. Create the power dyad.

Through the stones, she glimpsed Hammond in the field, half carrying Lady Margaret towards the wall. Almost safe.

Behind her, Helen heard the hiss of Philip's whips drawing back through the air. The smell of lightning erupted again, displaced air rolling like a wave against her skin. She ducked, slicing her knife in the air behind her, its blade connecting with a whip. Another whip clipped her back, biting into her flesh and smashing her ribs. Pain sucked all the strength from her legs. *Keep moving.* She staggered, only the pound of the battle in her blood pushing her onward.

She gathered her breath and yelled, "Carlston!"

He was still being battered back by Mrs Knoll, no more than fifteen yards away. He blocked an invisible whip, blood blooming across his arm, coat, shirt, his flesh laid open. He swung around, battle-fierce eyes connecting with hers for a second, then launched himself across the grass, cutting savagely at the whips that gouged the earth around him as he blocked and dodged.

The sound of Philip's breathing closed in behind Helen. So fast. She weaved to the right, the snap of a whip beside her face. Ten yards.

She felt the sweep of whips at her feet and leaped, clearing the prickling sensation of energy but landing awkwardly. She touched her hands to the ground and pushed off again.

Carlston broke free and ran towards her: five yards, four, three...

He stopped, eyes widening. The sharp pointed tip of a whip burst through his shoulder, its brutal shape made visible by the coating of his blood. He staggered another step, then fell to his knees. The whip slid out, leaving a gaping wound. He gasped and collapsed onto the grass.

"Carlston!" Helen propelled herself across the space between them and grabbed his outstretched hand, injured beyond use.

She screamed. The sound ripped through her throat: a primal

howl that dragged the oldest energy from the earth up through her broken body. She screamed up lightning that cracked above the stones, the sound shaking the earth. She screamed the stones into life, all twenty-seven boulders pulsing into glowing pillars of orange and red, as if set alight by her fear and fury.

Philip and Mrs Knoll drew together, their six whips raised for the coup de grâce.

Boiling energy roared through Helen, a blistering torrent that streamed from her hands into Carlston's body. He curled in agony from the force of it, the cords in his neck bulging with the effort of lifting his other hand to aim all their power at the two Deceivers.

The thick blue stream of energy exploded across the circle, engulfing Philip and Mrs Knoll in a flaming fireball that lit the night sky. For a second, Helen saw them within the conflagration – hair, clothes, skin alight, their mouths open in shock – and then the full fury of the blaze rose over them, the blue flames swirling into a ravening tornado of heat. The foul creatures, caught within their stolen bodies, writhed screaming as the earth power intensified into a white roaring inferno. The blinding heat shrivelled eyes, melted flesh, popped bones into black ash that swirled upward like a dark line to the heavens.

The Grand Deceiver. Incinerated into tiny specks of dust. Obliterated.

Helen screamed her savage glee – a long, ancient howl of victory. Yet the strength of the earth was already leaving her body, the blue flames dwindling in her hands. She released her hold upon Carlston, and the glorious power drained away with such speed that it slammed her back onto the grass, panting for air. A faint hum of it stayed in her blood, renewing her enough to let her roll onto her uninjured side, a new fear galvanising her past the loss of its glory, and the pain of her broken bones.

"Carlston!"

Not even a flicker of his closed eyelids at her call. His face was bleached white, and pale bone gleamed in the mess of blood and muscle that was his shoulder. She forced back her panic and listened for their Reclaimer bond. Yes, there, faint but still beating.

"Lady Helen!" Quinn's voice. Two sets of footsteps thudded over the grass at uncanny speed. "My lord?" Quinn crouched beside Carlston and undid his cravat. He pressed it over the terrible wound. "My lord?"

"He is alive," Helen said. "I can hear our bond."

Quinn nodded his relief. "He has already entered the fugue. We need to get back to the Hall."

He slid his arms under Carlston's back and legs and heaved himself upright, cradling the limp body of his Reclaimer. Helen slumped back, relief making room for her own pain to push forward.

Hallifax offered his hand to pull her up. "Can you walk? This has excited interest from the village and we need to go."

She glanced across the field to Stanton Drew. Some of the cottages now had flickering lights in their windows, and a few distant figures, hunched in thick coats, stood on the road peering towards the ancient monument. She took Hallifax's hand and allowed him to haul her upright, the movement forcing out a hiss. Even with the remnant of the earth energy fuelling her body, she was in pain. Broken ribs at least, she thought. And possibly something more vital, deep within, pierced by bone.

"There should be thousands of people here, hailing your extraordinary victory," Hallifax said. "But all you have is me and Quinn."

"And the stones," Helen said. So much power. She looked around the ring of cold, dark monoliths. Forever watching.

Quinn strode ahead, carrying Carlston as if he were no weight at all. Helen focused inward, feeling the soft steady beat of their Reclaimer bond. *We are impossible.*

She leaned upon Hallifax's arm and limped across the grass towards the road. By all rights, she should be rejoicing at the death of the Grand Deceiver. It was the fulfilment of her Reclaimer destiny. A new, safer life lay ahead. Yet it all seemed somehow smaller than she had expected. Or perhaps one's foes always seemed smaller once they had been defeated.

Chapter Twenty-Four

Helen breathed a shallow, pained sigh of relief as the dome of Chenwith Hall came into view, a gold lamp-lit beacon in the darkness, illuminating their way along the drive. From Faro's back, she looked over her shoulder at Quinn still carrying Carlston, his crunching steps upon the gravel slow but steady. Hallifax brought up the rear on Ares. All hail the conquering army, she thought tiredly.

Darby met them halfway across the front courtyard, muffled in a man's greatcoat. Had she stood on the portico watching and waiting all night? She touched Quinn's shoulder as she passed him – a silent check of his well-being – then ran to Helen.

"We are victorious," Helen said, her voice flat to her own ear. Six miles on horseback with broken ribs and an ankle laid open to the bone was enough to take the shine off any elation. The Reclaimer fugue dragged upon her mind too – a siren song of healing – but she could not succumb to it yet. First she must ensure Carlston's safety. Then make a report to Pike, and finally reassure Aunt, Andrew and Selburn that their fears were over.

"Thank God Almighty for your safe return," Darby said,

crossing herself. "Mr Hammond and Lady Margaret arrived no more than ten minutes ago, but they did not know the outcome of the battle. Are you injured?" She cast an assessing glance over Helen.

"How is Lady Margaret?" Helen asked quickly.

Darby glanced up, her face sombre. "She is hurt, my lady, but she is strong and I am sure she'll rally. But are *you* injured?"

"Some broken bones. It is nothing." She swung her leg over Faro's back and slid down to the ground, staggering at the stab of pain in her side and a sudden spike of agony in her ankle.

Darby took her arm, supporting her weight. "Nothing?" she echoed acidly.

"His lordship is far worse." She looked ahead at Quinn, head bowed from fatigue, Carlston senseless in his arms. "Your Mr Quinn has carried him the whole way."

"Getting him on and off Ares would have killed him. I think he is still in danger," Hallifax said, taking the reins from Helen's slack grasp.

She looked away from the warning. "His lordship is in his healing fugue, Darby, but Quinn will need your help to dress the wound."

"Of course. But I will see to you first, my lady."

"No, help Lord Carlston. Then me."

Helen limped towards the steps, lifting her head as her Reclaimer hearing picked up the sound of voices echoing in the huge space of the foyer. The front door opened and Selburn emerged, taking the steps at a run, closely followed by Mr Pike. Behind them, Aunt came down the steps at a more cautious pace on Andrew's arm, but Helen could see the strain and the relief in her trembling smile.

She braced herself as her betrothed approached. Would he see the kiss she had shared with Carlston etched upon her face?

She pushed away the foolish thought: a fancy born of guilt and exhaustion.

"Helen, you are safe! Hammond had no news. What happened?" Selburn stopped on the last step in front of her, taking her free hand. She could not quite meet his eyes. "Your face is cut open!" His own face flushed with fury. "How dare they hurt you."

She touched her cheek, but the burned gash had already started to close. "It is of no matter, Gerard. The Grand Deceiver is dead, and as you see, we survived. Lord Carlston, however, is badly hurt." She stumbled over Carlston's name.

Selburn looked around. "Is he being seen to? He will have the best care."

"Are you sure the Grand Deceiver is dead?" Pike demanded on the step behind him.

"Obliterated by fire," Helen said, latching upon the safer subject. A roaring image of the white-hot inferno melting flesh and popping bones overtook her for a sickening second. She blinked, rocking back on her feet. Darby's hold tightened.

"No chance of them shifting into another body?"

"There was none close enough, and the fire consumed them in seconds."

Pike squeezed his eyes shut for a moment. "Thank God. And thank you, Lady Helen." He addressed Selburn. "If I may, I will take you up on that offer of a coach and four to London tonight. I must inform His Highness that at least one threat to England is gone."

With her main duty done, Helen sagged against Darby's strong grip. The fugue dragged at her mind and limbs. She would not be able to resist much longer.

"The coachman awaits your order," Selburn said. "But do return to us, Mr Pike. This needs to be properly celebrated once our heroes have recovered. I know it is not a happy time for you, but this is your victory as well."

Pike hesitated, and Helen glanced at her betrothed. Surely Selburn knew the poor man was grieving.

"I insist," Selburn said. "I will not have you alone at this time of year. Return to Chenwith for Christmas."

Pike bowed. "As you wish, Your Grace." He turned back to Helen, his grief bright in his eyes. "At least it was not in vain."

A peace offering. Helen forced herself to focus. "Without her, it could not have been done," she said softly.

He nodded and continued down the steps, a dark, lonely figure heading towards the stables.

"Helen, my dearest girl," Aunt said. "I am so … I cannot say how glad, how…" She shook her head and touched Helen's arm, as if to reassure herself that her niece was indeed whole.

Helen tried to smile. "All is well," she managed. "But I need to sit down."

"Of course, my dear."

Aunt stood aside as Helen took another step. Lord, it felt like walking through thick mud. She stared at her feet, willing them to take the next step.

"Are you aware of the Reclaimer fugue, Lady Pennworth?" she heard Darby ask. "It is a deep sleep that will help Lady Helen heal. It is almost upon her, I think. Perhaps you could go ahead and have Mrs Clarke order up hot water to her room. And bandages."

"Of course. Anything." Aunt's footsteps receded.

Helen felt another supporting hand beneath her arm. "Come on, sprite, let me help you up the steps." Andrew, steadying her.

She tried to say his name, tried to smile, but a soft darkness swamped her senses. A cocoon of warm, black silence that called to her with the promise of sweet oblivion.

Helen opened her eyes, pulled from somewhere deep by a sense of unease. Above her stretched the canopy of her state bed, flickering firelight bringing a gleam to the heavy gold embroidery. She shifted, and a weight across her chest blossomed into agony. She gasped, mouth and throat parched.

A face appeared over her own, the long-boned features shadowed and sombre. "Helen, you are awake!"

She blinked away the blear of pain and managed a smile. "Gerard."

Darby's round face appeared next to him, frowning. "You should be in your fugue, my lady. Is something wrong?"

"I don't know."

She wanted to ask about Carlston, but Selburn's presence stopped the words. The impulse brought a rush of guilt that squeezed her eyes shut. She focused inward, her woolly mind slowly finding the Reclaimer beat between herself and Carlston. So faint.

"I hope it was not I who roused you from your healing, my dear," Selburn said. He touched her cheek, the gentle caress opening her eyes. "I shall leave you to the ministrations of Darby."

Helen managed another smile although even the muscles of her face ached. "I am glad you came. Thank you."

He nodded, blue eyes soft with concern. "Rest now." Then he added more lightly, "You do not want to miss your own wedding."

As the door closed behind him, Darby dipped the corner of a cloth into a pitcher and wet Helen's lips with an orangey taste of flowers. Orgeat.

"I'm sorry if His Grace woke you," she said. "He insisted on seeing you although I told him you were in the fugue."

"No, he did not wake me." Her voice was still little more than a croak. She touched her chest, above her heart. "I think it was more a feeling that something is wrong. Is Carlston healing properly?"

Darby nodded. "According to Mr Quinn, his lordship is deep in his fugue and healing well – like you should be, my lady. You're more hurt than you think. We could see the bone in your ankle, and I'm fairly sure all your ribs on the right are broken."

Sprat suddenly appeared at the other side of the bed, her expression bunched into blotchy ferocity. "You scared the bejabbers outta us, my lady. I thought you was a goner, like Miss Cransdon." Her voice cracked, and she touched Helen's hand. "Thought you wasn't comin' back."

"Sprat!" Darby scolded. "You must not speak to her ladyship like that."

"It's all right." Helen smiled at the girl. "I am returned, as you see, and I will be well soon enough."

Indeed, the fugue was calling her back, dragging at her mind and thickening her voice, but something was still amiss. Carlston was on the mend, yet a sense of dread soured her innards and stung her eyes. An image, made of cold night air and warm lips pressed upon her own, made her blink. Was it just her unquiet conscience that had pulled her from her fugue? The image shifted into the burning white inferno, bodies writhing, bones popping, flesh burning away.

"My lady, you're cryin'," Sprat said. "Is it the pain?"

"Sprat, go downstairs and ask Fairwood for some brandy. Now!" Darby ordered.

Helen turned her face into the pillow, panting from the remembered heat, from the gruesome fiery victory she had fuelled.

She heard the bedchamber door open and close – Sprat

departing. Warm fingers wrapped around her hand.

"I am here, my lady," Darby said. "We are alone now. What's keeping you from your fugue? Is it what happened? Quinn told me what he saw. The fire and the stones."

"I don't know," Helen gasped, her sight blurred by tears. She struggled to sit up against the pillows, the movement bringing a wash of pain from her ribs. She felt Darby's strong arm around her back, gently pulling her up. "All I can see are the Deceivers burning."

It was not true; she could also feel the trace of Carlston's hands upon her face.

"Do not trouble yourself about the Deceivers, my lady. They do not deserve pity. They didn't feel any when they killed the poor souls in the bodies they stole, or for all the life forces they sucked away."

"I do not feel pity for them."

Darby squeezed her hand. "Then what troubles you, my lady?"

Helen shook her head.

"My lady, we have viewed decomposing bodies, stabbed people, and even seen those Rowlandson prints together. You can tell me anything. I doubt I will be shocked."

Helen drew a steadying breath. "I kissed Lord Carlston, Darby. Not only that; he said *Amore mio* – my love – to me, and I said it back to him. It was before we faced the Grand Deceiver. I did not want to go into battle without telling him."

Was that what made her feel so wretched? Because she had crossed the line; declared her feelings?

"Surely that is not keeping you from the fugue?" Darby shook her head. "Do not dwell on it, my lady. Mr Quinn says that people do strange things before battle. It is the rising of the blood."

Helen wiped her eyes. "But I am little more than a week from my wedding."

"You are not married yet, my lady. The sin is perhaps not as great as you think."

Helen smiled at her Terrene's dry tone. "I am not like some others of my rank, Darby. I cannot marry one man and enjoy another with no care for who will be hurt."

"I know, my lady. Even so, you are a Reclaimer who has just destroyed a great enemy. You are not a woman without means, or a girl whose life is in the hands of others. If you wish to change your mind, you can. You have a choice."

It was true. Yet was she not hemmed in by the same walls that hemmed in every woman? If she chose to follow Carlston, it would hurt her family grievously and humiliate a good man. She would be forced to live outside society, not only as the worst kind of ruthless jilt – like poor Millicent – but as a fallen woman, the mistress of a married man. Did passion make up for all that pain? Was it not inconceivably selfish to think such violence of feeling had a right to overrun everything in its way?

Helen pressed the backs of her hands to her wet eyes. If she married the Duke, she would be fulfilling her family's wishes and she would, in effect, *be* society. A leader alongside a man who had proven his worth and his devotion over and over again. And there was passion there too. Not as intense, admittedly, but surely enough. And added to that, the possibility of a family and the promise she had made to Aunt and to Selburn to walk away from the dangers of being a Reclaimer. And yet...

"I cannot choose. I cannot!"

She feverishly plucked at the silk cover. Her mind felt so hot, as if the swirling thoughts themselves burned. She squeezed her eyes shut – all she could see was the white-hot inferno, bodies twisting, bone and ash.

Darby took her hand, stopping her from clawing at the cover. "I think exhaustion and pain are making this loom over-large in your mind, my lady. This is not the time to be making decisions, or even thinking on such matters. Let the fugue heal your body and rest your mind, and then consider it."

Helen nodded. The fugue was calling and it would wrap everything in blessed, soft darkness. An escape from her guilt and the creeping sense that everything around her was beginning to unravel.

She roused again in grey light. The curtains were closed, but the shutters behind them had been opened, light edging in at the bottom. Daylight. Her chest no longer felt as if two men knelt upon it. She stretched her ankle – no pain – and her mind seemed clear, the feverish whirl of impossible questions quiet, for now. The fugue had done its work. How long had she been in its embrace? Had Carlston emerged?

She concentrated, feeling the beat beneath her own heartbeat. Stronger than last time. That was something at least. She felt the tether too, still firmly in place, the Ligatus coiled but quiet.

The scene of fresh-cut evergreens and pine needles permeated the warm air. The smell of baking as well: pastry and roast fowl and the sweet earthiness of honey. Helen's stomach lurched into a hungry groan.

She pulled herself up onto one elbow. The green velvet chaise longue had been moved closer to the hearth and Aunt sat upon it, staring into the fire. She wore half-dress – it must be early evening then – the russet silk gown sporting a high frilled neck and long sleeves. How thin and frail she looked, Helen thought, her age showing in the stoop of her shoulders and the fold of jowls along her jaw.

"Aunt," she said. The strength of her voice had been lost to dryness. She tried again. "Aunt?"

Her aunt twisted around on the seat. "Ah, you are awake!" She rose stiffly and crossed to the bed with a smile. "How do you feel, my dear? Are you recovered? Darby said this fugue would completely heal you." Her voice held doubt.

Helen sat up, dragging a pillow behind her back, then received her aunt's kiss upon her cheek, breathing in the scent of Denmark Lotion, face powder and Johnstone's Royal Patent Windsor Soap; the comforting smells of her childhood.

"As far as I can tell, everything is whole again. How long was I ... *away*?" She paused, knowing the next question would seem significant to her ever-watchful guardian. Perhaps it was. "Is Lord Carlston awake?"

Aunt picked up a pitcher from the bedside table and poured a cloudy liquid into a glass. "It has been two days." She smiled again – a little strained – and passed the glass. "Merry Christmas, my dearest."

Two days; of course, it must be Christmas Day. "Merry Christmas, Aunt."

That accounted for the fresh-cut wood – holly boughs – and baking. She had clearly missed decorating the Hall and lighting the Yule log, two of her favourite festivities. She took a sip of the barley water, the liquid like a soothing oil upon the scratch of her throat.

She looked over the rim of the glass. "And Lord Carlston?"

Aunt crossed her arms. "Darby was here just a few minutes ago to say that he has also emerged from his fugue." She was keeping something back. It was in the hitch of her shoulders.

"Is he recovered?"

Aunt sighed, slightly exasperated. "There is no keeping any-thing from you. She said that he has emerged too early and is not fully healed. I did not wish to worry you."

"Not fully healed?" Helen repeated. How could that be? She took another sip, hiding her consternation.

"Darby said he is healed enough to be up and getting dressed."

Helen nodded. *Not fully healed.* Why then had he emerged from the fugue? Perhaps they were now so attuned that her own awakening had drawn him out.

Aunt sat on the edge of the bed. "We are all waiting, of course, until both you and Lord Carlston are recovered to properly celebrate your victory, and your return to *normal* life. Mr Pike is back from London and wishes to see you and Lord Carlston as soon as is convenient." She leaned closer, lowering her voice. "He is a most peculiar man, is he not?"

"He has just lost his wife, Aunt."

"Still, very abrupt manners. He has quite offended Lady Dunwick."

"Are they still oblivious?"

"Oh yes, and Lady Georgina and Lord Henry. I have taken over managing the house and hostessing for now until you are recovered. The story is that you are suffering from nerves again, and Lord Carlston has had another fall from his horse."

His lordship would not be pleased by that story, Helen thought. "And Lady Margaret?"

"She does not have the benefit of your fugue state, but she is doing as well as can be expected." Aunt's mouth pulled at the corner. "It is her mind, I think, that is most affected. Her brother believes something is weighing upon her most grievously. Even so, she is up from her bed."

Helen nodded. She understood only too well how dark things could prey upon one's mind and depress one's spirit. "I have been abed long enough too." She pulled back the covers and swung her legs out. Another kind of urgency was making itself known.

"Are you sure you are well enough?"

"Quite." She stood and flexed her toes in the thick carpet, then circled her ankle – all in good working order – then headed towards the dressing room and the chamber pot.

"So, my dear, shall I inform the Duke that you will be joining us for Christmas dinner?" Aunt asked. "The gong to dress is about to sound."

Food. That seemed like a very good idea. Helen looked over her shoulder as she entered the colder dressing room. "Yes, thank you."

"He will be happy to hear that Chenwith Hall has its hostess back. And its bride-to-be," Aunt called. There was a warning in her voice. Or was it a plea?

Helen did not answer, noisily opening the chamber pot cabinet. She stretched her hearing into the other room as she drew the pot out of its recess. Aunt had not moved, waiting for some kind of response.

Helen bowed her head. She should just agree, but something held her back. It felt as if she teetered upon a brink: one side, a dark, deep unknown full of yearning; the other, solid ground.

Finally, she heard the bedchamber door open and close.

Two hours later, Helen stared at herself in the dressing room mirror. She was wearing a new mull muslin evening gown, with the rosemary for Delia pinned upon its Brussels lace bodice, and her mother's gold and ruby cross at her throat. A return to normality. She traced the soft unmarked skin of her cheek where Philip's whip had laid open the flesh. She looked unchanged, and yet she felt immeasurably different from the Helen who had ridden out towards the circle of stones. She touched the gold cross. Would her mother have been proud of her Grand Reclaimer daughter? Lady Catherine had never had the chance to fully use her own talents, and in her last letter had begged her daughter to reject her Reclaimer heritage. Yet if Helen had rejected it, the Grand Deceiver would still be alive.

She picked up her lorgnette. One lens gone, the other a spiderweb of cracks. For a second, the room spun, her senses overwhelmed by the pain memory of her body slamming into stone. She drew a sharp breath, dropping the useless spectacles back onto the dressing table.

"Shall I send for Mr Pike and Lord Carlston, my lady?" Darby asked, returning from the bedchamber. "The dinner gong will strike soon, but Mr Pike said he wished to meet with both of you before you came down."

Helen steadied her breathing. "Yes, send for them."

She did not particularly want to see the Second Secretary. No doubt he wished to know her plans now that the Grand Deceiver had been defeated. What were her plans? She rolled her shoulders. She had made a promise to Selburn and Aunt to return to normal life, to retire from the Dark Days Club, and now it was due.

Her desire to see Lord Carlston, on the other hand, had been a constant battle to control since she had roused from her fugue. For two hours as she bathed and dressed, she had listened to the rhythm of their bond through her body, focused her Reclaimer hearing upon his steady breathing, and forced back a mad impulse to abandon all decency and propriety and go to his rooms. To look him in the eye and see if he still held their kiss within his heart. Perhaps it had not meant as much to him. Perhaps Darby had been right: it was no more than a rising of the blood before battle. It was all very well to be standing on a brink, but what if she stood alone? He had said they were impossible.

Well, it would not be long before she knew his truth.

Darby opened the door that led into the passage and gave the order to a waiting footman to fetch Mr Pike and Lord Carlston, then closed the door again. She picked up an abandoned drying cloth and hung it over the edge of the bath, smoothing it across the copper lip. Helen watched her in the mirror as she shifted the jewellery box, then returned it to the same position.

Helen turned in her chair. "You seem a little distracted, Darby. Is something bothering you?"

Darby rubbed her forehead. "I had a worrying thought, my lady. Do you think Lord Carlston could have been dragged out of his fugue by something to do with the Ligatus? He came out of his fugue in Brighton if you recall."

Of course Helen recalled; he had attacked Selburn and she had been forced to beat him into unconsciousness.

"That was the vestige madness, and he no longer has any vestige energy in his soul. It cannot be the same."

Darby nodded, yet did not seem relieved of her unease.

"What is it?" Helen asked. "You clearly have something else to say."

"I know you do not like gossip, my lady, but when I was down in the linen room, one of the maids told me that Mr Pike brought a package for his lordship. From France. A small box."

A cold certainty clenched Helen's gut. *From Lady Elise.* What had she sent him? "Does he already have it?"

"I don't think so. I believe he is dressing with Mr Quinn's help and has not yet seen Mr Pike."

Helen rose from her chair with one last anxious look at herself in the mirror. Darby had curled her hair becomingly in the latest dishevelled style, but she was no beauty, not like Lady Elise.

She walked through her bedchamber to her private drawing

room to await the arrival of Pike and Carlston. Her wait was not long; she had only just positioned herself before the hearth when a sharp double rap sounded upon the door. She listened. Only one set of breathing. Not Carlston.

"Come," she said.

Mr Pike entered the room, his black mourning jacket and stooped shoulders giving him the semblance of a watchful raven.

He bowed stiffly. "Good evening, Lady Helen. I am glad to see that you are fully recovered."

His eyes still held the strain of sorrow, but it seemed his duty had given him an anchor in his grief, for he closed the door and approached with an air of purpose, a leather satchel tucked under his arm.

"Thank you, Mr Pike. And yourself, how do you fare?"

"I am well, thank you," he said flatly. "We will wait for Lord Carlston." As brusque as ever.

She motioned to the opposite chair. "Will you take a seat?"

"No. I will stand."

Then so would she, Helen decided. They waited awkwardly before the fireplace, the sound of the mantel clock ticking, the log upon the fire popping and crackling. She stretched her hearing, following Darby along the passageway – she was humming a slightly flat "O Come All Ye Faithful". Of course, she would be heading to the servants' Christmas dinner.

"Does the Ligatus tether remain strong?" Pike asked.

The question, Helen realised, was not just from the Dark Days Club official; it was from Isabella's husband.

"Strong enough." She remembered the howling, hissing power slamming itself against its vestige shackle. "When I was fighting Philip, I absorbed some of his power and it seemed to feed the Ligatus, but the tether held it back."

He nodded, seeming to take some kind of grim satisfaction

in its resilience. "Did Mr King indicate if there was a way to remove the Ligatus from you?"

"No, but he did say that the tether would not last forever."

Pike rubbed his forehead tiredly. "If you feel it weaken at all, inform me. I suspect you will need to reclaim again in order to renew it and we can find a candidate immediately."

Even if she did retire from the Dark Days Club, as she had promised Selburn and Aunt, she would still be tied to it. Tied by a vestige tether; she smiled sourly at the pun.

"Is Mr Hallifax still here?" she asked.

"No. I had to send him to a possible reclaiming case in Wales. He did, however, ask me to send you his regards."

"I did not have a chance to thank him properly."

Pike's reply was lost in the sound of a familiar set of footsteps approaching. Carlston. She pressed her hands together, trying to control the leap of hope as his knock sounded.

She cleared her throat. "Come."

The door opened. Carlston stood in its frame, arm in a sling, his eyes finding her by the hearth. It felt as if her heart hovered between beats as she searched his gaunt face, and then it burst into hard joy. The kiss was in his eyes, in his smile, in the way he breathed. It pounded through their bond, racing through her blood, folding its truth into her heart. She did not stand alone on the brink. They stood together, looking into the dark unknown side by side.

He closed the door and limped forward with pained care, his usual ease of movement gone. Now that she could see past the joy of that first moment, it was clear he was still sorely injured. His skin held a grey cast, the strong bones of his face starkly angular, and the usual brightness of his eyes had been dulled by pain.

He saw her shock. *Do not worry. I am healing.*

How could she not worry? She fought back the desire to meet him halfway, to take his hands and help him across the room.

Pike observed his slow progress. "I am sorry to see you still so hurt, Lord Carlston."

"It was a hard battle," Carlston said. "Lady Helen fought magnificently."

"So I heard from Hallifax. He said the two of you were quite extraordinary."

Carlston smiled at Helen and it held more than agreement. "Yes. They tried to keep us apart – they knew about the dyad – but we prevailed."

"Did they attempt to activate the Trinitas?" Pike asked. "Hallifax could not give me a conclusive answer."

"No, but then they did not have the Ligatus," Carlston said.

"I did not even see the Colligat," Helen added. "Philip had it last, at Bath, but he did not bring it out at the stones."

An image of the Deceiver laughing at her on Quiet Street flashed into her mind. And then Delia, covered in blood. She closed her hands into fists, riding the inevitable wave of guilt and fury.

"Well, if he had it with him, it has been obliterated with the two of them," Carlston said. "Thank God."

"Well and truly obliterated," Helen confirmed.

Yet although the Colligat had been part of a heinous weapon, it was also the only portrait she'd had of her mother. Gone forever. She touched the cross upon its chain around her neck. At least she now had that keepsake.

"Do you have any idea why you have emerged from the fugue so early?" Pike asked Carlston.

Carlston gave a dry smile. "Perhaps for Christmas."

Pike lifted his brows, but motioned to the chair at his side. "Do you wish to sit?"

"I will stand, it is more comfortable." Carlston motioned with his uninjured arm. "What is it you wish to say to us?"

"Today, I am merely a messenger," Pike said. He shifted the satchel from beneath his arm and drew out two large letters sealed with red wax and ribbons. "I have been charged by His Royal Highness the Prince Regent to deliver these letters into your hands with the utmost expedience." He bowed, and passed one packet to Carlston and the other to Helen. "Read them and return them to me. I must burn them once you are done."

Of course: Dark Days Club procedure. Helen glanced at Carlston. By the surprise upon his face, he had not expected to receive a letter from the Palace either.

She turned her packet over. It had some heft to it, probably from the large Royal seal that held the edges together and the thick linen paper. She walked across to the window, sliding her forefinger under the red wax seal. It snapped open and she unfolded the single page, recognising the Prince Regent's elegant flourished hand.

Carlton House, Thursday, 24th December, 1812
Lady Helen,
Mr Pike has apprised me and my mother, the Queen, of the great victory that you and Lord Carlston have achieved against that most heinous of our enemies, the Grand Deceiver. Although your great service to this country is hidden from the majority of its people, please accept our eternal gratitude on their behalf. Your courage, adherence to duty and selflessness are exemplary. In recognition of your great service and on behalf of my father, I offer you a Royal boon: a favour, land, or a title. Make your request known to Mr Pike, and it will be arranged.
You have our fullest admiration and the thanks of a grateful nation.

May God's blessing be upon you.
In His Name and on behalf of His Majesty,
George PR

Good God, a Royal boon. Helen took a deep breath. Such an honour. And oddly synchronous: her mother had been given a boon by Queen Charlotte for services rendered. Lady Catherine had chosen to leave that last letter to her daughter in the care of the Queen, to be delivered after Helen's presentation. The letter that had, to some degree, brought her to this moment.

Helen looked up from the Royal signature. She knew exactly what she wanted.

Pike stood with his back to the fire, watching them read.

"Do you know what His Highness has offered?" she asked.

"I do," he said.

Carlston looked up from his own letter, his eyes feverishly brilliant in the pallor of his face.

"I want my mother officially exonerated," Helen said. "A complete denial of any treachery associated with our family name. Would that be possible?"

Pike inclined his head. "His Royal Highness indicated that he would do his utmost to grant your and Lord Carlston's requests."

Helen wet her lips. A gift not only to her dead mother and father, but to her dear aunt and brother too.

The distant clang of the dinner-hour gong sounded: the call to the drawing room.

"I also know what I want," Carlston said. He looked at her and she could almost feel the hammer of his heart alongside her own. "I want a divorce from Countess Carlston, or better, an annulment."

Helen drew a sharp breath. No need for years of waiting

and an Act of Parliament. All at once, his exoneration from any association with Lady Elise and his freedom. The marriage would be as if it never existed. Did it mean what she thought?

The answer was in his face. In the searching hope in his eyes. *Will you?*

It would bring so much hurt. So much recrimination. And yet there was only one answer. *I will.*

Pike looked at them both. "I thought that was all in the past..." He rubbed his eyes wearily. "You may need to reconsider that request."

Carlston frowned. "Can an annulment not be granted?"

"It is not that." Pike opened the satchel again and drew out a small square package tied with brown string. "Before you make any decisions, Lord Carlston, you should read the letter that accompanies this." He passed the package to Carlston.

Helen found herself walking closer – drawn by a terrible foreboding.

"It is from Elise," Carlston said, staring at the direction written across the front.

"It is," Pike said.

"You have opened it?"

"Of course. It is correspondence from a known spy."

Carlston's mouth tightened. "How kind of you to rewrap it," he said through his teeth. "But I cannot open it." He shifted his arm in the sling. "Not with this."

"Allow me," Helen said.

"Why don't you just tell me what it holds, Pike?" Carlston demanded.

"No. This is something you should see."

Carlston passed the package to Helen, the draw of his brows answering her silent query. *I don't know – one of Pike's sick games?*

Helen yanked the string off the box, then tore away the paper. It was like some ghastly mimicry of unwrapping a Twelfth Night gift. Inside, a letter, sealed with a wafer, and a small leather-clad case.

"Open the box," Carlston said.

Helen slid the clasp out of its home and flipped open the top. Carlston's breath released in a long hiss. On a bed of black silk lay a large oval gold locket, two inches long at least, with the letter E emblazoned upon it in diamonds.

"I had this made for her," he said. "Why is she sending it back?"

Pike motioned to the letter. "Read it."

Carlston nodded to Helen. "Open it for me, please."

She broke the wafer at the back of the letter, unfolded the page and passed it across, catching a glimpse of the salutation: *Mon cher Guillaume.*

She watched his eyes scan the slanting lines, his already pale skin blanching even more, his jaw clenching until she was sure he would shatter his teeth. What terrible news was in the letter?

He dropped it to the floor and picked up the locket from the box in her hands, his fingers trembling from the effort. Helen stooped and picked up the fallen missive. It took all her will not to turn it over and read the neat lines.

"Do you need some help to open—" she began.

"No." He finally lodged his thumbnail into the catch and flicked the locket open. For a long second, it was as if he would never take another breath, and then he drew a hard shaking gasp, as if he had run for hours.

"What is it?" Helen asked. "Carlston, what is it?"

He did not meet her eyes. "Read it."

She opened the folded page.

Calais, Monday, 21st December, 1812

Mon cher Guillaume,

I had hoped you would answer my previous letter, for the sake of what we once had together, but it is clear that you must bear me an insurmountable grudge. I am not surprised — you have always stood steadfastly by what you believe, and your nature is not bent towards forgiveness. Even so, it is imperative that we meet, mon chéri. I did not wish to coerce you, but I am left with no option. I have enclosed the locket that you gave me as a wedding gift. Do you remember how you threaded it around my neck? So much love, then, non?

Inside you will find a miniature that I have had painted. It is of your son, Francis William Standfield, Viscount Collingate. Believe me, I did not know I was enceinte when I left England four years ago...

Helen raised her eyes, her voice coming, it seemed, from very far away. "Your son?"

"I did not know ... she did not tell me," he whispered.

He passed her the open locket, the warmth of his tight clasp still upon the gold. It was a well-made portrait, the brushstrokes elegant and assured. The little boy wore a white stock and blue coat in the French style, his dark hair curling over a broad pale brow. The artist had brought light into his large dark eyes, and a flick of the brush had slanted his brows upward in a familiar way. Another deft stroke recorded the hint of a decided jaw in the sweet rounded curve of his face. Helen looked up at Carlston: the same brows, the same dark eyes, and that jaw. There could be no mistaking the boy's sire.

"But is it *possible*?" Pike asked.

Carlston dragged his hand down his face. "Of course it is possible."

Such a confusion of emotion in his eyes. Shock, hope, anger. God help her, it was the hope that cut her down. A thousand swords slicing at her heart. A child. They had a child together. An annulment would make the boy illegitimate. A divorce would make him the centre of scandal and the son of a traitor. There was nowhere to step.

"She might be lying," Carlston said harshly. And yet even in his words there was the hope that it was not so.

"Whether she is or not remains to be determined," Pike said. "Whatever the case, His Royal Highness the Prince Regent has asked me to impart the following to you. If the child exists and you claim him as your issue, then for the sake of your son and heir, His Royal Highness will guarantee a safe return to England for Lady Elise and a pardon for the charges against her of espionage and treachery. Not only that, but His Royal Highness and his mother, the Queen, will receive her at Court."

Carlston stared at Pike. "They would do that? Receive her?"

Pike nodded. "For the sake of your friendship with His Highness and for the boy's future." He glanced at Helen. "He says no child deserves to live under the taint of a parent's treachery."

Helen bowed her head. She knew the truth of that only too well. She would never wish it upon any child, let alone Carlston's son.

Pike cleared his throat. "His Royal Highness also said an English noble must not remain in France, living as a damned Frenchie."

Carlston allowed a mirthless smile. "That sounds like George." His eyes found Helen's, the pain in them matching her own. "I must discover the truth."

"You must," she said, forcing the words out. His honour –

her honour – would not allow anything else. "For the sake of the child."

She placed the locket in his palm, and his fingers closed upon hers for one beat of their hearts, one beat of their bond, the two steady rhythms now holding the promise of eternal loss.

Chapter Twenty-Five

Helen held tightly to one of the posts of her state bed, head bowed, afraid to move in case the howling misery locked in her chest burst forth. She should already be in the drawing room, the gracious hostess ready to lead her guests into Christmas dinner – but if she went down now, she would be laid bare before them.

Of course, she had no right to such pain. He was a married man *with a son and heir*, and she, brilliantly betrothed. There could be no claim to tragedy here. And yet she had stepped, and he had too: that breathless moment of hope and future entwined. What savage irony to make such a choice and then discover there had never been any choice at all. Or perhaps it was punishment for her selfish decision.

She dug her nails into the bedpost, feeling the solid structure shift under her strength. Stinging tears blurred her sight. No! She pressed the heels of her hands into her eye sockets, forcing the tears back. They must not fall, for if she started weeping she may not stop, and she had to make her appearance downstairs before her absence became an embarrassment for the Duke.

Twenty minutes later, Helen stood outside the drawing room. It took all her resolve to nod to the footman to open the door, and then to walk through it with a smile upon her face and the day's tidings upon her tongue.

The room smelled of the smoky remains of the huge Yule log burning in the fireplace and the evergreen boughs tied with red ribbons that decorated the tables and mantelpiece. Helen made her way further into the room, barely able to fix her eyes upon anyone in case they saw the truth behind her smile. Lord Henry stood in conversation with Andrew at the hearth. Pug sipped at a glass of ruby-coloured punch, her face flushed with pleasure, while her mother extolled the virtues of the hot baths to Aunt and Lady Georgina. Mr Pike stood alone, contemplating one of the portraits upon the wall. Finally Helen settled her gaze on Lady Margaret, seated next to the fire.

Darby had been right: Lady Margaret was sorely hurt. Her eyes held a heart-wrenching glaze – possibly too much laudanum – and she held herself as if she might break, all her graceful confidence gone. Mr Hammond stood behind his sister's chair. He returned Helen's smile, although his fair brows angled for a moment in concern. He had seen through her masquerade. A man who recognised the hurt of a heart.

"A Merry Christmas to you all," she said as gaily as she could manage. "My apologies for my tardiness."

"We were about to send out a search party," Selburn said, crossing the room. He took her gloved hand, kissing it in the old manner. "How well you look."

His smile held relief and questions, but above all, anxiety. He had not seen her since that brief emergence from her fugue. Little wonder he was worried. Through her anguish, she felt a cold nugget of guilt. Such a good man.

"I feel very well," she said. "I am fully recovered." She squeezed his gloved hand. *"Fully."*

He looked at her oddly, clearly sensing that the word held

more than a report of health. "I am glad," he said. "Fairwood is hovering outside with the call to dinner. I do not wish to hurry you, but are you ready to go in?"

"Of course."

He nodded, loath, it seemed, to give up her hand. With one last kiss upon it, he turned and, with a bow, offered Aunt his arm into dinner. Helen returned her aunt's smile, then realised that as hostess she would be escorted by Lord Carlston. He had already come to the same conclusion for he was on his way across the room.

He bowed, shifting his sling. "Lady Helen, I am afraid I can only offer you my company, not my arm."

At least she would not have to endure the torment of touching him. With her smile still firmly in place, she fell in beside him. He walked slowly along the corridor, allowing a little distance to open up between them and Selburn and Aunt.

"I do not know what to say," he told her, his voice pitched for Reclaimer privacy. "Only that, if it is true, I must get him out of France and bring him to safety. Can you understand that? Can you forgive me?"

"Of course I can," Helen said, her own whisper fierce. "You must do what is right."

She risked a glance at his face. Still grey with pain, and now more anguish in his dark eyes. He suffered too. One last stand together.

They entered the dining room. Garlands of holly and rosemary decorated the table around the central gilt epergne, their cinnamon and herb scents bringing lush green notes amidst the rich smells of roast goose and beef. Aunt, Mrs Clarke and Mrs Carroll had clearly worked together to create a beautiful and abundant feast.

Carlston escorted Helen to her seat at the end of the table.

"Lord Carlston, come sit alongside me," Aunt said, beckoning him to a place near the top of the table.

He angled his head for a moment, his desire to refuse as clear as if he yelled it, then bowed at the summons and took his seat at Aunt's side.

Pug passed Helen, eyes bright. She paused to whisper, "I am so glad you are well enough to come down. Is it not marvellous? We will have such a merry time."

"Very merry," Helen said, managing to keep the dryness from her voice.

Lord Henry took his seat at Helen's left, and called a footman over with a wave at his glass. "Not champagne. Can't stand the stuff. Claret." The footman bowed and removed the champagne glass.

Mr Hammond sat at Helen's right. She felt his scrutiny upon her. "What has happened?" he murmured.

"I am concerned about your sister," she whispered, deflecting the question.

He glanced along the table at Lady Margaret. "I am worried too. She will not talk about what happened to her and I think it is affecting her spirit, perhaps even her mind."

"She is a strong woman."

"I fear not strong enough." He drew a breath through pinched nostrils. "It should never have happened."

"You blame us," Helen said. "Perhaps you are right to do so."

He shook his head. "Not you, Lady Helen. I blame Lord Carlston. I know your attachment, but now you can see what happens to those who love him."

Helen was saved the need to answer by Selburn, who stood at the head of the table, drawing all attention.

"Tonight we dine *en famille*, for this is a celebration of

family and friends, the birth of our Lord, and the eternal defeat of evil by the righteous and the good." He looked around the table, his face sombre. "It is also a time to remember those who are no longer with us. May they rest in peace."

Lady Margaret bowed her head, her hand touching the knot of rosemary at her breast. Pike stared fixedly at the cutlery upon the table.

"Let us also give thanks to the Almighty for our heroes," Selburn continued, his eyes resting upon Helen, "and for the feast upon our table and for the joys of the season. Amen."

"Amen," Helen murmured with everyone else.

"Does he mean Wellesley?" Lady Dunwick asked Mr Pike at her side.

"I'm sure he does," Pike said. He glanced at Helen. "Although, of course, we have many heroes."

The first course was brought in and placed upon the table: two tureens of soup, and four types of fish with their sauces. Helen had thought her appetite consumed by misery, but upon the first mouthful of Mrs Carroll's excellent hare soup, her Reclaimer body demanded replenishment. A lesson, she thought dryly, on the unrelenting nature of life.

When the soups were finished, Selburn stood again, this time for the toasts.

"In seven days," he said, looking around the table, "Lady Helen and I will be married; a start of a *new* life together, the old one left behind. Allow me to toast my betrothed, the future Duchess of Selburn." He bowed.

Everyone around the table stood, except for Helen, and raised their glasses, chorusing, "To the future Duchess of Selburn."

The Duke tipped his glass to her in a private toast, his fair skin flushed, the blue of his eyes bright with something akin to jubilation. Helen forced a smile. She had been ready to walk away from him. He deserved better.

As polite society dictated, every guest around the table was duly honoured with a few gracious words from their host and a general raising of glasses, and then the footmen removed the soup tureens and the remains of the fish, replacing them with the second course. Two large roast geese, a roast beef, plump Yorkshire puddings, braised celery, a cauliflower in sauce, sautéed mushrooms, buttered kale, mincemeat pies, game pies, a glazed ham, rich creamy syllabub, an extraordinarily large trifle, nuts and dried fruits. Without the constrictions of formal dining, the conversation flowed across the table and around, the subjects ranging from the excellence of the meats, the prospect of more snow, the Saint Stephen's Day holiday for the servants on the morrow – "Rather inconvenient," Andrew muttered – and, of course, the upcoming wedding.

"Are the plans for the night fair completed yet, Selburn?" Lady Georgina asked as she toyed with a piece of braised celery upon her plate.

"They are. The day after tomorrow the lamps will be strung around the formal gardens." Selburn smiled. "I aim to rival Vauxhall. Then the stalls and roasting kitchens for the villagers will be set in the lower field."

"It will be most exciting," Pug said, sawing at a slice of venison pie. "I cannot wait to see the lights or the dance pavilion." She turned to Carlston seated at her side. "Dancing in the garden will be divine, do you not agree, Lord Carlston?" Her eyes travelled down to his sling. "Oh, but you will probably not be able to dance. How awful."

Carlston gave a tight-lipped smile. "I am afraid I do not stay for the wedding, Lady Elizabeth, so my inability will not cause me any distress."

Selburn turned from supplying Lady Dunwick with the sautéed mushrooms. "You do not stay, Carlston?" He glanced at Helen, but she busied herself with a slice of beef.

"I am called away by urgent business, and will be leaving early tomorrow morning," Carlston said. "My apologies to you and Lady Helen." He did not look her way.

Gone, tomorrow. The prospect clawed spikes into her heart.

"But you are still injured, Lord Carlston," Lady Dunwick said. "Surely you cannot travel yet."

"We must not detain Lord Carlston from his business," Selburn said briskly. He looked at Mr Hammond. "Will you and your sister go too?"

Hammond straightened in his chair. "No, Your Grace. My sister and I are not tied to Lord Carlston's plans." His gaze rested fleetingly upon the Earl.

Carlston's jaw shifted. "You will be missed, my friend."

Hammond picked up his claret glass and took a large swig, ignoring the comment. Nor would he meet Helen's eye again.

"I am not going," Lady Margaret said abruptly into the silence. "I am to be Lady Helen's attendant and I will not forfeit that honour." She leaned towards Helen, her voice thick with emotion. "You have already lost one attendant. You must not lose another."

"Do not fret, sister," Hammond said. "If His Grace allows it, we will stay."

"Of course you will stay," Helen said quickly, casting a firm glance at her betrothed. "And you too, Mr Pike. You are very welcome."

Pike bowed his thanks.

Lady Dunwick pushed the braised celery back into the order of plates, then glanced at Lady Margaret, plainly doubting that lady's facility. "It is, of course, dreadful about Miss Cransdon, but if you do require another attendant, Lady Helen, I am sure my Elizabeth would be honoured to assist you on the day."

"Mama," Pug said beneath her breath. She glanced sideways at Helen with a little beseeching shake of her head – she had not pressed her mother into such a declaration.

"I am sure that is an excellent idea," Aunt said. "Helen? You must have more than one attendant."

Helen smiled and nodded, pretending a full mouthful to avoid standing up and screaming out the anguish that was building momentum in her heart. *Please, don't go!*

The footmen arrived to remove the meats and place down the third course. Amidst the retrieval of plates and glasses, Helen risked a moment's regard of Carlston. He felt her attention and lifted his eyes from the contemplation of his wine glass, the expression within them raw. *I am sorry.*

But tomorrow?

I should not be here.

Helen looked down at the clean plate that had been placed before her by the footman. She understood that sentiment only too well.

After dinner, as the ladies waited for the gentlemen to finish their port and join them for charades and coffee in the drawing room, Helen managed to draw Lady Margaret to the window alcove for private conversation. Pug had claimed the pianoforte and was playing a soft and competent rendition of "Good King Wenceslas", while Aunt and Lady Dunwick appraised some tartlets upon the stand, and Lady Georgina yawned by the fireplace.

Helen and Lady Margaret sat side by side on the bench seat, the freezing night pressing upon the window behind them and bringing a slight chill to the air at their backs. Lady Margaret drew her shawl more tightly around her shoulders.

"You are not too cold?" Helen asked.

Lady Margaret gave her a sidelong glance. "I cannot recall you ever asking after my comfort before," she said, some of the old acid back in her voice.

A harsh judgment – and quite untrue, surely – but Helen did not want to quarrel. "I wish to thank you for your bravery," she said. "By keeping the secret of the Trinitas – of what I am – you helped us defeat them."

Lady Margaret gave a tight nod.

"I am also sorry – more than sorry, grieved – that the plan at the White Hart went so very wrong," Helen continued. "I have an odd feeling that something else was amiss there. Can you remember what happened?"

Now that she had said it, she realised just how deeply the sense of unease had woven its way into her mind. Was it just the sick weight of her own conscience?

"I cannot remember much at all," Lady Margaret said. "It happened so fast. Uncannily fast." She crossed her arms, cradling her body. "Afterwards, however, is completely clear."

There was a note in her voice that sent another kind of chill down Helen's back.

"Would it help to speak of it?" she asked.

Lady Margaret stared down at the floor. "Help? I do not know if anything can help. What they did..." She looked up and met Helen's eye fleetingly, her words barely a breath. "Both of them ... with that feeder tentacle they all have." Her voice cracked and she grabbed Helen's hand. "You must not tell Michael. Or anyone. Promise me."

Helen's scalp crawled with horror. She had no words to offer such a harrowing confidence. No wonder Lady Margaret's spirit was so oppressed.

She squeezed the cold hand within her own. "Of course, I will not say a word."

Lady Margaret eyed her for a long, heavy moment. "You say you feel something was amiss at the inn? I think so too."

"In what way?"

"I wonder whether the plan really went wrong."

Helen did not gather her meaning at first. "Are you saying you think we intended for you to be taken?"

"Not you." A flush mounted her cheeks. "My brother thinks that perhaps it was Lord Carlston's plan all along."

"That is not so," Helen said, the force of her words drawing Pug's attention from her soft playing. She lowered her voice again. "Surely Mr Hammond cannot believe such an awful thing? Or you?"

Lady Margaret lifted her chin. "I cannot see how else it could have happened. The protection of three Reclaimers and yet… Better to force an exchange that was not in a crowded city."

Helen shook her head. "It does not make sense. How could we know if they would ransom you? And we certainly did not choose the place of exchange. Besides, you cannot think Lord Carlston would be so ruthless."

And yet that sense of unease, still omnipresent.

Lady Margaret rose from the bench as the door opened to admit the gentlemen. "I know where your loyalty is coming from, Lady Helen. However, I think it for the best that Lord Carlston leaves us. And we leave him." With a grave nod, she walked back to the fireplace, her arms cradling her body.

It was not long before Mr Hammond made his way to Helen's side.

"Do you truly think Lord Carlston intended your sister to be taken at the White Hart?" Helen asked as he took a seat on the bench.

442

"You have spoken to Margaret?"

"Yes."

Hammond's eyes found his sister. "I do not know. Margaret seems to believe it, but I am not sure she is thinking clearly. She has lost faith in his lordship. In everything, it seems."

Helen bit her lip. She had promised Lady Margaret she would not share the terrible reason for the change in her disposition, but it was hard not to offer the explanation to her brother.

"And you? Will you really not go with him?" she asked instead.

Hammond's attention switched to Lord Carlston, who was in conversation with Lord Henry. Helen followed his gaze, and they both watched the long, lean line of his lordship's body, the tilt of his dark head, the bold bones of his face, a little too stark from the pain left after his uncompleted fugue.

"Even after all this, I do not wish to leave his side," Hammond said. "But I cannot abandon my sister. I cannot give her any further cause for distress."

Helen caught the desolation in his eyes. "I am sorry," she said. For him, for Margaret, and for herself.

She did not think for a minute that he and his sister could be right. Yet their disillusion about Carlston and the destruction of their friendship added another stone upon the heavy weight of her unease.

It seemed to Helen that the festivities in the drawing room would never end. Once Hammond had left her side, she focused fiercely upon her role as hostess, drawing Andrew and Lord Henry into a game of charades, pressing a glass of good cheer upon Mr Pike, reassuring Pug that she was a happy addition to the wedding party, entreating Lady Georgina to play upon the pianoforte, taking her own turn at the instrument, and dancing with Selburn and Mr Hammond. And all the while knowing exactly where Carlston stood or sat, reaching too often to feel the beat of their Reclaimer bond. It was like pressing her tongue upon a sore tooth, she thought wryly. The pain somehow oddly reassuring.

Finally, at half past one in the morning, the party disbanded. Helen followed Lady Georgina and Lord Henry up the grand staircase, bade them good night at their bedchamber door and, holding up her night candle, continued to her dressing room with a weary tread.

On opening the door, she found Darby on the chaise longue, darning a stocking by the light of a candle. Would she wish to leave with her husband tomorrow? Helen was not sure she could bear that loss as well.

"You look burned to the socket, my lady," Darby said. She rose from the chaise longue and put aside the stocking. Her eyes were puffy and red. Tears, or just her own fatigue?

"Too much Christmas jollity," Helen said, passing across her night candle and the gloves, then drawing her shawl from her shoulders. "Where is Sprat?"

"I sent her to bed." Darby folded the shawl and put it away. "I found her drinking gin with the grooms."

"Heaven forfend, what next?" Helen leaned her hands upon the dressing table, her head bowed. There was no reason to delay the next question, except cowardice. "Has Mr Quinn told you?"

"Yes," Darby said gently. "A son. He saw the painting. He says the boy is the spitting image of his lordship."

"The same eyes, brows and chin. It would be hard to argue they are not related." Helen paused. Whatever came next, she must accept it. She turned around, trying to keep her voice even. "What do you propose to do, Darby? Will you go with

444

your husband and Lord Carlston to Calais? I will not blame you if you do."

Darby crossed her arms. "You are about to be married, my lady. As if I would leave at such a time. I told Mr Quinn that I must stay for the wedding at least."

"Thank you." And after the wedding? Helen shied from the question.

"As it happens," Darby added, "he does not want me to go with them anyway. Says it's too dangerous with all the warships coming and going to France and America. Not to mention Bonaparte back in Paris." She gave a tight smile. "Besides, can you imagine Sprat trying to do your wedding hair?"

Helen laughed; a hiccup of relief more than mirth. "It would be a travesty." She sobered. "Oh, Darby, I do not know if I even deserve to be married now. I was ready to walk away from the Duke, to inflict such hurt upon him and so many people. My aunt, my brother. All to follow my own selfish heart." She bit her lip. "I must tell the Duke. He should know what he is about to marry."

"Good heavens, no!" Darby crossed the room and took Helen's hands. "My lady, you have not walked away. You have not even broken any vow. The only promise you have ever made to the Duke is that you will marry him. That may give him claim to your property, but it gives him no claim upon your thoughts or your body. Not yet. Not until you are married. As far as I see it, no one other than you has been hurt."

"But my heart walked away, Darby."

"That is between you and God, my lady. If you tell the Duke, there can be no outcome that will be in your favour. You will be confessing to something that has not even happened, and it will destroy any chance of your future happiness." She squeezed Helen's hands. "You must know I am speaking the truth. After all, it would be much more in my favour – and Mr Quinn's – if you were to go with Lord Carlston."

Dear Darby, ever practical – and right. One only had to look to Caro Lamb and poor Millicent for lessons against ill-judged love. Still, what about truth?

Helen pulled one hand from her maid's tight clasp and pressed her fingers against the welling of tears. "Surely the Duke deserves to know what is in my heart?"

"For what reason? Honour, or just to ease your own conscience? May I speak plainly, my lady?"

Helen smiled through her tears. If the last had not been plain, heaven knew what was coming next. "Please do."

"I am not high-born like you, my lady, and I've had some freedom to follow my heart. You've never had that freedom. Your marriage has always been about duty and family. The Duke seeks a wife of his own rank who will bear him healthy children, and you are the prize, my lady. Your Reclaimer healing will guarantee that you survive childbirth over and over again; and your children may even have special abilities. Not only that, but you have promised to leave the Dark Days Club and your Reclaimer duties once you are married. The Duke wins everything. Why else do you think he has tolerated your Reclaimer bond with Lord Carlston?"

Helen blinked. Would Selburn really have factored her ability to heal into his marriage proposal? It did not seem likely. After all, he had proposed before he had known she was a Reclaimer; and, frankly, if he had thought of such a thing it would be a little off-putting. As if she were a stud mare. Even she had not thought about that application of her heritage. In fact, she had not thought very deeply about mothering or the act of bearing children in any way, apart from a vague desire to have a family. There was very little information to be had about it all – the little she knew had been gleaned from the other girls at the seminary and her uncle's library – and marriage had seemed too far away in the future. Of course, that was no longer the case.

"It is a blessing that you and the Duke like each other," Darby continued, "but I do not think he would welcome being told to his face that he is second-best. I'm sure the Duke has his own secrets. Will you expect to know them all?"

A man of Selburn's rank and experience would certainly have secrets, Helen thought. The extent of his relationship with Lady Elise, for one, and probably other women as well. She certainly did not expect or want to hear about them. "No."

"Do you intend to be a good wife to him?"

"Of course."

"Then that is the only truth he will want to know, my lady. Trust me."

Helen drew a shaky breath. "And so I keep the secret in my heart?"

Darby nodded. "You keep it forever. If you are seeking some kind of penitential pain, I'm sure that will be enough."

Helen sniffed back her tears and squeezed Darby's hand. "You are right. I wish you could be one of my attendants at the wedding. You are more friend to me than either Lady Margaret or Lady Elizabeth."

Darby flushed. "That would not do at all, my lady."

"I know, but I wish it could be so."

Her maid smiled. "I'd like to see Lady Georgina's face if I did."

Helen tried to return the smile, but her breath broke into another sob. Darby stepped closer and wrapped solid arms around her sorrow, holding her tight.

* * *

Helen felt a hard shake upon her shoulder. She opened her eyes and looked up into Darby's face, lit by the night candle in her hand.

"His lordship and Mr Quinn are near ready to leave, my lady," she whispered.

Helen squinted at her little enamel clock. Quarter past seven. Coming up to dawn. She had not expected to sleep, but oblivion had found her almost the moment she had set her head upon the pillow. She pushed back the covers and sat up. The weight of Carlston's impending departure pressed upon her, its ache returning to the hole it had gouged into her heart. She focused beyond the pain and found the steady, comforting throb of their Reclaimer bond.

Darby helped her dress: no stays, a flannel petticoat for extra warmth, the wrap of a heavy woollen cloak, hair bundled into a cap. On any other day such a hurried toilette would not do for the future mistress of Chenwith, but today was St Stephen's Day, a rare holiday for the servants, and none of them would likely have risen from their beds yet.

With a candle each in hand, she and Darby slipped out of the dressing room, crept along the freezing first-floor corridor, then descended the grand staircase. The scent of Christmas remained in the boughs of evergreen tied to its ironwork. Helen looked up at the dome as she crossed the foyer. The embrace of Eros and Psyche was obscured in the gloom of the morning.

Darby pulled open the heavy front door, both of them gasping at the slap of freezing air that penetrated wool and flannel. They stepped out onto the portico and saw Quinn, muffled in his greatcoat, holding the reins of Ares and Faro, both burdened with heavy saddlebags. The two horses mouthed their bits, their breath puffing steam that rose into the foggy air.

Quinn looked up at their arrival, and a smile broke across

the grim concentration in his face.

"Excuse me, my lady," Darby whispered and took the steps down to her husband.

Carlston emerged from the direction of the stables. He had abandoned the sling, but still held his arm with some care. She recognised the moment he saw her – it was in the slight check of his stride, the angle of his head. She was not sure, however, if her presence was welcome.

It seemed to take forever for him to walk the distance across the gravel. He stopped at the bottom of the steps and looked up at her from under the brim of his hat, his gloves in his hands. Lud, he looked so drained.

"I was not expecting…"

"Darby wished to say goodbye to her husband," Helen said.

"Of course." He pulled his gloves through his fingers. "It is a hard parting for them."

"It is." She tried to keep the tremor from her voice. "I am sure her thoughts will be with him."

"As his will be with her," he said softly.

Helen clenched her hands. *Every day.*

"Every day," he said in agreement. He had seen it in her face. Did he see her pain too?

He pressed his hand across his heart for a fleeting moment. *Of course. It is mine too.*

He turned away and limped to Quinn and Darby, his approach breaking them apart from a kiss. Quinn touched Darby's cheek, then held Ares steady as Carlston mounted, his customary grace lost in a hiss of pain.

"Write," Darby said as Quinn swung himself up into Faro's saddle. "Please."

"I will." He nodded to Helen. "Good fortune to you, my lady."

"Thank you, Quinn. Good luck."

The two men urged the horses forward, the crunch of their hooves upon the gravel loud in the muffling wrap of the fog. Helen watched them ride along the drive, hoping Carlston would look back, but he did not. His back remained rigid, his neck stiff, face set resolutely forward. As they rounded the bend in the driveway and disappeared from view, she focused upon their Reclaimer bond, its quick rhythm hammering out her loss. *Gone, gone, gone.*

"If you'll excuse me, my lady, I'll get you some hot water," Darby said, her voice breaking. She bobbed a curtsey and started around the house towards the kitchens, head tucked to her chest.

Helen turned back to the front portico. A silhouette loomed in the doorway. She recoiled a step, her battle blood leaping through her body and clenching her hands into weapons.

The Duke stepped out, blowing upon his bare fingers. "It is a bitter morning." He eyed her raised fists.

"I am sorry, you startled me," she said stiffly.

"So I see." He peered down the driveway. "Do I take it Carlston has left?"

She gave a wordless nod, their bond still tolling through her body. *Gone, gone, gone.*

"So the Grand Deceiver is defeated and Carlston is no longer here, demanding your time," Selburn said. He took her hand and uncurled her fist, almost having to force her tense fingers straight. "There are no more battles to fight, Helen. It is time to focus on our wedding."

She stared down at her hand in his clasp. Yes, Carlston was gone, and from now on she must stop reaching for the solace of that beat beneath her heart.

Chapter Twenty-Six

FRIDAY, 1 JANUARY 1813

Helen drew her legs up under the warm bedcovers and rested her chin upon her knees, staring at the fire already lit in the hearth. Her wedding day. Just thinking the words brought a gripe in her innards. Here she was, a Reclaimer who had fought and killed the Grand Deceiver, and yet the prospect of saying her vows before family and friends made her feel sick to the stomach. Absurd.

Perhaps the nausea came from the prospect of walking down the aisle with her uncle. He had arrived late last night, his pouchy-eyed bluster still intact. Nothing about him had changed, except the wariness that had emerged on the night of her presentation ball had hardened into outright distrust. He would not look her in the eye, and spoke to her only through Aunt. He did, however, issue one comment through his small, flaky-dry lips when no one else was near. "Selburn is mad to take you, but I am glad you are going."

She contemplated the day beyond the open shutters. Grey and gloomy, but dry; the ball and night fair would not be ruined by rain. The evening was all prepared: hundreds and hundreds of lamps ready to be lit around the formal gardens, musicians hired, the dance pavilion – by all reports – finished, the Queen's rooms prepared, the supper cooked, and the stalls and kitchens ready for the villagers in the lower fields. A grand celebration for the marriage of a Duke to his new Duchess.

She listened, finding Darby's quick tread along the passage, the hot water she carried slapping against the sides of its pitcher, her breath quicker than it should be. Perhaps she was nervous too. After all, she was in charge of the bride's toilette.

Helen stretched her hearing further, but a house preparing for a Royal visit and a ball was not a silent place. With all the kitchen noise and the workmen and the cleaning, it was hard to discern anything particular beyond the passageway.

The door opened and Darby peered in cautiously. Seeing that Helen was sitting up, she widened the crack of the door with a deft bump of her hip and entered.

"I have a letter from Mr Quinn," she whispered as she shut the door and curtseyed. She bustled across the room to set the pitcher upon the washstand.

Helen sat up straighter. News of Carlston, finally. "What does he say?"

Darby drew the letter from her bodice. "Mr Quinn's not one for writing much more than the facts," she said wryly and handed it across.

Helen unfolded the paper; thick and rough, the kind supplied at inns. Quinn's hand was as big as the man himself, the single paragraph covering all of the page.

The Dolphin, Portsmouth, Wednesday, 30th December, 1812
Jen,
Here I write as promised, with little to tell. We've sailed the yacht from Southampton to Portsmouth, where all is busy with war – hundreds of ships coming and going, heading to America and France. No one can venture into

the Channel without escort. It's taken his lordship until now to secure a place in the Christian VII convoy that sets out for Cherbourg on the 1st January. As close as we can get to Calais. We will sail on the night tide. Tell her ladyship he is healing well.

Your devoted husband,
N

Helen released her breath, only now realising that she had been holding it. They were still in England, and he was healing well. Thank God. She hunched her shoulders, resisting the impulse to focus upon the Reclaimer beat. She had made her promises – to retire from the Dark Days Club, and to stop seeking that solace – and she must abide by them if her marriage was to work.

"They sail tonight," Darby said. "Cherbourg. Where is that?"

"To the south of the Channel. Quite a way from Calais."

"Does that mean they will have to go by land?"

"Probably."

They looked at each other. A dangerous journey in Bonaparte's France.

"They have travelled there before without incident," Helen said, as much to console herself as Darby. "They even went into Paris."

"True." Darby picked up Helen's dressing robe, holding it out. "I just wish they didn't have to go at all."

Helen thrust her arms into the sleeves and wrapped the robe around her body. God knew, she wished the same. That there was no Calais, no Lady Elise, and above all no little Viscount Collingate. A dreadful, selfish wish that she could not admit even to Darby.

* * *

Two hours later, Helen studied her image in the full-length mirror. Mrs Langdon – Bath's finest dressmaker, whose clients included such eminence as the Duchess of York – had worked a miracle in just five days. After Aunt's and Helen's hurried selection of fabrics, the dressmaker and her four assistants – two of them taken on just for Helen's order – had toiled around the clock to produce four wedding-day gowns.

For the marriage service, the celestial-blue velvet robe-pelisse trimmed in ermine that she was wearing now atop a fine white cambric gown. To greet the Queen, a pale olive cambric robe with plaited bodice and long, full sleeves to be worn with a lemon Cossack cloak. For dinner, a superfine round gown in the new Russian flame colour with a ribbon-trimmed bodice. And for the ball that evening, a round, low gown in willow-green satin, embellished with pearls and beads. All the latest styles, Mrs Langdon had assured Aunt, and perfectly suited to Lady Helen's tall, slim frame.

Helen turned to the side, admiring the rich fall of velvet from the three diamond fastenings under her bust. Aunt had insisted upon ermine rather than swansdown at the collar, lapels and cuffs; a nod, she'd said, to Helen's new rank as Duchess.

Darby had dressed her hair to sit in a tumble of becoming curls at either side of her face, only allowing Sprat to hand over the pins and warm the curling iron. The placement of the headdress – a small bandeau of diamonds, white roses, and folds of blue velvet from which a transparent Mechlin lace veil cascaded – had been a tense moment, and Darby had been forced to slap away Sprat's hand.

Helen glanced at the girl, standing sullenly near the door where she had been temporarily banished. "What do you say, Sprat?" she asked kindly.

"Yer look like an angel, my lady."

Helen leaned closer to the mirror, not quite convinced. The necklace of graduated turquoises that circled her throat – a gift from Selburn – seemed a little heavy. It was beautiful, of course, and had been chosen by him to suit the velvet robe-pelisse, but for the service she wanted something more delicate. And with more meaning.

"Darby, I think I would rather wear my mother's cross instead of these turquoises."

"The ruby cross?" Darby opened the jewellery casket.

"Yes."

They both looked up as the dressing room door closed. Sprat, gone without a by-your-leave.

"That girl's behaviour is getting worse," Darby said, shaking her head. She lifted a few of the boxes within the casket, finding the small leather case that housed the cross. She turned to Helen, opening it, then stared down, frowning. "It's not here."

"Is that the right box?" Helen asked.

"Yes. I put it back in here after you wore it on Christmas Day. I swear."

Helen glanced at the closed door. "I think I know what has happened to it."

Darby followed her gaze. "You think Sprat has taken it?" She snapped the lid shut. "Of all the ungrateful little wretches. Why would she do that, my lady? You've taken her in, given her a good livelihood, and she steals from you."

Helen sighed. "It is not that straightforward. I didn't tell you that she took a pearl ring from Miss Cransdon's room after her death. For her, I think it is like showing an attachment to the person."

"Stealing from them? A strange way to show affection." Darby shook her head and placed the box back in the casket. "She'll be

455

off to one of her hiding places. I'll get Geoffrey and that other footman to look for her."

"No, I do not want any chance of this coming to the attention of the Duke. Especially not today. I'll wear the turquoises, and when we return from the Abbey I will speak to Sprat. She will be sorry, I know, and I am sure she will return it."

Even so, the theft and Sprat's broken promise left a sour taste in her mouth. And it felt like a bad omen: her mother's cross, gone.

There was no time to dwell on such gloomy thoughts for at that moment her aunt, Lady Margaret and Pug arrived to oversee the last of her toilette.

They stayed until Helen asked for a few minutes to collect herself before they left for the Abbey. Finally alone, she opened her prayer book to read through the service, hoping to find some measure of calm within its pages.

At eight o'clock, a footman knocked on the adjoining bed-chamber door and informed Darby that the coaches were ready.

Helen put aside the prayer book, any calm she had recovered gone in an instant.

"Everyone is waiting downstairs to see you leave, my lady," Darby reported. "Are you ready?"

Darby had donned the navy-blue silk gown and paisley shawl that Helen had given her for her own wedding, and carried her own prayer book. Much to Darby's pleasure, and Aunt's disapproval, Helen had insisted that her maid have a place in one of the coaches to the Abbey. She was not going to be married without Darby nearby, and all of Aunt's arguments of what was right and proper for the wedding of a Duchess could not persuade her otherwise.

Helen rose from her chair, waiting for Darby to twitch out the veil at her back. "I feel so..." She stopped.

"Like you want to be sick?" Darby offered. She met Helen's gaze in the mirror with a sympathetic smile.

"Yes."

At least, that was part of how she felt. She was fasting prior to taking communion during the service, so some of the gnawing in her stomach was no doubt hunger. The other part was something she could not – no, must not – voice. A dragging sense of dread, as if she were making the worst mistake of her life.

"I felt the same way, my lady. It is just nerves. Every bride feels it."

They trod the length of the passage in silence. As they approached the grand staircase, Darby stopped. "I'll say good luck now, my lady, for I'm sure I won't get a chance at the Abbey."

Helen caught one of her hands. "Thank you. For it all."

Darby squeezed her hand. "We'll pray for them, my lady, at the Abbey. For a safe journey and a safe return."

She gave Helen's toilette one last assessing glance, then with a nod of approval headed for the side stairs.

Helen looked up at the dome above the foyer. The morning was bright enough to see Eros and Psyche in their embrace, the young god tenderly waking his lover from her sleep. Their story had ended in marriage too, after poor Psyche had suffered many trials. Perhaps a good omen for the day, Helen thought, except that she was seeing good and bad omens in everything and she did not even believe in them.

She looked down to where all of the household stood waiting to bid farewell to the bride. She searched their upturned faces: all, it seemed, except Sprat. And, of course, Selburn and Lord Henry. They had gone ahead to await the arrival of the bride at the Abbey.

Helen gathered the hem of her gown and descended the steps. She smiled at Mrs Clarke at the head of the line as she walked to the door. The housekeeper flushed at the attention and bobbed a curtsey, prompting all the servants to bow and curtsey, a murmur of blessings rising like a wave at Helen's back.

Uncle peered out of the coach window, scowling at the creep of their coach's progress alongside the Abbey. "Why don't the footmen clear these people out of the way?" he demanded, breaking the heavy silence. "We are already ten minutes late."

"They are here to see Helen," Aunt said flatly. "It is not every day a Duke gets married. Especially not at Bath."

It had been an uncomfortable journey. From the start, Aunt had maintained a monologue of inconsequentialities, mainly to do with the arrival of the Queen at Chenwith for the ball, and of course what they were going to wear and eat, and should they change the dance order? It was, to Helen's ears, just the dear lady soothing her own nerves, but Uncle had half risen from his seat near Corston and bellowed, "Silence, woman, for the sake of my sanity!", the spitting force of his temper pressing Aunt against the cushions. Helen had gripped the edge of her seat to stop herself responding in kind, but her uncle caught her savage glare. He sat back, his narrowed eyes and the truculent thrust of his lower lip clearly showing the bitter memory of her strong Reclaimer hand around his wrist at her ball.

The famous Abbey bells began to peal their arrival, the glorious sound resonating through Helen's ear bones. She leaned forward, startled to see how many people had gathered along the narrow street that led to the west entrance of the church: women on their toes to see into the carriage, children held high in strong arms, carts pulled up at the side with young men standing upon them. All to see the Duke's bride.

The coach eased its way into the yard and stopped outside the gothic frontage and stained window that graced the Abbey's west entrance. The huge arched doorway stood open, and Helen glimpsed the floor of the nave, paved in huge square stones.

The door opened and the footman let down the step. Uncle alighted first, growling another complaint about the gawking crowd.

Aunt smiled at Helen. "Do not mind him." She bent forward and pressed her lips to Helen's cheek, her skin warm and soft. "A kiss for luck, my dear. After this, I shall have to curtsey to Your Grace."

"You may always kiss me, Aunt," Helen said as the coach rocked under the lady's descent.

"Helen, do you come or not?" Uncle said, thrusting his head inside the door. "Do not make the Duke wait any longer."

She took his hand to descend the step, resisting the urge to close her fingers into another Reclaimer grip. Curious onlookers clustered around the yard; mainly fashionables, but also a good number of shop folk and beggars who had come for the largesse that would be thrown for good luck.

Helen looked up at the Abbey's frontage and the stone angels upon Jacob's ladder. She definitely felt in sympathy with the one looking over his shoulder, worried about where he would land.

Lady Margaret and Pug had already alighted from the coach behind and stood waiting at the doorway. Both had chosen to wear shades of lavender as a memorial to Delia – Lady Margaret in an elegant sarcenet and Pug in muslin. It had been Pug's idea, and had brought them all to tears at its inception.

"So many people outside. How marvellous," Pug whispered to Helen as she and Lady Margaret fell in behind her and her uncle.

Helen gathered her skirt hems and took the four steps down into the Abbey. She removed her hand from Uncle's arm for a moment to genuflect, crossing herself and casting a fervent prayer upward. *Protect them, please.*

The Abbey was remarkably bright for such an old church, the multitude of windows giving it an unusual airiness. Fifty-two in all, Helen remembered. She had counted them once during an interminable sermon. Beams of light streamed in through those on the east side, illuminating the high vaulted ceiling, elegant gothic arches, wooden pew boxes, and hundreds of carved stone plaques and memorials that decorated the clustered columns and floor.

Helen's attention, however, was swiftly drawn to the end of the nave. Selburn stood looking back at her, smiling, tall and straight in his black coat and breeches. Lord Henry was at his side, and the vicar stood before them, waiting with prayer book open.

Helen barely registered the small congregation of family and friends who stood as she entered. They were a blur of faces as she walked along the aisle, her hand resting lightly upon Uncle's arm, only Mr Hammond's smile and Darby's encouraging nod coming fleetingly into focus. Her heartbeat pounded in her ears along with the final peals of the bells and the pump and rise of the organ processional. And beneath it all, the ever-present pulse of her Reclaimer bond refusing to be denied; her other life-beat, thundering through her blood. *I will. I will. I will.* It was so dizzyingly strong, so insistent, that she looked over her shoulder, as if Carlston might have somehow appeared, drawn by its clamour. Or her prayer. But the doorway was empty.

She took a steadying breath and turned back to the nave. Back to Selburn. Ten more steps and she was beside him, her hand taken in a fleeting press of greeting. Uncle withdrawing. Selburn smiling.

The vicar cleared his throat, round face set into practised

sincerity, double chin quivering with every word. "Dearly beloved, we are gathered together here in the sight of God, and in the face of this congregation, to join together this Man and this Woman in holy Matrimony."

She tried to focus upon the familiar pronouncements, but most were lost in the hard thud of her pulse and the secret beat beneath her heart. The three causes of matrimony, the solemnity of their undertaking, and were there any just impediments? But the congregation were silent and no confessions were made.

The vicar turned to Selburn. "Gerard Stephen George Annisford, wilt thou have this woman to thy wedded Wife, to live together after God's ordinance in the holy estate of Matrimony? Wilt thou love her, comfort her, honour, and keep her in sickness and in health; and, forsaking all other, keep thee only unto her, so long as ye both shall live?"

"I will," Selburn said, his voice breaking slightly upon the vow. He smiled at her, as if to say they were almost there.

"Helen Catherine Wrexhall, wilt thou have this man to thy wedded Husband, to live together after God's ordinance in the holy estate of Matrimony? Wilt thou obey him, and serve him, love, honour, and keep him in sickness and in health; and, forsaking all other, keep thee only unto him, so long as ye both shall live?"

Forsaking all others. Helen glanced over her shoulder again. The doorway was still empty. She saw tears of pride in her aunt's eyes, her brother smiling.

And Selburn, waiting at her side.

"I will," she said, through the hard, heavy beat beneath her heart.

Chapter Twenty-Seven

Much to the disgruntlement of Uncle, the newlyweds and their guests were to return to Chenwith Hall for the wedding breakfast, rather than taking it immediately after the nuptials at the York Hotel or the White Hart.

As they drew up to the Hall at eleven o'clock, they were met by the servants waiting in line upon the gravel to officially welcome their new mistress.

To everyone's delight – especially Pug's – some of the men of the 10th Royal Hussars were there too; the advance guard of the Queen's detail. They were lined up upon their horses, wearing their handsome dark blue uniforms and busby hats with white plumes, and holding their rifles up to form an arch of honour to the front steps. A surprise organised by Lord Henry.

Helen and Selburn, hand in hand, walked under the arch, the men standing at impressive attention. Near the top, Helen stopped at a familiar face. "Mr Nesbitt! How good to see you again."

"Your Grace," he said, dipping his chin to the heavy yellow braiding upon his chest. "May I offer you the congratulations of the 10th Light."

Helen flushed. Apart from the vicar, it was the first time anyone had called her Your Grace. "Thank you," she said and looked down the line of smiling cavalrymen. "I know you shall soon be on duty, but I will have Cook send some cake for you all."

A ham was sent out too, under Helen's direction, and she also gave Mrs Carroll permission to hand out cake and a bowl of punch to the servants. Everyone must have their celebration.

An hour or so later, the official breakfast was coming to its close. Lord Henry rose and raised his glass.

"A toast to the new Duchess of Selburn!" he called over the hum of conversation in the dining room.

Selburn, seated beside Helen, eyed his brother with a smile. "Another?"

Helen waved her new brother-in-law to sit down. "Selburn is right, Lord Henry, I have been toasted enough. Let us toast Mrs Carroll instead, for this wonderful feast."

Mrs Carroll had truly outdone herself with the array of delicacies for the wedding breakfast: fresh baked rolls, hot buttered toast, coddled and fried eggs, pickled ox tongue, a ham, seed cake, cod, a poached trout, cold roast beef, colcannon, coffee, tea, pitchers of rich hot chocolate, and of course the wedding cake, full of fruit and iced in pure white sugar.

"Hear, hear!" Andrew said, raising his glass, his words slurred. "To Mrs Whatever-her-name-is."

Andrew had already had his fill of claret, Helen thought. It was definitely time to disband the breakfast and dress for the next part of the afternoon.

"Her Majesty will be arriving soon," she said quietly, casting a meaningful glance at her new husband.

They had not yet had a moment alone together, and it occurred to her that perhaps Selburn was not seeking one. An odd thought, since she could see the warmth and elation within his eyes whenever he looked her way. And in the coach on their return, he had taken her hand with its new gold ring and kissed her upon the mouth, right in front of Uncle and Aunt. Of course, there was no rush for more. They had their whole lives ahead of them to enjoy each other alone. Yet she could not help a private fear: perhaps her unseemly exposure to such matters as Mr Amberley had tainted her in some way, made her too *interested* in the physical side of marriage.

For a second, she felt the memory of another pair of lips pressed upon her mouth, her body alive with heat. Dark eyes, and fingertips that traced lines of fire across her skin. She bowed her head, the heat of the memory shifting into the heat of shame. Even now she thought of him. Even now as she sat beside her husband wearing the gold symbol of this new, sacred bond.

"My dear, are you quite well?" Selburn asked, resting his hand upon her shoulder. The weight of its tender regard seemed unbearable.

"I think we should adjourn," she said, managing a smile.

Selburn put down his glass and stood, obliging everyone else to rise from their chairs. "Her Grace, my wife," he looked down at Helen with a smile, "has reminded me that the Queen arrives in little over an hour."

"An hour?" Aunt exclaimed, tossing down her serviette. "We will barely have time to dress."

Back in Helen's dressing room, Darby rose from a low curtsey. She had changed from her navy best into her brown pin-tuck. Helen knew it to be Mr Quinn's favourite.

"Congratulations, Your Grace," she said and took the shawl from Helen's hands. "Thank you for allowing me to come to the service. It is strange, is it not? As I was listening to the words, I could hardly remember hearing them said over me and Mr Quinn. Yet they must have been."

"Did you pray for them?" Helen asked quietly.

Darby's smile faltered. "I did. And you, Your Grace?"

"Of course."

Darby stepped behind her and undid the catch of the turquoise necklace, sliding its weight from around her throat.

"I'm afraid Sprat is still hiding, Your Grace," she reported. "I asked Mrs Clarke if she had seen the girl, and apparently she had words with her this morning. Suffice to say, Miss Wainwright, Lady Georgina's maid, has complained that some gold ear-bobs have gone; and Lady Elizabeth is missing a comb from a set. Mrs Clarke is furious, but she doesn't want to raise it with you on your wedding day."

Helen closed her eyes. "It is getting worse." Sprat's thieving had to be stopped, before Mrs Clarke reported it to the Duke. She opened her eyes. "We need to find those things and give them back."

"She's probably sold them by now," Darby said dryly.

"She has had no chance. And I have a fair idea where we can look." Helen gestured to the skirting boards. "In Great Pulteney Street, Sprat showed me her cache. It was hidden behind the board in my dressing room wall. Perhaps she has done the same here."

"In *your* wall?" Darby echoed.

"I know. The girl is incorrigible." Helen crouched and ran her hand along the skirting board at her feet. "Look for a crack in the wood. If you find one, see if it lifts."

Darby kneeled at the opposite end of the room to peer at the boards, muttering under her breath. Helen crawled along the length of the side and far walls, digging her nails into four joins, but none of them lifted.

"Anything?" she asked Darby, who had crawled slowly along the other two walls.

Darby sat back on her heels. "I've found cracks enough, but none of them open."

"Damn," Helen said, finding a moment of relief in the vulgarity. She dusted off her fingers and pushed herself to her feet. "I thought it would be here."

Darby stood and surveyed the room with her hands on her hips. "You don't think she would have hidden it in your bedchamber, do you? Surely she would not be that impudent."

"Oh yes, she would," Helen said. She picked up her skirts and ran into the bedchamber, Darby close behind. "You take those two walls," she ordered, pointing to the right angle that housed the hearth and doorway. "I'll take the other two."

They set to work. Helen felt her way along the boards under the window. She found joins, but nothing loose. She looked at Darby, on all fours, her round face set into a frown of concentration as she investigated the boards beside the hearth. Clearly nothing there either.

Helen pulled her skirts out from under her knees and crawled towards the corner. She ran her fingertips along the right angle, finding another join. She dug her nails into the crack and pulled. It shifted.

"Here! Something moved."

She dug her nails in harder and pulled again, one side of the right angle coming away just as Darby crouched at her side. Helen thrust the board behind her and they both peered into the cavity. Atop a folded letter lay a tortoiseshell comb, two gold ear-bobs, Helen's ruby cross and a round diamond hairclip.

"Stashed in your bedchamber." Darby shook her head. "I cannot believe it."

Helen pulled out the letter by its corner, dragging the other pieces from the cavity with it. She slid the jewellery and comb into her cupped hand, sending dust motes swirling into the air.

"Everything accounted for. And if I recall correctly, the diamond hairclip belongs to Lady Margaret."

"And the letter?" Darby asked.

Helen placed the handful of stolen treasures onto the carpet and brushed the dust off the letter. By the creases in the paper, it had at some stage been screwed up and then smoothed out again, perhaps to act as the tray for the other treasures. She unfolded it and stared. The neat hand was sickeningly familiar.

Calais, Monday, 21st December, 1812
  Mon cher Guillaume…

"It is a letter from Lady Elise. To Lord Carlston," Helen said. She read on:

I had hoped you would answer my previous letter, for the sake of what we once had together, but it is clear that you must bear me an insurmountable grudge. Even so, it is imperative that we meet. I did not wish to coerce you, but I am left with no option. I have enclosed the locket that you gave me as a wedding gift. Inside you will find a portra—

The word *portrait* had spread into a large inkblot. It was the letter about Carlston's son, except it was *unfinished*. How could Sprat have stolen an unfinished letter from Lady Elise?

The words blurred, her vision narrowing into a grey tunnel as the horror of the answer crashed down upon her. The letter had been written in this house. *This house*. Helen swayed. The enormity was too much to comprehend.

"My lady—" Darby checked herself. "Your Grace, what is it?"

Helen thrust the letter towards Darby. "This is in Lady Elise's hand – I recognise it. It is unfinished, Darby, yet Sprat stole it. It must have been written here!"

Darby frowned at the page. "That is impossible. That would mean Lady Elise is in the house."

The letter was definitely in Elise's hand, but the woman herself was patently not at Chenwith, Helen thought, scrabbling for the logic of it. Surely it could only mean that someone else in the house had written both this unfinished letter and the one that Carlston had ultimately received. Someone who wrote in Lady Elise's hand and held possession of the locket Carlston had given her. Dear God, Lady Elise must have been a Deceiver, Helen realised. Carlston would be devastated.

Darby shook her head at the suggestion. "Are we sure this letter and the other cannot have been forged, Your Grace?"

"I would think the reference to the locket seals their authenticity." Not to mention the intimate details that Lady Elise had revealed in the first letter. "She must be able to shift into any body," Helen added in a whisper, her horror growing. "Darby, I think she is part of a Grand Deceiver."

"No! That's not possible. You and Lord Carlston killed the Grand Deceiver."

Did they? The doubt hit her like a hard punch to the stomach.

"I think it was a ruse, Darby. We were meant to think we had killed the Grand Deceiver, but we didn't."

"Yes, you did. Mrs Knoll was once Berta – she had the ability to shift into any body. She was a Grand Deceiver." There was a pleading note in Darby's voice.

"True, but we only assumed Philip was the same. Perhaps

Mrs Knoll was one half of a defunct Grand Deceiver, like Mr King."

They looked at one another, the possibility hardening into certainty.

"God help us, the Grand Deceiver is here," Darby said. "They could be anyone."

Anyone. Helen held up her hand for silence. If the Grand Deceiver was truly in the house, they could be listening. Maybe they had already heard what had been discovered.

She held her breath and stretched her Reclaimer hearing, but no one stood outside the room or in the passage, and the background sounds of the busy house made it impossible to discern anything beyond that distance.

She sighed in relief. "We are alone. We can speak freely."

Darby nodded and looked at the letter again. "So this whole business about the son in Calais – it is just a ruse to separate you and Lord Carlston. None of it is real."

Not real. The son a ruse; and Lady Elise a ruse too, for if she had been one of the bodies inhabited by this Deceiver, she would be long dead. Long gone from Carlston's life.

Helen drew a sharp breath. But now she herself was married, the ring upon her finger, the union made before God. The heartache of that had to wait. Right now, she had to focus. The Grand Deceiver had managed to separate the Grand Reclaimer. To what end? Clearly, to open the door to their realm so the rest of their kind could enter this world – that was their raison d'être. But when and how?

Another terrifying realisation rocked her back upon her heels.

"The Grand Deceiver probably knows that I hold the Ligatus within me. They probably know I am the Trinitas."

"You think they are within the Dark Days Club?"

Helen pressed her hand upon her head, as if to hold in the

terror of it. "How else could they have manipulated us so masterfully?"

"But they would have had to hide any sign of feeding. Any sign of their Deceiver strength."

"It would have been a great risk," Helen agreed. "Perhaps it has not been for long."

Darby gasped. "Lady Margaret and Mr Hammond! Could they have been inhabited at the stone circle?"

Helen froze. Was it possible?

"No, the letter must have been written well before we went to the stones," she said, thinking it through. "It was sent up to London to be brought back by Mr Pike. That itself would take a few days. Besides, if we are right, then only Mrs Knoll had the ability to transfer, and both Lady Margaret and Mr Hammond were too far away."

"But Lady Margaret was with them all that time by herself."

"Yes, but Mrs Knoll was alive and well at the stones, until we killed her. She had not inhabited Lady Margaret."

Darby sighed. "Of course." She stiffened again. "Mr Pike brought back *both* of Lady Elise's letters from London."

"Because they had been sent to the Home Office." Helen touched Darby's arm; a call for restraint. "We don't know when these creatures infiltrated our friends. It could have been months ago or years ago. We need to find Sprat and ask her whom she stole this letter from. Then we will know the identity of at least one of them." She stood up, her legs trembling. "And we must also stop Lord Carlston and Mr Quinn from sailing tonight."

"But how? Portsmouth is near Southampton, hours and hours away."

"I will take one of the Duke's best horses," Helen said. "If I change a few times on the way—"

"You can't go, my lady," Darby interrupted, hands on hips. "If you go, the Grand Deceiver will know immediately that they have been discovered and they will escape or transfer into new bodies. Besides, the Queen is about to arrive, and the whole place will be in an uproar if you are not beside the Duke."

Helen slumped. "You are right."

"I will go," Darby said.

"No, I need you to find Sprat. As you say, the Queen will be here and I cannot run around looking for a missing maid."

Helen paced across the room. Who to send to Portsmouth? Someone who could not possibly be one of the creatures. Someone who would be discreet. Someone who could ride the distance without flagging. Ah, of course. She had just the man.

She grasped Darby's shoulders. "Go to the 10th Light and find Mr Nesbitt. Bring him to my private drawing room as quietly as possible."

As soon as Darby closed the door, Helen picked up Elise's unfinished letter and headed into her drawing room. She sat at her secretaire and stared out of the window at the workmen checking the lamps in the garden in readiness for the ball. Her mind felt full of terror, nothing else. A sheer, blanking horror.

She squeezed her eyes shut and opened them again. *A still target is an easy target.*

She needed two letters.

She pulled out the tiny drawers on the desktop. Paper, pen, ink, sand and two wafers. She inked the quill, tapped the excess off, and began to write, the scratch of the nib loud in the silence.

Chenwith Hall, Friday, 1st January, 1813
   Carlston,
   Enclosed is an unfinished letter from Lady Elise that Sprat stole from someone in this house. We did not destroy

*the Grand Deceiver. They are here, at Chenwith, and
they have separated us. Calais is a trap.*

*It seems that Lady Elise was once one half of the Grand
Deceiver, which means she is long gone from this world,
and your son is a ruse. I am sorry.*

Please, return as swiftly and quietly as possible.

Helen

She paused, then added *Selburn*. It was her name now.

She folded the page into a packet, tucked Elise's letter inside,
then wet the wafer and affixed it at the back. Considering the
fact that anyone could be the Grand Deceiver, it was a risk
entrusting the letter to Mr Nesbitt. A small risk admittedly, and
one that had to be taken. Everyone in the house must now be
suspect. She swallowed, her mouth dry. That included Selburn,
Aunt, Uncle, Andrew, Hammond, Lady Margaret and Pike.
Even Pug, Lady Dunwick and Sprat must be included, although
they were unlikely.

Everyone except Darby and Lord Carlston. She held a blood
bond with both of them, and a Terrene bond with Darby;
surely anything awry would have been noticed by now. And
by that logic, that included Quinn too, since he held a Terrene
bond with Carlston. She had to trust them – she had to trust
someone – for the sake of her sanity. She could not stand with
this terror alone.

She pressed her fingers more tightly upon the shaft of the pen
to stop them trembling, then wrote *Lord Carlston* on the front
of the packet, sanded it and put it aside. Now for the second
note, to the Commanding Officer of the 10th.

She inked her pen, tapped it and frowned down at the empty
page as an awful line of thought overtook her mind. If the
destruction of Philip and Mrs Knoll had indeed been a ruse, then

the Colligat – the third part of the Trinitas – was still in play. The real Grand Deceiver would still have it. If they knew she was the other two parts of the weapon – which she had to assume they did – their plan must be to unite her with the Colligat in some way and force her to open the doorway to their realm.

She clenched her teeth. She would never do so, of course. Yet it was inevitable they would try. But when? Carlston had been gone for five days now and there had been no attempt; and it would surely be madness to make a bid at her own wedding ball in front of so many witnesses. She would have too many allies, even without Carlston. It would be far more logical to wait until they could draw her somewhere alone. Then again, anything was possible when it came to an enemy like the Grand Deceiver.

Whatever the case, it was essential that Carlston return. And Quinn too. The four of them – the only members of the Dark Days Club each of them could trust – must hunt down this Grand Deceiver as soon as possible. And as secretly as possible.

To that end, she started the second note. A few lines that instructed the Commanding Officer of the 10th Royal Hussars that the Duchess of Selburn had sent Mr Nesbitt on an errand that would take him from his duties for a day and required complete discretion.

She had just finished writing the direction upon its front when a knock sounded on the door.

"Come."

The door opened to admit Darby and Mr Nesbitt. Helen brushed off the sand, picked up the two packets and rose from her chair.

The cavalryman bowed, his busby with its distinctive white plume cradled in his arm. "Your Grace."

When they had danced together in Brighton, it had been clear to Helen that Mr Nesbitt had seen and suffered a great deal in his life – she had heard it beneath the surface of his wonderful stories about India. She had also seen that those hard experiences had brought with them an admirable level-headedness and tough courage; two qualities she was about to count on.

"Mr Nesbitt, you told me at the Upper Rooms that His Highness the Prince Regent instructed your company to assist me or Lord Carlston if ever we required it. Do you recall?"

He nodded, watchful. "Of course, Your Grace."

"I require that assistance now, most desperately, and it is not a small request. I need you to ride post-haste to Portsmouth to stop Lord Carlston from sailing to Cherbourg in the convoy of the Christian VII. They depart on the evening tide. You must find a way to give this to him."

"Even if he has sailed, Your Grace?"

"Yes. He must not go to France." She handed him the packet. "Give him this and bid him act immediately upon it." She gave him the other note. "And this is for your Commanding Officer to confirm you are acting on my instruction. You must inform no one else."

"I understand."

"Do you know the way to Portsmouth?"

"I do, Your Grace."

"How long do you think it will take you to get there?"

"With changes, I believe I can do it in five hours, Your Grace."

Five hours there and five hours back, more or less. Even if all went well, Carlston would not be back until midnight. By then, she hoped to know the identity of at least one half of the Grand Deceiver.

Chapter Twenty-Eight

By three o'clock, the Queen's travelling carriage and its procession of entourage coaches were ponderously making their way along the gravel driveway under the cavalry escort of the 10th Light Dragoons. Helen waited on the front portico with the Duke, twisting her hands together in her new olive-green gloves, dyed to match Mrs Langdon's half-dress creation and its fur-lined, lemon Cossack cloak.

After finding the letter and dispatching Mr Nesbitt, she and Darby had barely had time to change her into the new gown and its accoutrements and make it back downstairs in readiness for the Queen. As it was, Helen was sure her fashionably dishevelled curls had tipped a little too far towards the unruly.

On the gravel below, she could see Darby waiting next to Mrs Clarke in the line of senior servants, shifting from foot to foot, her restlessness earning a glare from the housekeeper. The press of Darby's lips said it all: they had to find Sprat, and standing in line waiting to greet the Queen was not going to do it.

"You need not look so anxious, my dear," Selburn said. "Her Majesty has a genuine interest in you. It was she who initiated her visit here today."

"Of course." Helen smiled to hide the leap of suspicion that came with his words.

Good Lord, did she suspect the Queen now? Her Majesty had every reason to take an interest in her: daughter of Lady Catherine, the Reclaimer who had rendered her a great service. She had also, by Pike's report, just rid the country of a terrifying enemy.

Helen laced her fingers together in an effort to stop wringing them. Somehow, she must find a private moment to warn the Queen that the Grand Deceiver was not in fact dead; that she and Lord Carlston had been duped and there was every possibility the Grand Deceiver was hidden within the guests or staff at Chenwith Hall. Under the circumstances, it would be prudent for the Royal party to leave as soon as possible.

She cast a glance over her shoulder at their guests, standing in order of rank to greet the Queen. Her uncle, his chin tucked into his bull neck against the cold, and Aunt, almost standing on her toes with the pride of the moment. Beside them, Lord Henry and Lady Georgina, who was quite ravishing in a rose-pink pelisse, silently watched the approach of the Royal cavalcade. Surely they could not be the Grand Deceiver? Or Lady Dunwick and Pug next to them, whispering together? Helen focused briefly upon their conversation: Lady Dunwick was instructing poor Pug on how to conduct herself in front of the Queen.

Lady Margaret stood beside Pug, clearly trying to ignore their exchange, and leaning quite heavily upon Mr Hammond's arm. Could it be the brother and sister? It seemed inconceivable they could be so duplicitous. Just as it seemed beyond belief that Mr Pike, beside them, could be the enemy. And yet that enemy was somewhere in the house.

She concentrated on the Reclaimer pulse beneath her heart-beat, ignoring the tiny flick of guilt. While the Grand Deceiver was still alive, she had to use everything at her disposal to destroy it, and that included ignoring her promise. The beat was steady. God willing, in just over four hours it would start to get stronger as Carlston rode towards them.

"Will you come to the terrace at nine o'clock, before the ball?" Selburn whispered, jolting Helen from her focus. "I want to show you the pavilion before it is overrun with guests. I cannot wait for you to see it in all its glory."

Of course, her wedding gift. She met the sweet anticipation in his eyes and smiled. "The terrace, at nine o'clock."

The State Coach drew up to the front steps, the two red-liveried footmen riding on the footboard behind leaping down as it stopped. They hurried to the coach door, one opening it, the other letting down the step and rolling out a crimson carpet across the gravel. They stood to attention as a figure inside rose stiffly from her seat, her rather stout silhouette blocking the window.

The Duke took Helen's hand and together they descended the steps to meet their guest.

Both footmen took a Royal hand to help Queen Charlotte alight, and she slowly descended the step onto the carpet, one of her ladies-in-waiting lifting the train of her navy-blue sable-trimmed pelisse to ensure it did not become caught in the doorway.

Helen sank into a low Royal curtsey as the Duke bowed.

"Your Majesty," he said, "may I present to you Her Grace, the Duchess of Selburn."

"Ah, Duchess, how that pleases me," the Queen said in her accented English. She gestured for Helen to rise as three ladies-in-waiting emerged from the carriage behind.

Helen did so, and met the pale blue and rather shrewd regard of her Queen. She had aged since they had last met, eight months ago at St James's Palace, no doubt due to the recent decline in her husband's condition. It was said the King had now sunk irretrievably into madness. Her face had settled more heavily into its jowls, and her mouth had lost any softness to become a grim line of forbearance. She wore a cap over her grey hair, which was frizzled high in the old-fashioned way, and her famously bright eyes were somewhat dulled by weariness. The journey would have no doubt contributed to her fatigue, Helen thought. The Royal lady was, after all, near seventy years old.

"Thank you, Your Majesty," she said and glanced at the three carriages behind the Queen's. More of her retinue were alighting. How was she to draw Her Majesty away from so many ladies-in-waiting and Royal officials?

The Duke gestured to the house. "We have tea in the drawing room, Your Majesty, if you would like to take some refreshment."

"Later, I think," the Queen said. "It is a long way from London. I feel the need to walk. Duchess, will you accompany me?"

"I would be delighted, Your Majesty," Helen said.

The Queen peered across the front lawn towards the thrum of activity in the lower field. "I shall view the fair. Let me take your arm, my dear."

Together they began to walk slowly towards the ha-ha, the ladies-in-waiting falling in behind.

The Queen turned and waved them back. "No. Wait here."

The order was met with curtseys and the ladies drew back to the gravel drive. Helen and the Queen proceeded onward in silence across the grass. The yellow snuff stains on Her Majesty's flared nostrils were vibrant against the pallor of her weariness, and she leaned heavily upon Helen's arm, but her expression was one of determination. It seemed as though the Queen intended to contrive a private conversation.

"Your Majesty," Helen started.

"Not yet," the Queen said. "A little further."

They walked on, the smell of roasting mutton and beef from the kitchens in the field below scenting the slight breeze. Clusters of workmen, musicians and stall holders were gathering beyond the ha-ha, clapping and calling out blessings and "God Protect the King". The Queen acknowledged them with a gracious wave.

She finally spoke. "So, you have something of import to say to me?"

"How did you know, Your Majesty?"

She smiled; a flash of small yellowed teeth. "My dear, I have lived in Royal courts all my life. I know when someone has important information to impart."

"I fear we may be overheard."

The Queen raised her brows. "Even out here?"

Helen gave a nod.

"I see." The Queen considered the field below, then pointed to two young men, one holding a fiddle, the other a flute. She beckoned to them. They looked at one another and began to scramble up the ha-ha. "I am known to be a great admirer of music," she said, observing Helen from the corner of her eye.

The two men, dressed in shabby breeches and heavy woollen jackets, approached and bowed low.

"Play for me," the Queen ordered. "Something lively and loud. Keep upon the task until I tell you to stop."

"Yes, Your Majesty," the fiddler said. He cleared his throat. "Would the 'Spri—'" He took a breath, closing his eyes for a moment to collect himself. "Would the 'Sprigs of Laurel' be to Your Majesty's taste?"

"An excellent choice," she said and waved them to start.

The fiddler raised his instrument and nodded to his companion. They started the tune, one that Helen knew well from Assembly Balls.

"Louder," the Queen said. They increased the volume. She nodded her approval, then steered Helen a few yards away. "Well?" she asked.

Helen met the Queen's unblinking pale stare and straightened her shoulders. She must confess their failure. "Your Majesty, I have every reason to believe that Lord Carlston and I did not in fact destroy the Grand Deceiver as Mr Pike reported. We were tricked into thinking we had killed our enemy. I offer no excuse. We were outmanoeuvred."

"That is … disappointing," the Queen said, her eyes upon the crowd in the field below. Two straggling rows had formed to dance to the music. As the tune rounded back to the start, the men bowed and the ladies curtseyed, the pairs launching into the first set. "So the Grand Deceiver is still out there?"

"Not out there, Your Majesty. I believe the Grand Deceiver is currently staying in this house."

The Queen turned her penetrating gaze back to Helen. "For what purpose? To attack me?"

"I do not believe that is their aim, Your Majesty. Even so, you and your retinue should leave, for your safety. It is the Grand Deceiver's mission to open a doorway between their realm and ours to invade our world, and the way to do that is through my power. I do not intend to allow myself to be used in such a way, but they have managed to separate myself and Lord Carlston. I have taken steps to bring Lord Carlston back as soon as possible. He should be here by midnight."

"You think the Grand Deceiver intends to strike tonight?"

"No, Your Majesty." Helen drew herself up. "The Grand

Reclaimer intends to strike tonight."

If, God willing, Mr Nesbitt found Carlston in time.

The Queen gave a small smile. "Well said, Duchess." She looked back at the people waiting for her return on the Hall's driveway and portico. "The Grand Deceiver is standing up there somewhere?"

"Yes. I must suspect everyone."

The Royal brows lifted. "Even the Duke?"

"Although it pains me to say so, even the Duke. Even my aunt and uncle, and my brother."

"And myself? Am I to take it by this conversation that I am above suspicion?"

Helen paused. "Not above, Your Majesty. I am merely taking a calculated risk by speaking to you."

The Queen gave a small snort of laughter. "Most people would have fallen over themselves to demur at such a thought. You are very like your mother. She too said her piece candidly." She sighed. "We were friends, you know. Two women with power they could not use. I, who had promised my poor dear husband that I would not meddle in state matters, and your dear mother, prevented from taking up arms by the Dark Days Club. I believe she would have been very proud to see her daughter rise into such a warrior, fighting to protect England." Her eyes met Helen's kindly. "Our lost ones walk with us every day, yes? We must be glad that they are with our Lord in the glory of heaven."

Helen bowed her head. Her mother proud of her; it was a precious idea. Yet, in truth, she had failed her mother and her father, with their killer – the unknown VC – still unpunished, and the information inside the Ligatus restrained along with its terrible howling savagery.

The Queen pursed her lips. "If I were to leave now, surely

that would alert the creatures that something is afoot."

"Possibly," Helen admitted.

"Not to mention the social ramifications for yourself and the Duke. Everyone knows I have come to bless this union and to show my interest in you – an action that should help remedy any rumours about your dear mother. If I leave now, the opposite will be achieved." She shook her head. "No, I will stay. I am the Queen of England; I do not run from an enemy. I will trust in God and you, Duchess, to protect me."

Helen curtseyed. "I am honoured by that trust, Your Majesty," she said, finding it hard to swallow past the sudden dryness in her throat.

Helen had hoped to find Darby waiting with Sprat in her dressing room, but it was empty. She stretched her hearing, listening for Darby's firm tread, but the clatter and conversation throughout the house obscured everything beyond the passageway outside.

She drew off her gloves and placed them on the dressing table. Dinner had seemed interminable, every minute sawing upon her nerves. The Queen had elected to take a small meal in her rooms to rest before the ball, so the dinner company had been more or less everyone she suspected of being the Grand Deceiver, interspersed with guests from London who had arrived early to take advantage of the daylight travelling. Every time she had looked down the table at her friends and family, she had fancied she saw a sly glance or an odd expression. A Deceiver hidden in everyone.

As she reached behind her neck and found the clasp of her pearls, she focused upon the Reclaimer bond. Still at its mid-distance beat. The hands of the little clock on the mantel had not moved since she had last looked. Ten past eight. Mr Nesbitt should have arrived at Portsmouth by now, yet she felt no change in the bond. Perhaps he had not been able to find Carlston. Perhaps the convoy had already sailed. Or, more likely, she would not be able to discern any change until Carlston was almost upon Chenwith.

She drew the pearls free of her throat and dumped them upon the table beside the gloves. This waiting would send her mad.

She pulled her jewellery casket towards her, lifted its lid, and unpacked the neatly stacked boxes within. At the bottom, she found the flat green leather case she sought. She drew it out and flicked up the two brass clasps. Inside, her touch watch lay upon its bed of white silk. She lifted it up by its fob ribbon. The light from the room's abundant night candles shimmered across its sea-green enamel case, diamond-encrusted central arrow, and twelve emeralds that marked the hours around its edge. As beautiful as the day she had received it from Carlston. Now that her lorgnette had been destroyed, she must use the touch watch once again. At least the colour of the case would suit her ball gown.

Where was Darby? She listened, but still no sign.

With a flick of her thumb, she opened the enamel case, then lined the three crystal lenses up together to form the Reclaimer glass. All in perfect working order. She folded the lenses back into the watch case and returned it to its white silk.

Finally, she heard Darby's quick tread along the passage. But only one set of footsteps. She was alone.

The door opened. Darby stepped in and closed it with a press of her back against the wood. She dipped into a curtsey.

"Nothing yet?" Helen said, more statement than question.

Darby gave a small tired shake of her head. "I have looked in all the usual places." She crossed the room, pausing to gather the pile of clean linen for Helen to change into for the ball. "You don't think she could have run away, do you? One of the footmen said Mrs Clarke threatened her with dismissal if she didn't tell the truth."

"I think it unlikely." Helen turned her back for Darby to unfasten the gown ties. "She does not want to end up at another bawdy house, and she would not try to walk to Bath at night. She would freeze to death."

"I'll try beyond the house and outbuildings," Darby said. "Could we risk asking Geoffrey for help?"

"No, this must stay between us." Helen looked over her shoulder as she felt the first of the ties release and the gown slip a little. "Keep searching, and keep me informed during the night. When you find her – if you find her – bring her straight to me."

"Even at the ball?"

Helen nodded. "Even at the ball." She glanced at the clock again. Twenty past eight. "We must hurry. The Duke has asked me to join him on the terrace at nine o'clock."

Darby drew the back of the gown open, pulling the sleeves off Helen's shoulders. "Do you think some ill may have befallen Sprat?" she asked quietly. "Could the Grand Deceiver have discovered that she could identify them?"

Helen bowed her head. "I cannot see how, but that is my fear."

The ball was scheduled to start at ten o'clock, but a number of carriages had already pulled up in the front drive and were discharging their passengers into the warmth of the foyer, where a glass of mulled wine and Aunt's welcoming smile awaited them.

Helen, intent on reaching Selburn for their nine o'clock assignation without being seen by either Aunt or the eager guests, slipped past the grand staircase, taking the corridor that led directly to the terrace. The same route she had taken when she had desperately, and unknowingly, sought the replenishment of earth energy from the ley line that ran through the Chenwith estate.

Was she heading out to meet one half of the Grand Deceiver on the terrace? Or perhaps she had just slipped past the creature greeting the guests in her dear aunt's body. She squeezed her eyes shut for a second, past the pain of those two possibilities. She must not keep speculating in such a way – it brought too much fear crashing in behind it. She must focus upon her own pretence of normality, and wait. For Sprat, and for Carlston.

She pushed open the door and shivered as the night air pressed upon the bare skin of her décolletage. Hopefully Selburn had made sure the new pavilion was warm, otherwise all their female guests would freeze to death. She clutched her Norwich shawl more tightly around her shoulders, but its thin protection did little against the low cut of her bodice and the cold air.

Selburn stood looking out upon the gardens, gloved hands laced behind his back, the line of his broad shoulders accentuated by the fit of his Weston jacket. Beyond him, hundreds of lanterns lit the formal gardens. They were threaded through tree branches, set around the base of the Atlas fountain, strung from poles along the pathways like paper garlands, their glow holding back the moonless night. And beyond the maze of lamps, an even brighter glow and the shape of a dome. The pavilion.

He turned as he heard the terrace door close, his light show catching the gleam of his blond hair. The anticipation on his face made her smile.

"Ah, there you are. What do you think?" he asked.

"Gerard, it is beautiful," she said, her delight momentarily subduing the strain of the day.

"Your own Vauxhall Gardens, my dear. It lights the way to your wedding gift." He held out his hand. "Come, let me show you."

His clasp was firm and strong around her hand. They were

the only people out there and it was eerily calm, as if the gardens were drawing a breath before the Queen emerged from the drawing room and the other guests made their way to the ball. Helen could just make out the music from the lower field, a see-sawing scratch of fiddles and trill of flutes. The villagers' celebration was well underway.

Selburn led her down the steps onto the path, and her reticule, heavy with the touch watch inside, swung on its drawstring between them. The earth energy thrummed through the thin leather soles of her dance slippers. It felt stronger than the day when she had arrived – perhaps because of the new moon due the following night. It was one of the two peaks of Reclaimer power, and could be an advantage if it came to fighting the Grand Deceiver.

Helen's mind flashed to Sprat again. Where was the girl? Was she even alive? The ghastly thought clenched her teeth.

Selburn led her past the fountain, the lamps around its base casting the hunched figure of Atlas and the Earth upon his shoulders into gold relief, then through the formal garden. "You seem a little distracted," he said, tucking her hand into the crook of his arm.

She waved her other hand airily. "It is the prospect of the ball."

"There is no need to worry. All is in order. Now close your eyes and let me guide you the last part of the way."

They had reached the end of the formal gardens, where paths led off into the wilder Capability Brown landscapes.

"Close my eyes?" Helen could not keep the suspicion from her voice. "I will stumble and dirty my ball gown." A lame excuse, even to her own ears.

And clearly his as well. "Do you not trust me?"

In all truth, she trusted no one except Darby and Carlston. Not what Selburn would want to hear.

"Of course I do." She closed her eyes, stretching her other senses around him, creating his tall, familiar figure in her mind through the sound of his breathing, the heat of his skin near her own, the smell of his cologne.

Slowly, he led her along the path, his hand beneath the length of her forearm. The gravel crunched under her feet, and the light from the lamps in the trees danced across her closed eyelids. She felt the warmth of the pavilion as they approached, heard the footsteps of the servants within, and the building's huge rectangular shape formed in her mind.

"Open your eyes!" Selburn said.

She blinked, a gasp drawn from her at the sight. The pavilion was at least the length and breadth of the grand ballroom inside the Hall. Three of its four walls were a series of glass doorways set into white and gilt arches. The fourth wall, made of white marble, had been extended into a narrow, curved antechamber. Inside the pavilion, three huge crystal chandeliers held hundreds of candles, their light reflected in the huge gilt mirrors set between the arches. The building was made almost completely of glass.

"I can see right through it," she said, astounded. "Gerard, it is magnificent."

He had steepled his hands against his mouth, watching her over his fingertips. "Come. Let me show you inside. It is even better."

The footman at the door opened it with a bow. She stepped in, the reflection of her wonder caught in the multitude of mirrors. A gust of heated air eased the chill on her skin, and the earth energy still thrummed beneath her feet. In the corner next to the antechamber door, the waiting musicians rose from their seats and bowed.

"How is it so warm?" she asked.

Selburn pointed to a large edifice in the far corner, decorated with blue and white panels of pastoral scenes. "It is a Delft porcelain heating stove," he said proudly. "The same as inside the Catherine Palace in Russia. I have based it all on the Palace."

He turned in a circle, gathering the whole pavilion in a wave of his hand that ended in a flourish at the wide doorway that led into the antechamber. Helen glimpsed a rich carpet, and gilded seats set up to view the dance floor.

"That is for the Queen and her retinue," he said. "I have organised a toast for Her Majesty at midnight, and then an early supper so that she does not tire."

"It is beautiful." Helen walked across the chalked dance floor. The surface – whatever it was – seemed rather hard for dancing. "What is the floor made of?"

"Compacted earth with clay upon it." He turned in a circle again, admiring his creation. "It is meant to be as if you are dancing in the garden itself." He bowed. "Will you dance with me, wife? Shall we be scandalous and try the new waltz?"

Dancing in the garden – such a grand, romantic gesture. She curtseyed, then stepped into the circle of his arms. "Dance the waltz? You shall ruin me, sir," she said, pretending maidenly horror.

"It is my aim," he said, smiling. He waved an order to the musicians. "Play the 'Duke of Kent's Waltz'."

The music filled the pavilion. Selburn's hand found its place upon her waist – so intimate – his other hand holding her arm arched above her head. She took a deep breath and released it. Almost a sigh, for there was no threat here; no savage whips or vile feeding tentacles. Just a moment to enjoy. A rare gift, even more beautiful than the pavilion in which they stood.

She rose onto her toes, the earth power warm under her feet, and felt herself swirled into the new, dangerous dance.

Three hours later, the addition of two hundred guests had intensified the pleasant warmth inside the glass pavilion to an almost unbearable heat. Rivulets of condensation had formed upon the glass arches; and the air was thick with the smell of hot bodies, sweet melting beeswax and earthy chalk being ground underfoot. The music and loud hum of conversation seemed to bounce off the windows, amplified ten times over.

One of the glass doors stood open, letting in the chilled night air, but Helen still felt clammy sweat in the small of her back as she grasped the hand of her dance partner, the new Russian ambassador, Count Lieven. If her body felt overheated, her mind felt as if it were ablaze with frustration and suspicion. Twice during the night Darby had appeared at one of the arched glass doorways like a ghost and shaken her head. Still no sign of Sprat. To make matters worse, the Reclaimer beat within Helen's body had not changed. Either Mr Nesbitt had failed to reach Portsmouth in time, or her own strained nerves were preventing her from sensing Carlston's approach. At least she had managed to click together the lens in the touch watch once and swiftly scan her guests. Every figure had been surrounded by pale blue energy, but even that had not provided much reassurance. It had been early in the evening, before she was in constant demand, and not all the guests had been inside the pavilion.

Mr Hammond, for instance, had not been present. He and Pug now promenaded two couples ahead, although Hammond did not seem to be concentrating upon his partner. His gaze kept turning to Lady Margaret, seated on one of the gilt chairs at the side of the dance floor, where she conversed with another lady. The little lace cap upon Lady Margaret's dark hair signalled that she did not intend to dance, and Helen had seen her refuse even the Duke for this set. He was four couples ahead, dancing with Countess Lieven, the fascinating wife of the ambassador.

The promenade circle slowly turned, sending Helen and the ambassador past the doorway to the Queen's antechamber. To Aunt's obvious delight she had been invited to sit with Her Majesty, and as Helen trod by she met her eyes. So much pride in her aunt's smile. It was too unnerving even to consider her as one half of a Grand Deceiver.

"Your husband says this pavilion was inspired by the Catherine Palace," the ambassador said over the music. "We call it Tsarskoye Selo. I can definitely see the influence. Has he visited my country?"

"I do not believe so, ambassador," Helen said. She searched her limited Russian, taught to her by a fellow student at the seminary, a young and very homesick Countess. *"Pravda krasivo?"* It is beautiful, yes?

The ambassador smiled. "You speak my language?"

Helen made a small demurring gesture with her hand. "Only a little." Mainly, she thought, words of love. The young Countess had been a great romantic.

"Tsarskoye Selo is indeed a beautiful palace," the ambassador said. "There is a room within that is made entirely of amber…"

Helen drew in a sharp breath as she felt something shift in her chest. A change within the Reclaimer beat. Finally, or was she imagining it? She focused inward, the heat and the music and the courtly man at her side all fading into the steady pulse within her body. No, it was not her imagination.

She pressed her hand to her bodice as if her heart might burst out of her chest. Carlston was nearby. Thank God!

"Duchess, are you quite well?" the ambassador asked, wrenching her focus back to the hot pavilion.

490

"I beg your pardon. Yes, I am very well."

She added a polite smile, then peered out of the arched windows as they circled past. Was Carlston already on the grounds? She fought back the impulse to abandon the dance floor and run out to search for him.

She nearly missed the cue to break the promenade circle, only the firm hand of the ambassador alerting her to the new figure. She led the row of ladies up towards the antechamber, the gentlemen lining up behind the ambassador. They were near the end of the dance. Could she contrive to slip away after it had finished?

She skipped down the row of ladies sweating in their muslins and silks, and glimpsed her uncle in conversation with the dashing Lord Carnarvon. Pike stood nearby, drinking a glass of punch with Andrew. He nodded as she passed.

She met the ambassador at the end of the row and took his hand, skipping back up the centre to return to the top of the line. As she turned back to her place, her eyes caught upon two figures standing at the far glass door. Darby, firmly holding Sprat by her thin shoulder. Helen's heart leaped with relief. The girl was alive and well.

Darby turned, tipping her head towards a line of trees. The lamps strung in the branches had been extinguished, but Helen could just make out two tall figures. Carlston and Quinn.

She flexed her fingers, trying to relieve her frustration. She could not leave the dance floor. It would be the height of ill manners, and besides would bring too much attention upon herself. Fixing a smile on her face, she trod the last figures, the shadowy figure of Carlston always at the corner of her eye.

The music finally drew out into the finishing chords. Helen curtseyed to the ambassador and allowed him to take her hand to lead her from the floor.

"Shall I procure you some punch, Duchess?" he inquired.

"No, thank you." She smiled. "If you will excuse me, I must attend to a small matter."

She barely stayed for his bow, launching herself past a group of thirsty dancers clustered around a tray of punch held by a footman.

"Duchess!" Lady Dunwick called. She was barrelling towards Helen with Pug in tow. "Do you think you—"

Helen pretended she did not hear and veered to the right, trying to move as if she were not in a hurry, her gaze unfocused and sliding past the faces of those who tried to claim her attention. The Reclaimer bond pounded in her ears.

Almost at the door. Darby and Sprat were no longer in view. They must have retreated into the shadows too. Helen looked over her shoulder – Selburn was engaged with Lord Desmond. She pulled open the glass door and stepped outside, the cold air instantly chilling the sweat on her skin. She quickly shut it behind her, ignoring the curious stares of those behind the wet glass, and crossed the gravel surround of the pavilion. She peered into the shadowy foliage, her Reclaimer sight adjusting. No one was there. Where had they gone? She rubbed her arms, the cold air beginning to raise gooseflesh.

A shadow shifted along the path, near some trees. Darby stepped out and beckoned. She wore Quinn's mud-spattered greatcoat over her shoulders. Helen smiled. Quinn, always looking after his beloved Jen.

"I found Sprat in the Venus temple," Darby whispered as she led Helen off the path and into a dark copse of trees. "Little minx won't tell me anything."

Helen nodded, but all her attention was upon the figures ahead. There were no lanterns strung in these branches, but the ambient light from the pavilion was like false moonlight, casting cold shadows across the grass. Quinn lounged against a tree, arms crossed over his jacket; but even after five hours of hard riding, Carlston stood straight and unyielding. Road dust smeared his face, and his greatcoat was spattered with mud and wet up to his knees.

She could smell his familiar wet-wool and warm-skin scent. She took a deeper breath. It was like breathing in courage and comfort all at once. What was she to say? How was she to act now? She had thought only to bring him here as fast as possible, not how it would be once he had arrived.

He stepped forward and caught her outstretched hands, his dark eyes intent. She had not meant to touch him, but there it was, their hands somehow entwined. And her heartbeat, as quick and hard as the Reclaimer beat they shared.

"Your note," he said. "There is no Elise in Calais? No boy?"

"It was a trick too, like the false Grand Deceiver. I am sorry."

His face held such a pained mix of loss and fierce relief. He smiled, full of hope, but she could not meet it. Yet equally she could not let go of his hands.

"Helen, I—"

"I am the Duchess Selburn now." She said it too sharply, like a slap. But what else could she do? Today was her wedding day. She let go of his hands.

"Of course." He bowed. "Congratulations."

Behind him, Quinn also bowed, murmuring his good wishes.

Helen gave a nod of acknowledgment, glad to be able to crouch down before Sprat and focus upon the task at hand. She took the girl's cold bony hand in her own. Darby had wrapped Sprat in her own cloak, but she was still shivering.

"I have something very important to ask you, Sprat."

"I told her you weren't angry, but she won't believe me," Darby said.

"Mrs Clarke said I was gunna be dismissed," Sprat said, scowling at Darby. "I ain't coppin' to nuthin'."

"You are not dismissed," Helen said. "Do you understand?"

Sprat squinted at her. "Truly?"

"Truly. Now, tell me, where did you find the letter you hid in the wall in my bedchamber? From whom did you take it?"

Sprat chewed her lower lip. "You sure you won't get mad?"

"Absolutely not."

"Lady Margaret."

Lady Margaret? Helen looked up at Carlston. Beneath the road dust, his face was a ghastly grey. He leaned his hand against the nearest tree trunk, drawing deep deliberate breaths. No wonder. If Sprat were telling the truth, that meant Lady Margaret had written in Elise's hand, which also meant that Margaret, Carlston's trusted aide, was now inhabited by the same Deceiver that had once been his wife. A double betrayal.

"Are you sure?" Darby demanded, shaking the girl's shoulder. "This is no time for lies."

"I ain't lyin'," Sprat said, wriggling out of Darby's grip. "I saw her put it in the fire grate in her room, ready to be burned as part of the mornin' fire, so I figured she didn't want it no more. I swear it."

Dear God, had Lady Margaret been a Deceiver all the time they had known each other? Or was it more recent? How did she manage it? How did she feed?

"Is it possible, Carlston?" Helen asked.

He lifted his head. "She pointed us in the direction of Philip and Mrs Knoll as the Grand Deceiver. It would also explain our failure at the White Hart," he said heavily. "It has always troubled me that Dunn never sensed any Deceiver approaching. Now I think he didn't sense one because she was already there, with him. Lady Margaret laid him out from behind, and Pike too, then placed the note and retreated at Deceiver speed, apparently spirited away by her abductors."

It made sense, Helen thought. Awful, duplicitous sense.

"Did she kill Miss Cransdon too?" Sprat asked. "Wasn't she the one holdin' her in the street?"

"I don't know, Sprat," Helen said. "Possibly."

"Does that mean Mr Hammond is the other half of the Grand Deceiver?" Quinn asked quietly.

Helen stared at the ground. Surely not Hammond. The idea felt like a punch to the heart. Yet he and Lady Margaret were twins; how could he not know his sister was a Deceiver? And he too had been with them right from the beginning.

"They are twins," Carlston said, echoing her thoughts.

She looked up. "He insisted on staying here and not going with you. They both did."

"Do we truly think it is Mr Hammond too?" Darby said, her voice small.

Carlston rubbed his face with both hands as if trying to clear his mind. "I am not convinced, but it does not matter. In the end, we only need to destroy one of the Grand Deceivers to destroy the dyad, and we know Lady Margaret wrote those letters. We must finish this tonight before they realise we know who they are."

"Do you have a plan, Your Grace?" Quinn asked Helen. "When is the best chance to draw the creature alone?"

"I think after the toasts," Helen said slowly. She stood stiffly. It felt as if every joint in her body ached with shock. "Once the toasts are finished, everyone will walk to the house for supper and the pavilion will be empty."

Carlston nodded. "Ask Lady Margaret to walk with you, then lag behind. We can set up an ambush on the path away from the pavilion."

"I managed to check earlier and she showed no Deceiver energy in evidence, no weapons built," Helen said. "A ley line runs through the grounds. We will have more than enough earth power to draw upon."

"Then that is the plan," Carlston said. "We shall obliterate this creature and finally have done with the Grand Deceiver."

Chapter Twenty-Nine

Helen walked back to the bright pavilion, her arms wrapped around her body in an effort to hold back the bitter cold that came from shock as much as the freezing night. Lady Margaret was now the enemy. And at some point, to enable the creature to inhabit her body, the real Lady Margaret had died alone and unmourned. Perhaps years ago. The brutal pity of it sent a shiver across Helen's shoulders.

And Mr Hammond: was he the other half to Lady Margaret's Grand Deceiver? Something within Helen refused the possibility. Logic pointed to it, but it did not sit right in her innards. Then again, she had not seen the Deceiver within Lady Margaret. How could she trust her intuition when it had already proved so blind?

She stopped just outside the halo of light from the pavilion and watched the dancers through the series of arched doors. The glass muffled the music a little, but it was still loud; a lively duple dance. The swirl of pale gowns and dark jackets reminded her of an aurora flask she had once seen at a natural philosophy lecture: electrical fire, dancing inside a bottle.

Sprat's question still played upon her mind. Had Lady

Margaret killed Delia? Or was there another explanation, just as horrifying and heartbreaking? Perhaps Delia had been the Deceiver, and she had shifted into Lady Margaret on Quiet Street. Delia had, after all, eloped with Mr Trent, a Deceiver. Had he inhabited her a year ago, killing the real Delia? Helen shook her head. Trent had been a man, and the female Grand Deceiver needed female bodies. Maybe Delia had been a Deceiver all along, before she had even eloped with Trent.

Whatever the case, these creatures left hidden carnage in their wake and it had to stop tonight. At least now the Grand Reclaimer was reunited, the beat between her and Carlston a steady pulse of hope and determination.

The closest set of glass doors opened and Selburn stepped out. "Where have you been, my dear? We are about to toast the Queen and Crown. I could not find you."

"I needed some air. It is quite hot within."

He looked over his shoulder. "Yes, I will have to rethink the ventilation." He smiled, holding out his hand. More of an ushering than an invitation. "Shall we? The Queen wishes to go to supper."

An excellent idea, Helen thought. The sooner their guests went to supper, the sooner she and Carlston would be able to destroy the Lady Margaret Deceiver.

Inside, silk and ivory fans fluttered quickly, and brows and décolletages shone with sweat. The dance set had finished, the musicians laying down their instruments for a much-needed respite, the music replaced by chatter and laughter. Footmen weaved through the company carrying trays of champagne in readiness for the Royal toast.

Helen searched the gilt chairs at the side of the dance floor, but Lady Margaret was no longer there. Where had she gone? And Mr Hammond? She rose onto her toes. So many slight, dark-haired ladies. Was Lady Margaret even still in the pavilion?

A group of people disbanded from their conversation, finally showing Mr Hammond, and next to him Lady Margaret. Their expressions were identical – a fierce intensity – although Hammond's focus was upon his sister, whereas Lady Margaret seemed fixed upon the Queen, who was seated at the doorway of the antechamber. Helen looked away in case her rising fury somehow drew their attention. One of them, at least, had killed Delia and the real Lady Margaret. And Lady Elise too.

Selburn beckoned to a footman holding a tray with only two vessels upon it: glass goblets, each encased in an elegant holder of chased silver.

"I had them made for our toasts," Selburn said, lifting them from the tray. He passed one to Helen, the silver casing cold against her fingers.

Lud, every nerve within her body was stretched tight with dread. Would she and Carlston be able to obliterate Lady Margaret? They had access to the earth power – indeed an excess of it from the ley line that ran through the grounds – but every attack held risk.

Fairwood stood waiting with a staff in hand, ready to announce the toast. Selburn nodded and the butler walked to the middle of the dance floor and plunged the staff against the hard clay. Once, twice, three times. The sharp slams cut through the chatter, shifting guests to either side of the pavilion as if Fairwood were Moses parting the Red Sea.

"Pray silence for His Grace the Duke of Selburn," he called. "The Royal toast."

Helen looked through the path of parted guests to where the Queen sat, attended by her ladies-in-waiting. Aunt sat beside Queen Charlotte, her face flushed from the heat, her glass of champagne already delivered. One of the ladies-in-waiting fanned Her Majesty; another stood with a glass of champagne at the ready.

The Queen met Helen's eyes across the length of the pavilion, a lift of the Royal brows posing the obvious question. Helen gave a slight nod. Yes, the Grand Deceiver had been found. Her Majesty's eyelids fluttered, but she gave no other sign of acknowledgment.

The Duke cupped his hand beneath Helen's elbow and steered her forward a few steps to stand amidst their guests.

"Lords, Ladies, gentlemen," he said, raising his glass. "A toast to Her Royal Majesty the Queen!"

"The Queen," everyone chorused, turning towards the antechamber and drinking to Her Majesty. The Queen graciously inclined her head.

Helen lifted her glass to her lips and took a mouthful. It was a bitter champagne, not to her liking at all. Oddly grainy. She lowered the glass and looked inside. Little black specks had gathered around the edge.

"And to His Majesty the King!"

"The King!" Helen repeated with everyone else, raising her glass and taking another mouthful.

She licked her lips. The after-taste was ashy. Her vision clouded for a second. She blinked, then heard a soft hissing murmur at her back. She looked around, but no one stood behind her or, indeed, whispered nearby. The sound was inside her head: a soft buzzing that rapidly increased in volume – her swarm of bees rising – and melded with a low familiar howl. The Ligatus.

She looked at the glass in her hand. Ashy? Inside her mind, the Ligatus heaved against its tether, writhing with new-found energy. She looked down at her feet, trying to flex her toes in her soft kid-leather slippers. The warmth of the earth energy from the earthen floor had turned into a stinging burn. The heat climbed through her body, the feel of it dangerously different – heavier in some way – its relentless path locking her bones and muscles and sinews together.

"Selburn, something is wrong," she managed. It was hard to form the words.

Near the antechamber, Lord Henry stepped forward to make the wedding toast, all attention upon him. "Your Majesty, Lords, Ladies, gentlemen, it is my pleasure to wish the bride and groom…"

"It will not be long now," Selburn whispered. He took her free hand and pushed her glove down her arm, slowly working it over her hand and fingers, smiling at an older lady nearby who watched, scandalised.

Helen tried to draw her hand back, but her body felt as if it were caught in treacle. What was he doing?

He pulled the glove free, then drew something from his fob pocket. A gold oval frame, its edge made of filigree. Helen's innards clenched – she knew that frame. He turned it over. Beneath the oval of glass, her mother's delicately painted face stared up at her, blue eyes bold and challenging.

"Another wedding present," he whispered, placing the portrait face down on her bare palm. The back compartment was empty; the three woven strands of hair that had once been set under its glass, gone. The hair, Helen realised, needed for the Colligat alchemy.

His fingertip tapped the empty glass oval. "The third strand – the blond Deceiver hair – was my own," he said softly. "You have just drunk the Colligat, my dear. The three parts of the Trinitas, finally united. Now the realm will open."

Her eyes flew to his face. Selburn was the other half of the Grand Deceiver. Not Hammond. Dear God, how could she have missed it? For a moment, her mind was blank, the danger so overwhelming that no thought was possible. Only the terrifying sensation of falling into a black abyss.

"How?" It came out slowly, little more than a breath. Yet behind the one tortured syllable, she silently screamed. At his betrayal. At her stupidity.

"It has been a long time planned," he said, tightening his hold upon her wrist. "Well before I took over the young Viscount Chenwith's body."

Viscount Chenwith: VC. Helen rocked back on her feet as if she had been physically hit. *Cannot trust VC.* She had married the man – no, the *creature* – who had killed her parents.

"You surprised us by absorbing the Ligatus," he added softly, "but in the end it does not matter. Your body is just the vessel for the Trinitas power."

He turned her hand over and the miniature dropped to the floor in a hard clink of gold. He caught her champagne glass as it fell from her other hand.

Hate surged through Helen, the bright cold force of it punching a shaft of light through the darkness. A path out of the airless black hole of his betrayal. She was far more than a vessel. She was a Reclaimer.

She tried to wrench her hand away to strike at his smiling face, but her body would not move. Muscles and flesh fused into the strange position – her arm outstretched as if she reached for a dance partner's hand.

"No!" She forced the word out through her locked jaw. Yet even as she said it, the relentless momentum of the Colligat power erupted through her body. A rush of Deceiver and Reclaimer energy.

It crashed over the Ligatus, feeding its savagery, causing the howling, hissing power to slam against the restraint of the vestige tether. It swept through her blood, hooking into the earth power rising through her feet, hauling it up through her body – a raging pathway searing through veins and muscles and bones towards the Ligatus. The two energies slammed together, a collision of life and death, rocking Helen upon her feet, only Selburn's brutal hold keeping her upright. The tether was going to break. She could feel it weakening under the brutal onslaught.

Her heartbeat thundered through the Reclaimer bond, drumming out her terror to Carlston. She could barely sense his presence through the crashing storm of alchemical energy. Her vision warped and shifted, pale blue energy springing up around every figure within the pavilion. Human life force. Even the foul creature that stood at her side. He had not glutted, not even fed.

She forced her eyes to move – a grinding, dry shift to the right. The other one – Margaret – was bathed in pale blue too. And around everything, a pulsing swirl of darker blue energy. How could she see it all?

Of course, through the Colligat. By holding her mother's miniature, she had once been able to access the alchemy and see the energy in the world. Now it was within her body, raging through her, fusing with the other parts of the Trinitas to rip open a doorway between this world and the Deceiver realm. Millions of starving creatures waiting to pour through.

Dear God, she had to stop them.

Frantically she strained against the alchemical fetters upon her body, forcing her eyes to move across the crowd. She found Uncle, only a few yards away, standing with champagne glass in hand, and beside him, Lord Carnarvon and Lord Desmond. All intent upon Lord Henry's toast. Half the House of Lords was in the pavilion. And the Queen too. Was that the Grand Deceiver's plan? To kill them all?

No, Helen realised, horrified, it was worse than that. The Queen and the Upper House – the leaders of England – were the bodies for the new Deceivers coming through the doorway. She had to get them out. Get them as far as possible from the pavilion and the Deceiver doorway.

Desperately, she searched the crowd of guests. There, beside a pedestal holding an urn of flowers, a thin hunched figure in black.

Gathering her fury and fear into one precious lungful of sound, Helen screamed, "Pike, the realm is opening!"

It came out barely words, more a muffled howl. Selburn's hand tightened painfully around her wrist. Everyone turned from Lord Henry's speech, faces shocked at the unseemly interruption. Helen locked her eyes upon Pike's gaunt face, silently begging him to understand. To act.

For a long, agonising moment, Pike stared at her and then his gaunt face drained into a ghastly grey. He launched himself towards the antechamber, where the Queen sat. *Yes*, Helen thought, giddy from the tiny victory. *Yes!*

The euphoria was quickly swamped by waves of earth power and Ligatus energy clashing inside her, over and over, ramming the vestige tether, weakening its dark noose of power. The restraint could not last much longer.

She tried to brace herself, to hold back the storms of power that crashed together, but they rose in one last huge wrenching twist that slammed against the vestige. The tether strained, then snapped, her body heaving with the sudden surge of energy.

"Get down!" Selburn yelled to Margaret.

The two Deceivers dropped to the ground as the combined force of the Colligat, Ligatus and Vis roared out of Helen's bare outstretched hand and slammed through the pavilion in a shock wave. It thundered through the air, ramming everyone in its path to the ground and rolling them, screaming, along the hard earthen floor, ripping clothes, tearing skin, gouging flesh.

Helen tried to scream as the blue energies around the figures merged, warping into each other, the pavilion awash with twisting shades of blue. The three huge chandeliers swung wildly, half their candles extinguished and pelting down like hard wax hail.

She saw Pike collide with the Russian ambassador, both men hitting the ground. Hammond flung against a bank of chairs. Pug screaming as she slid across the bloodied floor. And the Queen, a heap of rich topaz brocade upon the antechamber floor, Aunt sprawled at her side.

The awful power within her surged again, bursting out of her into another shock wave that rolled over the room. Bodies tumbled again, limbs flung out in flashes of flesh and under-clothes, those still conscious shrieking. The pavilion windows bulged outward from the force, then shattered, the smashing cascade of glass swamping the screams and groans, and raining down upon the gardens outside.

Every part of Helen felt alight, a pulsing conduit for the Vis earth power. It pumped through her in a deafening hum, millions of swarming bees joining the screaming howls of the Ligatus, an inexhaustible supply of power that erupted from her in a blue torrent of fire. The flames crackled across the warm, wet air three yards from her face. Tiny snaps of lightning fused thousands of droplets of water together, the links building and spreading into a huge flat circle in front of her, like a wall mirror the size of two doorways. Solid air that bent and oozed as if it were molten glass, the rest of the room behind it lost in the sliding shift of its swirling grey surface. Helen could sense space behind it, like a huge hole punched in the air.

Margaret scrabbled to her feet. "It is working! The portal

is opening." She ran to the edge of the circle, avoiding the blue fire that poured from Helen's hand, and pressed her fingertips against the melting air. The light pressure sent ripples across its taut darkness.

The floor was strewn with unconscious people, their finery smeared with dance-floor chalk, earth and blood. Others hauled themselves up and scrabbled for the archways, their screams slicing through the humming roar of the blue torrent. To the right of the portal, Pike crawled around bodies towards the opposite end of the pavilion and the Queen, his progress becoming lost behind the huge dense circle of rippling air.

At the corner of her eye, Helen saw a blur of Reclaimer speed. Carlston, running across the glass-scattered lawn, his fury and rising battle blood thundering through their Reclaimer bond. Quinn and Darby followed, slower but not far behind. They did not know that Selburn was the other Grand Deceiver. She fought to move her hand. Her finger. Anything to warn them. But all she could move were her eyes, everything else locked within the alchemy power that roared through her into the portal.

Selburn had seen Carlston coming too, for he rose onto his knees beside her and plunged an obscene purple-brown feeding tentacle into the chest of the nearest body. Her uncle. She watched, immobile and horrified, as Uncle's senseless body lifted off the floor a few inches then thudded back, his legs flopping obscenely as the pulsing tentacle sucked out his life force. An ultramarine whip rose from Selburn's back, weaving like a snake.

Silently, Helen screamed her fury at him. How dare he rip away life in such a sickening, ignoble way.

"It is taking too long!" Selburn yelled to Margaret. "Get the realm open. I will stop Carlston."

Margaret whirled around and plunged her own feeding tentacle into the chest of a young woman lying unconscious on the floor – the sweet daughter of a local landowner. The force lifted the girl's form up as if she sat, then dropped her back to the ground. A whip curled over Lady Margaret's shoulder, its tip thickening into a club.

Uncle and the girl, both dead, just like that. Hot tears slid down Helen's cheeks. She watched, impotent, as both creatures plunged their foul tentacles into living bodies again, glutting to build another whip. A young footman and an older woman. Two more innocent people dead.

Helen focused fiercely upon her right hand, trying to close it into a fist, to check the searing power. Nothing. Not even a twitch. She roared silently with fury and frustration.

The Margaret half of the Grand Deceiver turned back to the dark, glassy circle of air and hammered at it with her hands and whips, sending up sparks and the smell of spent lightning. The portal bowed and rippled under the attack, a faint black line spreading from its centre. The beginning of a crack.

Helen ground her teeth together. Within the power streaming from her, she could feel the pressure of the Deceivers on the other side of the undulating surface, an avalanche of destruction waiting to pour through.

"Come on!" Margaret screamed. She kicked at the faint crack. "Open!"

On his knees, Selburn dragged the dead footman across the dance floor to lie next to Uncle's body and the sprawled figure of Lord Desmond, who was still alive but senseless. Selburn stretched out on his side then pulled the footman's corpse over his own body, as if all four of them had been thrown together, a tumble of arms and legs. An old soldier's trick – but he had miscalculated, Helen thought with savage delight. Carlston would see his whips, their blue energy folded back like wings.

Carlston had slowed back to human speed and now looked through the ruined archways near the Queen's antechamber. Helen saw his head jerk back as he recognised the torrent of blue power and the circle of darkness rippling in the air. He knew what was happening. He had seen it at the stone circle.

He grabbed the shoulder of a young 10th Light Hussar who had just hauled himself upright from the lawn. Desperately, Helen focused her hearing through the screaming people and the roar of blue fire from her hand.

"Rally your men. Get the Queen and as many people out as you can," Carlston ordered, drawing out his touch watch from his fob pocket.

The man saluted. "Yes, my lord. Where to?"

"As far from here as possible! Just get them out. Do not approach the Duchess or myself. Tell your company."

Helen's eye caught upon three still figures standing in the shadows on the path behind them – men, villagers, a single whip extruding from each of their backs. More Deceivers. From where? From everywhere, she realised, despair knotting her gut. Mr King had said all Deceivers nearby would gather to add their energy to the portal.

Carlston assembled his touch watch, then pushed his way through the shattered doorway to Helen's left, shouldering past panicked men and crying women as they staggered out onto the lawn. He lifted the lens and scanned Lady Margaret, still kicking at the dense rippling circle of energy, and then Helen, his lips tightening at her frozen imprisonment. In the periphery of her vision, Helen watched the arc of his sweep, waiting for him to stop at Selburn's whips. He scanned right over them, then lowered the glass, frowning.

No! Why did he not see them?

Quinn and Darby picked their way over the broken glass to enter the pavilion, both gaping at the circle of melting air.

"It is the Trinitas," Carlston said, the battle blood in his voice. "Lady Helen's power is opening the realm."

Quinn eyed the blue energy streaming from Helen's hand. "How do we stop it?"

"I can stop her power through the blood bond," Darby said. "Just one touch." She hoisted up her gown and stepped forward.

"Wait!" Carlston grabbed her arm. He scanned the pavilion once more through the lens, then snapped it back into its case. "There is too much energy – I cannot make out anything. But I'll wager that creature in Margaret has whips, and the other Grand Deceiver is in here too. Stay alert."

Dear God, the Reclaimer lens could not distinguish the whips from the excess of power. Helen silently screamed, *Selburn*. But no one could hear her.

In one fluid movement Carlston slid his glass knife from his boot scabbard and gave Quinn and Darby the sign to move forward.

At the far end of the pavilion, one of the 10th Royal Hussars edged through the archway and slid his hands under the arms of the senseless Russian ambassador, hauling him through the doorway. Three other soldiers moved cautiously into the antechamber and helped the Queen and her ladies to their feet. Helen saw Aunt amongst their careful retreat from the pavilion and felt a sharp moment of relief. At least they were alive.

Carlston, Darby and Quinn cautiously picked their way between the unconscious and dead guests, every step taking them closer to Selburn, lying in wait on the floor. Helen watched, agonised, as Carlston stopped a mere yard from the portal, his head to one side, eyes narrowed. Could he sense Selburn's whips?

Selburn must have thought the same, for he launched the dead footman at Carlston with Deceiver strength. The corpse flew through the air in a heavy arc, limbs spreading as if still animated. Carlston whirled around and caught its full weight against his back. Selburn propelled himself after the corpse, his two whips aimed at Darby's head, the vicious slicing blows on a trajectory of inevitable connection.

In a blur of speed, Carlston shouldered the dead footman to the ground and grabbed Darby, wrenching her aside as the two tips snapped past her face. He shoved her towards Quinn and spun around, slicing one whip through with his knife. Selburn hissed with pain.

Carlston bounced backward on his toes, a snarl of understanding on his face. "You!" He ran at Selburn, blocking the Deceiver's path to Darby as she darted towards Helen.

"Stop Darby!" Selburn yelled to Margaret, then lunged at Carlston.

Lady Margaret ran forward, whips curling, ready to slam down upon Darby, but Quinn threw himself between them, screaming a blood-curdling war cry. As the whips drew back, shifting their aim, a figure rose up behind Margaret, a gilt chair held high above his head.

"You killed my sister!" Hammond screamed and swung the chair at the Deceiver's back.

Margaret twisted around, her whips snapping forward to block the blow, smashing the chair into splinters and propelling Hammond back. He hit an archway with a sickening thud.

It was only a moment of distraction, but it was enough. Darby threw herself across the floor and grabbed Helen's ankle, her fingers digging into the flesh.

An arc of power exploded between them, an incandescent flash that blinded Helen for a second as it flung her back from the shivering air. She hit the hard floor and rolled, gasping, the blue fire gone, the Trinitas connection extinguished by Darby's touch. The sudden loss of power curled her into agony, every nerve ablaze. She squinted through the pain. The roar of energy had disappeared; only shrieks and sobs now, and the smash of Selburn's whips slamming into the ground as Carlston dodged the vicious blows.

A face hovered over her: dark eyes, dark skin, a swirl of moko. Quinn. She grabbed his forearm. "Did it work?"

"No." His voice was flat with defeat.

"Darby?"

"Senseless, my lady, but breathing."

Helen hauled herself to her feet. Darby lay a few yards away, crumpled in a heap. Beyond her, the shimmering circle was intact. Margaret had returned to clawing and hammering at the dark crack within it, the surface bulging and rippling under her attack.

The hum of earth power and the chittering howl of the Ligatus still surged through Helen's body. She swayed, grabbing Quinn's shoulder for support. Now the tether was gone, the dark energy was trying to claw its way to meet the darkness in the Deceiver realm. Only her strength of mind, her will, held it back. And she could feel that slipping.

"Helen!" Carlston yelled as he ducked away from Selburn's whip. He sliced at Selburn's arm with his knife, the tip of the blade catching flesh. Selburn roared and snatched his arm back.

"I am free, but the portal is still here!" Helen shouted.

She could see that the battle was taking its toll upon Carlston. He was doing his best not to stand on the senseless people sprawled on the ground, but the added obstacles made it hard for him to keep his balance as he dodged and spun away from the plunging whips. His greatcoat had already been sliced open, the wool soaked dark from a deep gash across his forearm and chest.

Helen pressed the heel of her hand against her forehead, trying to hold back the cacophony in her head. *Think!* Darby's touch had broken the circuit of power and destroyed the Trinitas, but it had not closed the portal. Why?

Enough power must have flowed between the realms to fix the pathway in place.

So how could they close it now?

She looked at Carlston as he leaped away from a low bludgeoning blow. Would a firestorm of directed earth power blast the portal away? If they tried it, what would it do to her tenuous hold upon the Ligatus?

One fireball, she decided. She could hold back the Ligatus to make one fireball.

"Quinn, wake up Darby," Helen ordered, pulling off the glove from her right hand. "We may need her to stop my power again."

It was almost impossible to avoid standing upon an arm or a leg as she closed in on the battle between Selburn and Carlston. She would not have thought it would matter to Selburn, but even he was making small leaps and hops around those still prone on the dance floor. Then, sickened, Helen realised why. Those still alive would be the vessels for the Deceivers waiting behind the portal. He did not want them damaged.

"Carlston! The stones!" she yelled, hoping he would understand.

Both Carlston and Selburn swung around. As Helen expected, Selburn attacked immediately, his whip snapping back over his shoulder then swinging in a blistering curve of speed towards her head.

She braced her feet – one more second – then ducked, and

felt the whip's power prickling across the top of her head. She caught the lethal pulsing tip in her hands and staggered a step, dragged by its momentum. The whip seared through the skin and flesh of her palms. For a moment, she feared she had made a mistake and then the Deceiver energy rushed through her body. Fierce animal savagery that flooded her muscles and mind. The Ligatus, still clicking and gibbering its song of death, rose within her to claim the dark energy, clawing at it with howling delight.

Selburn screamed with pain and fury, his whip heaving against her bloodied grip.

"Now!" Carlston yelled.

Helen let go of the whip. Selburn reeled back, whips flailing, as she focused inward, wrenching the earth energy up through her body. The buzzing energy swarmed through her muscles, through her blood, the blue flames springing into her bloodied palms.

Carlston grabbed her hand and swung around to face the portal, her power swirling into a fireball in his hand. She felt him gather all his Reclaimer strength, and then he hurled it at the shimmering doorway.

Helen held her breath as the ball of fire slammed into the viscous air, bowing it backward, then spreading in a roar of flames. The Margaret Deceiver recoiled, shielding her eyes. The doorway sprang back, shivering under the force. The flames flickered, dancing for a second upon the rippling surface, and then were gone. Extinguished? No, Helen realised, aghast. Not extinguished, consumed. The black crack across the undulating grey surface had lengthened. The portal swirled with darkness, a sense of endless depth behind it.

Margaret stepped closer to the crack and gave a tinkling laugh. "You have made it even bigger. Don't you realise your power comes from the earth? It is the energy of life. That is what we feed on. The portal is almost open – I can hear them coming."

Helen could hear them too: a high-pitched shrieking that crawled across her nape and shivered down her spine.

Carlston sank to his knees, drained of energy, like the first time at the stones. Quinn ran over and hauled him back to his feet as Darby silently moved to stand beside Helen. A gesture of solidarity.

At the corner of her eye, Helen saw movement outside. Thirty or so villagers and servants, each with a Deceiver's ultramarine energy, were heading towards the pavilion, compelled to add their power to feed the rupture between the realms.

Helen slumped. They were, in effect, surrounded. Carlston saw them too, his hands clenching into fists.

She glanced at him: *Outnumbered.*

His mouth tightened: *We fight to the end.*

She drew in a steadying breath: *Of course.*

"You are defeated, Carlston," Selburn said, backing up slowly to the portal, keeping the two of them in his field of vision, his whips curled, ready to strike. "You were always going to be defeated. We have planned this for generations while we waited for a female direct inheritor to be born." He bowed to Helen. "Our Vis, the energy source of the Trinitas. Then all we had to do was wait for you to come into your power, my dear, all the while feeding information to mad old Benchley, whispering the way to build his book of death bound together with his own Reclaimer blood. We could not have done it without him."

The Ligatus – Benchley's obscene weapon. Still gibbering and howling within Helen's mind, barely held back now. She could feel it hammering at her control.

"You are the VC in Benchley's journal. You killed my parents," she said, edging forward an inch. If she had only one strike before the portal opened, she would destroy the creature who had ripped apart her family. "Why?"

"To cast you adrift, of course. Your Reclaimer mother had already recognised your abilities. We did not want you trained," Selburn said. "As it is, you have surprised us with your quick proficiency."

"You – the creature in Lady Margaret's body – you were Elise as well?" Carlston rasped, the question taking him a half-step closer too. "When did you take her body?"

Margaret paused from digging at the doorway and looked over her shoulder. "Before you met her, *mon chéri*." Carlston winced at the endearment. "We were having so much fun, were we not? But I had attracted some suspicion, and you were close to taking over the leadership of the Dark Days Club from Benchley. We could not have that – we still needed his madness. So I disappeared, leaving a trail of blood leading to you. I shifted from body to body until it was time to move back into Lady Helen's orbit in that silly girl, Delia."

Helen clenched her teeth at the insult to her friend. She edged forward another inch. "When did you steal Delia's body? At the inn with Mr Trent?"

"No. Mr Trent was just to catch your attention," Margaret said, as if Helen were failing some kind of test. "A girl as kind as yourself would never allow her friend to be ruined. It is your kindness, your tenderness, that makes you so easy to manipulate."

"And your fear of your own power that defeats you," Selburn said.

Helen lifted her chin. He was right, but she would not let him see it. All along she had feared these forces within her, tried to hold them back. To control them. Even abandon them. Particularly the heinous power of the Ligatus, Benchley's alchemical weapon that was never meant to sit within a human mind and heart.

The thought stilled her breath. The Ligatus was indeed in her mind and heart. The book had nearly dragged her and Carlston into the chaos of its anguished madness. To save them both, she had opened herself to the howling pain and fear and fury of the slaughtered within it. She had sung their lament, comforted their pain with pity and compassion, drawn their blood-soaked power into the solace of her own understanding. She drew a shaking breath. The Ligatus was not Benchley's weapon. It was her own.

Selburn motioned to the gathered Deceivers on the lawn. "Approach," he ordered.

Helen stared at the dark crack that was slowly splitting apart the shivering circle. The Deceivers sought life energy. And within her she held death. Mr King had said the Ligatus could level a world. Could it level a Deceiver world?

Her heart quickened, the terrifying hope drumming through the Reclaimer bond.

Carlston glanced sideways. *You have something?* Fierce hope in his eyes.

She gave a slight nod. *A huge risk.*

His half-smile. *I trust you.*

His faith filled her heart, but did she trust herself? This could just as easily destroy all of humanity. Yet if they did not try, the Deceivers would come through and ravage the world anyway. They had to take the risk.

Outside, two of the Hussars had realised something was awry with the villagers and servants marching towards the pavilion. The soldiers launched themselves into the middle of the advancing Deceivers, tackling two of them to the ground.

Selburn's attention was diverted to the skirmish. "Kill them and get in here," he commanded the Deceivers.

Helen caught Carlston's eye and nodded towards the portal. *We go through.* She touched her forehead. *The Ligatus.*

She watched the understanding, the realisation of sure death, dawn in Carlston's face: a tensing of muscle in his jaw, the jut of his chin. *Yes.* His eyes narrowed at Selburn and Margaret. *And we take them with us.*

Helen gave the slightest of nods. Yet how could she release the Ligatus from her mind? It was forged through her Reclaimer bond with Carlston. Would that bond release it as well?

She drew a sharp breath – it was not only a bond between her and Carlston. It was Darby too. A blood bond of three forged through the Ligatus. They were a Trinitas. Or more to the point, an anti-Trinitas. The mechanism that Mr King had said could stop the Deceivers.

Bring the blood, bring the bone, bring the dead: the old verse from the Montblanc archive. Now she understood. *The blood*: their bond. *The bone*: their bodies. *The dead*: the Ligatus.

She turned her palms over; the gashes from grabbing Selburn's whip still seeped blood. Of course, she *was* the Ligatus now: her blood could reforge the bond. But would that release the Ligatus power? It was their last hope.

Helen checked on Selburn: he was directing the compelled Deceivers into a semicircle in front of the portal. Margaret still hammered at the crack.

She glanced at Darby at her side. "One way left," she whispered, the truth raw in her eyes. It was the way they had feared. They had always known they might not survive the Ligatus.

Darby bit her lip, her gaze shifting to Quinn standing beside Carlston. Tears sprang into her eyes. "I understand, my lady."

"Do not let go of me," Helen added softly, taking Darby's hand, her clasp sticky with blood. Their bond should give them a moment of protection.

Darby tightened her grip, and looked past Helen to Quinn. So much love in her face. Her soft mouth twisted into an anguished smile. A farewell.

Quinn stiffened, his eyes darting to Carlston. He knew something was about to happen.

Helen spoke to Carlston, her voice little more than a breath. "Take my hand only when we go through. We must forge the bond in their world, not ours."

He nodded.

Dear God, Helen prayed, *let it work.*

"Add your power to the portal," Selburn commanded the other Deceivers. "It is almost open, and we must keep it open for as long as we can."

There was no more time.

Helen gathered herself. "Now!"

She launched forward at Reclaimer speed, pulling Darby in her wake, her bones and sinews on fire as her Terrene's weight dragged upon her hand. Carlston ran beside her, their Reclaimer beat thundering in rhythm with their steps. She caught sight of another runner behind them. Quinn. No! He must not come through. He did not have the protection of their triad bond.

"Quinn, stay back!" she yelled.

It was only ten yards to the doorway and yet it felt like an endless, stretched moment. Helen saw Selburn's mouth draw into a snarl, Margaret's eyes widen. And then she collided with Selburn, a hard slam of flesh meeting flesh, her body angled to take him with her through the wall.

"What are you doing?" he screamed in her ear. "You cannot survive in there."

"Neither can you!"

She reached for Carlston's hand as he slammed into Margaret, their combined momentum carrying all five of them towards the undulating wall. Selburn wrapped his whip around Helen's waist, trying to stop their fall. They swung together in a ghastly mimicry of their waltz, Darby dragged behind.

Helen caught a flash of Carlston, his hand groping in the air. The three of them had to forge the bond through blood if it was going to work – her blood on her hands. She lunged towards him and their palms slammed together, fingers curling into each other as their bodies hit the wall's thick glutinous surface. It held them suspended for a terrifying moment, then they fell through, Helen's nose and screaming mouth filling with the smell and taste of lightning.

There was no landing on the other side. No ground. Or air. Just bitter cold and pressure, as if a thousand stones had tumbled on her chest and arms and legs.

In the dim light that seeped through from the pavilion she saw Selburn's bulging eyes and open mouth gasping for air that did not exist; Darby, clawing at her throat; and Carlston's snarl as he threw off Margaret. The Deceiver tumbled backward, her whip flying past his face.

Pulsing sound – an unholy shrieking – reverberated around Helen. She fought back wild panic, her mind filled with its own howling power. The Ligatus. A ravening beast made of blood and death rising to meet Selburn's whip, still wrapped around her waist. The power clawed at his dark Deceiver energy, consuming it in a boiling wave of fury, pulling it into her body for a sublime moment of savage animal victory. A foul bridge to Selburn and the screeching multitude of Deceiver energy beyond.

Go! she screamed in her mind, her own fury, her own loss, joining the rage of the slain.

The blood-ink voices howled their liberation, roaring through Selburn's whip power. A molten force of blood-soaked rage and despair that ripped all the blood energy from her mind and heart, and blasted through Selburn's human body. In the pale borrowed light, Helen caught a flash of his once-loved face – bulging eyes, mouth screaming – and then he was a thousand pieces of flesh and bone flying into the darkness around them. Obliterated.

The power rolled over Lady Margaret, ripping her into an arc of bloody pieces, then swept through the Deceiver realm in an oily inferno that boiled across the shrieking darkness, silencing everything in its path.

A shock wave of power like a pistol's recoil slammed Helen backward into Darby and Carlston. With their hands still locked together, they hit the thick barrier between the worlds. Helen caught sight of Darby's agonised eyes, Carlston's corded throat.

Dying. No air. Helen's lungs were aflame in her chest, her vision grey and blurred. With the last of her strength, she tightened her grip around Carlston's icy hand. Around Darby's hand. At least they were all still together.

A brutal yank on her arm wrenched Helen backward, slamming Carlston against her body, and then she was sliding through the gelatinous surface of the portal, its weight dragging at her arms and legs as if it fought her escape.

She landed hard on the pavilion floor beside Carlston and Darby, all three of them gasping for breath, the impact breaking their grip upon one another. Above them, the portal wall shivered, bowed, then collapsed and hit the floor. A splashing, sparking deluge that swirled around them in a muddy mix of chalk, earth and blood.

Helen rolled painfully onto her side and sat up out of the freezing muck. A few feet away, Quinn wrapped Darby into the tight curl of his arms.

Carlston groaned, and slowly sat up too. He waved his hand through the air, fingers spread in a tense sweep. "It is gone. The realm is gone." He looked at Helen and smiled. "You closed it."

"No, we destroyed it," she said. "We were a Trinitas too, through the Ligatus blood bond."

Quinn nodded. "I knew it had something to do with that bond you all forged in Barnes Terrace."

"Did you pull us out?" Carlston asked him.

"Of course I did, my lord." Quinn's rare smile appeared. "I was not going to leave my wife in a Deceiver realm."

"A good thing, then, that the Duchess and I were holding on to her," Carlston said. He leaned across and gripped Quinn's arm. "Thank you, my friend." He turned to Helen, a jerk of his chin directing her gaze beyond the archways. "Look."

The Deceiver villagers and servants had retreated and were disappearing into the shadows. Released, it seemed, from the Grand Deceiver's compulsion.

"They really are gone." Helen closed her eyes, letting the overwhelming relief and savage exultation wash over her for a precious moment. She had avenged her mother and father. And, perhaps, redeemed herself.

"And our bond through the Ligatus, that is gone too, isn't it?" Darby said, lifting her head from her husband's shoulder. "I cannot sense it any more."

"The Ligatus ripped it out of us," Helen said. "And all of the dark energy as well."

She focused inward, and a cold realisation curled her fingers into the wet mud.

Something else had been ripped out too. The Grand Reclaimer bond. She focused inward again, searching, hoping she had been mistaken, but found only her own heartbeat. The steady pulse of her bond with Carlston was gone.

She looked at him and their eyes met in a fleeting moment of shared loss.

Chapter Thirty

Lord Henry leaned forward in his chair in the Great Hall, his long face still smeared with blood from a cut to his cheek. "My brother is dead? Are you sure, Mr Pike?" He looked at Helen. "Is he sure?"

His voice penetrated the subdued murmur in the huge room, drawing everyone's attention. The Hall was still set up for the wedding ball supper, but the gilt chairs were now full of injured and shocked people huddled in blankets supplied by Mrs Clarke and her maids. The 10th Royal Hussars had done an excellent job of evacuating the pavilion and, according to Pike, were now carefully moving the bodies of those who had died to the cool store under Lord Carlston's direction.

"It is confirmed by unimpeachable eyewitness accounts, Your Grace," Pike said. "The Queen, and Helen, Duchess of Selburn."

Lord Henry straightened at the reminder of his new title. Helen glanced at Pike, impressed. He had, in just one masterful sentence, deftly reordered their precedence and distracted Lord Henry from the rather problematic demise of his brother. Lord Henry was now the Duke of Selburn; and Helen, his brother's widow, thus a Duchess by courtesy. At least Lady Georgina, the new Duchess, would be happy.

Helen had been a bride, a Duchess and a widow in one day. And a Grand Reclaimer too, victorious and disbanded all at once. She pressed her hand against the filmy fichu that Darby had pinned over the worst of her torn and bloodied bodice. Perhaps it was always meant to be that way: once the enemy was conquered, the Grand Reclaimer was no longer required; their powers separate again. It had become such a solace to reach for that beat within her – the pulse of his presence – but now it was gone and she felt numb from its loss. Did Carlston feel the same way?

They had realised almost at the same time that their bond was gone, and he had looked as hollow and bereft as she had felt. The sudden loss had been so overwhelming it had seemed to freeze all other feeling. Even the glory of victory. Then people began to wake and scream, and everything became a blur of emergency: tending the injured, marshalling the servants, concocting lies with Pike. There had been no time to understand what had happened and what it meant. No time for words of love. Besides, Helen thought dryly, she could hardly have declared her devotion to Carlston amidst the wreckage of her own wedding ball.

The new Duke turned to her, sincere sorrow on his tired, bruised face. "Duchess, I cannot imagine how appalling this day has been for you. It is a terrible blow for our family."

Helen murmured her agreement. To Lord Henry, his older brother had died only a few hours ago, when in all truth he had been murdered years before by the Grand Deceiver. Even so, at some point a real brother had been lost and Lord Henry had every right to grieve. As did she: her own uncle and six other guests and servants dead. And the two young Hussars who had tried to stop the compelled Deceivers. The harsh price of victory.

The new Duke threw off the blanket across his shoulders. "I must see my brother for myself."

Pike held up his hand. "I am afraid that is not possible, Your Grace." He glanced sideways at Helen – they both knew the official story was specious at best. "The porcelain heater installed in the pavilion exploded, and he and Lady Margaret Ridgewell were incinerated."

"Incinerated?" the Duke echoed. He looked up at Helen. "But you were standing next to him."

"He pushed me out of the way. Saved my life." She cleared her throat and forced out, "Noble to the end."

"True. He was an exceptional man," the new Duke said gravely. "You are saying there is nothing left?" His shoulder twitched at the thought of it.

"I am afraid so," Pike said. "The Queen witnessed it. She is upstairs in the drawing room and even now awaits you and your wife, the Duchess of Selburn."

"Why did you not say so immediately?" The Duke hauled himself to his feet and beckoned a passing footman. "You, help me find Lady Georgina." With a nod to Helen, he departed.

Pike looked around the full room. A number of people still lay senseless upon the blankets and bedding. Others had roused to be plied with wine and brandy. "This is going to be a challenge to contain," he said softly.

"We do seem to have bad luck with our lighting and heating," Helen remarked.

Pike's wintry smile appeared. "The perils of innovation." He nodded towards the doorway. "Your brother is attempting to gain your attention. I think it best if he is not apprised of everything that has happened tonight. For the time being anyway."

Helen turned to see Andrew rising from a chair next to Pug. His left eye was swollen shut, but otherwise he seemed whole. She had checked on him and Aunt straight after their victory, but he had been one of the many knocked unconscious by the waves of power.

"Andrew, you are awake. I am so glad. Has the physician seen you? He is the local man, but I believe he is competent."

He waved away the necessity. "There are others worse off than I." His mouth thinned into regret. "I've just heard about Selburn; I am so sorry, sprite. And Uncle too. Poor Aunt. Is she…?"

"Shaken, but remarkably stalwart," Helen said.

"No doubt she will wish to take him back to London for the funeral. I will arrange it," he said.

"Would you?" Helen looked at him in surprise. "That would be most helpful."

"I take it you will return to Aunt's house? She will need you, of course, and I am sure you do not wish to be alone."

"No, I will be setting up my own house," Helen said.

It was the one thing she had decided upon. Uncle had been a disagreeable man, but he had also been a shrewd negotiator and had set her money in trust and ensured a handsome jointure in the event of Selburn's death. She had already sent Darby upstairs to supervise the packing. The sooner they left Chenwith Hall, the better. She would take rooms at the Clarendon, or maybe Grillon's, until she found a suitable residence.

"A house by yourself? No, you cannot do that, sprite. You are still a young girl. How will it look for you to be living alone?"

"It will look as if a widow is setting up her own house," she said flatly.

"But you cannot—"

She held up her hand, stopping him. "I am quite done with *cannot*, brother. I appreciate your concern, but you know that I am capable of looking after myself."

He eyed her for a long moment. "I only want you to be safe."

"No, Andrew, you want everything to be as it once was, and that can never happen. Everything has changed."

Especially herself, Helen thought. She had grown from a naive girl to Grand Reclaimer, and now she sensed more change within her power. A strengthening, as if the removal of the Ligatus had somehow cleared a pathway to the forces within the earth. She flexed her fingers. Her skin prickled with energy even though she was not standing upon bare ground.

Pug rose from her chair beside Andrew, a blanket clutched around her torn gown. "I am so sorry, Your Grace," she said. "The Duke ... on your wedding day ... it is just awful. And your uncle too."

"Thank you, Lady Elizabeth. Are you and your mother in any way injured?"

"Just some scrapes. Mother thinks we must not intrude upon Chenwith Hall or you at this time, so we will be leaving soon." She looked up at Andrew and smiled. "Lord Hayden has offered to escort us back to Bath."

"Then I will wish you farewell," Helen said. "And, Andrew, please see a physician."

"I will make sure of it," Pug said and bobbed a curtsey.

Helen turned, hiding a quick smile. The girl had a good heart and a steely resolve. A good match for Andrew. The thought was a respite from the heaviness of her heart.

She returned to Mr Pike, and felt the press of eyes on her as she crossed the room. She sighed. Such attention was going to be her lot until some other sensation overtook the tragedy of her wedding day.

"Where has Mr Hammond gone?" she asked Pike.

They had seen Hammond only briefly in the aftermath, still somewhat dazed by the blow he had received from the false Margaret. Helen could only imagine his distress. His sister – his twin – murdered and her body used as a vessel for the Grand Deceiver.

Pike bent his head to the doorway. "I have put him in the dining room with a decanter of brandy."

Helen found Hammond sitting in a chair at the window and staring at the front driveway, light from the outside lamps and flambeaux flickering across his face. He held a glass of brandy in one hand, its sharp fruity smell scenting the warm air of the room.

"Duchess." He rose and bowed. "Quite a wedding day for you."

"Quite a day for you too." She pulled a chair across to sit with him at the window. "I am sorry about Margaret."

He nodded. "Pike told me your uncle was killed too." His voice held the lilt of condolence.

"Yes. Nine people in all lost their lives. May God protect them."

"It makes me sick to think we were living beside those creatures. That my own sister..."

"When did you realise she was a Deceiver?"

He sipped the brandy. "For certain? When she was ripping at the realm portal." He took another mouthful. "Probably before that, however, in some way."

"After Delia's death? When she changed?"

He gave a nod. "I should have realised, but I thought it was her distress. Anyone would be distressed by watching a friend bleed to death in their arms. And then the abduction." He swallowed hard and tucked his chin to his chest, waiting for the grief to subside. "Did the creature in Delia kill her, do you think? Or was it Mrs Knoll?"

"I believe Mrs Knoll cut Delia's throat so that the Deceiver in Delia could shift into your sister through the blood."

"Why move into Margaret though?"

Helen wet her lips. She had to tell him. "I think it was my fault. The Deceiver in Delia thought I was suspicious of her."

"Were you?"

"Not really. I accused her of gossiping about the return of Lady Elise, and now I think back on it, there was a connection between her and Selburn too, which I put down to Delia's flirtatious nature. I think that was the success of their deceptions – there was always a more reasonable explanation." She paused, the truth of that idea gathering momentum. "When Carlston attacked Selburn in Brighton—"

"Twice," Hammond said, the word a little slurred. He was, she realised, a trifle foxed.

"Yes, twice, we all thought it was the vestige madness – that was the obvious reason. But I think that Carlston, in his mania, had actually sensed the truth." She pressed her hands to her mouth as another possibility flashed into her mind. "And Selburn called out during the street fight with Lawrence in Brighton. I thought he was just horrified, but it was probably an order to Lawrence to stop attacking me."

"And the Grand Deceiver is well and truly dead now?"

"Yes. Both of them blown into pieces by the Ligatus power."

"Good. I wish I had seen it." He drained his glass, the lamps outside the window digging dark shadows of grief under his eyes and in the grim lines at the corners of his mouth. "I feel as if I am half missing."

To some degree she thought she understood how he felt. The loss of the Reclaimer bond was a constant ache in her heart.

"What will you do now?" she asked. "Do you stay with his lordship?"

He picked up the decanter and poured a large measure, the liquid sloshing into his glass. He motioned the decanter towards her, but she shook her head.

"I think my turn as an aide is over," he said, raising the glass to his eyes and observing the courtyard through the amber liquid. Another coach had been brought round for departing guests, and the horses' breath steamed in the freezing air. "It is time to forge my own path." He glanced sideways at her. "And you? Do you stand alongside him?"

"The Grand Reclaimer bond is gone," she said.

"Ah." He twirled his glass. "That must be a relief."

She blinked at him. That was not the response she had expected. "In what way?"

"You were worried that your love was made of blood alchemy. Now that alchemy is gone." He waved a hand as if conjuring the next step in his logic. "Thus you will now know whether it is a true bond or not." He frowned at her fixed stare. "Am I wrong?"

She smiled. "No. You are quite right." She stood, and closed her hand upon his shoulder.

He craned his neck back to look at her with intent navy eyes – not quite as foxed as she had thought, or perhaps as he wished to be – and pressed his hand upon hers for a moment. "It is a true bond, my friend. Write to me about your adventures. Perhaps you could mention him now and again, in passing."

She heard the heartache in his voice. "I will."

Helen found Pike at the side bureau in the foyer, dispatching yet another messenger into the night.

"The Queen wishes to see you and Lord Carlston," he said,

already folding the edges of another letter into a packet. "Miss Darby and Mr Quinn too."

"Now?" Helen looked down at her torn and smeared ball gown. She could not attend the Queen in such ruined clothing. "I would prefer to wash and change if possible."

"At your convenience," he said, bowing. "You will find Her Majesty in the drawing room. Will you inform Miss Darby? Or should I say, Mrs Quinn."

"Still Miss Darby for now," Helen said. "I shall bring her with me. She is upstairs, supervising our packing."

He paused in folding the packet. "You have made plans? Where do you go?"

"Anywhere but here. In the short term, London."

"The very short term, I suspect."

"What do you mean?"

He lifted a thin shoulder. "You are still a Reclaimer." He eyed her narrowly. "Unless you have decided otherwise?"

"Do I have a choice in the matter?" she said, unable to keep the acid from her voice. Pike had, after all, coerced her and Hammond into a dangerous lack of choice. "I thought you would hold me to my oath."

"If anyone has earned the right to choose her own path, Duchess, it is you."

She did not know what to say to such a volte-face. He bowed into the silence, picked up the folded packet and departed, his stooped shoulders even more lopsided than usual.

Helen slowly climbed the grand staircase, turning over his words. For the first time in her life, she had complete say over her own destiny. It was a dizzying thought. For so long, she had conceded the path of her life to the expectations of family and society and, she had to admit, her own limited idea of what she could be. Now she knew her own capabilities, knew that within her lay a core of steel that she could rely upon. Where would she step from here? And would she be stepping with Lord Carlston?

The question carried her to the door of her dressing room. Inside she heard Darby instructing Sprat about the right way to fold linen. Helen sighed. After all her heroism, Darby deserved more than styling hair and packing trunks. She deserved to choose her own path too. If that included leaving Helen's service to be with her husband, then so be it.

She drew a breath and pushed open the door. Darby and Sprat turned from surveying the contents of a travelling trunk – one of four lined up against the wall – and curtseyed.

"Yer Grace, is it true we're goin' back to London?" Sprat asked.

"Quite true," Helen said. She glanced at Darby. So many questions still to be answered between them.

Sprat leaned forward, her voice dropping into a whisper. "An' the Duke was the other Grand Deceiver?"

"True again."

Sprat sniffed. "I always knew he was a wrong 'un."

Darby crossed her arms. "Come now, Sprat, that is a lie. You did not."

"I ain't lyin'. You knew too, Yer Grace, didn't yer?" Sprat turned back to Helen. "Well, in 'ere you did," she thumped her bony chest, "like me. You never told him 'bout the kerchief I nabbed or the other stuff. You never really trusted him, did yer?"

"I think you grant me too much perspicacity," Helen said. Even so, Sprat was right in some respects: she had kept a great deal from Selburn. Perhaps some deep part of her had distrusted him, but she had not listened to her intuition. She would carry the burden of that mistake forever.

Sprat's narrow brow knitted. "I ain't got no perspi—" She

shrugged. "I ain't got none of that, Yer Grace. I swear."

Helen met Darby's eyes in amusement. A welcome moment of levity.

"I wouldn't be so sure, Sprat," she said gravely, then addressed Darby. "You and I have been summoned by the Queen."

Darby straightened. "Me?"

"And Lord Carlston and Mr Quinn too." Helen picked up the torn, soiled edge of her ball gown bodice. "I need to wash and change."

"Sprat, go get some hot water from the kitchens," Darby ordered. "Two pitchers." She cast a questioning glance at Helen. "If you allow, Your Grace? I'll need a wash too."

"Of course."

Sprat dashed out on her errand, the door closing behind her in a small slam.

"She can't even leave a room properly," Darby said. "Do you know why the Queen wants to see us, Your Grace?"

"I would say she wishes to hear the truth of what happened."

Darby circled her hand at the base of her throat. "And are we telling her the whole truth?" she asked delicately.

"We are. She knows all about the Deceivers."

Darby sighed her relief. "Good. I did not wish to lie to the Queen." She crossed to the clothes press and surveyed its reduced contents. "I have already packed most of your gowns, and we do not have any mourning black with us. I assume you must wear it for the sake of the new Duke and Duchess. The darkest colour we have is your navy-blue carriage gown."

"Darby," Helen said.

She turned around. "Your Grace?"

"We no longer have our Reclaimer and Terrene bond."

"I know." Darby's face was stricken.

"If you wish, I will release you from service. You can go

with Mr Quinn. I could even arrange a release from your oath to the Dark Days Club." Helen cleared her throat. "If that is what you want."

Darby bit her lip. "Is it what you want? Do you no longer need a Terrene?"

"Of course I need a Terrene!" Helen stopped, her mind catching up with her heart. So she had made her decision after all. She was to stay a Reclaimer. "But I do not want to stand in the way of your happiness. You have a chance now to live a normal life."

Darby gave a tremulous laugh. "I do not want a normal life. Besides, Mr Quinn knows who he married. He knows I have made two vows in my life and I must honour both."

Helen caught her hands. "I do not want a normal life either. We will live our lives like no other women before us. Are we mad?"

Darby laughed. "Quite possibly, Your Grace."

"I do not know how it is going to work," Helen admitted. "I do not wish to pull you away from your husband."

"But you and Lord Carlston are in love, are you not? We will all be together. At least, once you have made a show of mourning."

"I am not certain that will be the case," Helen said, releasing her Terrene's hands.

"What do you mean?"

"Lord Carlston and I have not had a chance to speak about such matters yet. I do not know how he feels. Not any more."

"So you are tormenting yourself with thoughts that he has stopped loving you?" Darby shook her head. "Why would you think that? You both declared yourselves at the stones. You were ready to abandon your wedding to be with him."

"That was before the Grand Reclaimer bond was destroyed.

I do not know how much of our regard was made of that alchemy. We were linked in such an *essential* way. Like another pulse. And now it is gone."

"Has it changed your love for him?"

Helen tilted her head. "No, I do not believe so. Even through the pain of the lost bond, my heart reaches for him."

"Then why would it be different for him?"

"Maybe it is not, but I will not make the mistake of presuming another's mind or sensibility."

Darby looked at her narrowly. "Then you must speak to him. Tell him how you feel."

"I must. And if he no longer feels the same…" She stopped. If he did not feel the same way, that was something she would have to endure.

She would not borrow heartache now, not when there was true heartache downstairs in that line of silent bodies laid out under sheets.

Helen, clad in navy blue and wearing her mother's cross for comfort, arrived at the drawing room with Darby at her side. The Queen's ladies-in-waiting stood in the corridor, murmuring softly, apparently banished from Her Majesty's presence. Helen felt their eyes upon her as the Queen's own footman opened the door and announced them.

"Her Grace, Helen, the Duchess of Selburn, and Miss Darby."

Helen led the way into the room. The atmosphere held a curious weight, as if an intense conversation had suddenly been halted by their arrival. The Queen sat in an armchair, the topaz gown exchanged for a sombre grey silk, her face a little puffy and pale from fatigue. Her eyes, however, were as lively as ever.

To Helen's surprise, Aunt sat on a sofa at the Queen's side, wrapped in a paisley silk shawl, a wan smile of welcome upon her worn face. She had been crying, Helen noted. Uncle had never deserved such a kind and generous woman.

Pike stood a little to one side of Her Majesty, a black-clad sentinel guarding his sovereign and his secrets.

Helen sank into a low curtsey. From the corner of her eye she saw Carlston standing near the side bureau. He had, of course, removed his torn and bloodied greatcoat, and had clearly borrowed clothes for he wore clean buckskins and new linen. His jacket, however, still bore the stained cut of Selburn's whips, the white of his shirt showing through the sliced cloth when he moved.

Helen blinked, once again feeling the terrifying sensation of the Deceiver's whip around her waist and the horrifying sense of suffocation. She drew a steadying breath. They had been so close to defeat. But they had prevailed. All of them together.

She aimed a small smile at Carlston, but he had angled his head away as if to avoid her glance. Or was she imagining it? Beside him, Quinn smiled proudly at Darby, who had sunk into her own deep obeisance.

The Queen motioned them to rise. "Ah, Duchess, we were just talking about you. And is that Miss Darby behind you?"

Darby stepped forward. "Your Majesty."

The Queen inclined her head and motioned them forward. "Lord Carlston has been informing me of the events of the evening. He says we are to thank you, Duchess, for coming to the solution that saved us all from the creatures. And you, Miss Darby, we commend for your great courage and sacrifice."

"Mr Quinn too, Your Majesty," Helen said. "We would not have survived without his quick thinking."

She turned to gather Quinn into the conversation, her gaze catching for a moment upon Carlston's face. His dark eyes were set upon the Queen, jaw clamped shut, expression at its most impenetrable. Why did he not look her way?

"I also wish to commend a young cornet by the name of Nesbitt in the 10th Light," Carlston said. "He rode to retrieve me from Portsmouth. Without his effort, we would not have prevailed against Selburn and Lady Margaret."

"Mr Pike, make a note of that name," the Queen said. She shook her head in bemusement. "Every time I think of it I feel such shock that Selburn was one half of the Grand Deceiver. I have had him to many a dinner. Quite unsettling to think about it. Do we know when he inhabited the real Duke's body?"

"I believe it must have been at least ten years ago," Helen said. "Possibly when the older brother – Oliver, the heir – died."

"And their plans had been in place for generations?" The Queen looked at Carlston. "You said that Selburn orchestrated the deaths of Lord and Countess Hayden?"

"It would seem so, Your Majesty," Carlston said, stepping forward. "The Grand Deceiver wished to isolate the Duchess Helen from her mother, who, as you know, was also a Reclaimer."

Still no glance in her direction, even though he talked about her and her parents.

The Queen leaned across to Aunt. "As her Royal boon, your niece asked that the name of her mother – your sister and my friend – be exonerated. I will indeed act upon that request."

Aunt smiled, new tears springing into her eyes. "Thank you, Your Majesty."

Helen touched the gold cross at her throat. Finally, her mother would receive the honour she deserved.

The Queen returned her sharp attention to Helen. "Your aunt has agreed to come to me as a senior lady-in-waiting once she has mourned. It will be a great relief to be able to talk freely with someone about all this terrible business."

A great honour. Helen met her aunt's eyes – beyond the sadness there was a spark of excitement.

"And, Lord Carlston," the Queen continued, "Mr Pike tells me your earlier request was to be divorced from Lady Elise. She was the other Grand Deceiver at some point, was she not?" Again, she shook her head. "Such a charming girl."

"Yes, Your Majesty. The Duke of Selburn introduced me to her, and I am ashamed to say I was young and easily manipulated into striving for her hand," Carlston said grimly. He glanced at Pike. "I was the only member of the Dark Days Club who was willing to entertain the idea that the Duchess – Lady Helen as she was then – was a direct inheritor. I believe Selburn and Lady Elise wished to ensure that I did not step in to train Lady Helen, and also to keep Benchley at the head of the Reclaimers. He was under their sway; they were playing upon his madness to build the Ligatus. Thus, the false disappearance of Lady Elise and my subsequent exile."

"Ah, the Ligatus." The Queen shuddered. "Mr Pike has informed me of its origins."

"It was the missing part of the Trinitas," Pike said. "Benchley had hidden it, and so we and the Grand Deceiver were searching for it at the same time. The race ended, rather surprisingly, with Lady Helen absorbing the alchemy."

Helen remembered the bloody battle at the house in Barnes Terrace. She had found Selburn at the top of the stairs with a knife in hand. Her new knowledge suddenly reordered the image into a stunning realisation.

"Carlston, you did not kill Mr Stokes," she blurted out.

That finally made him turn and look at her, his face rigid with shock. "What do you mean?"

"I think Selburn did it. I found him upstairs, although I had told him to stay outside. I thought he had come to protect me, but he was kneeling beside Mr Quinn with a pistol and a knife." Helen pressed her hand to her mouth as the vision of the two men sharpened in her mind. "Good Lord, I think he was going to kill you, Mr Quinn, but my arrival stopped him."

Quinn nodded slowly. "I do not remember much about it, but I remember his face above me," he touched his abdomen, "and more pain."

Darby crossed to him. "Perhaps he stabbed you again. It did not make sense that you were not already healing by that time."

Quinn took her hand and said in his matter-of-fact way, "Well, he did not succeed."

Carlston shook his head. "I cannot remember it at all." He drew a breath. "It would be a relief to know I did not kill my friend."

"It seems more likely that the Grand Deceiver would have killed Stokes," Pike said.

Not what he had originally believed, Helen thought waspishly.

The Queen raised an eyebrow at Pike. "I take it this is an internal matter?"

Pike bowed. "An internal matter, as you say, Your Majesty. And at an end now, I think."

"Then let us return to Lady Elise. Since she is dead, more or less..." She leaned towards Aunt again. "It is very difficult to keep track of who was who, don't you think, Lady Pennworth?"

"Indeed, Your Majesty," Aunt said.

The Queen nodded and looked at Carlston again. "Since the real Lady Elise is deceased, Lord Carlston, I think it would be more expedient to officially declare her dead rather than arrange a divorce; and then have her name, and thus yours, exonerated from any taint of espionage. I hope that will be satisfactory."

Helen caught the slide of his eyes towards her, and felt her heart leap. She tried to meet his gaze, but it was gone again, fixed once more upon the Queen.

He bowed. "Thank you, Your Majesty."

"Now, we wish to speak to the Duchess and Miss Darby alone." She waved a dismissal at Carlston and Quinn. "You may go."

Carlston's shoulders tensed, but he did not look Helen's way again. Why was he avoiding her so assiduously?

The two men bowed and departed the room.

The Queen waited until the doors had been shut, then said, "Well, Pike?"

Pike stepped forward. "On behalf of Her Majesty, I ask if you will be continuing your duties as a Reclaimer, Duchess? The Grand Deceiver may have been defeated, but there is still the Pact and thousands of the creatures in England."

Helen glanced at her aunt. "Yes, I believe I will continue. I am sorry, Aunt. I know you wish me to retire."

Aunt shook her head. "I understand, my dear. This is what you are meant to do. Tonight you were ... magnificent."

Helen felt a sting of tears in her eyes. She blinked them away.

"I am glad to hear you will be staying with the Dark Days Club, Duchess," Pike said. "And do you stay as Terrene, Miss Darby?"

"Yes, I do." Darby glanced at Helen. "Although we no longer have our bond, do we, Your Grace?"

"The blood bond that Darby and I forged through the Ligatus is gone," Helen explained. "Do you think we will be able to establish another, Mr Pike?"

"I believe so," he said. "It will just be a matter of performing the ritual."

The Queen held up her pale palm; a rejection of the conversation. "I do not wish to know about this godless alchemy, Pike."

Helen met Pike's eyes. The Queen was famed for her piety and strict morality.

Pike bowed. "I beg your pardon, Your Majesty."

The Queen leaned closer to Helen. "An hour ago, I had an *interesting* discussion with Count Lieven, the Russian ambassador, who, it transpires, is also aware of the Deceiver presence in our world. He told me Bonaparte's retreat from Moscow has left the city in a terrible state and the population is being attacked by Deceivers. The Russian Reclaimers are doing all they can, but he has asked for reinforcements. At least two Reclaimer envoys. Lord Carlston has agreed to go, and we thought that if you were willing, you could also go, Duchess. Mr Pike assures me that for all your youth, you are more than capable to discharge such a duty with great skill and honour."

"Moscow?" Helen echoed. *With Carlston?* She glanced at Aunt. Her mouth was so thin it had almost disappeared. Clearly she did not like the idea. But it was not her decision.

"I know it is a most uncomfortable time to be travelling," the Queen added, "but I think it a good idea for you to leave England for a short while, at least until this past evening's events are not so high in everyone's mind. Think about it for a day or so, but we must have your answer soon."

"I understand, Your Majesty. I will think on it."

"Then you and Miss Darby may go, Duchess. England thanks you for your most courageous service." She turned to Aunt. "Lady Pennworth, tell my other ladies they may enter."

Helen and Darby curtseyed as Aunt rose from the sofa.

"I return to London with the Queen," Aunt whispered to Helen as they retreated to the door. "Will you sit vigil with me for your uncle tomorrow night?"

"Of course I will."

"I cannot like this idea of Russia, my dear," she admitted softly.

"Because of Carlston? Surely he has proven himself a man of worth now? Rather more so than Selburn, do you not think?" Helen gentled the jibe with a smile.

Aunt bit her lip. "I am sorry I pushed you so hard towards the Duke. It still staggers me that he was one of those creatures."

"We were all taken in," Helen said grimly.

"Even so, you vanquished them." Aunt pressed a slightly damp kiss upon her cheek. "I am so proud of you, my dear." She turned to touch Darby's arm. "Look after her, will you?"

Darby bobbed a curtsey. "That is my sworn duty, Lady Pennworth, and my honour."

In the corridor, Helen swept past the ladies-in-waiting, looking for Carlston. He was not there. He had not waited. She felt a rise of dry apprehension in her throat.

"Will we go to Russia, Your Grace?" Darby asked, hurrying to keep up.

"I hope so." Helen ducked through the connecting corridor to the grand staircase. "Lord Carlston barely looked at me in there, Darby."

"Yes, I saw, Your Grace."

"Do you think it is because – ah, there is Mr Quinn. But where is Carlston?"

Quinn stood quite alone at the bottom of the staircase, a greatcoat draped across his arms. He bowed as Helen approached, his eyes meeting Darby's for an eloquent moment.

"Lord Carlston asks that you join him at the temple of Venus, Your Grace," he said quickly.

Away from the house. Away from prying eyes. The place where they had controlled their power.

"Did he say why?"

"Only that he hopes you will join him, Your Grace." He held out the greatcoat. "It is very cold out."

Helen was glad of its heavy wool as she slipped out of the door that led to the kitchen yard, ignoring the curious glances from the kitchen staff still supplying hot drinks and food to the injured. She made her way swiftly across the lawns. It was near three o'clock in the morning and a frost had settled upon the grass, crunching beneath her feet. Even so, she felt the warmth of the earth power through the soles of her boots. No need to stand upon the ground in her hose any more. Change was definitely afoot.

She smiled at her own pun, yet beneath it was a bubbling sense of excitement. Granted, she was no longer part of the Grand Reclaimer – a loss that still ached – but she had powers beyond those of a normal Reclaimer.

She broke into a trot, accelerating to the cusp of Reclaimer speed, every step thudding down and bringing the flow of power into her body, pumping it up through the stretch of muscle and the throb of blood through her veins. So glorious. So easy. No foul, chittering Ligatus tainting it with darkness or death. Just pure life energy. The force of the earth. Her skin prickled, her hands curling with the presence of it within her body. She rubbed her fingertips across her thumb and felt a spark. Unusual.

She slowed and stopped, sliding fingers across thumb again. A small blue flame sprang into the air and hovered above the apex of her fingertips. She held her breath, but it did not break up or even flicker. She opened her hand, concentrating upon the flame, the shape and sense of it in her mind. The flame expanded. *Ball*, she thought, and the flame curled around itself into a sphere, still suspended inches above her palm. She focused, willing it to rotate. Slowly it began to turn. She shifted her hand and the ball of flame moved with it. Gently she jerked her hand up. The flame lifted and dropped back to hovering above her palm, like a ball being bounced. She laughed. Lud, she could completely control it.

She shook her head at her own dullness. Of course she could; even before the Ligatus, she had been able to draw and store energy. And now, without the chaos of the Ligatus within her, she could control it too. By herself.

She walked on, using the ball as a lamp before her, the flame casting a cold blue path of light across the frosted grass. A trifle showy, she thought with a smile, but it was her power and she could not bear to extinguish it quite yet. Besides, there was no moon and she wanted the illumination.

Finally, she approached the temple. It was dark – Carlston had not lit a lamp – but she could easily make out his silhouette, turned towards her as she climbed the small hill. Out of habit she reached for their bond, but of course it was not there. Just her own heartbeat, hard and fast in her chest.

She stopped in front of him, holding the blue flame ball between them so it lit their faces. The cold light made the bold lines of his jaw and cheekbones seem cut from marble. His expression was still impenetrable.

"That is new," he said, eyes upon the light.

"I can still draw upon the earth energy." She moved her hand away, letting the flaming ball hang in the air. It was set there now, no need for concentration. Like a tiny moon in the sky.

"Of course." He nodded, coming to the same conclusion she had. "It was always your gift." He smiled, a fleeting softness in the grim cast of his face. "Thank you for coming here. The Queen requires me to escort her to London tomorrow and I could not bear to leave without seeing you. Alone." He glanced at the temple wall behind him. "Of course, it was only as I arrived here that I remembered Elise's portrait within. Hardly the company either of us wants."

Helen peered into the temple, but the portrait was lost to the shadows. Where it belonged.

"It must have been such a shock for you to realise she had been with us as Delia and then Lady Margaret," she said.

"It makes my skin crawl." He shook his head. "I am sick to the core to think of how many people she and Selburn killed in the most heinous way. Destroying their souls, stealing their bodies. I should have realised sooner. Saved our friends. Saved you from him."

Helen bowed her head. Poor Delia and Lady Margaret. And the true Gerard, taken so long ago. It would be some time, she knew, before her fury at the Selburn Deceiver abated. And her shame, too, that he had manipulated her so masterfully. A sudden realisation lifted her eyes to his. "Is that why you have been avoiding me? You think all of this is your fault?"

He gave his half-smile and the sad curve of it pierced her heart. "Of course it is my fault. I have been a Reclaimer far longer than you. I should have known sooner."

"How?" she asked flatly. "They said themselves they had been planning this for generations. We barely had any true information – everything was obscured by lies and inaccuracy, and Benchley's mad scrawlings. We had to piece it all together ourselves. And we did."

Neither of them, she realised, had anything to be ashamed about.

"We did," he agreed. "The Grand Reclaimer prevailed."

"But now the bond is gone." She stared at the ball of blue flame. It seemed easier to look into its bright light rather than his face for the next question. Still, it must be asked. The truth must be known. "Did you ever think that our regard for one another could be the blood alchemy rather than true feeling?"

"No, never!" The force of his reply brought him a step closer. "I loved you well before we made the Grand Reclaimer bond. Besides, even if the alchemy once formed a part of it, we are now forged by so many other, stronger bonds. Faith. Honesty. Love."

She released her breath. "Trust."

"Yes. Trust." He lifted his hand to her face, his finger tracing the corner of her mouth and the curve of her chin. "Even without the Grand Reclaimer bond, Helen, you are my heartbeat. My pulse. You are the fire in my blood and the laughter in my soul."

She blinked, her tears blurring the bare truth in his dark eyes. She laid her hand against his chest, the quick thud of his heart matching her own. Together, aligned.

In the steady blue light of her power, she pressed a kiss upon his mouth and breathed two words into the soft caress. *"Amore mio."*

She felt his arms circle her, his lips curling into a smile against her own.

"In Russian," she added, "it is *lyubov moya.*"

Enjoyed *The Dark Days Deceit*?
We'd love to hear your thoughts!

#TheDarkDaysDeceit   @AlisonGoodman
@WalkerBooksUK   @WalkerBooksYA

@WalkerBooksYA

Author's Note

I hope that one of the delights of the Lady Helen series is the blend of real history, people and places with the fictional world of our heroine. In this final instalment of the trilogy, the action is set in and around the beautiful city of Bath – the mothership of Regency history and architecture, and a hub of Jane Austen appreciation. A most fitting place, I think, for a Regency heroine to meet her nemesis.

The Royal Crescent, Lansdown Crescent, the Circle, the Assembly Rooms, the Cross Bath, the Abbey, and the Pump Room and Yard are all still standing in all their glory, although some have had a bit of Victorian and modern tinkering. I can report that the afternoon tea at the Pump Room is delicious, and the hot spring baths are sublime. The "waters", however, still taste disgusting.

The shops on Milsom Street that Lady Helen and her friends visit are those that were in existence in December 1812 – I built a map of the shops and other amenities from the newspaper advertisements in the 1812 *Bath and Cheltenham Gazette* and *Bath Chronicle*. A research nerd's dream task!

The Stanton Drew stone circle is real and still stands

in the middle of a field without much in the way of touristy embellishment. I found fascinating old newspaper reports of strange phenomena at the stones, including a dramatic burst of power similar to the one that I describe in the novel.

Mr King was the real Master of Ceremonies at Bath in 1812 (according to the polite society, one was always *at* Bath, never *in* Bath). Beau Nash and Captain Wade were also real MCs. The historical Mr King was, by all accounts, a very gracious man and most probably not a Deceiver – a bit of literary licence on my part that I hope is not seen as a slight upon his character. At the time of writing, the statue of Beau Nash still stands in the Pump Room and the portrait of Captain Wade graces the Octagon Room at the Assembly Rooms. However, there is no carved fob on the statue, and the decoration on Captain Wade's lapel, while existing, is hard to make out in any detail.

Other real historical figures include Queen Charlotte, the Prince Regent and Count Lieven, the Russian ambassador, whose wife, the Countess Lieven, became one of the patronesses of Almack's.

The Duke's estate, Chenwith Hall, is based on the floor plans and grounds of Castle Howard, the ancestral home of the Carlisle branch of the Howard family. The house in Great Pulteney Street did exist, but did not actually explode.

Christmas in the Regency was a much more subdued affair than the Victorian Christmas tradition from which many of the modern traditions arise. In the Regency, there was no Christmas tree, presents were more often exchanged on the Twelfth Night rather than on Christmas Eve or Christmas Day, and many people went about their day as normal with only an extra attendance at a Christmas service and a more elaborate dinner. The same applies to weddings – they were far more subdued with the bride often wearing a coloured gown or something that could be used for best after the ceremony, and only family and a few close friends in attendance. Weddings had to be conducted in the morning by law, and so the celebratory meal afterwards was literally a breakfast, thus the term "wedding breakfast". It was mainly the gentry and nobility who went on a honeymoon or, as it was more likely called, a wedding tour, with most other folk getting back to ordinary life the same or following day.

Mesmerism was a real movement at the time and Abbé Feria was one of the main players in the field. I have, however, pushed the knowledge of hypnotism into a bit more depth than was around at the time.

The upcoming play at the theatre and the concert at the Assembly Room were actual events on those days, although I invented the acrobats advertising the play.

The Bath sedan chairs were also a real mode of transport, and the chairmen were often recruited as the eyes and ears of the city, since there was no organised police force in Bath or, indeed, in England during the Regency. A formal police force did not come into effect until 1828.

Sadly, the murder of the infants is a true event and the newspaper article that Aunt reads is from the 16th December 1812 *Bath and Cheltenham Gazette*. I could not discover if the killer was ever brought to justice.

If you ever want to experience a little bit of the Regency, I recommend visiting Bath and, if possible, the annual Jane Austen Festival where you can dance at a ball and promenade along the streets where Jane herself once walked with her dear sister Cassandra.

Keep an eye on the shadows though. And remember, don't wear any metal…

Alison Goodman, October 2018

Acknowledgements

As ever, my thanks to my wonder team: Ron, my husband, my best friend Karen McKenzie, and my parents, Douglas and Charmaine Goodman. I couldn't have finished this series without their unstinting love and support.

My thanks also to my brilliant agent, Jill Grinberg, and her talented associates: Cheryl, Katelyn, Denise and Sophia.

I feel very lucky to have worked on the Lady Helen series with such a fabulous publishing team at Walker Books. My eternal gratitude to my editor, the very lovely and eagle-eyed Emily McDonnell, and my sincere thanks to Maria Soler Cantón and Chloé Tartinville for the gorgeous covers, Ed Ripley and his innovative Sales and Marketing team, and Rosi Crawley and her nimble Publicity team.

A special shout out and thanks must also go to Gill Evans, who originally bought the Lady Helen series, and to Nicola O'Shea for her gentle but ruthless editing pen.

I belong to two writing groups – The Y. & J. Writers and Clan Destine – who provide endless inspiration and camaraderie. Thank you!

I'd also like to acknowledge the work of Daniel Alan Livesay and his dissertation on "Children of Mixed Race", and the work of Trevor Fawcett, who has written a number of interesting articles on the history of Bath, including the sedan chairs and chairmen, the shops and luxury trade, and the black population in Georgian Bath.

Finally, I must acknowledge my dear, departed sweet hound from Hell, Xander, who was with me for most of this book. He died at the grand old age of seventeen. We mourn him, but we have also now welcomed Buckley into our hearts, a sweet little Australian terrier mix rescue who steals socks and is quickly learning how to be a writer's dog. He still hasn't quite got to the level of snoring that Xander did, but he has developed an excellent paw-tap on my leg at 4pm to remind me that it is time for our daily constitutional.

Alison Goodman is the author of the international bestselling and award-winning *Eon/Eona* duology, as well as the acclaimed *Singing the Dogstar Blues* and the adult thriller *A New Kind of Death* (originally titled *Killing the Rabbit*).

Alison lives in Melbourne, Australia, with her husband, Ron, and their rescue pup, Buckley. She is working on her next novel.

Visit her website at www.darkdaysclub.com

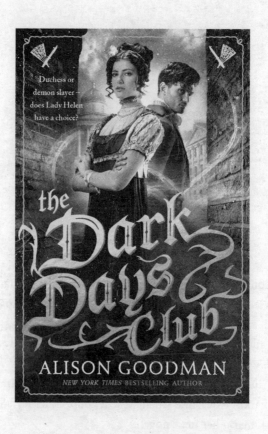

"A great mix of fantasy, history and romance ...
I would definitely recommend it to fans of
The Infernal Devices or The Diviners series."

Bookish at Heart

London, April 1812

Lady Helen Wrexhall is set to step into Regency Society and find a husband. But this step will take her from glittering ballrooms and the bright lights of Vauxhall Gardens into a shadowy world of demonic creatures and deadly power.

Drawing her into this underworld is Lord Carlston, a man of dubious reputation and infuriating manners. He believes Helen has a destiny beyond the ballroom; a sacred duty to protect humanity. Not the usual aspirations of a young lady in her first London Season.

A delightfully dangerous adventure of self-discovery and dark choices, set against a backdrop of whispered secrets, soirées and high society.

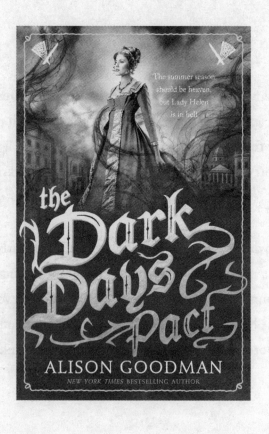

The summer season should be heaven, but Lady Helen is in hell

the Dark Days Pact

ALISON GOODMAN

NEW YORK TIMES BESTSELLING AUTHOR

"Lady Helen is intelligent, lively and brave, and one of the best YA protagonists I have come across."

Emer, teen reviewer, *Lovereading.co.uk*

Brighton, July 1812

Lady Helen Wrexhall has taken refuge in Brighton following the scandalous events at her presentation ball. Now she must complete her Reclaimer training, ready to battle the Grand Deceiver believed to have arrived in England.

Her mentor, Lord Carlston, is facing his own inner battle, and as he fights the violent darkness within his soul, Lady Helen's loyalty is tested. Entrusted with a secret mission by the Home Office, she must make the agonising choice between betraying those around her or breaking her oath to the Darks Days Club.

"A delicious collision of Regency romance and dark fantasy." Publishers Weekly